Other books by Je...

Covenant Series

(Full series com...

Sentinel

Lux Series
(Full series completed- Upper Young Adult Paranormal)
Shadows
Obsidian
Onyx
Opal
Origin
Opposition

The Dark Elements
(Upper Young Adult Paranormal)
Bitter Sweet Love
White Hot Kiss
Stone Cold Touch

Standalone Titles:

Don't Look Back
(Romantic Suspense Upper Young Adult)
Cursed
(Upper Young Adult paranormal)
Obsession
(Adult spin-off the Lux Series)

Jennifer L. Armentrout

www.jenniferarmentrout.com

Wicked

Published by Jennifer L. Armentrout
Copyright © 2014 by Jennifer L. Armentrout
All rights reserved

Library of Congress Cataloging-in-Publication Data
Wicked/Jennifer L. Armentrout—First edition
ISBN 978-0-9889829-5-6 (Paperback)

Cover Design by Sarah Hansen. All rights reserved.

This book is for you, the reader. Without you, this book wouldn't be possible. None of this would be.

Chapter One

Sweat dotted my brow. Tendrils of red hair clung to my neck. My legs felt like I'd been sitting in a sauna. I was pretty sure there was a waterfall of sweat coursing between my breasts, and that alone put my mood somewhere between slapping someone and pushing them in front of a trolley.

It was so hot and sticky humid that I was seriously beginning to believe that New Orleans was one of the seven circles of hell and the outdoor seating area of the Palace Café was the gateway. Or the waiting room.

A fat drop of sweat slipped from the tip of my nose and smacked off my Philosophy of Human Person text, leaving a little damp circle in the middle of a paragraph I could barely see through the sheen of sweat blinding me.

I always thought the title of my class was missing an 'A' somewhere in there. It should be Philosophy of *A*

Human Person. But oh no, that wasn't how Loyola rolled.

The small table rattled on its legs as a large iced coffee slammed down directly in front of my book. "For you!"

As I peered over the top of my sunglasses, my mouth watered like I was one of Pavlov's dogs. Valerie Adrieux plopped into the seat across from me, her hand like a claw on top of my iced coffee. A mix of Spanish and African heritage, Val had an absolutely beautiful skin tone, a rich and flawless shade of brown, and she looked *awesome* in bright oranges and blues and pinks and every freaking color of the rainbow.

Like today, Val wore a loose, orange halter that defied gravity, a purple necklace, and as I glanced down, I saw a turquoise peasant skirt. She looked as if she had stepped off a catalog featuring urban chic. If I wore any color other than black, tan, or gray, I looked like an asylum escapee.

Sitting up straight, ignoring how the backs of my thighs stuck to the chair, I made grabby fingers at the iced coffee. "Gimmie."

She arched a brow. In the sunlight, Val's hair had a burnt auburn sheen to it. Pretty. Mine looked like a fire engine. Scary. No matter the level of humidity, her head full of corkscrew curls always looked great. Again, pretty. Between the months of April and November, the curl in my hair got lazy and turned into a frizzy wave. Again, scary as hell.

Sometimes I wanted to hate her.

"Don't you have something else to add to that?" she asked.

This was one of those times.

"Gimmie . . . my precious?" I added.

She grinned. "Try again."

"Thank you?" I wiggled my fingers toward the coffee.

She shook her head.

I dropped my hands in my lap with a tired sigh. "Can you point me in the right direction of what you want to hear? Play a game of hot and cold or something?"

"While I love that game most of the time, I'm gonna pass." Lifting the iced coffee between us, she smiled broadly at me. "The correct response would be, 'I love you so much for getting me iced coffee that I'd do anything for you.'" She waggled her brows. "Yeah, that sounds about right."

Leaning back in my chair, I laughed as I kicked my legs onto the empty seat to my left, stretching out the muscles. The reason I was probably sweating so much was because I was wearing lace-up boots that ended just below my knees and it was like two-hundred degrees, but I was working tonight, and flip-flops really weren't conducive to getting the job done or hiding the things necessary to get said job done. "You know I can totally just kick your ass and take the coffee, right?"

Val stuck out her lower lip. "That's not nice, Ivy."

I grinned at her. "It's true though. I could ninja-kick your ass all up and down Canal Street."

"Maybe, but you would never do such a thing because I'm your best-est friend-est in the world-est," she said with another wide smile, and she was right. "Okay. What I want isn't a big deal." She moved the straw jutting out of the iced tea close to her mouth, and I groaned. "Not at all."

"What do you want?" My second groan was lost in the hum of foot traffic passing the café, and the sound of sirens most likely heading toward the Quarter.

Val shrugged one shoulder. "I have a date Saturday night—a hot date. Well, hopefully a hot date, but Daniel has me on the schedule to work the Quarter, so . . .?"

"So, let me guess." I reached behind me, draping my arms over the back of the chair. Not the most comfortable position, but it helped me air out. "You want me to take your shift in the Quarter . . . on a Saturday night? In September. Smack dab in tourist hell?"

Her head bobbed an enthusiastic yes. "Please. Pretty please?" She shook the iced coffee, and the chunks of ice rattled in the plastic container enticingly. "Please?"

My gaze moved from her hopeful face to the iced coffee and stayed there. "Sure. Why not? Not like I have a hot date."

"Yay!" She shoved the coffee forward, and I snatched it out of the air a half second before she dropped it. A heartbeat later, I was slurping away happily, totally transported to a chilly, caffeinated heaven. "You know," she began, placing her elbows on the table, "you could have a hot date, if like, you went out on a date once every year or so."

I ignored that comment and continued drinking at brain freeze speed.

"You're really pretty, even with all that hair." She made a circle with her hand in the general vicinity of my head as if I didn't know I looked like a Q-tip with my hair piled atop it. "And you have really great boobs and a total tap-that-ass kind of ass. I'd totally do you."

4

I continued to ignore her as a dull ache started behind my eyes. I so needed to slow down on the coffee, but it was so damn good.

"Do you even like boys, Ivy? You know, I swing both ways. I'm more than willing to help a girl out."

I rolled my eyes then immediately winced. Lowering the iced coffee, I pressed my palm to my forehead. "Ow."

Val snorted.

"I like boys," I grumbled as the icepick sensation faded. "And can we not talk about boys or swinging both ways or helping me out? Because this conversation is going to lead to the lack of orgasms in my life and how I need to get naked with some random dude, and I'm not really in the mood to talk about that."

"What do you want to talk about then?"

Taking a slower sip of the coffee, I eyed her. "How come you're not sweating?"

Val tipped her chin back and laughed so loudly an older couple strolling by with matching fanny packs stared at her. "Babe, I'm born and raised in Louisiana. My family can be traced back to the original French settlers—"

"Blah, blah. Does that somehow mean you have some kind of magical ability that makes you absolutely resistant to the heat while I'm drowning in my own funk?"

"Can take the girl out of the north but can't take the north out of the girl."

I snorted at that. It was true. Having moved to New Orleans only three years ago from northern Virginia, I still hadn't adapted to the weather. "Do you know what I'd do for a polar vortex right about now?"

"Not have sex, that's for sure."

I flipped her off. Truthfully, I didn't even know why I didn't miss a single day when it came to taking my birth control pills. I guessed it was habit from when it actually mattered.

She giggled as she leaned against the table, her dark brown eyes surveying my philosophy book. "I just do not get why you're going to college."

"Why not?"

The look on her face suggested the heat had fried a few of my brain cells. "You already have a job—a job that pays extraordinarily well, and you don't really need to get another one like some of the others do. We don't have a lot of bennies, and we have probably the shortest lifespan of any job out there that doesn't involve sky diving without a parachute, but that's another reason to not waste your time on that crap."

My shrug was my response. To be honest, I wasn't sure why I started going to Loyola a year ago. Maybe it was boredom. Maybe it was the weird need to do something most twenty-one-year-olds were doing. Or maybe it ran deeper than that, and whatever *that* was, was the reason behind taking sociology with a psychology minor. I toyed with the idea of being a social worker, because I knew I could do both things if I wanted to. Maybe it had to do with what happened to—

I cut those thoughts off. No reason to go there today, or any day. The past was in the past, dead and buried with the entirety of my family.

Despite the sweltering heat, I shivered. Val was right though. Our lifespan could be brutally short. Since May, we'd lost three Order members—Cora Howard, aged twenty-six. She was killed on Royal, neck snapped.

Vincent Carmack, aged twenty-nine. He met the end on Bourbon, his neck torn open. And Shari Jordan, thirty-five, was killed just three weeks ago, her neck also snapped. She'd been found in the warehouse district. Deaths were common, but three in the last five months had all of us uneasy.

"You okay?" Val asked, head tilted to the side.

"Yeah." My gaze tracked the trolley as it rolled past. "You're working tonight, right?"

"Yeppers peppers pots." Shifting back from the table, she clapped her hands and rubbed them together. "Want a friendly wager?"

"On?"

Her smile turned downright evil. "Most kills by one in the morning."

An elderly man shuffling past our table sent Val a strange look and then picked up his pace, but the truth was, people heard stranger crap on the streets of New Orleans, especially when you were only a handful of blocks from the French Quarter.

"It's a deal." I finished off the coffee. "Wait. What do I get when I win?"

"*If* you win," she corrected. "I'll bring you iced coffee for a week. And if I win, you do the . . ." She trailed off, eyes squinting. "Lookie. Lookie, artichokie." She lifted her chin.

Frowning, I twisted around and immediately saw what Val was talking about. I sucked in a shallow breath as I bent my right leg so my boot was closer to my hand. There was no missing the chick.

To most humans, like ninety-nine percent of them, the woman in the flowing maxi dress walking down Canal Street looked like the average person. Maybe a tourist. Or possibly a local out shopping on a Wednesday afternoon. But Val and I weren't like most humans. At birth, a lot of mumbo jumbo was said, warding us against glamour. We saw what most did not.

Which was the monster behind the normal façade.

This creature was one of the most deadly things known to man and had been since the beginning of time.

Sunglasses shielded her eyes. For some reason, her race was sensitive to the sunlight. Their true eye color was the palest of blue, a shade leached of all color. But using glamour, a dark magic, their kind could choose what humans saw, so they came with a variety of physical traits, shapes, and sizes. This one was blonde, tall and willowy, almost frail looking, but her appearance was extremely deceptive.

Not a single human or animal in this world was stronger or faster, and their talents ran the gambit, anywhere from telekinesis to igniting the most violent of fires with a brush of their fingertips. But the most dangerous weapon was their ability to bend mortals to their will, enslaving them. Fae needed humans. Feeding off mortals was the only way the fae slowed their aging process down to a lifespan that rivaled immortality.

Without humans, they'd age and die just like us.

Sometimes they played around with their victims, feeding off them for months, if not years, until nothing was left but a dry husk of what used to be. When they did that, they poisoned the human's body and mind, turning them into something just as dangerous and unpredictable as the fae. But sometimes they just outright slaughtered their victims. People like Val and I couldn't be warded against the feeding and the effects at birth, but centuries ago, the simplest and smallest thing had been discovered to null their abilities to manipulate us.

Nothing was more unexpectedly badass like a four-leaf clover.

Each member of the Order wore one. Val had a clover encased in her bracelet. I wore mine inside my gemstone tiger-eye necklace. I even wore it at home when I showered and slept, having learned the hard way that no place was truly one hundred percent safe without one.

Seeing through the glamour that enabled them to blend in was how we were able to spot and hunt them. Their true forms were equally beautiful . . . and disturbing. Skin a silvery color, kind of like liquid nitrogen, and incredibly smooth. Their beauty was eerily flawless, with high angular cheekbones, full lips, and eyes that tilted up at the outer corners. Everything about their true form was creepily alluring, in a way that made it hard to look away. The only thing the fairytales and myths got correct was the slightly pointed ears.

"Fucking fae," muttered Val.

My sentiments exactly since they had taken everything from me. Not once, but twice, and I hated them with the passion of ten thousand blazing suns.

Other than the ears, the fae were nothing like Disney painted them, or the ones Shakespeare had spun tales about, and they, like all their distant relatives, did not belong in this realm. Long, long ago, the fae had discovered a way to breach the divide between the mortal realm and theirs, what was known as the Otherworld. The summer and winter courts, if they'd ever existed, had been dissolved, and there was just one ginormous group with one really scary, totally typical goal.

They wanted to take over the mortal realm.

And it was our job to send them back to the Otherworld. Or kill them. Whatever worked the quickest.

Problem with that was the fact they weren't easy to do either of those things to, and they'd woven themselves into every facet of the mortal world.

As the fae passed our table, Val smiled up at her, all friendly innocence, and the fae returned a tight smile, having no idea we saw right through it all.

Val looked at me and winked. "That one is mine."

I flipped my textbook shut. "No fair."

"Saw her first." She stood, smoothing her hand along the wide leather belt she wore over the waist of her skirt. "See you later." She started to turn. "Oh, and seriously, thank you for Saturday night. I'll get laid and you'll be able to live vicariously through me."

I laughed as I shoved my book into my bag. "Thanks."

"Always thinking of others. Peace out." Spinning around, she easily sidestepped another table and disappeared into the throng of people crowding the sidewalk.

Val would catch up to the fae and lure it to a place where she could quickly dispose of it without the general populace witnessing what would probably look like cold-blooded murder.

Things got really awkward really fast when an unsuspecting human stumbled upon that mess.

Other than the mortals that fae kept around for a multitude of nefarious reasons, most of mankind had no idea that the fae were very real even though they were everywhere. And in cities like New Orleans where a whole crap ton of weird could go down without anyone batting an eyelash, they were a plague upon the city.

As I lifted my gaze and stared out at the swaying palms, I wondered how it was to be like everyone walking up and down the street. To, well, live in blissful ignorance. If I'd been born into any other family than the one I was, so many things would be different.

I'd probably be graduating from college in the spring. I'd have a large group of friends where memories instead of secrets linked us together. I might even have a—*gasp*—boyfriend.

Boyfriend.

Immediately, the busy street I sat on faded away. It was just me and . . . God, three years later and it still cut deep to even think of Shaun, and it took no effort to picture those soulful brown eyes. Some of the detail was beginning to fade—the image of his face had begun to blur, but the pain had not lessened.

A seed of sadness rooted deep in my stomach, and I desperately ignored it. Because what did my mother used to say? Not my real mom. I had been too young when she was killed to remember anything about her. My foster mother—Holly—used to say if wishes were fishes, we'd all cast nets. It was a quote she picked up from some book, loosely translated into there was no point in spending time on wishes.

At least that's how I took it.

It wasn't as if I didn't know how important my job—*my duty*—was. Belonging to the Order, a widespread organization full of knowledge that had been handed down through families, generation after generation, meant my life had more meaning than most.

Or so they said.

Each of us was marked with a symbol signifying that we belonged to the Order, and the tattoo, which were three interlocking spirals reminiscent of a Pre-Celtic design. Ours had three straight lines underneath it, though. It had been adopted as the Order's symbol of freedom.

Freedom to live without fear. Freedom to make our own choices. Freedom to thrive.

Mine was next to my hipbone. None of us wore it an area visible to mortals or fae.

So what I did with my life *was* important. I got that. The Order *was* my family. And I didn't regret any of what I had to do or what I'd given up. Even if the vast majority of people had no clue what the Order and I were doing, I was still making a difference with my life. I was saving lives.

And I was one badass ninja when I wanted to be.

That brought a grin to my lips.

Slinging my bag over my shoulder, I grabbed my empty iced coffee and hopped to my feet. It was time to work.

~

The fae I spotted outside of a bar on Bourbon Street reminded me of Daryl Dixon from *The Walking Dead*. Which was made of suck since I was going to have to kill him.

He was wearing a tan button-up shirt with the sleeves cut off at the shoulders, the edges frayed and worn, and jeans almost faded out completely at the knees. He had that weirdly hot redneck vibe about him, especially with the shaggy haircut.

The whole silvery skin tone and pointy ears really ruined the redneck ambiance though.

In and out of the bars on Bourbon Street, the fae reminded me of a tourist, because each time he walked out, he had a new container in his hand. Rumor had it that human alcohol didn't affect the fae, but nightshade, a plant toxic to humans, worked just like liquor did.

After seeing him with so many different containers and watching him for the past hour, I began to suspect that each of those bars might have a fae in them, because he was walking like he was three sheets to the wind by the time he wandered off Bourbon and passed the Gumbo Shop.

I made a mental note to call David Faustin, the head of the New Orleans branch of the Order, to see if he'd heard anything from the other members about nightshade being served at the human bars. But first I needed to take care of the Daryl Dixon reject.

I couldn't just walk up to the fae and get all stabby with him in front of people. I didn't want to spend a night in jail. Again. The last time someone saw me take out a fae, the police were called, and even though there was no body, I was loaded up with weapons, and that was kind of hard to explain.

And I really didn't want to listen to David bitch about all the strings he had to pull and blah, blah.

I'd probably sweated a pound off my boobs by the time the fae stumbled down an alley. Halle-freakin'-lujah. I was starving, there were beignets with my name written all over them, and since it was Wednesday night, there weren't a lot of fae roaming around, so I was totally going to lose my bet with Val.

The weekend would be a totally different story. When there were more mortals to mess with and it was easier for them to do what they wanted and get away, they came out in droves.

Kind of like cockroaches scurrying around at night.

The fae blended in with the thick shadows of the narrow alley, and I was quiet as I followed him, keeping close to the damp brick walls. Sliding my hands off the straps of my backpack, I groaned when the fae stopped halfway down the alley and faced the building.

His hands dropped to his zipper.

Was he seriously going to pee? Really? Ugh, that was so not on my list of things I wanted to hear or see tonight. And could I really kill something while it was peeing? Seemed kind of unsportsmanlike to kick a dude with his pants down.

I was so not going to wait for him to do his business. At the rate in which he was moving, I'd be here for about ten minutes before he got his zipper down.

Keeping my gaze trained on the fae, I reached down and slipped my hand around the non-business side of the iron stake secured inside my boot. Iron had always been epically destructive to the fae. They didn't go anywhere near it. Just the touch of it singed them, and if you stabbed one in the center of the chest, it didn't kill them but sent them right back to their world.

However, separating their heads from their bodies ended them. For realsies.

But sending them to the Otherworld was enough, thank God, because obviously chopping heads off was messy and gross. Gates, hidden all over, were the doorways between our worlds. They'd been closed for centuries, but were still well guarded. Sending them back was a one-way ticket.

I stepped away from the building, stake in hand as I moved swiftly down the alley. At my back was the hum of the busy street, muted conversations, and the distant drone of laughter.

My fingers tightened on the stake as the fae shifted his legs, spreading his thighs. I didn't make a sound as I walked right up to him, but some kind of inherent instinct alerted him to my presence. Fae couldn't sense us, but they knew the Order were around.

The fae twisted at the waist; his milky blue eyes met mine but were unfocused. Confusion splashed across his striking features.

"Hi!" I chirped, cocking my arm back.

His gaze flickered to my hand and he sighed. "Fuck."

Even intoxicated and about to pee, the fae was freaking *fast*. Whirling around, he deflected my blow with one arm and lifted his knee. Spinning to the side, I narrowly avoided a kick to the stomach.

I didn't glance down to see just how far he got with the zipper as I sprung forward and dipped under the arm he swung at me. Popping up behind him, I planted my foot in the center of his back.

The fae grunted as he staggered a step then turned to me as I rushed forward, ready for this to be over. Swinging my hand with the stake, the sharpened edge wasn't even an inch from his chest when he spat, "Your whole world is about to end. He's—"

I shoved the iron stake into his chest, cutting off his words. The stake cut through his skin like he was made of the cheapest tissue. For a second, he stayed completely intact, and he opened his mouth, letting out a high-pitched howl that sounded like a coyote getting run over by a Mack truck.

Holy shark teeth!

Four incisors were razor sharp and elongated. They reached his lower lip and reminded me of a mutant saber-toothed tiger. Fae could bite. It wasn't pretty. Actually, all creatures from the Otherworld had a tendency to get nippy.

Snapping back, I lowered the stake as the fae was sort of sucked into itself. From the top of his shaggy head to his sneakers, he folded like a ball of paper being crumpled, going from over six feet to the size of my hand before there was a crack of sound, like one of those bang snap fireworks, and a flash of intense light.

Then there was nothing.

"As last words go, that was kind of cliché and lame," I said to the spot where the fae had stood. "I've heard better."

"I'm sure you have."

Heart slamming against my chest, I whirled around. Visions of spending the night in the city jail danced in my head. Despite the fact that I'd probably already been caught red-handed, I shoved the stake behind my back.

Thankfully, it wasn't one of the city's finest standing at the mouth of the alley, but a man wearing black pants and a white shirt. As he lazily walked forward like he was out for a midnight stroll, I felt no measure of relief.

The dude obviously saw me stab the fae. This could only mean one of two things. The man belonged to the Order, but wasn't a part of the New Orleans branch, because I didn't recognize him. Or he was a servant to the fae, a human entranced to them. They could be just as dangerous.

And when you stabbed them, they didn't pull the poof, be-gone act. They bled. They died just like everyone else did. Sometimes slowly. The Order didn't have a no-kill human policy because it was a necessary evil at times, but it had to suck something fierce to kill one.

My fingers spasmed around the stake. *Please don't be a servant. Please be some whack job who thinks I'm his redheaded stepchild or something. Please. Please.* "Can I help you?" I asked, bracing myself.

The man cocked his head. Oh, I didn't like this. Every muscle in my body tensed. He stood a few feet inside the mouth of the alley, and then I saw it.

Pale, washed out blue eyes, slanted at the outer corners—fae eyes. But his skin wasn't silvery. It was a rich olive color that stood out against blond hair so pale it was almost white, and that hair was long, like Legolas in the *Lord of the Rings* long.

Legolas was kind of hot.

Okay. I so needed to focus because this dude was not right. Every instinct in me fired off warnings. I took a step back as I eyed the newcomer. There was no glamour on this guy, and he didn't carry the typical glazed over look servants favored. He looked human but not, and there was something about him that screamed he wasn't going to get friendly in any way I'd be happy with.

The man smiled as he lifted his arm. Out of thin air, a gun appeared in his hand. Just like that. Hand empty one second and the next he was holding a gun.

What in the holy hell?

"I wish you could see your expression right about now," he said, and then lowered the gun, aiming it right at me.

Chapter Two

The man pointing a gun at me was so not a human, because the last time I checked, we didn't have nifty abilities that enabled us to conjure guns out of thin air. I didn't even think fae could do that.

But this man—this *thing* had to be a fae.

"Not cool." I backed up, no longer bothering to hide the stake. "Kind of tacky to bring a gun to a knife fight."

The thing laughed, and the sound was as chilling as winters in the north. No humor. No empathy or humanity attached to it. "Kind of stupid to let you walk up behind me and stab me like the last one just did."

"That's a good point." I kept slowly moving backward as my heart pounded. I was nearing the other side of the alley. There was only one option for me. "You're not a normal fae."

A tight-lipped smile appeared. "And you're not a stupid cow?"

"What are you?" I ignored the derogatory term fae called humans. Cow. Cattle. Sustenance for them. Whatever. I'd been called worse.

He opened his mouth, but that second of distraction was all I needed. Like I'd been trained a hundred times over, I centered myself and cocked back my arm. Stepping forward, I let the stake fly.

It struck true, just like I knew it would.

The pointy end embedded deep in the thing's chest, knocking him back a step. A slow, satisfied smile split my lips. "Wait, I know what you are. A dead fae."

He glanced down and his shoulders rose with a deep, irritated sigh. "Really?" Annoyance colored his tone as he reached up with his free hand and proceeded to pull the stake out of his chest. He tossed it aside, and my eyes widened as the iron stake clanged off the pavement. "How weak do you think I am, cow?"

Holy shit.

Fae did not do that. They *couldn't*. But this one did, and this was so bad it wasn't even funny. I did the only thing left I could do, proving I wasn't a stupid cow. If you couldn't be sure you could win the fight with a fae? When in doubt, get the fuck out.

I turned and ran.

That's what we were taught when we were going down shit creek, nearing shitville, population unlucky you, without a shitty paddle. A good warrior knew when to retreat, and this was totally one of those moments.

My backpack thumped off my back as I hauled ass, picking up speed as I neared the narrow opening in the alley. Something popped behind me, and almost immediately a fiery pain exploded along the left side of my stomach, knocking the air out of my lungs.

The bastard shot me!

For a moment, I couldn't believe it. Surely he did not shoot me with an actual bullet from an actual gun. But the pain told me he had.

My step faltered, but I didn't stop. If anything, I ran faster—harder. Pain shrieked through me, and I felt like a lit match had been pressed against my side. I cleared the mouth of the alley and didn't look back.

Dodging drunks and tourists, I darted around the packed sidewalk and kept running as I reached into the back pocket of my cutoff jeans and pulled out my cellphone. Crossing Royal Street, I hit David's name and could barely hear the phone ringing over the sound of my pounding heart and the street traffic. I needed to tell him what happened—how the fae required no glamour and had summoned a gun out of nothing. This was huge. A total game changer.

The phone rang and rang until I cursed and disconnected the call. Clutching the cell in my hand, I slowed down to a jog, not because I wanted to, but because my toes were starting to tingle and my breath was wheezing out of me.

I'd never been shot before. Stabbed? Yes. Thrown around? Most definitely. Almost set on fire? That too. But being shot . . . wow, this sucked donkey balls.

Reaching out with my other hand as I stepped around two college-aged guys who were seconds from toppling over, I pressed my palm against my stomach. Wincing, my vision blinked out for a second then came back fuzzy before I could see clearly.

Oh dear.

Doubting I'd make it to a hospital in time, I hung a left onto Dauphine Street. The Order's headquarters was located on St. Phillips above an Order-owned gift shop called Mama Lousy that sold all kinds of cool iron stuff amidst an obscene amount of fake voodoo crap and authentic *n'awlins* spices and pralines.

God, I'd really love a praline right about now. I would shove two in my mouth.

Except there was a good chance I was bleeding to death.

In the back of my head, I thought it might've been a good idea to give Val a call, but I didn't want to worry her. I was so close to the Order anyway. I just had to keep walking.

My breathing was labored, and the hand I had pressed to my stomach was feeling way too wet and sticky, but as I spied the deep burgundy three-story building with its intricate wrought iron railings and thick, bushy ferns, I told myself I could do this. Just a couple more steps and I'd be okay. The wound couldn't be *that* serious. I doubted I would've been able to walk this far if so. Doc Harris would be there. Having a small one-room apartment on the second floor, he was always there.

The rest of the walk was a blurring of faces and sounds. Already closed up for the night, the gift shop was dark and unwelcoming as I pushed myself past the entrance and to the side door. Gripping the handle with a shaky hand, I yanked it open and stumbled into a dimly lit stairwell, panting as the pain dulled to a steady ache.

I didn't want to, but I had to take a moment before I climbed the damn stairs. They seemed so long, and the door looked as if it was a mile away. Yelling would've been pointless. The halls were soundproof, as were the rooms above.

"Get up the stairs, Ivy," I told myself. "Get up the damn stairs."

Putting one foot in front of the other was *hard*. I made it six steps before the sweat on my brow turned cold and tiny bursts of white light danced in front of my eyes. That couldn't be good.

The steps zoomed up to meet me as my knees turned to jelly. I caught myself with one hand before I face-planted, then my arm got all wobbly, and before I knew it, I was on my back slipping down a step or two. The pain from the bumpy ride didn't even register.

Dammit, all that progress for nothing.

In my hand, my cellphone vibrated. Maybe it was David finally calling me back. Or it could be Val rubbing it in my face that she already got two, possibly even three kills, and here I was, bleeding out on steps that kind of smelled like powdered sugar ... and feet.

Ew.

I needed to answer the phone, but the buzzing stopped and I couldn't will the energy to move the phone to a point where I could use it.

Someone would find me. Eventually. I mean, there was a security camera at the top of the stairs, and Harris had to check the monitor at some point. Plus, other members of the Order would be in and out during the night.

Maybe I'd just take a nap.

In the back of my head, a tiny voice ranted how bad of an idea that was, but I was so tired and the steps were becoming surprisingly comfortable.

I had no idea how much time passed, but I heard the door above me open, and I thought I heard Harris's accented voice echoing through the stairwell. I wanted to lift my arm and give him a happy little wave, but that required effort. Then, there was another deep voice. One I didn't recognize.

I blinked, or I thought that was all I did, and when I opened my eyes, I seriously considered that I might have died.

As cheesy as it sounded, as my vision focused on who was above me, I was staring into the face of an angel. Or at least that's what the paintings of angels in the million and one churches in the city told me they looked like.

The guy couldn't be very much older than me or it was the head full of curly brown hair that made him appear so young. One matching eyebrow arched as I stared into eyes the color of leaves in the spring, a rich almost unnatural green. Cheekbones were broad, jaw strong and cut like it was made of marble, and those lips were impossibly full as they curved into a slow grin on one side, revealing he had a deep dimple in his right cheek.

Shaun had dimples.

My breath caught sharply as the lancing pain in my chest that always accompanied thoughts of Shaun warred with my side for attention.

The guy's extraordinary emerald gaze flicked away from mine and up the stairs. "She's alive."

That voice. Whoa. Deep. Smooth. Cultured sounding. Yummy.

"And she's staring at me really intensely. Kind of unnerving. Like the blank stare of a sociopath."

I frowned.

24

"Who is it?" asked another voice, and yeah, that was Harris. "I can't tell who it is on the monitor and I ain't got my glasses on."

Harris couldn't see two feet in front of his face without his glasses.

Green Eyes met my gaze again, and that grin spread across his face. Dammit. He had a matching set when it came to dimples. "How would I know? But she kind of looks like that chick from the movie *Brave*. You know, the one with the really curly red hair."

What. In. The. Hell.

"She's got really pretty blue eyes, though."

Though. *Though?* As if that somehow made up for the fact that I had frizzy red hair like a Disney character.

"Shit," said Harris. His footsteps thudded down the stairs. "That'll be Ivy Morgan."

Seriously? That's how people know me? They could say I looked like the chick from *Brave* and they were like oh, that's Ivy?

I needed to dye my hair stat.

Wait, why was this dude watching Disney movies?

Green Eyes hovered over me, his head tilted to the side as his gaze drifted off my face. "She's bleeding along the stomach." He reached between us. "I think she's—"

I snapped out of whatever stupor I was in, and with a burst of energy I managed to catch his wrist before he got very far. His skin was warm and smooth. "Don't touch me," I gritted out.

His eyes met mine again, and for a moment, he didn't move, and I was struck again by his handsomeness. It wasn't often one saw a mortal male that rivaled the beauty of the fae. Then he easily slipped his hand free and rocked back on the lower step, kneeling. He raised his hands to his sides. "Not something I usually hear from the ladies, but your wish is my command."

I would've rolled my eyes if I wasn't concentrating on not seeing double. "That's . . . original."

A deep, rolling chuckle rumbled out of him as he rested his hands on his bent knees. "If it works, don't fix it is my mantra."

"Classy," I rasped, planting my hands on the step.

"I wouldn't do that if I were you," he commented helpfully.

Ignoring him, I pushed up into a sitting position, and a harsh burst of air parted my lips as the dull ache fired to life.

"Told you."

My narrowed gaze swung to the guy, but before I could say anything, Harris was at my side, his large body swallowing the stairwell. "What happened to ya, girl?"

"Got shot." I lifted my chin, my mouth dry as a desert. Since Green Eyes was with Harris, I took a leap of logic and assumed he was with the Order. "A fae shot me."

Harris bent over, settling a hand on my shoulder. The deep wrinkles around his eyes increased. "Girl, the fae don't use guns. Not sure why. They just never did it, and I ain't gonna look a gift horse in the mouth."

I gestured at my stomach with my bloodstained hand. "Obviously, I've . . . been shot, and it was a fae—a fae that didn't need any glamour."

"What?" Green Eyes asked sharply, and I looked at him.

26

His face started to get a little fuzzy around the edges, but that didn't detract from his attractiveness. "This fae didn't have silver skin. I couldn't . . . see his ears, but he had fae eyes. There was no glamour that I could tell. And he . . . conjured a gun out of thin air."

Green Eyes' brows flew up.

"Okay. Imma thinking ya might have hit ya head," Harris said, gripping my upper arm. "Let's get ya upstairs and take a look at ya."

"I didn't hit my head. I'm . . . telling you what I saw. He was a fae and he . . ." As Harris hauled me to my feet, Green Eyes rose, and the stairwell blinked out for a moment like a switch was thrown. "Whoa."

Harris said something, but all I could hear was this strange roaring sound, like the ground was shifting underneath and reaching up to grab me. I opened my mouth, but my tongue felt heavy and foreign, and utterly useless.

The entire building seemed to spin, and the last thing I heard before the world went black was Green Eyes sharp curse, and the last thought in my head was if I was going to be number four to die.

~

When I opened my eyes, particles of dust danced in the daylight streaming through the windows across from me. For a moment, I had no idea where I was or how I got here, but as I watched those tiny particles shimmer and fall, my memories slowly pieced back together.

I was at headquarters of the Order, most likely on the third floor, away from all the meeting and training rooms that thrummed with activity during the day. It was a huge infirmary room, outfitted to handle several patients at a time. There was another room, next to the bathroom that I'd never been inside of. I didn't think anyone except David went into that room. Val and I were convinced they were hiding a nation's worth of treasure in there.

The cot I lay on wasn't the most comfortable, but it was better than having the edge of the step pressing into my back, and someone had tucked a thin blanket around me.

Probably Harris. He was a big bear of a man, but he had a soft spot in his chest the size of Lake Pontchartrain.

I'd been shot.

Oh God—shot by a fae that didn't have silvery skin and could conjure a gun out of nothing. This was major news, and it changed everything. If the fae no longer needed glamour, how could we tell them apart from everyone else? It's not as if they were the only ones with pale eyes, plus there was a thing called contacts. And even more important, what I forgot to tell Harris was the fact that I stabbed the fae and it had done nothing.

A door opened, drawing my attention. I squinted as a form appeared, crossing through the bright streams of light toward my bed. An image of Green Eyes, the stranger who seriously looked like an angel, formed in my thoughts, and a strange tumbling sensation hit me in the stomach.

I didn't like the feeling.

But it wasn't Green Eyes who took shape the closer he got to my bed. It was our fearless leader, David Faustin, and he looked annoyed as usual.

David was sort of ageless, in a way where he could be in his forties, his fifties, or even his sixties, but no one knew. His skin, a shade or two darker than Val's, was mostly free of wrinkles, and he kept his body in rigorous shape. He wasn't smiling as he grabbed a folding chair and plopped it down next to my bed.

He dropped into the seat, arms across his chest. "You're alive."

"You're full of warm and fuzzies," I croaked.

One dark brow arched. "I'm assuming this is why you called me last night. Would've answered, but Laurie would be downright pissed if I left her hanging, if you get my drift."

My nose wrinkled. I totally didn't need that image that was just painted in my head. David and Laurie had been married for about a decade, having met when Laurie was transferred by the Order to New Orleans. Two Order members hooking up was pretty much the norm since the knowledge of the fae and our duty was passed down from one generation to the next, and our life expectancies weren't the greatest. Many Order members never married. Others that did and had kids, like my real parents, ended up being killed, and another family involved in the Order cared for them.

Having already lost my real and adoptive parents, and my . . . boyfriend to the fae, I couldn't wrap my head around falling in love again. Getting close to Val and a few others in the Order was risky enough, because I knew that at any moment they could die on the job. So it was hard for me to see so many of the Order members coupling up and opening themselves up to a world of hurt that never truly faded no matter how much time passed.

But Laurie and David were deeply in love despite all that, even though David had the personality of a rabid chupacabra and Laurie was as sweet as a praline.

"Talked to Harris when he called me. He said it was just a flesh wound that bled a lot, probably made worse by you running."

Pink crept into my cheeks as I stared at David. "I didn't run because I'm a coward. He had—"

"I didn't say you were a coward, Ivy. The man had a gun. You cannot fight a bullet."

Still, the tone of his voice stung like a sting from a hornet. I wet my lips. "It wasn't a man."

David eyed me for a second then reached toward the table next to my bed. "Thirsty?"

"Yeah. My mouth feels like sandpaper."

He poured water into a plastic cup, and just the tinkling sound was enough to drive me crazy. "Need help sitting up?"

Members of the Order weren't weak, so I took a deep breath as I shook my head and forced myself to sit up. There was a dull twinge of pain along the left side of my stomach, but not as bad as I expected.

"Harris gave you a shot while you were out, so you shouldn't be feeling too much pain." David noted what must've been reading my mind as he handed over the water. "You want to drink that slowly."

The moment the cool wet stuff hit my lips, it was hard not to gulp it down, but I managed to not look like a horse at a trough.

David leaned back, grabbing a bottle out of his pocket. "Here are some pain meds to use if your stomach starts hurting, which Harris said probably would for a day or so since he had to stitch you closed."

He tossed the bottle toward my lap, where it landed with a little rattle. "I'm gonna pull you off rotation until next Wednesday."

I lowered my empty cup. "What? Why? I can—"

"Your wound could reopen when you're fighting. We don't need you bleeding all over our steps again like a stuck pig. You're off until next Wednesday."

I was knocking off points for lack of empathy. "But I'm working for Val this Saturday."

"Not anymore. She needs to find someone else or do it herself. Not your problem." He refilled my cup from the pitcher. "Do you have class today?"

It took me a moment to catch up with what he was asking and figure out what day it was. "It's Thursday, right? I don't have class again until tomorrow." Normally, I worked Monday through Friday and had the weekends off. "About what happened last night. David, the fae—"

"I know what you said to Harris and Ren, but—"

"Ren? Who's Ren?" Then it hit me, and my tongue silently worked around the name. "Is he the guy with green eyes?"

David tilted his head to the side as he scowled. "Well, I haven't really been checking out the boy's eye color, but he was with Harris last night when you bled on my steps."

"I didn't bleed on your steps on purpose," I snapped.

His brows flew up. "Are you taking a tone with me? Because I'll take that cup of water right away from you."

"I'll never let go." I cradled the cup of water to my chest as I eyed him. "Never."

David's lips twitched as if he wished to smile, but he was too cool to do that. The man was a brick of ice.

"Anyway, Ren Owens is from Colorado, transferring to our sect."

Oh. Colorado. Never been, but always wanted to visit. And what kind of name was Ren Owens?

"But back to what you said you saw, there's no way that's how it went down," he said. "The fae must've had the gun for some reason, and yes, that is concerning but expected. We knew eventually they would start using human weapons."

Frustration pricked at my skin like a heat rash. "The fae wasn't using glamour. Or maybe he was, but it didn't matter. His skin wasn't silver. It was . . . I don't know. Like a deep tan—an olive color."

He leaned forward, resting his elbows on his knees. "Are you sure it was a fae, Ivy?"

"Yes! I'm sure, David. He made a gun appear out of thin air, and I threw my stake at him. It hit him in the chest, and it didn't do a *thing* to him. He pulled it out and tossed it aside."

He opened his mouth and seemed at a loss for words as he stared at me.

"Yeah. Exactly. The man wasn't human, David. He was a fae that didn't have silver skin, could conjure a gun out of nowhere, and the iron stake did nothing to him. Didn't burn him. Didn't send him back to the Otherworld. It did nothing."

"Impossible," he said after a moment, and my shoulders tensed with irritation.

"I know what I saw. And you know me. I'm not unreliable. Never once have you ever had to question me or—"

"Except the time you ended up in jail."

"Okay. Except that one time, but what I'm telling you is the truth. I don't know what it means, but . . ." A trickle of fear moved through my veins, forming a ball of unease in the pit of my stomach. I downed the glass of water and sat the plastic cup aside, but it didn't lessen the feeling. "If hitting a fae with iron does nothing to them, then they would be unstoppable."

"No, they would be an ancient," David said, and then stood.

My eyes widened at a word I hadn't heard spoken in a long time, not since I was a child and Holly and her husband Adrian would tell me stories of the race of the oldest and deadliest of fae—the warrior knights of their courts, the princesses and the princes, and the kings and queens. Fae that could change shape and form, and had abilities beyond our understanding. None of the fae that walked the mortal realm lived as long as the ancients had in the Otherworld, at least not as far as any of us knew. Basically, the ancients were the kind of fae that could wreak untold havoc in the mortal world if they ever crossed over. It never even occurred to me that the one I faced last night could've been an ancient.

"I thought they were all sealed in the Otherworld," I said. "When the doorways were closed, they—"

"They were." David walked to the window and pulled the flimsy pale blue curtain back. "It could be possible that a few remained here undetected, but it's very unlikely."

That ball of unease doubled in size. "But not impossible?"

Letting the curtain fall back into place, he rubbed a hand over the tight curls that were sheared close to his skull. "Very unlikely. It seems far-fetched that there'd be

33

one who survived this amount of time without our knowledge—without anyone seeing it."

"I saw it," I said. "And this one could easily blend in. If you weren't looking straight at it, paying attention, you wouldn't even know it was a fae."

David faced me. "We don't know what you really saw." He held up his hand as I opened my mouth to protest. "We don't, Ivy. That doesn't mean I'm disregarding what you're reporting to me. I'm going to contact the other sects and see if they have had any experiences like this, but until I hear back from them, we need to keep this quiet."

At least he was starting to take what happened seriously. For that I was grateful. Reaching down, I tossed the blanket off my legs and carefully swung them off the edge of the bed. "Shouldn't we warn the others?"

"And create a panic situation, one where we have members killing humans because we think they might be an ancient?"

"But—"

"Ivy," he warned. "I cannot afford for any of our members to panic, or for innocent lives to be lost."

I didn't like it, but I conceded. "I'll keep quiet."

Doubt crossed his features. "That also means not telling Valerie, who, by the way, you might want to call before she flips her shit."

"Ye of little faith," I murmured, tugging at my bloodstained shirt. Thank goodness it was black or I would've scared the bejeezus out of a bunch of people last night, running all bloody.

"I'm being serious." He pierced me with a stern look. "Tell no one until we know what we're dealing with, especially when we have suffered as many losses as we have this year. You understand me?"

I kind of felt like a misbehaving child when he looked at me like that. The man was hard to deal with, but since I'd lost my family, he was the closest thing I had to a . . . to a father figure. "I understand, David."

"I would hope that you do." He placed his hands on his hips. "Look, take as long as you need here, then go ahead and head home. Remember, you're off until Wednesday, but I expect to see you at the meeting tomorrow."

Baby Jesus could land in front of me, and I wouldn't miss the weekly bitch session.

He started to leave but then stopped. "Did the fae say anything to you?"

Sliding off the bed, I ignored the tender pull of the skin over my stomach. "Nothing really. I mean, he creeped up on me after I got rid of another fae—a normal one who said the same old 'your world is about to end' crap, but this one? He called me a cow, that's about it."

David nodded, almost absently, and then with another swift reminder that I was off rotation, he left the room, leaving me staring into nothing. As I searched for my boots, I couldn't help but notice that the unsettled feeling in the pit of my stomach hadn't faded, even with David saying he was going to contact the other sects.

The thing was, as I found my boots under the small table by the bed, I couldn't shake the feeling that while David didn't appear to be too overly concerned about the potential of an ancient roaming around, this was just the beginning of something big.

Chapter Three

Getting home took a little longer than normal since I wasn't feeling up to hoofing it anywhere, which meant dealing with traffic. I caught a cab and used the time to inconspicuously—because the cabbie was starting to give me a weird look—reassure Val that I wasn't dead, currently dying, or going to die anytime soon.

That I knew of.

"I have bad news," I told her as we neared the Garden District.

Val snorted. "Other than getting shot by some punk?"

I decided to tell her it was some random jerk on the street that shot me, which didn't take a leap of faith to believe. The fae weren't the only dangerous things on the streets of New Orleans. The cabbie had hit the break at that point, and I thought he was going to kick me out of the car or something. "Yeah, besides that. I can't work Saturday night. David pulled me."

"Honey, the moment you told me you were shot, I expected that. And honestly, that's the last thing you need to worry about."

"Thanks," I murmured, glancing out the window then doing a double take. A guy was riding a . . . unicycle on the side of the road, wearing a . . . blue cape. What the hell?

Only in New Orleans.

"Do you want me to swing by before I head out tonight?" she asked.

I glanced at the driver. "Nah. I'm just going to clean up and sleep."

"Call me if you need anything. Promise."

The urge to tell her what really happened last night was hard to resist. Not because I wanted to gossip, but because I wanted to warn her to be on the lookout. Sighing, I gripped my cell tightly. "Promise, but hey, be careful. Please?" The very moment that left my mouth, icy fear wriggled into my chest. Losing Val, the only real friend I'd made since moving here wasn't something I wanted to even consider. "You promise me that, okay?"

Val's laugh was airy. "I'm always careful."

Hanging up the phone after saying goodbye, I realized we were on Coliseum Street and edging to a stop against the curb shaded by thick oak trees. I dug into my bag and handed over some cash before climbing out.

The cabbie looked happy to be getting the hell out of there.

I was lucky with the place the Order had helped me find upon arriving in the city. While most of the Order lived closer to the Quarter, I was thrilled to be in the absolutely stunning Garden District, with its tapestry of trees, rich history, and old homes.

The house, about a ten-minute walk from Lafayette Cemetery No.1 was an antebellum home converted into two apartments, one up and one down. There were separate balconies with the entrance to the first floor at the front, and the entrance to my place along the back, which was accessed through a gorgeous courtyard overflowing with potted plants and flowers.

The iron cornstalk fence surrounding the entire property was an added benefit.

Well, up until now.

A shudder worked its way down my spine as I latched the gate behind me, and before I headed through the courtyard, I stared out at the cars flowing down the street. A warm breeze caught the loose curls at the nape of my neck and tossed them as I drew in an unsteady breath.

General mankind had no idea that fae existed because the Order had been able to protect them so far. Yes, some we couldn't save, but as a whole, we did a damn good job keeping them safe. But if that fae I ran into last night was an ancient, and if there were more around, or if they were no longer susceptible to iron, we were so screwed.

I wondered who I could even talk to about an ancient. David was obviously not going to be that helpful. The only person who came to mind was Brighton Jussier's mother Merle, a woman who knew a lot about virtually everything, but she was kind of . . . whacked.

Rumor had it that Merle got caught by fae without the protection of a clover and it messed with her head.

Before then, she had been well-known as a brilliant mind in the Order, but now her mental state changed by the day.

I turned from the road, walking down the cobblestone path in the courtyard. Normally I lingered, plucking off the dead petals from the flowers, but I was more tired than I realized.

I guessed bleeding like a '*stuck pig*' was exhausting.

At the top of the outdoor stairs, I groaned as I spotted three small boxes from Amazon stacked in front of my door, just under the awning. "Oh, come on."

I did not order anything from Amazon recently, but I bet I knew who did. God, I really needed to change my password to my Prime account and turn one-click ordering off.

Cursing under my breath, I picked up the boxes. They were light, but my tummy was feeling tender. I unlocked the door and stepped into the living room, quickly scanning the couch. The peach colored blanket was no longer draped along the back but half on the cushion and half on the floor.

The TV was on, a movie playing where a boy wearing glasses was riding a broom, trying to escape a very angry, very large dragon. As I closed the door behind me, locking it, I murmured, "Harry Potter . . . and the Goblet of Fire? What the . . . ?"

I sighed.

I placed the boxes in a low sling back chair by the door that had a footstool placed in front of it, walking over to the slider behind the couch and pulling the drapes back. Potted flowers swayed in the breeze, but the wicker chairs with the awesomely thick cushions I'd paid an arm and a torso for were empty.

So was the bathroom in the hallway, but I grabbed the shower curtain with pastel colored fish on it and yanked it back. Bathtub also empty.

Opening the door to my bedroom, I was relieved to find everything in there the way I liked it and had left it—blinds and curtains closed. The room was a good twenty degrees cooler than any other place in my apartment, and I couldn't wait to face plant in my bed and snuggle with the super comfy chenille bedspread.

After I showered.

There was a smaller, second bedroom on the other side of the kitchen that faced Coliseum Street, and had another balcony accessed from it. People loved their balconies around these parts. I entered the kitchen, and my gaze immediately went to the open cabinet door where I kept my cereal boxes.

All twelve of them.

I liked my variety when it came to cereal.

Dropping my backpack in the chair near the bistro table by the large window that overlooked the courtyard below, I walked around the island and stopped in front of the cabinet.

On the counter, the box of Lucky Charms—how ironic—was tipped to the side, the plastic wrapper split open and the top of the box resting against the rim of a huge blue and purple bowl.

Having really no idea of what I was going to see, I slowly approached the bowl. A surprised laugh bubbled up my throat and I clapped my hand over my mouth to squelch it.

Lying in my bowl was a houseguest I wasn't quite sure how I ended up with but couldn't seem to get rid of. Tiny arms and legs were sprawled across a bed of cereal.

Not a single marshmallow was in sight, and I'd bet all the money in my savings account that the best part of the cereal was in the distended belly of the brownie passed out in my cereal bowl.

Could brownies get intoxicated from sugar?

I had no idea.

Two and a half years ago, I stopped a fae from luring a small girl away from her family, and ended up chasing the sick bastard into Saint Louis Cemetery No. 1 where I was able to send him back to the Otherworld. But as I was in the process of leaving, I got distracted by the rumored tomb of Marie Laveau, and that was where I found the little brownie.

Brownies were a rarity in the mortal realm. Frankly, from what I'd heard, they hated it here, supposedly preferring the forests of their realms, and honestly, there was no hiding what they were.

The gossamer wings kind of stood out.

Myths always portrayed them as being wingless, but they had them. They were also tiny, little things about the size of a Barbie doll. The brownie had been injured, suffering a tear in his frail wings and a broken leg. The moment he stared up at me with those big, pale blue eyes, I knew I couldn't just leave him there, hiding behind a vase with dried out flowers in it, standing among crusty Mardi Gras' beads. So I picked him up and put him in my backpack.

I'd taken the brownie home with me.

I knew—God, I knew—it was my duty to finish the job. No creature of the Otherworld was allowed to survive in our world, but I couldn't bring myself to do it, even though I knew I'd be in a world of trouble, maybe even kicked out of the Order. But I'd taken him home, created a leg splint out of popsicle sticks, and wrapped his wing with gauze while he sat there, a forlorn and pouty look on his cute face. I don't even know why I did it. I hated anything from the Otherworld—no matter their size or what breed they were—but for some reason, I took care of the little brownie.

And he'd stayed.

Probably because he discovered the Internet, the TV, and my Amazon Prime.

So yeah, I knew *exactly* how I ended up with the brownie, and just didn't understand why I had a weak spot for the little douche I'd named Tink.

I snorted.

Tink hated that nickname once I played the movie Peter Pan for him.

Peering into the bowl, I shook my head. He was shirtless, and cereal was stuck to his pale white wings, but at least he had pants on. Tink was wearing a pair of Ken doll trousers. Black ones with satiny stripes running down the sides.

I poked him in the belly.

He jerked away, arms flying as he sat up, snapping at my finger with wicked sharp teeth, coming dangerously close to making contact.

"Bite me," I warned, "and I will bury you alive in a shoebox."

His mouth dropped open as he popped out of the bowl, hovering above it. Pieces of cereal flew across the counter as his wings moved soundlessly. "Where have you been? You didn't come home. I thought you were dead, and no one knows about me, and I would just be left here. Forgotten. I'd starve, Ivy. *Starve.*"

I folded my arms across my chest. "Doesn't look like you were starving. Looks like you were pretending to be a chipmunk and storing food for the winter by eating all of it."

"I had to eat to get through the stress of being abandoned!" he shouted, raising a hand and shaking a fist the size of a thumbnail at me. "I didn't know where you were, and you don't engage in any bow-chick-a-wow-wee so you always come home."

My lips turned down at the corners.

Tink flew up until he was eye level with me, clasping his hands together over his belly as he gave me those big eyes. "I ate so much sugar. So. Much."

Shaking my head, I turned and started picking the cereal up off the counter and tossing it into the bowl. "I don't even want to know what your blood sugar levels are."

"We don't have blood in our veins." He buzzed to my shoulder and sat down. His small fingers gripped my earlobe. "We have *magic*," he whispered in my ear.

I shrugged him off with a laugh. "You do not have magic in your veins, Tink."

"Whatever. What do you know?" He landed on the counter and started kicking cereal across it. I sighed. "So where were you, Ivy Divy?"

"I got shot last night."

"What?" Tink shrieked as he slapped his hands on his cheeks. "You got shot? Where? How? By who?" He zipped up in the air, darting left to right, right to left. "Did you cry? I would've cried. A lot. Like a river of motherfucking tears."

A whole half a minute went by as I stared at him. "Okay. You're normally like a little fairy on crack—"

"Just because I have wings doesn't mean I'm a damn fairy!" He then slipped into a language that sounded faintly like ancient Gaelic before saying, "I had a lot of sugar, okay? Is that a crime? You left me here alone all night! What else was I supposed to do?"

"Can brownies have strokes?" I asked, a little concerned by the way the vessels were starting to pop out along his temples.

He cocked his head to the side as he screwed up his face. "Is that when you blow something in your head? I don't know. Wait. Oh my, Queen Mab, do you think I'm having a stroke?" He zipped up to the light fixture in the ceiling, disappearing behind the silver dome-shaped shade. A second passed, then he peered over the side. His white-blond hair was sticking up in every direction. "I'm having a stroke. Shite."

"Get down from there, Tink. Good God," I muttered as the fixture swayed. "You're not having a stroke. Forget I said anything."

"I hate it when you call me Tink."

I grinned. "I know."

"Evil woman." He hesitated and then made his way back down to the counter, where he sat with narrowed eyes. "So . . . anyway, you got shot?"

I nodded as I finished scooping up the cereal. "A fae shot me."

"When did they start using guns?"

Grabbing the box and bowl, I took them over to the trash and dumped them. Not like I'd be eating any of that after he'd taken a nap in it. It wasn't weird talking about my job with Tink. He seemed to take it in stride. "I don't know, but the fae didn't have silver skin either."

44

When Tink didn't respond, I turned around, half expecting him to have passed out, but he was awake and his eyes were wide. "And the fae conjured a gun out of thin air," I said.

Tink swallowed.

"And I stabbed him with an iron stake and it did nothing," I added, walking over to him.

He hopped up to his feet. "That sounds like an . . ."

"An ancient?"

His head shook back and forth. "They are badass. Scary, but badass." He tip-toed to the edge of the counter. "Was he near you when he shot you? Like was he far away?"

That was a strange question, but then again, it was Tink. "He was a good distance away from me. If he'd been close to me, I doubt I'd be standing here right now."

He paled. "I've never seen an ancient here."

"Exactly how long have you been in this world, Tink?"

One shoulder rose. Not like I expected an answer, or at least a helpful one. Tink didn't even know what gate he'd come through or how he ended up here. He said that he woke up in our world, in the cemetery, and had no idea how it all happened. Based on the condition he'd been in and his personality, I suspected he'd gotten the crap beat out of him and someone pitched him through a gate. Tink also never told me his real name since knowing any Otherworld creatures' real name gave you power over them, even the fae. All I did know was that he loathed the fae as much as the Order did. From what I gathered, his kind had been hunted to near extinction by the fae in the Otherworld, and Tink's entire family

45

had been slaughtered. His hatred of the fae put us on the same team, even if other Order members wouldn't agree.

"I've seen the ancients in the Otherworld," he said in a stage voice. "I've even seen the prince."

"Really?"

He nodded. "The prince . . ." Throwing out his arms, he spun in tight circles that were actually dizzying to watch. "The prince is dreamy."

Uh.

"But so are most fae, aren't they? Gorgeous but deadly, arrogant bastards." He stopped spinning. "The prince is also really scary."

I leaned against the counter, ignoring the steady ache that was increasing in my stomach. "You've seen the prince? Like the real prince of the Otherworld?"

"Yep. Saw him three times." Eagerness crept into his expression. "Once he was in this meadow. Kind of like the meadow in that movie with the sparkly vampires and crazy hair."

Oh Lord.

"He didn't see me, which was a good thing. The second time was when I was near their palace. It kind of looks like something on the show you watch where everyone dies."

"Game of Thrones?" I suggested. "King's Landing?"

He jumped as he nodded. "And then the third time was . . . well, he was doing something you never do."

There were a lot of things I never did. "What was that?"

Cupping his hands around his mouth, he stretched up as his wings arced behind him. "He was having sex."

"Tink," I muttered, hanging my head.

"With three females. Three." Tink settled back, shaking his head in wonder. And I was kind of in wonder myself. Three females, one male? Then again, I wasn't surprised. The fae were full of sexuality. Another weapon they used against mortals. "How is that even possible?" he asked.

"It takes talent," I replied, eyeing the little dude. A moment passed while he danced around. "Do you know anything about ancients being here?"

He stopped and looked up at me. "No."

"What about why an ancient would suddenly make his presence known?"

A shake of the head. "I have no clue."

"You wouldn't lie to me, would you, Tink?"

"No." He grinned. "You have Amazon Prime."

I snorted. "Good to know how I can secure your loyalty." I pushed off the counter and headed toward my bag. "By the way, while you were passed out, there were deliveries for you. I put them on the chair by the door."

"Ah!" He flew up in the air. "Why did you wait until now to tell me?" Heading toward the living room, he stopped beside me. "But you're okay, right? You're not going to die on me while you sleep? No one knows about me, so no one will know to come looking for me, and I already ate all the marshmallows out of the Lucky Charms."

Laughing softly, I shook my head. No one knew about Tink, not even Val. Whenever anyone came over, Tink knew to hide. "I'm fine. Just a little sore, but they gave me some stuff for that. I'm going to take a shower then probably sleep."

"It's only four in the afternoon."

"You were passed out when I came in, so I don't want to hear it." Grabbing the bottle of pills out of the front zippered pocket of my backpack, I scooped one out and chased it down with a root beer I fished out of the fridge.

"Don't get addicted to those. I don't want to be roomies with a junkie because then you'll move on to harder shit and end up doing bath salts and eating my face off." Then he flew out of the room.

Tink . . . Tink was weird.

I'd made it to my bedroom door when he flew past me, clutching a tie-dyed troll doll. He collected them, and I honestly really didn't want to know what he did with them.

Once inside my bedroom, I placed my drink on the nightstand, and flipped on the bedside light. Although I kept the room dark, everything inside of it was bright— the fuchsia pillowcases and deep purple chenille bedspread, the blue and pink paisley bench at the foot of my bed. Even the two dressers and the nightstand were painted a bright blue.

Since I couldn't wear colors like Val did, I lived knee-deep in them.

I got undressed, leaving my clothes in a pile by the door to the en suite bathroom. I was lucky to have two, especially since Tink liked to turn the hallway bathtub into a swimming pool. This bathroom was simple and gorgeous, and I loved the old claw-foot tub with the shower rod.

I cranked the water on to as hot as I could stand it and made sure the bandage covering my stitches was secured before I stepped under the steaming stream.

The moment the water hit my skin, I let out a sound of pure bliss. It felt like I hadn't showered in days.

The water ran a deep pink until the basin of the tub cleared and all the dried blood was washed away. I cleaned my hair twice, and as I stood under the pounding stream, I let the events of last night finally catch up to me.

I slapped my hands over my face, but the tide of emotion rose up swiftly, settling in the back of my throat. My eyes burned fiercely as I squeezed them shut, refusing to let the tears fall.

I hadn't cried since the night my adopted parents were slaughtered, the same night Shaun was killed, and I had cried so many tears back then I think there was a good chance I'd soaked up a lifetime's worth of heartache. Getting shot was like pricking open old wounds with a butter knife. I wasn't sure why exactly, other than the flash of mortality, but I saw Holly and Adrian's lifeless stares as if I were standing over them again. Then I saw Shaun, him paling as . . .

Running my fingers over the Freedom symbol inked into my skin next to my left hip, I turned my back to the shower and forced myself to take steady, deep breaths until the knot in my throat lessened and the images of that dark night retreated.

The ache in my stomach had started to fade by the time I stepped out of the shower and dried off, but the antsy feeling that always accompanied thoughts of what happened that night had surfaced and was going strong. So was the feeling of unease as I walked into my cool bedroom. There could be an ancient out there right now, doing God knows what, and I was going to bed?

It wasn't even six in the evening, but the bed did look super appealing. Glancing at my dresser, my gaze skipped over the daggers lined up neatly. They were only slightly different from a stake. The blade was thinner and the handle made them easier to use.

Curling my fingers around the edges of my towel, I blew out an annoyed breath. I knew what I wanted to do, but David would have my ass in a sling since he told me to take off until Wednesday.

But he didn't tell me I had to stay home.

A grin pulled at my lips as I started toward my closet. Technically I wouldn't be working. I'd just be out for an evening walk, and if I happened to come across any fae, even a possible ancient or whatever, then it wouldn't be my fault.

With that thought circling around, I changed into a fresh pair of jeans and a loose t-shirt Tink had ordered for me a few months back. It was black with a drunken fairy on it. Leave it to Tink to find that shirt online . . . and buy it with *my* money.

I strapped a dagger inside my boot and tugged the hem of my jeans down. I twisted my hair into a knot, securing it with a thick bobby pin. Tink was nowhere to be found when I entered the kitchen and pulled my textbooks out of my bag, making the backpack lighter.

I headed to the closed bedroom door and rapped my knuckles on it. "Tink?"

"I'm busy!" came the immediately shout.

The troll doll he carried into his room earlier appeared in my mind, and I mentally recoiled from that with a quickness. "I'm heading out. Okay?"

A second later the door cracked open and Tink stuck his blond head out. His pale blue eyes narrowed. "You're not going out to work, are you?"

I shook my head. "I'm just heading out." Which wasn't entirely a lie. "I won't be late."

His lips pursed. "I don't believe you. You're up to shenanigans! I can tell."

"Want me to bring back some beignets?"

Tink's eyes widened and a look of childlike glee crept into his expression. "Would you? For me? A whole plate for me? All mine? Not yours?"

I rolled my eyes. "Yes, Tink."

"From Café Du Monde?"

"Yes." I sighed.

"Then get the hell out of my face and get going!" Tink slammed the door shut.

"You're welcome," I muttered, shaking my head.

Conserving energy, I caught a trolley to Canal Street, and as I stepped out under a palm, I really hoped I did not run into David. No one could make you feel like a misbehaving thirteen-year-old quicker than he could. I crossed the street and headed toward Royal. The sky was overcast, and the air was cloaked with humidity. I couldn't wait until the cooler temps rolled in.

As I made my way toward the Quarter, I thought of Green Eyes. Was he out here tonight? And who in the hell was he? What did David say his name was?

Why was I even thinking about him?

Though I bet money the moment Val laid eyes on him, she would be laying a lot of things on him.

For a Thursday night, the Quarter was packed, but as one hour turned into three, I hadn't caught sight of a single fae. The whole thing was turning out to be a bust, but I guessed that was good news, right?

But it was . . . strange.

Probably because there was a darkness that lingered over the city, a tangible feeling of something building in the background that wasn't all puppies and rainbows. Over the last couple of weeks I'd noticed it. Even some of the other Order members had mentioned it. Val had said no more than a handful of days ago that it reminded her of how it felt before a bad storm rolled into the city. I didn't know what the feeling truly signified, but I couldn't help thinking it had something to do with the fae I'd run into last night.

I roamed up and down Bourbon, where the fae typically congregated. I should've seen at least three by this point. This was weird, and the sense of unease grew stronger, trickling through my veins like the icy rains I used to hate up north.

Thinking of the bar I'd seen the fae stumble out of the night before, I pivoted around and nearly slammed into an older man. "Sorry!" I sidestepped him, and I was pretty sure he had no clue I almost plowed him over.

I slowed my steps as I neared the bar. From the outside it looked like almost every other bar on Bourbon—a little sketchy, slightly rundown, and teaming with people who were in various stages of drunkenness. I usually stayed out of the bars, because my patience thinned quickly, but I took a deep breath and stepped through the open door.

And immediately regretted it.

The scent of stale beer and mold smacked me in the face. Yuck. Trying not to breathe too deeply, I moved around the edge of the group surrounding the bar. A TV hung from the ceiling, broadcasting a baseball game. Shouts erupted. Arms shot into the air. Droplets of beer flew in every direction. I stepped back, hoping I didn't get drenched.

"Ivy."

My fingers tightened on the strap of my bag. I recognized that voice. Crap. I turned around to see Trent Frost, member of the Order, and certified ass kisser.

I plastered a smile on my face that felt painful. "Hey. . ."

Trent looked me in the eyes for a full two seconds before his gaze dropped to my breasts. Typical. "Didn't you get shot?"

Good to know what happened last night had spread through the Order. "Yeah, but it was a flesh wound." I turned, glancing back at the bar. I was going to have to kung-fu people out of the way to get a look at the bartenders. "Nothing big."

"Also thought you were off rotation until Wednesday," he said.

"I am. I'm not working."

He was like a wolf with a cornered rabbit. "Then why are you out here?"

I shrugged. "Why are you?"

"Wanted to see the score on the game."

I faced him, arching a brow. "Seriously?"

His dark eyes dropped again, and I resisted the urge to plant my fist in his face. "Actually, no. I caught a couple of fae coming out of this bar over the last week. Wanted to check it out."

Well hell bells, I wasn't the only one who noticed that. Trent might have a perverted, wandering eye, but he was good at what he did. And the deep scar under his lip spoke of all the times he'd tangled with the fae. "I saw one come out of here last night, so I was curious to see what was going on."

"Thought you weren't working."

I shot him a peeved glare. "Just because I'm checking something out doesn't mean I'm working."

"Uh-huh." He chuckled as he nodded up at the bar. "Bartenders are normal tonight. Not sure if that's how it is every night or if one of them is working for the fae." He folded muscled arms across his huge chest. For what he lacked in height, he sure made up in width. The man could probably knock down a small house with all the muscles he was packing. "Either way, I'm going to hang here, see if I can catch anything."

"Streets are dead, aren't they?" I asked as a guy bumped into my shoulder.

He nodded. "I heard that you said a fae shot you," he said, and I cursed under my breath. Harris must've talked because I doubt David would have. Me trying to cover up what happened didn't help if someone else was talking. I wanted to do what David had ordered and keep my mouth shut and all, but I couldn't help thinking it was wrong and put other Order members at risk.

Screw it.

I faced Trent. "It was a fae who shot me, and I'm sure you also heard that it made a gun appear out of thin air. It wasn't a normal fae, Trent. I stabbed it with iron and it did nothing."

His lips twitched as he looked over my head and at the screen behind the bar. "That sounds . . . batshit crazy. Like as crazy as Merle sounds."

I stiffened as if cement had been dropped down my spine. I felt a lot of sympathy for that woman. A huge part of me . . . well, I could understand her, and I didn't like hearing anyone talk like that about her.

"That's ignorant," I said, my voice calm even though I was seconds from introducing his face to the power of my uppercut. "She was a member of the Order, and you should respect everything that woman has sacrificed."

Trent tipped his head back and laughed through his nose. "With or without my respect, that doesn't change the fact that she's crazy." Shaking his head, his gaze flipped to mine then dropped to my chest. "Man, I gotta say, it was a bad idea when the Order started allowing females in. You guys just can't handle—"

I didn't even think.

Grasping his shoulders with both hands, I leveraged myself as I brought my knee up and forward, slamming it between his knees. Air punched out of his lungs, along with a harsh curse. Letting go of his shoulders, I stepped back with a smile as he doubled over.

"Handle that, asshole." Then I spun on my heel and practically flounced out of the bar.

I was definitely going to get yelled at for that if Trent ratted me out, but whatever lecture I'd be facing was so worth it. What a freaking pig. The sad thing was a lot of the guys in the Order felt that way. Idiots.

The sun had long since gone down, and the scent of rain clung to the air as I headed toward Jackson Square. I needed to call it a night, pick up some beignets, and head back home. I crossed the intersection, and as I glanced to my left, I came to a complete stop in the middle of the street.

Holy crap.

There, right in the middle of Orleans Avenue, was the fae from last night. I couldn't believe it, but it was him. My heart kicked in my chest as I veered to the left, hitting the sidewalk and sticking close to the buildings.

He was standing with his side to me, out in front of the cigar shop. A human male was with him, and it was just the massive size of the fae that made the human look like a strong wind could blow him the rest of the way to the square. He was strung out, frail, and sickly looking as he stood beside the fae, itching at the skin above the day's growth of beard. The fae who shot me turned, his back to me, and the human tried to follow but stumbled off the curb and fell, cracking his knees on the road.

That was the effect of a fae feeding off a mortal's essence, slowing stripping away their life until nothing but dust and bones was left behind.

The fae didn't even look back at the mortal as he started walking down Orleans, toward Royal. I picked up my pace as the guy managed to stand. Disoriented, he turned in a wide circle until he spotted the fae several feet ahead. He lurched after him like a lost puppy—an unfed, flea-infested puppy.

So incredibly wrong.

Fury rose in me as swiftly as a fierce storm blowing in. My hands curled into fists, and my blood boiled with anger. My entire being was focused on the bastard as I stalked forward. I made it a couple of feet when something—a person—stepped out from between two buildings and grabbed a hold of me.

An arm curled around my stomach, just below my breasts, securing my arms to my sides. I was up and off the sidewalk in a nanosecond, taken into the narrow pathway between the two buildings. A hand clamped down on my mouth. Instinct kicked in, and I brought my knees up, planning to throw my weight forward.

"I wouldn't do that," said a low, deep voice directly in my ear. "I'm going to put you down, and you're not going to spin around and punch or kick me. You understand?"

How was I supposed to voice my understanding? His hand was over my mouth!

"Come on, Merida. Nod your head if you feel me."

Who in the hell was Merida? It didn't matter. All I needed was for him to let me go, and I wasn't going to punch or kick him. I was going to beat the living crap out of him. I nodded.

"I'm trusting you. The last thing I want to see is for you to hurt yourself," he said.

Oh, someone was going to be hurting, and it wasn't going to be me.

A second later, the arm around my upper stomach disappeared and so did the hand. Without hesitation, I spun around and looked up into a pair of startling emerald colored eyes.

Chapter Four

It was him. Green Eyes. *Ren*. That was his name. Now I remembered. I started to step forward, but he beat me to it. Moving as quickly as a damn snake striking, he caught my wrists. He didn't yank my arms to my sides. All he did was hold my fists away from his face.

A lopsided grin appeared on those full lips. "Can't say I'm entirely surprised you took a swing at me."

"Then I guess this won't surprise you either." Leaning back, I shifted my weight onto my left leg, but again, Ren outmaneuvered me with a quickness that was sort of embarrassing.

He stepped into what would've been a fantastic kick and forced me back against the wall. Then there was nowhere to go, no space whatsoever. My back was against the building, and the entire length of his hard body was pressed against mine.

Son of a bitch.

As if he could read my mind, that grin spread and the dimples played peekaboo. "Now I think we can have a conversation without me ending up bloody."

I blew out an aggravated breath. "I wouldn't bet on that not happening."

He chuckled, and the sound rumbled through me. I couldn't even remember being this close to a guy since . . . since Shaun. "Look, I'm sorry for snatching you off the street like a kidnapper, but you were about to make yet another huge mistake."

His apology was lost on me. "Make another mistake?"

"Yeah, like the one last night that ended with you getting shot." He dipped his chin, and the yellow glow of the light attached to the wall above us glanced off his broad cheekbones. "I know what you were about to do."

"I didn't make a mistake last night. I was doing my job," I spat. "And I doubt your job includes grabbing chicks off the street."

"That would be a hell of a lot more entertaining, but the moment you thought you could engage that fae last night, you made a mistake. And you were about to do it again, you little ass."

"Little ass?" I sputtered. "You grabbed me off the street like a serial killer!"

"And I've apologized for that even though you should be thanking me. I just saved your life, sweetness."

Floored, all I could do was stare at him for a moment. "You're insane."

"I'm a lot of things, but today I'm your fucking saving grace."

"Wow. You're so incredibly modest," I said. "Let me bake you some damn cookies."

That grin spread into a smile that I could easily see stopping hearts across the nation. "I like sugar cookies. With extra sugar sprinkled on top."

"Oh, go fu—"

"You were about to get your ass handed to you by an ancient, Ivy. I stopped you," he said, proving that he knew my name wasn't Merida or whoever the hell he called me. "And I know you're one bundle of kick ass hotness, but you're not ready to face off with one of them."

I opened my mouth, but two things struck me into silence. First off, he called me a bundle of kick ass hotness, and that really did sound like a cool compliment. But more importantly, he called that fae an ancient more than once, and that got through the haze of fury.

Staring up at him, I simmered down. "He really is an ancient?"

"Yes."

My heart rate jumped. "How . . . how do you know?"

"I know."

"I don't know you enough to even begin to trust you or what you're saying," I told him. "So a little detail would be nice."

"I didn't ask you to trust me." He tilted his head to the side as his thumb moved on the inside of my right wrist, gliding in a small circle in a way that was distracting. "What I am telling you, is that fae you met last night and were following tonight isn't a normal one. He's an ancient, and he's not the only one here."

"How do you know?" I repeated.

A muscle thrummed along his jaw and a moment passed. "Aren't you supposed to be taking time off?

What are you doing out here? Because I cannot believe you came out here to hunt, not more than twenty-four hours after you almost bled out on my boots."

"You didn't answer my question." I paused. "And I didn't almost bleed out on your precious boots."

"You were bleeding pretty bad. How are you feeling?" His thumb was still moving.

"Obviously, I'm not dead," I snapped. "Tell me why you're saying that's an ancient. David said—"

"Let me guess, he said it was highly unlikely that it was an ancient because none have been seen in decades, if not centuries? Of course he said that." His gaze darted to the sidewalk as a scream sounded from off in the distance. "You wouldn't believe me if I did tell you."

Frustration snapped at my heels, but without warning, he let go of my wrists and stepped back. The whole front of my body tingled from the contact or lack thereof. As he stood in front of me, I realized his entire right arm was covered in tattoos. Nothing like what each Order member had inked on their skin. There wasn't enough light to check out the detail, but it looked like a vine curling down his forearm, over the top of his hand, and disappearing between his thumb and pointer.

Ren widened his stance as if he expected me to attack, but I managed to refrain from doing so. "You need to go home, Ivy."

My mouth dropped open. "You need to get your head checked if you think you can tell me what to do."

That slow curve of his lips happened again, forming a rather devastating smile that showed off his dimples. "If you don't go home, I'm going to call David and tell him you were out here hunting."

Now my jaw was on the ground. "You wouldn't."

"Hmm. I wonder how he'd react. He doesn't seem like the kind that seems cool with people disobeying his orders."

David would probably throw a fit. Hell, he might already be in the process of throwing a fit if Trent had called him. And if he got another call from Ren? He'd probably suspend my ass, maybe even fire me, and I . . .

I really didn't have anything if I didn't have the Order.

And I hated Ren for using that against me. "You're a dick."

Some of the humor slipped out of his eyes. "You know, I've been called that a time or two."

"No big surprise." Without saying goodbye, I turned and walked toward the sidewalk. I started to turn back toward Bourbon, but stopped when I remembered the damn beignets I promised Tink.

If I came home without beignets, Tink would probably cut my hair off while I slept. Sighing, I spun in the other direction and headed toward Café Du Monde. At this time of night, the place was going to be packed.

"Where are you going?" Ren asked from behind me.

I cursed under my breath. "Not that it's any of your business, but I'm going to get some beignets."

"Right now?" He fell in step beside me. "Are they really that good?"

Sending him a disbelieving stare, I shook my head. "You haven't tried them yet? That's like the first thing everyone does when they come to New Orleans."

"No." He scanned the sidewalk, frowning as he passed a couple that looked like they were about to make a baby on the sidewalk. "I haven't had a lot of time."

I wanted to ask him what he was doing, but then again, I really didn't want to chat with him either. He wasn't going to tell me how he was so sure that fae was an ancient or anything of real value, and I wasn't sure I even believed him.

If David didn't think it was a real threat and Trent obviously thought a brick in my foundation was loose, then why would Ren, a complete stranger, be the only person who believed that the ancients were around?

Ren didn't talk as he followed me to the Café, and I did my best to ignore him, but it was hard to pretend he didn't exist when he was a six foot four prime specimen of a man walking beside me.

He also waited in the long ass line, under the bright ass lights, a quiet presence behind me. At least I was able to see more of the tattoo. What traveled down his arms was a network of intricate vines, shades of deep greens and grays. The ropey design twisted together, reminding me of a Celtic knot. The vine curved over the top of his hand and between his fingers. I couldn't think of a time I'd seen a tattoo like that before. When I placed two orders and stepped aside, Ren looked at me curiously.

"I'm super hungry," I muttered.

He grinned.

Our orders came around at the same time, and it was weird as we walked out together, as if we really *were* together. Part of me wanted to see his reaction when he had his first bite of the sugary beignet. The first time was always an experience to treasure.

But we weren't friends. We barely knew each other, and he practically kidnapped me off the street. Curling my fingers around the bag, I shifted my weight from one foot to the other then glanced over at him. "Well, I'll see you around."

He didn't say anything but tilted his head to the side. For a moment, I wondered what it would be like if he and I met under . . . well, under normal circumstances. Like if we shared a class at Loyola. I probably would've been thrilled to get to know him better, to see how far that tattoo traveled, but we weren't normal, and this was just awkward. Sighing, I turned away.

"Ivy?" he called out.

As if compelled, I turned to face him again.

Ren stood mostly in the shadows, just outside the light spilling out of the café and across the sidewalk. "Don't do anything stupid. Go home. Be safe."

Then he was gone, disappearing into the group of people crossing the street.

~

With only a few hours of sleep before my morning class at Loyola, I was Cranky McCranky-Pants, especially since I skipped the pain pill so I didn't risk the chance I'd start drooling on myself any more than normal.

On days like these, when I was recovering from a bullet wound and had little sleep, I wondered the same thing Val did. Why in the world was I going to college? I could be in bed, all cuddled up and shit, dreaming about hot men with abs covered in powdered sugar.

Okay. That just sounded weird.

But I had two classes on Friday—Philosophy and Statistics. The first I didn't mind, and I actually found it interesting. When it came to Statistics, I'd prefer plucking my eyelashes out with a rusty pair of pliers.

I was able to grab a sandwich before Statistics, and forced myself into my seat. As I waited for the professor to find his way, which would be a while because even he seemed to dread attending the class, my thoughts drifted back to last night—to Ren.

One thing that had kept me up almost all night was the fact that I hadn't asked him what he was doing following what he claimed was an ancient—what had to be an ancient. I'd been so wrapped up in the fact that he'd grabbed me and known the fae was an ancient that I hadn't thought to question what the hell he was doing.

The only thing I could figure out was that Ren was hunting the ancient, but what made him—

"You look like crap today."

I turned to the left, watching as Jo Ann Woodward dropped into the seat beside me. "Thanks. I feel even better now."

She laughed softly as she pulled the massive Statistics text out of her bag and tucked thick, almond colored hair behind her ear. "That was mean of me." The text thumped off the desk—the book was so big and thick, I was sure I could turn it into a deadly weapon. "Seriously, are you feeling well?"

I really liked Jo Ann. I met her my first year at Loyola in one of my Intro to Psych classes, and I'd immediately hit it off with the curvy brunette. She was genuinely nice and as sweet as a strawberry dipped in sugar. Like one of those rare people that honestly didn't have a bad word to say about anyone, she was the kind of person I really wanted to be best friends with, and when I hung out with her, I felt . . . normal.

That feeling was rare and priceless.

Although Jo Ann and I had shared many late night study groups and we'd even gone out a few times, she really didn't know what I did or who I was. Keeping the Order a secret put up a huge wall between us that no matter how close we got, would never breach.

And that sucked.

Glancing at my notes I'd taken from Wednesday, I shook my head. "I think I might've had a stomach bug yesterday or something." Such a lie. "I'm feeling better." Kind of not a lie. I wasn't dying from pain, but my stomach was tender.

"Oh no, do you need anything?" she asked as her brown eyes grew to the size of mini spaceships.

For some reason, Jo Ann labored under the belief that I needed mothering. Not in an overbearing way, but it worried her that I lived alone in the city and she knew my immediate family was gone. Unable to tell her the truth of how they died, I'd gone with the trusty and tragic car accident.

"I'm okay. I promise," I told her as I glanced at the clock. Two minutes past the start of class. Maybe we'd get lucky, and the professor would be a no-show.

Jo Ann watched me as she twirled a pen between her fingers. "Are you sure? I can make a mean bowl of chicken noodle soup. Straight out of the can."

I laughed. "Yeah, I'm sure."

She grinned. "You want to grab something to eat before I head into work?"

Jo Ann worked at a halfway home in town, proving she was near sainthood. I almost said yes but remembered I had to head to the Quarter for the weekly meeting. Disappointment surged. "I can't. Maybe this weekend?"

Her lips split into a big smile. "Yeah, just text me. I'm off on Sunday."

Finally, our professor found his way to class, and again it appeared as if he dozed off mid-lecture. I wasn't sure I actually learned anything by the time class wrapped up, and I still hadn't figured out why it was a prerequisite.

I walked out of class with Jo Ann, ignoring the stitch in my side as we tried to navigate the packed hallway. "By the way," she said, nudging my arm with hers, "I like your hair like that."

"Huh?"

"You have it down," she pointed out. "You never wear it down. It looks good like that."

"Oh." Feeling self-conscious, I reached up and my fingers tangled with the curls as we hit the stairwell. "I really didn't do anything with it this morning."

That part was true. I'd showered and let it air dry while I shoved my leftover beignets in my mouth.

She laughed. "Then you should do nothing more often. You . . ." Trailing off, she nearly walked into the railing as we headed down the steps.

"Whoa. You okay?" I asked.

Her naturally tanned cheeks turned red, and she seemed unable to form a word. A moment later I understood why. Coming up the stairs was Jo Ann's future husband.

Except Christian Tran didn't realize that.

I hid my smile as he rounded the landing and looked up. Black baseball cap twisted on backward, a shock of black hair curled out from under the band. His dark eyes were warm and friendly as they landed on Jo Ann.

"Hey," he said.

Jo Ann beeped. That's what her response sounded like, and that was all she was able to do as Christian continued up the stairs. The two of them worked at the halfway home, but on alternate schedules. She didn't know a lot about him. Hell, she didn't even know if he was single or if he even liked the ladies, but she was madly in love with him.

I grabbed her hand, pulling her down the stairs. "You really need to talk to him."

Her eyes were wide again, panicked. "I can't. You just saw that. It happens every time I try to talk to him. I sound like Beaker."

Tossing my head back, I cackled like a cracked out hyena. "Oh my God, you totally did sound like Beaker."

"I know," she lamented. "He probably thinks I can't talk."

"He knows." I wanted to somehow give her better, more useful advice, but I was so out of it when it came to dating that last night was the closest I'd been to a member of the opposite sex.

The moment I thought of Ren, I was simultaneously angry and . . . and I didn't know what else. There wasn't a single word I could use to describe it. My heart did this weird flipping thing, and that made me not want to even think his name.

Exasperated with myself, I missed half of what Jo Ann was saying, and she had to rush to her next class to be on time. As always, she hugged me tight, like we'd known each other since we were in diapers, and I promised to text her over the weekend before we parted ways.

I caught a trolley to the Quarter, and with some time to kill, I made my way to Aunt Sally's Shop to pick up a box of pralines for Tink. Not that he needed more sugar in his little body, but I knew it would make him happy.

Stowing the box in my backpack, I headed down Decatur. It was early Friday evening, and the streets were crazy. Tonight would be off the hook, and the fae would be everywhere. It didn't feel right not hunting tonight, especially since I knew I could do it without hurting myself.

Mama Lousy was pretty busy as I passed by and peeked in. Jerome was behind the counter, looking as grumpy as an old man sitting on the front porch watching kids run across his lawn. He was retired, out of the Order for the last ten years, and he really was a poor choice when it came to working the shop.

Jerome was not a people person.

Grinning, I waved at him from outside.

He scowled in my direction as someone ambled up to the counter, dropping a fake skull on it.

I entered through the side and climbed the stairs. After a couple steps up, I glanced down, and relief coursed through me when I saw that the steps weren't covered with my blood. That would've been gross.

The door at the top opened about ten seconds after I rang the buzzer. Expecting Harris when I stepped through, I bit back a sharp curse when I saw Trent.

One side of his mouth curled up. "Oh, look. It's the crazy bitch."

I arched a brow. "Oh, look. That's so unoriginal." I stepped to the side, planning to walk around him, but he moved to block me. My patience dangled by a rope. "I'm surprised you're still walking today."

Two red spots blossomed on his cheeks. "I'm surprised they still let you in the Order after you spouted that crazy shit."

So many words rose to the tip of my tongue, but my patience was now hanging by a thread, and the last thing I needed to do was knee him in the balls again. So I was going to be the bigger person and walk away. Like an adult. I was going to be so proud of myself if I pulled this off.

I moved to walk around him, but he stepped to the side again, and this time he put his hand on my shoulder. The weight was heavy, and his palm trapped several strands of my hair, pulling on them. Our gazes connected, and I knew I was seconds from not only kneeing him in the groin but also permanently ensuring he would not reproduce.

A shadow fell across Trent's face and he jerked his hand away, stepping a foot back from me. Perhaps he read his impending neutering in my expression alone.

But a familiar deep voice filled the room. "Everything okay, Ivy?"

Every muscle in my body tensed as I realized Ren was behind me, and my fierce expression alone hadn't warned Trent off. I wanted to turn, but I would not give Trent my back. And I wasn't entirely comfortable with Ren at my back either. I was stuck between an asshole and a hot weirdo who was also a potential asshole. "Everything is peachy."

"Seems like it," he drawled.

Trent's jaw locked down, and I could tell by the way his cheeks were now mottled that he wanted to say something, but he nodded curtly at Ren. Total bullshit. Because did Ren's superior manliness warrant respect even though Trent had known me for three years? I hated people sometimes.

"I don't think everything is okay," Ren commented as I watched Trent's retreating form.

Having no idea what to even begin to think when it came to Ren, I turned to him. That clenching deep in my chest occurred again, a feeling I wasn't too happy with. But he was possibly the hottest mortal guy I'd seen, and that tattoo? With his short-sleeved black t-shirt, there was no missing the intricate tattoo as it wrapped down his ripped bicep and strong forearm. I dragged my gaze up to the almost angelic beauty of his face.

God, I was so incredibly vain.

Bright green eyes danced as they met mine, and his lips curled up in amusement. It was then that I realized he was waiting for my response. "What?"

His grin spread until the dimples appeared. "I was just kindly pointing out that it doesn't seem like everything is okay."

Oh. I'd missed that. I so needed to get a grip. "What makes you think that?"

He shifted his weight as he folded his arms across his broad chest. "Probably has to do with the fact that jackass called you a crazy bitch."

"Whatever." I waved my hand dismissively. "It's nothing."

"Is it?" One dark eyebrow rose. "Sounds like it might be more than nothing, especially since he was just in that room over there." Ren nodded at the double, paneled wood doors to the right, where the meeting would take place, and where Trent had just disappeared into. "He was talking."

I tensed as I felt my stomach start to drop. "Talking about what?"

"About what you said you saw Wednesday night and what happened. He was telling a whole room full of people." Ren's green eyes met mine. "Your sect leader was in there."

Barely able to keep the wince off my face, I struggled to keep my expression blank. I didn't think it worked because a shadow of a sympathetic look crossed his handsome face. I looked away, my hand tightening around the strap of my backpack.

"I do not think it is wise for you to speak so openly about what you saw," Ren advised quietly.

My spine straightened even further. Hindsight was a bitch. Of course, I probably should've kept my mouth shut when I spewed everything in Trent's face, but I didn't need him rubbing it in mine. "Thanks, but I didn't ask for your opinion."

A moment passed and then Ren sighed. He stepped so that he was directly in front of me again, and he looked like he wanted to say something more, but he never got the chance.

The door to the meeting room opened up and David strode out, letting it slam shut behind him. Ren turned at that moment, unfolding his arms and widening his stance in a way that had a weird, protective vibe to it. I couldn't really tell what mood David was in because he looked like he always did.

Which was pissy as hell.

I braced myself nonetheless. If Trent had been in there running his mouth after David told me to keep quiet, I knew this was not going to be pretty, especially as the dark skin around his eyes wrinkled as they narrowed.

David stopped in front of me, his deep brown eyes moving between us. "I'm actually glad both of you are here." Completely confused by that statement, I lifted my chin as the sect leader's gaze met mine. "You don't need to go to the meeting."

My jaw unlocked. "What?"

"I told you to keep your mouth shut." His gaze hardened. "You did not do that. Kind of like you had one job, Ivy. You failed at that."

The entire nape of my neck burned. To have David say something like that to me at any point sucked monkey balls, but with an audience, and that audience being Ren, it made me want to pitch myself off the balcony outside the window. Knowing my luck, I'd end up in a piss-filled puddle. But what David was saying wasn't fair. "I only said something because Trent already—"

"I didn't ask for an excuse," he fired back. "It doesn't matter what Trent said. You know he's full of shit half the time, and you should've left it at that."

That was such bullshit, but before I could voice that startling accuracy, Ren chimed in. "Seems like the issue is with Trent and not Ivy."

Surprised, I cut a look at him. Considering the fact I had not been relatively nice to him at any point since I'd met him, the last thing I should've earned was his defense.

"And I didn't ask for your opinion, did I?" David's gaze flipped back to him.

Ren gave him a half grin that was part smug and part daring. "All I'm saying is, from someone on the outside, if he brought the shit up first, how is that Ivy's fault?"

He just earned cool points. "Totally agree with that statement."

"Here's the thing. I have about forty-five members of the Order in a room where the fucking air conditioning isn't working, running their mouths like a bunch of old women now. Half of them think Ivy's got a screw loose, and the other half think we have a fucking ancient running around. Trent wouldn't have said shit before the meeting if Ivy hadn't bruised his balls. Literally."

My eyes widened.

His eyes narrowed even further, until just a thin slit of brown was visible. "Yeah, I know that, too. He wanted to file a goddamn complaint against you, and you're damn lucky I fucking hate paperwork and already had to file one on your ass once this week."

"You had to file one because I got shot since maybe we do have an ancient on the streets," I said, then twisted toward Ren as my arms fell to my sides. Our gazes locked, and this was the perfect time for him to speak up, to say what he'd told me the night before.

Silence.

And I waited—waited for Ren to say what he said to me last night when I spied the same fae that shot me and he stopped me from following it. I waited while I heard a burst of laughter from the room the rest of the Order members were holed up in and told myself that laughter had nothing to do with me. I *waited*.

Ren said nothing.

Another half a minute passed as I stared at his profile. I sucked in a sharp breath as realization kicked in. A muscle had begun to thrum along his jaw as the seconds ticked by. He wasn't going to say a damn word, nothing that really backed me up. The burn that now traveled across my cheeks deepened. I didn't understand. Anger rose, but so did something I honestly felt stupid for even feeling. I was *hurt*, and that was dumb. I didn't know him and had no reason to trust him.

David scratched at his jaw. "You, on the other hand, do need to get your ass in there as soon as we get done with this annoying ass conversation. The other sect members need to know you so they don't end up accidentally trying to kill you." Then he turned back to me, and the edges of his expression softened. "I know I pulled you off rotation until next Wednesday, but I can't spare anyone else, so I need you to show Ren around town until then. You won't be hunting. If you do happen across a fae, he will handle it until then. You will basically be shadowing him and making sure he knows his way. You'll start tomorrow night."

Oh hell.

"Sounds good to me," Ren said.

Oh—oh hell to the no.

I took a step back, because I was really afraid I might turn into a rabid squirrel. "No can do."

Ren looked at me sharply.

"You don't have a say in this, Ivy. Let that sink in for a second before you continue with whatever you're about to say," David replied calmly.

My hands curled into fists.

"Are you letting that sink in?" he asked.

Man, it was so sinking in. David was giving me a direct command, which meant if I refused it, I was in

75

breach of the Order. And that meant I'd get a formal write-up. You only got three before you were kicked out, stripped of your tattoo, and even your wards. They were hardcore like that.

Holly and Adrian would've been so disappointed in me if that happened. The same with Shaun, because none of them had disobeyed the Order at any point in their lives, but I already did once, and they had paid that price with their lives.

As much as I hated the idea of having to do anything with Ren, especially after he let me throw myself under the fully-loaded bus with the ancient thing, I couldn't dishonor the memory of those who burned inside me. Disobeying the Order over something so simple would be exactly that.

"I got it," I said hoarsely.

David didn't look so thrilled for some reason. "Good. Meet him back here tomorrow at five. You're no longer needed here tonight."

There was a beat of tense silence then Ren exhaled softly.

One of the hardest things I'd ever had to do was walk away from David and Ren with my back straight and my chin up, but I did it and I did it without even looking back at them. I gathered what felt like a torn shred of pride, and I walked out of there before those fragile slivers of control broke.

~

My phone dinged twice by the time I was opening the door to my apartment and dropping yet another stack of Amazon boxes on the chair. Part of me hadn't wanted to look at it, but as I slipped the phone out of my bag, I saw it was from Val.

U were shot by an ancient? Thought it was a thug?

That was the first text.

The second text read, u need to call me girl, bc every1 is saying cray cray shit.

I needed to talk to Val, but I really wasn't feeling it at the moment. Sending a text back that read I'll call you tomorrow, I was relieved when I got an okay from her.

Sighing, I opened up my door and nudged it shut behind me. The TV was about ten decibels too loud and was one of the *Twilight* movies—maybe *New Moon*. Tink was nowhere in sight as I walked across the hardwood floor and picked up the remote, turning the volume down. Placing it back on the old chest I'd converted into a coffee table, I gasped when I saw the couch.

A troll doll with bright green hair peeked out from behind the tan throw pillow, and its face, the color of suntan lotion, was frozen in a wide smile. It was also naked.

Sometimes Tink did that. Placed the damn dolls in weird places for me to find and be creeped out over. I snatched it up then walked down the hall and into the kitchen.

Tink sat on the island, crossed-legged in front of my laptop. I sighed. Yet another thing I needed to change the password to. He was so caught up in whatever he was watching, he didn't hear me walk up behind him. I bent over and blew on his bare back.

He shouted and shot up in the air, his wings beating rapidly as he whirled around, placing his hands like he was about to break out some kung fu. Despite the crappy evening I was having, a laugh bubbled out of me.

Tink dropped his hands to his chest and dragged in several deep breaths. "I think you gave me a heart attack. I can feel it in my chest. It's the big one." Pressing his hands to his front, he staggered back. "Oh no. It's happening. I'm about to die."

I tossed the doll at him. "Stop leaving these things laying around the house. It's weird."

He caught it, dropping slightly under the sudden weight. "I did no such thing. I told you what they do. They come alive when I'm sleeping. It's not my fault."

Rolling my eyes, I looked at the laptop. "Why do you have one of the Twilight movies on in the living room and Harry Potter on my laptop?"

"I'm doing research." He landed in front of my computer and placed the doll next to it. "Important research."

"Okay." I headed over to the table and shrugged off my backpack.

Tink flew over, hovering next to me. "How was your day, *honey*?"

I smiled faintly as I dropped the bag into the seat then zipped it open. "Not the greatest."

He cocked his head to the side. "You want to tell Dr. Tink all about it?"

"Thought you didn't like to be called Tink."

"Don't question my inconsistencies."

I laughed again. "I don't really want to talk about it." I pulled out the box of candies. "But I have pralines."

You'd think I pulled out a handful of naked brownies that were willing to live and serve Tink by the way he reacted. Buzzing around the kitchen excitedly, I was worried he was going to accidentally fly into one of the windows. Eventually he calmed down, and we ended up watching the rest of what turned out to be *Eclipse* and then *Order of the Phoenix* for whatever research purposes he wasn't ready to share. I was okay with the brain candy. It kept me from stressing over everything that had happened and what I'd have to do going forward.

I crashed a little after nine like a total loser, but I ate five more pralines before I rolled myself into bed, my stomach not appreciating the overdose of sweetness. Unable to fall asleep and striving to keep my mind free of all the crap, I grabbed a worn novel off my nightstand, cracking open *Rule*. A little after ten my eyes grew too heavy for me to keep open. I put the novel down, flipping off the light, and shifted onto my side. I wasn't sure exactly when I fell asleep, but when I blinked open my eyes, my bedroom was lit with a soft glow.

It took me a couple of seconds for my brain to process that there were only two lights in my bedroom. The ceiling one, which was much brighter, and the lamp on the nightstand, but I'd turned that off.

Thinking that Tink was being a freak again and had sneaked in my room, I started to roll onto my back, expecting to find a damn troll doll on the pillow next to mine, but my hip hit something warm and hard.

I froze as my heart skipped a beat.

Something was there, something that was way too big to be Tink, and then it moved, no longer resting against me. Instinct shot to the surface, and I shifted onto my back and sat up.

Déjà vu smacked into me, except this time I wasn't in an alley, but somehow unexpectedly staring into a pair of eyes the color of spring grass.

Son of a bitch.

Chapter Five

Part of my brain couldn't fathom what he was doing in my apartment—in my *bedroom*, sitting on my bed, giving me a half grin that revealed one deep dimple.

Was I dreaming?

He tilted his head to the side, and several dark, russet colored curls fell across his forehead. "You do this a lot? This stare at me and not speak kind of thing?"

Yeah, not dreaming.

Instinct was still firing within me, and I pulled my legs out from under the bedspread as I rolled back. I was more of a kick ass first and ask questions later girl. Ignoring the pull of the stitches, I planted my feet into Ren's chest.

He was knocked back, but caught himself before he fell. On his feet, he rose to his full height as I slid off the bed, landing in front of him. How did he get in here? Had he found Tink? Oh my God, what if he'd done something to Tink? Concern blossomed.

Not giving him time to recover, I spun on one foot and caught him in the stomach with my other foot. Ren's grunt told me that it hurt, and I snapped forward, aiming my fist for his face—his *really* nice face. What a shame I was going to have to bloody and bruise it.

He moved like lightning striking, catching my wrist and using my momentum to spin me around. An arm gripped tightly just below my breasts. "Whoa, Ivy, you need to chill."

I so didn't need to chill. I shoved my free arm back, catching him in the stomach again, but this time I could feel exactly how hard that stomach was. His abs didn't even budge. I went to do it again, but he did something that was going to piss me off until I took my last dying breath.

He shoved one leg between mine, hooking his foot around my ankle. One second I was struggling against him and the next I was falling forward.

"Crap," I muttered.

Ren didn't let me freefall. Instead, he controlled my weight and where I was heading. Before I knew it, I was on my stomach and he was above me, his knees on either side of my hips, and his hands wrapped around my wrists, pinning my arms to the mattress. My cheek pressed into the bedspread, and from my not-so vantage point, I could see that the bedroom door was open.

How quickly he incapacitated me yet again was humiliating, and I was too damn angry to be *that* afraid. "If you don't let me go, you're going to regret it."

"Jesus, is this going to happen every time we meet?"

"If you keep doing shit like this, then yes!"

He shifted so that his breath danced along my cheek. "I'm not trying to hurt you."

82

"You're practically crushing me." I tried bucking my hips, but he squeezed his knees in, stilling me. "I swear to God, if you don't let me go, I'm—"

"You're really feisty, aren't you?" He chuckled, and that ticked me off even more. "Look, I didn't come here to fight you. I need to talk to you."

"This is a really funny way of talking." I tried to twist my arms, but all I managed to do was make the position even more uncomfortable. "How did you find me?"

"Looked at your file in David's office."

My fingers curled into the bedspread. "He's going to kick your ass."

He chuckled again. "Nah, I don't think so."

God, he was so lucky I couldn't get my hands on him right now. "If you looked at my file, then you would've seen my phone number. You could've tried, I don't know, calling me like a normal person."

"I did call you," he replied, and again his breath stirred the hair along my temple. I hadn't been close to a guy since . . . since Shaun, and go figure, it was a dude breaking into my apartment that was the one. "You didn't answer."

For a moment I couldn't remember where my phone was, but then I remembered it was in the kitchen, next to my laptop. I started to fire back, but Tink suddenly appeared in the open doorway, and *what the?* He had one of those skillets just large enough to cook an egg in, and he was holding it over his head like a battle-axe. I was kind of surprised that he could carry the pan, but Tink was buff for a little guy. He had a six-pack—a brownie six-pack. His face was contorted in a silent battle cry as he started into the room.

Wide-eyed, I shook my head. As much as I appreciated the effort, his interference would not end well. That small as hell frying pan was not going to do any damage. Thankfully, Tink froze and lowered the pan. A second passed then he zoomed out of the doorway.

"Are you calm yet?" Ren asked.

Calm enough to shove a spike through his startling green eyes. "Okay. So you admit to being creepy and looking at my *personal* information, but how did you get in here?"

"I don't think taking a tiny peek at your file is that creepy." His hands shifted, and I jerked as his thumbs moved along the insides of my wrists. God, if he started that thumb thing again, I was going to lose it. "But to answer your question, the balcony doors off your living room were unlocked. So, technically, I didn't break in."

Unlocked? Dammit. That had to be Tink. "You didn't break in, but you had to have scaled a wall to get to that balcony,"

"Actually, I scaled the vines."

Damn, that . . . that took talent. I refused to admit I was any bit impressed. And he was doing that thumb thing again, slow tracing circles that created a deep, unsettling feeling that *had* to do with him being a creeper. "So you looked at *my* stuff, scaled *my* wall, let yourself into *my* house, then came into *my* bedroom and sat on *my* bed. And watched me sleep? That's got creep factor written all over it."

"I thought girls liked being watched by some random dude. Here I had it wrong this whole time," he replied.

Tink appeared in the open door again, his wings rapidly moving, and in his hands he held a . . .

84

slingshot? Oh sweet baby Jesus take the wheel. Where did he get a slingshot? Off of Amazon? That didn't matter. The brownie had taken the time to paint his face. One half was red, the other blue. He looked like he wandered off the set of *Braveheart*. I mouthed the word *no* at him.

He threw up a hand, and I think I saw a middle finger.

"Are you talking to someone?" Ren's grip loosened as he rocked back and turned to the door. My heart stopped, but Tink zipped away before Ren could see him.

"No," I said.

Ren paused. "Huh."

His knees widened, letting up on my hips, and with the lax grip on my wrists, I took advantage of the distraction. Yanking my arms free, I rolled as Ren cursed. I sat up, wincing as that really pulled at the stitches, sending a bite of pain across my midsection. Gripping Ren's shoulders, I flipped him onto his back and straddled him as I reached under my pillow, grabbing the iron stake I always kept there.

Before he moved, I placed the *very* pointy end against his throat, right over a *very* important artery. "Role reversal, bitch."

Ren let his arms fall to the mattress as he stared at me through impossibly thick lashes. "That move was really kind of hot."

I narrowed my eyes.

"You really are Merida."

"Who in the hell is Merida?"

One side of his mouth kicked up again. "The chick from the movie Brave with—"

"The frizzy red hair. Got it. Thanks. I'm seriously going to stab you."

"She didn't have frizzy hair," he argued. "And besides, she was hot."

I stared down at him. "You think a Disney character is hot?"

"Have you seen some of those Disney characters?"

"She was not hot. She's like the least hot of all Disney characters." I hadn't seen the movie, but I remember catching glimpses of it. The chick didn't even have boobs. Why couldn't he say I reminded him of Ariel or something?

Then again, Ariel was kind of stupid, giving up her voice for a dude.

His brows lifted. "She could kick ass, therefore she was hot."

My fingers tightened on the stake. Okay. So Merida was a badass, and I guessed that was better than saying I reminded him of Belle, the Stockholm victim, and now I was oddly flattered. "This conversation has taken a weird turn."

"Yeah," he drawled lazily, and then moved his arms. I tensed, but he didn't move to grab me. He lifted his head and pressed the vulnerable section of his neck against the stake, carefully folding his arms behind his head. "It has."

Annoyed at his lack of fear and concern, I scowled at him. "Comfy?"

His grin spread, turning downright wicked. "Very."

"Don't call me Merida anymore." Using my other hand, I pressed down on the center of his chest, then kind of wished I hadn't. Good Lord that was one hard chest. Did he have pecs? He totally had pecs. My gaze darted to his right arm, to the extraordinary tattoo for a brief second before I met his stare.

Ren appeared to consider my order. "Since you asked nicely, I won't do it again, but you can call me whatever you want."

"Are you hitting on me?" Shocked, I shook my head. "Are you for real?"

"My momma probably thinks I'm real."

I ignored that. "While I have a stake at your throat?"

"You're also sitting on me, and sweetness, if you slide about an inch or so down, things are going to get real awkward."

Holy shit.

"Or fun," he added, and his lips did that slow curl again, like he savored the whole process of smiling. "I told you I found that move you made to be fucking hot. But I don't think you're going to be down for that."

That unsettled feeling returned, and I didn't like it, didn't even know what to do with it, so I dismissed it and his comment. Needing to pull this conversation back to what was important, I focused. "Why are you here, Ren?"

"I told you. I needed to talk to you, and I didn't really want to wait." He wet his lower lip, and that action, for a second, snagged my attention. "I probably should've. I can see you didn't like my impromptu visit, but I'm going to be a good boy and just lay here."

Based on the way his green eyes glimmered, I doubted he knew how to be a good boy.

"I know you're pissed at me," he added, and I frowned at him. "Not just over this, but because of tonight."

I curled the fingers of my free hand around the collar of his black shirt. Pissed wasn't an accurate description of how I felt. "I know what I saw Wednesday night."

"I haven't said you didn't."

"You were all chatty Thursday night, but you didn't say anything to David. You made me look like a fool."

"I also didn't make you look like anything," he replied. "However, I do remember clearly telling you that David wouldn't think there was an ancient here."

"You did absolutely nothing to back me up last night."

He tilted his head to the side, completely unfazed by the dagger I had at his throat. "Why would I?"

Whoa. Startled by his blunt honesty, my grip on his shirt loosened. "Wow." That was all I could say. "You are something else."

He blinked those damn lashes, surprised, and finally that cocky smile faded. "You don't understand."

"Of course not. It's okay that almost the entire Order thinks I overreacted or made it up. Worse yet, they probably think I'm losing my mind or something," I said, and no sooner had those words left my mouth when the truth of my expectations smacked me upside the head.

I knew exactly why I expected Ren to have my back earlier tonight. Because Shaun would have. No matter what craziness I'd get myself involved in, he had my back. Thinking that Ren would, because of Shaun, was the height of ridiculousness. I'd known Shaun for almost all my life and Ren only a handful of hours. I just didn't understand why I thought a stranger would be like Shaun, but I did recognize that was a huge flaw inside me.

"Whatever," I finally said. "It's not your responsibility to step in. I lost my cool with Trent and ran my mouth. That's my fault."

"But you said Trent already knew," he challenged. "Don't you find that strange?"

I shook my head. "No. I think Harris has an even bigger mouth than Trent and me combined."

Ren didn't respond to that.

A moment passed. "Wait. How do *you* know that Trent knew?"

His gaze met and held mine. "You said something about it last night after I stopped you from getting yourself killed."

Had I said something about Trent? Searching through my memories, I couldn't really recall if I had. Wary, I stared down at him. "Why would I trust you?"

"You don't have a reason to trust me, Ivy. But you know what? I never asked you to," he said, repeating the same words he said to me last night.

Then he moved.

Snatching my wrist, he pulled the hand holding the stake away from his throat and flipped me on my back before I could take another breath. He tossed the stake on the bed beside me, and then moved away, stopping in front of my dresser.

I popped up, swiping the stake off the bed. Breathing heavily, I moved so that his back was to the door just in case Tink tried another rescue.

Ren opened his mouth, but his gaze dropped and he snapped his jaw shut. I might have been experiencing an epic dry spell when it came to fun times with guys, but I wasn't blind. Those bright, forest green eyes were checking me out in a slow, appraising way. It was then that I realized I was in my sleep clothes. Both the shorts and the tank top were thin, especially the top. I didn't have to look down to know he was noticing that a certain area of my body thought the room was chilly.

Immediately, I wanted to cross my arms over my chest, but I refused to show him that I was at all bothered by his blatant stare. Warmth crawled across my face. My arms practically shook with the control required to keep them away from my breasts.

"See something you like?" I asked.

"Oh yeah." His voice had deepened in a way that sent a tight shiver over my skin. "I bet your boyfriend is one happy man."

"My boyfriend is dead," I snapped before I could stop myself.

Ren's eyes met mine. For a moment he didn't speak, and I felt my cheeks burn even hotter. "I'm truly sorry to hear that."

I pressed my lips together.

"Was he a part of the Order?" he asked quietly.

For some reason, I found myself nodding.

His lips parted slowly. "Was it recent?"

I shook my head. I didn't even know why I was nonverbally answering his questions. Val was the only person I really talked to about Shaun. My tongue started moving. "It was three years ago."

Something flickered across his face, and before I could figure out what it was, it was gone. "You're twenty-one, right?"

"You really took more than a peek at my file."

He ignored that. "You turn twenty-two in December if I remember correctly."

I lowered the stake a fraction of an inch. "Wow. Okay. How old are you?"

"Twenty-four. My birthday just passed, but I accept late gifts." He flashed a quick grin that didn't reach his eyes. "He was your first love then."

Drawing back like I'd been kicked in the chest, I blinked. What he said wasn't a question but a statement, and I wondered if I had an announcement of such information written across my forehead . . . or my breasts.

A new wave of anger rushed through me. "That's none of your business, and I also doubt that it's relevant to any reason why you're here."

"You're right." He raised a hand and I tensed, but all he did was drag it through his mass of waving curls. "I'm here, because like I said last night, I know there are ancients in New Orleans. That's why I'm here. I'm hunting them."

Out of everything I was expecting him to say that didn't even cause a blip on the radar.

Ren grinned again, and this time it was real. "I can tell by that what the fuck look on your face that you don't believe me. That's okay. I guess. But the look is about to get even more extreme."

I braced myself.

"What I'm about to tell you is something that many would kill to keep a secret. And the only reason why I'm telling you is because we're sort of stuck together for the next couple of days, and I cannot afford to waste time by keeping you in the dark. I have a job to do." The mischievous and almost charming grin made a brief appearance. "Plus, it helps that everyone thinks you're crazy now. Even if you did repeat what I'm about to tell you, no one would believe you. That's got bonus points written all over it."

My eyes narrowed. "Gee. Thanks."

"You're welcome," he replied blithely. "I belong to the Elite, an organization within the Order. No one outside of the Elite knows about us. We put the secret in Secret Squirrel."

I shook my head slowly. "You . . . I've never heard of such a thing."

"Like I said, you wouldn't. Neither would your fearless leader David." Raising his arms above his head, he stretched and the shirt he wore rose, exposing what turned out to be a tantalizing glimpse of his lower stomach. Pants hanging low, I got an eyeful of those side muscles near the hips, the ones that formed the vee. Then he put his arms down. "Look, I'm starving. Have you eaten today?"

Goodness, he switched topics as fast as Tink. It was disconcerting. "I haven't eaten anything since this afternoon." Not counting the pralines. That didn't count as food.

"There's this place a few blocks down that I passed that looked good, so we should get some food. You don't have to change. I'm loving this getup." His step forward was measured, as if he half expected me to throw the stake at him. "Come grab something to eat with me, and I'll tell you what I know, Ivy. I know a lot. And you can tell me exactly what happened Wednesday night."

Half of me knew I needed to tell him no and kick him out of my place. Probably even call David, and report everything that Ren was saying, but . . . he was right. David had said he'd talk to the other sects, but after tonight I was convinced he didn't really believe me. And

I know what I saw Wednesday night. I wasn't going crazy or overreacting. That fae had done things only an ancient could, and if there was a chance Ren wasn't crazy, and everything he was saying was true, I needed to know.

I flipped the stake in my hand and said, "Okay."

Chapter Six

While I was still wary of Ren, going out to eat was a safer bet than hanging around in my apartment. Banging pots and the sound of cooking was a call that Tink could not refuse. The brownie would make himself known, and I wouldn't risk that. So I kept Ren in my bedroom while I quickly threw on a pair of jeans, snapped a bra in place under the tank top, and added a loose three-quarter-sleeve shirt.

I caught a glimpse of myself in the mirror. Well, my hair. It was doing its own thing, curls going everywhere, and I didn't even attempt to try to tame them into submission. I let them fly. Whatever.

I grabbed an extra iron stake from my dresser and secured it to the inside of my boot. Although I wasn't hunting, I didn't want to get caught unprepared.

On the way out, I saw Tink peeking out from behind the couch, and he still had his war paint on, looking like a demented pixie. It took every ounce of self-control not to laugh. As Ren walked outside, I sent Tink a thumbs up, and he responded by doing something inappropriate with his hand. Obviously he didn't like that I was going out with Ren.

The temps had dropped, and even though it was late, the hole in the wall diner Ren was talking about only had a few booths open. The place smelled good—like food and not a septic system, which is how a lot of places tended to smell. I'd eaten here a few times in the past and the food was good, so Ren was lucky being a newbie to the town and picking a place to eat where you probably wouldn't get listeria.

We sat down in a booth near the door, the exhausted looking waitress quickly filling our requests—coffee for Ren and a coke for me. "I'll give you two a couple minutes," she said, nodding at the grease-stained paper menus resting on a clean table in front of us before spinning around and tackling another set of customers in a nearby booth.

Ren glanced at the menu as he grabbed the white caddy and started pulling out the packets of sugar. "Awesome. They're serving breakfast." He ripped a packet open and dumped the sugar in his coffee. "I could go for some grits. What about you?"

"Breakfast does sound good," I said, and watched as he emptied a second packet into the coffee. "I guess I could eat some gravy and biscuits. And bacon."

"Extra crispy bacon." A third packet went into the coffee. "Bacon tastes different here than in Colorado. That might sound stupid, but it's true."

"No, you're right. It does. I guess it's just the way they fry it."

He glanced up, and even in the horrible fluorescent lights, his skin still looked golden, as if it were kissed by the sun. I hated to even think about what I looked like or what color of red my hair was in this lighting. "So, you're not from here?"

I shook my head as I picked at the edges of the menu and he moved on to the fourth packet of sugar. "I'm from Virginia."

"That's where you were born?"

"Yeah. You born and raised in Colorado?" I asked.

"Just outside of Denver." He emptied the fifth packet into his coffee.

Sitting back, I arched a brow as he picked up the sixth packet of sugar. "Do you want some extra coffee with your sugar?"

He gave me a quick grin. "I like things sweet."

"I can tell," I murmured, and I glanced up as the waitress reappeared. She took our orders then rushed off like the devil was snapping at her heels. "So, you going to tell me about this thing called the Elite?"

"I just need my first gulp of caffeine." He lifted the cup and took a hefty swallow. The sound he made afterwards actually made the muscles in my lower body tense. It was such a deep, throaty groan that warmth crept into my cheeks. "Ah, that is so much better," he said.

Then he winked.

"You are..." I shook my head. There were no words. I kept my voice low so we weren't overheard. "Tell me about the Elite."

He took another sip and thankfully didn't sound like he was having an orgasm afterward. "The Elite have existed since the beginning of the Order, and they've handled different things throughout history. Remember the Knights Templar? They branched off from the Elite"

"You're joking."

"When I joke, I'm usually funnier than that. But back to the point of this, the Elite has been in operation for a long ass time, and just like the Order, the members of the Elite are generational. It runs in the family."

I glanced over as the door opened and two college-aged girls stumbled in, looking like New Orleans chewed them up and spit them out. "Okay. Let's say, hypothetically, I believe you. The Elite hunt ancients?"

"We hunt the fae like everyone else, but we are trained to handle the ancients," he explained, cradling his hands around his cup of coffee. He had nice fingers, long and elegant. I could picture him strumming a guitar. I had no idea why I was thinking of his fingers. "Did you manage to stab that fae?" he asked quietly.

My stomach flopped at the memory. "I did, but it didn't do anything to him. He pulled it out and tossed it aside. I told David, but he . . ."

"He probably said he'd contact the other sects, right? I'm not talking shit about David. He seems like a good guy, but most of the Order is unaware of the ancients still being here. He probably thinks you didn't stab him."

"If people in the Order—people like you—know that they are, why wouldn't it be common knowledge? Not knowing is dangerous. Obviously." I gestured to myself. "We need to know what we're dealing with, and not having that knowledge has us at a disadvantage."

And it also made other Order members think I was crazy.

"I get what you're saying." He leaned forward. "But the ancients are rare, Ivy. The fact you ran into one is damn near unbelievable. They don't engage the Order.

They stay hidden and surrounded by their own kind. When I say we hunt them, we literally have to *hunt* them down. There's no reason to have people panic when the likelihood of them ever running into one is nearly nonexistent."

I didn't agree, because obviously I proved someone could just stumble across an ancient, but I wasn't going to spend the entire time arguing with him. "How can you kill one?"

"Iron doesn't work."

My jaw dropped. "What?"

"Iron doesn't work," he repeated, then leaned back as the waitress delivered our food. Gravy steamed off my plate, and the scent was downright enticing, but my appetite had taken a big hit.

Ren grabbed the remaining packets of sugar and dumped them in his pile of lumpy looking grits. "There's no sending them back to the Otherworld. The only thing you can do is kill them, and there's one thing that will do that. A stake fashioned from a thorn tree that grows in the Otherworld is virtually a bullet to the brain."

"From a tree that grows . . . in the Otherworld?"

He nodded as he scooped up a mouthful of grits. "Yeah, so you can imagine getting that shit isn't easy. The weapons one can use against the ancients are limited, but the thorn stake works just like iron does. But as you know, ancients are far more dangerous and skilled."

I picked up a piece of bacon. "They can conjure things."

"Yes. As long as they have touched something, they can pretty much recreate it. They can also invade people's dreams, and they can move things around just

98

like normal fae can. They're powerful, Ivy, and you're damn lucky that you got away from one of them with just a flesh wound."

I didn't need him to tell me I was lucky. Facing down an ancient, a fae, or even a human with a gun usually didn't end well, no matter how awesome you thought you were. "And you have one of these weapons?"

"Of course." He ate politely and cleanly, despite the fact I'd only eaten two slices of bacon and almost all of his grits were gone. "And before you ask, yes I've killed ancients before. Four of them, and no, it was not easy. I have the scars to prove that, and yes, if you ask nicely, I might be convinced to show them to you later." He glanced up through thick lashes. "You going to eat? Your food is getting cold."

I looked down at my biscuits and gravy and absently picked up a fork. "Why do you think the ancient is here?"

"It's always been here. That's the thing. There aren't many, but there are enough ancients that were in this realm when the doors were sealed. The right question is why was it engaging with you? Like I said, ancients are like . . . mob bosses. Fucking dangerous, but they don't get involved unless they have to. The fact this one was out on the street and *hunted* you down means something."

The savory gravy turned to sawdust in my mouth. "Hunted me down?"

"That's the only plausible explanation. No one in the Elite—no one, Ivy—has heard of an ancient seeking out a member of the Order. Hell, can you think of a time when a fae has hunted down an Order member?"

Yes, I could think of a time when a fae had hunted down members. It rarely happened, but it had. Three years ago.

"This is a big deal." Pushing his empty bowl aside, he attacked his plate of bacon. "The question is why?"

Only half of my biscuit was gone, but I was done. My thoughts spun with what Ren had told me. He could be lying—could be completely delusional, but I know what I saw. That wasn't a normal fae, and David had even confirmed that ancients had those abilities. Deep down, my instinct told me Ren wasn't lying. Just like it had told me that Tink was harmless.

And my instincts had told me not to meet Shaun that night, but I hadn't listened to them then.

Something occurred to me. "Maybe it wasn't just hunting me. Maybe it was hunting Order members in general. We've lost three of them since May. That's not entirely abnormal—the deaths, but these were good and skilled members."

"If they're hunting members, we need to know why."

"And this is why you were sent here? Because of an ancient being in New Orleans?" I asked after the waitress refilled our drinks.

Ren eyed me for a moment. "We've been tracking movement of the fae. At least a hundred have left the west and ended up here or in surrounding cities, but I bet you haven't seen an increase."

Thinking on it, I shook my head. "There's always a lot here, so it might be hard to recognize that there's an increase."

"These fae are laying low. They're up to something." He paused, tilting his head to the side. "And we know there's a gateway to the Otherworld in New Orleans."

I leaned forward, gripping the edge of the table. "How do you know that? Only a few know where the gates are and who guards them."

A blasé look crossed Ren's handsome face. "I'm a part of the Elite. We know what city the gates are in, but we don't know the exact location or who guards them."

Only the guards knew where the gates were, and maybe the sect leaders. It was a safety precaution once the Order discovered that the fae only knew the location of the gate they came through but not any of the others. Many decades ago, a member of the Order had been caught without protection and was tortured into giving away the location. The doors were sealed, but they could be reopened, and shit would get real bad real fast if that happened.

"You don't happen to guard the gate, do you?" he asked. "Because that would make my job so much easier, because I have a feeling the ancients are also looking for the gates."

I snorted. Yep. I snorted like a little piglet. "Uh, no. And I have no idea where it is either."

A burst of laughter came from the table the two girls sat at, drawing my attention. Their faces were flushed, and one looked like she was laughing so hard she was about to pee herself. Two guys had joined them. One of them had an arm draped along the red cushioned booth, his arm behind the girl who was laughing the loudest.

"Do you ever wonder what it would be like to be one of them?" Ren asked.

My attention snapped back to him. The question ricocheted through me. I slipped my hands off the table and I leaned against the seat, as if I could somehow put distance between the question and me. "No."

Glancing over at the happyland table, Ren propped his forearms up and leaned toward me like he was about to share the biggest secret. "Sometimes I do. Can't help it. Those four people over there? They can't even comprehend some of the shit we've seen and have had to do. They're lucky. We never had a chance to be them. We were born into this."

"But . . . but our job is so important. We're making a difference . . ." I stopped myself because I sounded like a recruitment video.

"I'm not saying that we aren't. Just pointing out the fact that those four over there will probably live long, happy lives," he replied, meeting my gaze. "Doubtful that any of us will."

That was a damn sad truth I didn't want to dwell on. "So you're here to find the gate?"

"And to figure out what the fae are up to." Ren tapped his hands off the table. "You know what's coming up, right?"

Of course I did. "The fall equinox."

"The gates are always weaker during the equinox and the solstice," he said, saying what I already knew. "They could be gearing up for something to do with them."

"This can't be the first time that they're planning something," I pointed out.

"It's not. We've just always been able to stop them."

I stared at him blankly as his words floated around in my head. Here I thought I was in the know, being that I was in a secret organization, but apparently, I didn't know everything.

"Do you believe me now?" he asked, reaching for the plate my bacon was on.

Snapping forward, I caught his hand around the wrist before he got a hold of my bacon. "I *might* believe you, but that doesn't mean you can steal my bacon."

Those full lips split in a grin. Our gazes locked, and the tumbling sensation in my belly resurfaced. I could see how easy it would be to fall into the green depths of those gorgeous eyes or be wooed by the charm he seemed to wear like a second skin. His grin spread into a smile, revealing his dimples. And that dipping feeling in my stomach turned into something richer, fiercer.

I dropped his hand, grabbed a slice of bacon, and shoved it in my mouth. I didn't have any use for swoon-inducing guys.

Ren sat back, his eyes seeming to glimmer as he watched me. "When you get done eating, I want to show you something I think you need to see."

My brain so went in the wrong direction with that, because for some reason I thought about seeing more of those abs, and I so didn't need that. Not at all. Nope.

I shoved another slice of bacon in my mouth.

~

It was a little before one in the morning, and the party was just getting started in the city. People were everywhere despite the fact we weren't even in the Quarter but near the business district, and my patience with walking around the tools that simply stopped in the middle of the sidewalk was already wearing thin.

Whatever I needed to see was in the warehouse district, and as I walked beside Ren, I couldn't help but notice he got a lot of attention. Women of all ages checked him out. So did a lot of men. He had that angelic face but was rocking a grin that had bad written all over it. I was beginning to hate that grin, because . . . well, because of *reasons.*

The buildings were more formidable and the modern mixed well with the traditional. Bars and clubs were different than the ones found in the Quarter; this was a place locals seemed to favor over the crazytown that went down on Bourbon.

"So . . . what are you trying to show me?" I asked, starting to tire out. "The traffic here sucks just as bad as it does during the day."

Ren chuckled. "You should see Denver."

I opened my mouth to respond, but he suddenly grabbed my hand and pulled me back against him. Immediately, I dug my feet in, but his strength was impressive. One second I was walking along and the next we were against the brick front of a hotel, my back pressed against the front of his body. He curled an arm around my stomach like he had in my bedroom.

Every sense fired at the rush of warring sensations. There wasn't an inch of softness to his body, and he smelled clean, like the woods in Virginia. "If you don't let me go, so help me God, I will—"

"You are so full of threats." He dipped his head so that his cheek almost touched mine. He pointed with his other hand. "Look. Watch this car."

My heart pounded fast as I tracked where he was pointing. A black Town Car with tinted windows slowed and pulled up against the curb. Within seconds, a valet appeared out from underneath the awning, striding toward the back door.

"That better be Theo James or Jensen Ackles getting out of that car," I muttered.

Ren chuckled. "I have a feeling you're going to be disappointed."

"Figures." As long as I'd lived in New Orleans, I'd never seen a damn celebrity. It was like I wore anti-celebrity spray. "And why do you have to be so grabby? Jesus."

"I like the way you feel against me," he said.

"Ugh." I rolled my eyes, but there was a part of me, a teeny tiny part of me, that liked the way he felt.

The valet opened the back passenger door and a man stepped out. A tall man dressed in a suit that looked like it cost as much as my monthly rent. He had light brown hair and a face that would've been perfectly pieced together if it weren't for the pale, cold blue eyes.

My pulse moved faster.

The man had that deep olive complexion and high, angular cheekbones. The air around him seemed to sizzle with electricity as he buttoned the front of his jacket closed.

"He's . . .?" I couldn't bring myself to say it.

Ren's arm tightened below my breasts, and I felt his thumb swipe over my ribs. I shivered, unable to suppress it. "He's an ancient," he spoke low in my ear. "Looks like a high-powered businessman, huh?"

The dude looked as if he stepped out of GQ.

He took one step forward, his pale gaze swinging up and down the sidewalk, not stopping on us. But it stopped on a woman who was standing with a man—her boyfriend or husband I guessed based on the way her arm was wrapped around his waist. I held my breath as a scented breeze rolled down the street, way too . . . appealing for a natural aroma. It smelled like an island would smell—fruity, heavy, and sensual. The breeze was warm, teasing the senses. I'd never smelled anything like it before. I started to squirm but stopped when I realized how close Ren and I were.

The breeze picked up the woman's blonde waves, tossing them lightly. She tensed, and my breath caught as she looked over her shoulder.

I started to step forward the moment the woman's gaze landed on the ancient, but Ren held me back. "Don't," he murmured.

It went against every part of my being. I wanted to intervene, needed to, as the woman stepped away from the man she'd been with and approached the ancient as if she was walking in a daze. Sickness rolled through me as the ancient fae smiled.

I gripped his forearm. "We have to do something, Ren."

The woman was almost at the ancient's side when Ren shifted, moving in front of me and blocking what was happening. I started to step to the side, but he caught my chin, forcing my gaze to his. "I know how hard it is to stand here and let that happen, but there is nothing we can do right now. You think he would hesitate to put you down right here on the street in front of these people? He wouldn't."

"But—"

"He'll glamour everyone into thinking someone else killed you. I've seen it happen, Ivy. I've lost many of those I considered friends because they thought they could treat an ancient as a normal fae. I cannot stress enough how dangerous they are, and I don't mean this as an insult, but you are not ready to fight one of them."

Closing my eyes, I willed the anger and frustration firing up inside me to slow its roll. Ren was right. I knew that, but that didn't make it any easier. I spoke once I was sure I wasn't going to drop a bunch of F-bombs. "How did you know he would be here?"

He dropped his hand from my chin. "I've been in town for about a week, and before that suspicious look on your face grows into a lets-stab-Ren look, I checked in with David the moment my ass—my fine ass, I might add—stepped foot in the city. I spent every night hunting and found that bastard last night."

"Then you don't need someone showing you around town," I pointed out, not even bothering to hide the accusation in my tone.

"David doesn't know that, and he doesn't need to. As far as he knows, I've been hanging out. He can't know why I'm really here, Ivy."

My spine straightened as I met his hardened gaze. "Why? Why does it have to be so secretive?"

A muscle thrummed along his jaw. "Why does the Order remain a secret?"

The answer was easy. The general public would not believe us. People had to see things to truly believe in them, but that wasn't the same with us. We knew fae existed. We knew that ancients had walked this realm at one time. If enough members came forward, everyone would believe.

"Anyway," Ren continued. "Did some research on the bastard. He's registered in this hotel as a Marlon St. Cyers. Living in one of those semi-permanent suites while his new home is being built."

I frowned. "Wait. That name—he's some kind of huge developer in the city, I think."

Ren nodded. "Yeah, he is."

"Holy shit," I whispered. The fae masqueraded as humans all the time, but never one in such a public position. The fae aged much more slowly than mortals did. To us, they would appear immortal. Marlon looked like he was in his mid-thirties, but he had to be several hundred, if not more, years old. They could glamour people into thinking whatever they wanted, but with the Internet and everyone having a camera phone, and the ability to post anything to any website, technology wasn't like it was even twenty years ago. Someone would find pictures of people who didn't age. Fae existing in the public eye was risky for them.

Ren dipped his head again, and before I could process what he was doing, he swooped in and pressed his lips to my cheek.

I jerked back and stared up at him. "What in the hell?"

A wicked grin appeared. "You looked like you could use one."

My cheek tingled from where his lips made brief contact. "I looked like I could use a kiss on the cheek?"

"Yeah," he replied. "Everyone could use a kiss on the cheek once in a while. Plus, the expression you make when you're confused is fucking adorable."

I started to reach up to touch my cheek but stopped myself before I ended up looking like a complete idiot. "You are bizarre."

"I think you kind of like my bizarreness."

I shifted my weight. "I don't know you well enough to like anything about you."

"Now you know that's not true. You know I'm from Colorado. I use a lot of sugar in my coffee. I steal

108

bacon." He dropped his voice. "And you know I hand out cheek kisses to those in need of them."

"I . . ." What the heck did I say to that?

Ren stepped to the side, and my gaze landed on the man the woman had been with. Angry shouts erupted as he pushed the valet, trying to get inside the hotel.

The devilish smile slipped off of Ren's face as he glanced from the altercation to the entrance of the hotel. His hands curled into fists as his jaw locked down. As I studied him, I thought of Merle again. If anyone knew where the gates were, it would be her.

Chapter Seven

Ren and I made plans to meet up after the meeting on Friday. I didn't tell him that I thought I might know someone who'd have info on the gateway. I wasn't about throwing names out there, and he hadn't pushed it. Instead, he insisted on seeing me home, which was ridiculous considering I roamed the streets at all hours of the night due to my schedule, and he hadn't done so the night before.

Unless he had followed me home Thursday night and lied about checking my file just for the contact info, but if he hadn't done that, making sure I didn't get abducted on the way home or something was kind of sweet. Barely. However, the whole scaling the wall outside and letting himself into my apartment uninvited totally canceled out the sweetness.

Tink was passed out on the throw pillow when I locked the door behind me a little before three in the morning. His war paint was faded on his face and smeared across the fabric. I couldn't even begin to know how to get that out without it staining. Could you wash pillows? Ugh, Tink was going to owe me for this.

He must've been exhausted, because when I scooped him up and carried him into his bedroom, he remained asleep. I placed him on the small dog pillow he'd fashioned into a mammoth-sized bed.

Most of the time I avoided going into his bedroom, and as I backed out of it, I quickly realized that had been a good idea. He had an army of troll dolls lining the built-in bookcases that covered the length of the wall opposite his bed.

"Ahhh," I murmured as at least three hundred glassy black eyes seemed to be sizing me up. "So creepy."

I closed the door behind me and grabbed a Capri Sun pouch out of the fridge. Then I checked the French doors that led to the balcony off the living room. Pulling back the soft blue curtains, I found that the door was locked. Had to be Ren, because I doubted Tink would lock them.

After drinking my fruit punch, I poured myself into bed, and this time when I fell asleep I wasn't woken up hours later with some random dude sitting next to me. Close to ten in the morning, I forced myself to put on my running sneakers and not go into the kitchen and overdose on sweet tea or some other form of caffeine. That would be my reward if I made it back to my apartment alive.

Being a part of the Order required that I stay in shape, so I made myself run at least three miles four times a week. Combining that with the various mixed martial arts training we did with other members was the only reason why I didn't weigh a billion pounds since I ate pretty much everything and anything in front of me.

I needed to run since I hadn't done anything truly physical for any length of time since Wednesday morning. Couldn't fight the fae if I was winded easily.

Luckily the temps remained cool as I hit the outside stairs and the courtyard below, and I hoped that meant the cold season was coming sooner rather than later. Putting my earbuds in, I powered up the music app on my cellphone then opened the gate. I straightened the band on my nylon shorts and then started off, heading toward Kindred Hospital at a slow jog.

As always, my thoughts wandered when I ran, and not surprisingly, they drifted right to Ren. I still couldn't believe he actually kissed my cheek. Did he go around doing that randomly? For some reason, I wouldn't be shocked if that was the case. Ren was definitely a huge flirt, something a lot of the men in the Order were. Maybe it had to do with how dangerous our lives were, and they were all seize the moment kind of guys. So were the ladies. Except I liked to think we were a little more inconspicuous about it.

Ren was stupid hot, as in the kind of hotness that made you want to do stupid, fun things you'd most likely regret later, but that didn't mean I trusted him a hundred percent. He was a stranger, but all the Order members were strangers at some point, each one a complete unknown. When I came to New Orleans, I immediately had to put my life in the hands of people I'd only just been introduced to. If I needed backup, I had to believe that one of them would answer the call, and they had to trust that I'd do the same for them. We had to go welcome and join others without the fear of betrayal. Under the Order, we were one cohesive unit. We had been since its creation.

But that still didn't make it easy to trust newcomers. Ren had been up front with me about the Elite. Sharing that kind of information should've caused me to trust him more, but in a way, it only made me more wary. Why was he so willing to trust me with such old, secretive information? Then again, he knew that David hadn't taken my claims seriously and that half the Order probably thought I was riding the crazy-pants train. But if Ren was up to something shady, I couldn't fathom what it would be. What did he have to gain by making up the existence of the Elite or by lying in general? Still, I was uneasy about the whole thing.

I needed to talk to someone, but David was a no go at this point. I knew I could trust Val with the info, and I would, but I needed to know more before I opened my mouth. As I successfully crossed Foucher Street without getting plowed by an ambulance, I thought about Brighton's mom Merle. If anyone knew where the gate was, and if there was one in New Orleans, it would be her.

But did I really want to bring Ren to her?

That was the question that plagued me the rest of the run and throughout the afternoon. It was one thing for me to make risky choices, but to put others in the path of what could lead to disaster wasn't something I planned on ever doing again. I had to trust Ren before I introduced him to Merle.

I just didn't know if I could get to that point.

I made a plan to visit Brighton's house tomorrow. From previous experience, I knew Merle was usually up and out in their garden in the afternoon, and Sundays were usually . . . good days for her. I didn't need Ren there to ask the questions I needed to ask. The only thing I had to do was get through tonight.

Which I had a feeling was going to turn into a really long, really annoying night.

~

Five minutes late to meet up with Ren, I wasn't surprised when I neared Mama Lousy and saw him waiting for me outside the gift shop, leaning against the building. Dressed in dark denim jeans and a loose shirt that hid the weapons I knew were most likely attached to the sides of his waist and under his shirt, he looked almost like any regular hot dude hanging out in the shade. He wasn't looking at me, and all I got was the strong line of his jaw, but I could tell a half grin teased his lips. My stomach dipped as my steps slowed.

Ren had a certain aura of danger surrounding him, an impression of coiled and barely restrained power. He might have look relaxed with his hands shoved into the pockets of his jeans and his legs crossed at the ankles, but anyone who walked by him knew he could strike at any given moment.

"I was beginning to wonder if you were going to show," Ren drawled without looking at me.

I frowned. He must have one hell of a peripheral vision. "Traffic sucks." I stopped beside him, quickly glancing at the tattoo on his arm. "I'm not sure what I'm supposed to do with you today since you know your way around the city."

Tipping his head back against the wall, he exposed the masculine length of his neck. I never thought a guy's neck could be sexy before, but I realized just then that it really could be. His eyes were closed, and the long fringes of his lashes fanned out, dark and spiky. The soft grin continued to play along his lips. "I'm sure there are places you can show me."

The tips of my ears burned. For some reason, with that smile and that deep voice, his words held a different meaning. I shifted, smoothing my hands over my jeans as a gaggle of older women teetering on heels stumbled passed us. "Louis Armstrong Park is a great place to hunt at night."

He looked at me then, eyes narrowed. "I think you're trying to get me killed."

I cracked a smile. The park could be a wee bit on the dangerous side, which was a damn shame, because it was beautiful as were all the sculptures inside it. "You could feed the ducks."

Ren laughed then, and I liked the sound. It was deep and infectious. "Next you'll suggest I head out to the Lower Ninth Ward and wander aimlessly while holding several hundred dollar bills."

"Make sure you head east of Frenchmen Street while you're at it. Check out north of Rampart also."

"You're terrible," he murmured, shaking his head. "You know, New Orleans is really no different than any other large city. It has its good and bad parts."

"True," I agreed, watching the group of ladies cross the street. Two young guys were tailing them. I hoped those women kept a close hand on their purses. "Except we have a lot more fae here."

"That you do." He pushed off the wall, turning to me as he pulled his hands out of his pockets. "I like your hair like that."

Tilting my head back, I frowned in confusion. "Huh?"

"You have it pulled up." Reaching out, he caught the end of a stray curl along my temple. "It's cute, but when it's down? Fucking hot."

"Um . . ." I snapped my mouth shut, and for a moment I stared at him. "Thanks?"

He chuckled as he tugged on the curl until it was straight, and then let go, watching it bounce back into place. "I could play with it all day."

I blinked slowly. "Wow. You don't get out much, do you?"

Ren grinned. "So you have a game plan in mind for tonight?

"Not really." I started walking down the already congested sidewalk.

Not surprisingly, he caught right up and fell in step alongside me. "Why not?"

Keeping an eye on the cluster of people at the corner of Bourbon, I stepped around a young woman with a bright green drink container. She was eyeing Ren like she'd rather be slurping him up through a straw. "Saturday nights are usually crazy. You can make all the plans you want and it's all going to go to hell in a matter of seconds."

Ren didn't respond.

I glanced at him quickly. His gaze was trained ahead also, but that grin had faded like a ghost. "You have a problem with that?"

"Nope," he replied, surprising me. "But I think we might have a problem up ahead."

The crowd had grown in the last couple of seconds. You saw a lot of strange things on Bourbon. People wore wings. Some people walked around in nothing but body paint and tiny shorts. Others dressed like vampires that crawled out of an Anne Rice novel. If you were naive enough to try and snap a picture of them, they expected you to pay. Then there were the tourists who couldn't handle all the decadent indulgence and passed out wherever they stood. There was also the sad, random violence that infested the city and had nothing to do with the fae—simply humans hurting other humans for no real reason. So as we neared the group of people, a mixture of tourists and locals, it really was anyone's guess.

Stepping off the curb, I walked around a parked truck attempting to unload full kegs for a nearby bar. Ren followed me as I made my way onto a street so packed with people it was almost impossible for a car to make it down a block in a timely manner . . . or without clipping a few pedestrians.

I edged around the horde of bystanders, aware of the strained laughter of some and the growing sense of unease that seemed to be hopping from one person to another. Something was most definitely going down at the corner of Bourbon and Phillip.

Over the drifty jazz music spilling out from the bars, a shrill sound erupted from whatever the crowd was blocking from our view, sending chills down my spine. A cross between a shriek of pain and one of rage, it was an inhuman scream.

"That's doesn't sound normal," murmured Ren, his hand closest to me moving to his side.

Pushing through the crowd, I ignored the sharp looks directed at me. Ren was right beside me, clearing a much larger path. A guy in front of us stepped to the side, and I caught a glimpse of disheveled brown hair and a hunched over, broken form, and then the man was shaking his head as he turned.

"Man, crack is a powerful drug," he muttered, scratching at the black beard along his chin. "Bitch done lost her—"

The eerie howl drowned out whatever he was saying. All I saw was the brown hair, matted and greasy, charging forward. The thing leaped like a damn cat from several feet behind the man. It landed on his back, screaming that horrible sound as it wrapped scrawny, dirt-covered arms around his shoulders. The legs were the same, filthy and scuffed, poking out from a torn skirt. It was a female—a rabid female.

And I had a sick suspicion she wasn't on drugs.

The woman threw her head back and howled as the man grabbed her arms, staggering to the side. People scattered, giving them a wide berth as the man struggled to get the woman off his back. Someone shouted for the police.

Heart pounding, I launched myself forward as Ren did the same. My stomach sunk when I realized there was no reaching them in time. The woman dived for the man's exposed neck, her mouth wide open.

Shit.

The man's pain-filled screams blasted us as her blunt teeth tore into the side of his neck. Other shouts joined in as the crowd realized what was happening. People started running in all directions, dispersing like dropped marbles. Deep crimson sprayed out from his neck as the man stumbled, falling onto one knee. He couldn't shake the woman, and she was still gnawing at him like some kind of freaking *Resident Evil* zombie.

I reached them first.

Grabbing a handful of tangled hair with one hand, I reached under her head with my other hand and gripped her jaw. I pressed with my fingers until she let go, then hauled her crazy ass back.

Blood spurted once and then twice before pouring down the front of the man's shirt as he fell forward onto his side. Ren was right there, dropping to the ground beside the fallen man, placing his hands tightly over his torn neck. He didn't hesitate for a second, didn't even check to see if I could get the woman under control. He *trusted* that I would.

"You're going to be okay, man. Just hang in there," Ren said, lifting his chin toward the shocked cluster of people. "Someone better be on the phone with 911."

The woman was going nuts, arms flailing and fingers clawing at the air. Red smeared her mouth and her chin. She was a gory mess, and I knew the minute I let her go, she was going to come after me.

I did just that.

Releasing her nasty hair, I backed away as she spun on me. She let out another scream that hurt my ears before she lurched forward.

I stepped into her attack, planting one hand on her shoulder as I cut her under the chin with the other, snapping her head back. She went down like a bag of rocks, alive but out cold.

Sirens whirled in the distance as I drew in a ragged breath and checked out Ren. He still had his hands on the man's neck, but the poor guy was turning a ghastly shade under his dark skin, and the entire length of his shirt was covered in blood. He wasn't looking good.

119

Suddenly Val was there, pushing through the crowd, her eyes flicking from Ren to me and then the woman sprawled on the street. "What in the hell?"

"She took a bite out of that guy," I said, swallowing hard as Ren kept talking to the man who now appeared unresponsive.

Val's teal green skirt billowed out around her as she kneeled next to the woman. "Good God," she said, reaching out and gripping the woman's shirt. The green and yellow bangles circling Val's arm jangled as she tugged the collar down. "Damn it."

There it was, proof that this was no case of drug use gone really bad.

Across the woman's chest, the veins leading to her heart looked as if they were infused with black ink. When a fae fed off a human for an extended period of time, it poisoned their blood and polluted their mind.

And apparently made them want to bite people.

Val let go of her shirt. "Such a waste."

The woman was past the point of no return. Once the veins turned, that was it. There was no coming back from it. She would die, probably by tonight or tomorrow, and those darkened veins would fade quickly afterwards, leaving no oddities on the body. Toxicology reports would show no drugs, and death would usually be ruled as some sort of heart failure.

"Shit." Ren's golden skin was a shade lighter as he leaned back, withdrawing his hands. My gaze moved to the man. His chest was still and his eyes wide and unseeing. Heaviness surrounded my heart. He was gone.

Ren's shoulders rose as he looked over and our eyes met. Shadows crept into them, dulling the green hue.

Rising fluidly, he turned and walked toward those standing near the curb. People parted and he disappeared behind them.

I started toward him then stopped, turning back to Val. "You didn't go on your date," I said.

She raised her chin and a weak smile formed. "Couldn't find anyone else to cover, but there's always later tonight." She glanced in the direction Ren had gone. "You need to track down the new hottie?"

"Yeah," I said, stepping around the prone woman. "You got this?"

Val nodded. "Don't forget, we need to talk."

"I haven't." Wiggling my fingers, I went after Ren, aware of the curious looks. It was a good thing to disappear before the police showed because of all the questions. Val would do the same once they had the woman secured. It worried me that she would be in police custody, dangerous until her body gave out, but there was nothing I could do once they carted her away unless I put the woman out of her misery.

And I couldn't do that—some could, but not me.

David once told me that it was a weakness, one that I needed to work on overcoming. He hadn't been a total jerk about it, just matter of fact.

Over the top of the crowd moving both ways on the uneven sidewalk, I saw Ren's coffee colored waves, and then he appeared to vanish. What the hell? I picked up my pace, breaking into a jog. I passed a bar then saw him.

He was in a narrow alley, kneeling by an outdoor spigot, washing the blood from his hands. It pooled on the dirtied ground in a murky puddle.

He didn't look up as I approached him. "It doesn't get easier," he said, rubbing his hands together. "You'd think eventually that it would, but it doesn't."

I didn't respond because there was nothing to say. Not being able to save someone and watching them die? Yeah, it never got easier.

Sighing heavily, he turned off the spigot and stood, wiping his hands along the front of his jeans. A wavy lock fell across his forehead and into his eyes. "That man back there? When he got up this morning, he probably thought he was coming home tonight."

"Probably," I whispered, not even sure he heard me over the partygoers on the street and sidewalk.

Ren lifted his chin to the small balconies above. "He had no idea."

"No."

Shoulders tensing, he lowered his chin and met my gaze. Several moments passed and neither of us said anything. The world outside the alley washed away, all the noise retreating to a distant hum. The sorrow in his expression was palpable, and I knew he felt the stranger's death in a way most Order members didn't. Not that they didn't care about a human loss, but when you were surrounded by so much death, you not only expected it but became a part of it.

Without giving myself time to really think about what I was doing, I stepped forward and reached out, wrapping my hand around his damp one. His eyes flared back to life with surprise. Feeling warmth in my cheeks, I squeezed his hand then let go.

His gaze traveled over my face then flicked up. He grabbed me by the shoulders, jolting me. I gasped out of shock as he pulled me against his chest and turned, pressing me toward the building.

Not even a second later, a blue and white moped flew down the alley, moving so quickly the force created a sharp burst of wind. Eyes wide, I watched it breach the entrance on the other side, hanging a sharp right.

"Oh my God, I . . . I almost got run over by a *moped*," I said, turning my bewildered stare back on Ren. "That would've been so embarrassing to be taken out by one of them."

His lips twitched as his striking features softened. "Good thing you have me around, saving you from reckless moped drivers."

"You're a hero," I replied.

Ren laughed, and I felt a measure of satisfaction at hearing the sound. Although I'd only known him for a short period of time, I hadn't liked the burden etched into his features. It didn't seem right on him.

He drew in a deep breath, and mine caught. In that moment, I realized we were chest-to-chest, so close I thought I could feel his pounding heart, but it might've been mine. Probably was mine, but there wasn't an inch of space between our bodies, and unlike the last time we were like this, I was so not feeling anger.

His arms draped loosely around my waist, and a heady warmth trilled through my veins. I stared at the vee of skin exposed above the collar of his shirt and realized dimly that my hands were on his chest. I had no idea how they got there. They had a mind of their own. That headiness dropped low in my belly, tightening muscles that had been on vacation for a fairly long amount of time.

Holy crap, I was actually experiencing a case of insta-lust. Sure, I'd noticed guys since Shaun, but nothing more than a passing interest that lasted all of ten seconds and was easily forgettable, but this . . . this was like basking in the sun.

Good news? My lady bits still worked—oh yeah, they were really working, like, overtime. The tips of my breasts tingled where they touched his chest. A blade of desire pierced me sharply, and it was the first time in three years I'd felt this level of attraction.

And Val, who had a healthy obsession with the functionality of my lady bits, would be thrilled to know they still worked.

Bad news? I wasn't sure exactly what was bad about any of this yet, but I was sure I'd come up with a few things as soon as there was some kind of space between us and my brain started working again.

"You okay?" Ren asked, voice deeper and rougher. "Your stomach?"

Don't look up. Don't look up. My gaze roamed up his neck, over lips that really were way too nicely formed, along a nose I realized must've been broken at some point due to the slight hook in its structure, then I was staring into eyes surrounded by thick black lashes. Dammit, I had looked up.

But gosh, his eyes were really beautiful.

One side of his mouth curled up. "Ivy?"

I blinked. "Yeah, my stomach is fine. I actually ran this morning, and it didn't bother me at all."

"That's good." The tilt of his lips spread into a full smile, and oh me, oh my, those dimples came out and those muscles low in my stomach tightened even more. "Ivy?" he said my name again.

124

"Yeah?" I was proud of the fact that I didn't take forever to answer, but the breathless quality of my voice sounded strange to my ears, because even with . . .

I didn't want to finish that thought.

He dipped his chin, and my heart jumped. "You going to let go of my shirt? I mean, you don't have to, but you keep tugging on my shirt like that, I'm going to get all kinds of naughty ideas that I will, without a doubt, act on."

At first I didn't get it. What the hell was he rambling on about? Parts of my body got hung up on the naughty ideas he'd act on and got all kinds of happy about that. My gaze dropped and I saw my hands were fisting his shirt, and . . . his arms weren't around me anymore.

Oh my God, I was groping him—*his shirt*. Could you grope a shirt? I was pretty sure I was groping his shirt.

Dropping my hands, I took a step back and bounced into the brick wall. Total stealth move right there. I wanted to kick myself.

Ren's eyes glimmered in the fading sunlight filtering between the buildings. He didn't speak for a moment, just holding my stare with his and then, "We should probably clear out of the area."

Good idea. Great idea. Witnesses could have given our description, and those we had on the force might not be around to play interference. Drawing in a deep breath, I reined in my newly discovered active lady bits as he stepped aside gracefully. For such a large guy, he moved as if he was made of air. Actually everything about the way he moved was fascinating to watch.

Or I really, seriously, just needed to get laid.

I sighed.

125

Then the worst possible thing in the history of mankind and beyond burst out of my mouth. "Do you have a girlfriend?"

Holy shit balls on Sunday, I did not just ask that. Ren looked over his shoulder at me, one eyebrow arched. I did ask that. Those words really did come out of my mouth and I wanted to maim myself, but I waited to hear his answer.

Ren's grin was like dark chocolate, smooth and rich. "Not yet."

Chapter Eight

The rest of our shift was pretty uneventful compared to what happened at the start of it. I tried not thinking about that poor woman and the innocent man, the life that was lost in a matter of minutes, the life that would be lost, and all the other lives that would be impacted. Not thinking about it, as callous as that sounded, was the only way we could continue hunting. And I tried not to think about the tension-filled moment Ren and I had shared or the absolutely stupid question I had asked or his mysterious response. That was the only way I could still walk beside him without wanting to pitch myself in front of a moving vehicle.

We found three fae—normal fae—during our patrol. As much as it killed me to stand aside and let Ren handle them since I'd been ordered to not engage, I was already tired of arguing, at least for the night. Both of us would be off on Sunday, and I was thinking by Monday I'd be able to fight without risking much damage to the stitches.

When it was time for our shift to end at one, I wasn't entirely surprised when he attempted to escort me home. "I'm going to get a cab," I told him. "It's too far of a walk, even in the day."

Standing on the corner of Canal and Royal, he cocked his head to the side. "True."

I really had no idea how to part ways from this point, and I felt like I could give a class on awkward. I could see the cab coming and I glanced at Ren. "Well, I guess I'll . . . see you on Monday then?"

A slight smile appeared. "Sure."

My eyes narrowed as the cab pulled up to the curb. Opening the back door, I stopped. "Where are you staying?"

"I'm renting a place over in the warehouse district."

I was relieved to hear he wasn't sleeping on the streets. Not knowing what else to say, I waved goodbye and climbed into the cab. I gave the driver my address, and not a minute afterward, my cell dinged.

I pulled it out of my back pocket, noticing that it was from a number I didn't recognize, and all it said was thank you.

Curious, I typed back who is this?

The response was immediate. Ren

Oh. I'd forgotten he'd seen my number in the file and honestly hadn't considered that he saved it even though he said he'd called me. I hadn't even checked to see if he had, so I did just then. There was a missed call Friday night from the same number. I typed back what are you thanking me for?

No response came by the time I made it to my apartment, but I saved his number, and it was a little weird entering his name when I realized I didn't know what his last name was.

UPS must've been to my house after I'd left, and I stopped to pick up two boxes. Carrying them inside, I placed them on the chair just inside the door.

Tink was in the kitchen when I walked in, nibbling on a praline that was the size of a pizza compared to him. "Hey! You're back. And you didn't get shot." Lowering a chunk of candy that he held, he frowned up at me as I dropped my keys on the counter beside him. "You weren't shot again, right?"

"No."

He raised the piece of candy as if he was toasting me then shoved it in his mouth. How he stayed in shape was beyond me. Jumping to his bare feet, he placed his hands on his narrow hips. "You know what I've been thinking?"

"Yeah?" I yawned, reaching up and tugging out the bobby pins.

"That guy that was in here last night?" He picked up the pin I'd placed on the counter and twirled it like a baton as he marched back and forth. "I think you want to get it on with him."

"Uh. What?" Moving my fingers through my hair, I eased the knots of curls. "What in the world makes you think that?"

"You left the house with him even after he obviously broke in. I'm telling you what, you females are freaks. Guys break in and you all swoon like B&E is a desirable trait," he ranted, still twirling the hot pink pin. "Females of my kind? If you did that they'd eat you for dinner. And not in the fun way. They'd start off by eating the man parts." He grabbed his junk as if I needed a visual aid. "And then they'd—"

"Okay. I get it. First off, I don't think breaking into my apartment is something to swoon about. I don't think most girls do. Secondly, Ren didn't break in, because someone," I pointed at him, "left the French doors unlocked."

His eyes widened. "I did no such thing."

I arched a brow.

"Okay. I might've done that, but he climbed a wall to get in, and that's kind of . . . well, that's actually kind of impressive." He lifted the pin, shaking it at me. "I bet that means he could pick you up and—"

"Oh my God, Tink, really? He's a member of the Order. He's new to the area. And he's apparently impatient and didn't want to wait for me to return his call. Does that mean we're going to get naked and pretend to make babies? No." An odd sense of disappointment washed over me, and I pushed the sensation away. "So not going to happen. And I'm not talking about sex with you."

The pin clattered when he dropped it on the counter, and he rose into the air so I was eye level with his bronze chest. "Let's talk about sex."

"No." Rolling my eyes, I walked away.

"Sex is good!"

"Shut up, Tink."

"Sex is fun!" he continued to shout.

I shook my head. "The only thing you're having sex with is inanimate objects, so what do you know?"

He ignored me. "Sex is best when it's one on one!"

Stopping in the hall, I turned to where he was doing a pelvic thrust. "Isn't that a George Michael song?"

"Maybe. But he was wrong. I like to think sex is best when it's like three on three or something. Seems more adventurous."

"Whatever. Goodnight, Tink."

I closed the door as he broke out in a Salt-n-Pepa song. "You're living in the wrong decade, Tink!" I yelled through the door then giggled when it sounded like he kicked it and went into a fit of curse words.

After getting ready for bed, it took a while for me to get to the point where I could doze off, and when I finally did sleep, I dreamed I wasn't alone in the bed, that there was a hard male body pressing against the length of mine. Hands were everywhere, touching me softly, caressing me in places that were far too intimate, and in ways that I had little experience with. I heard my name, the voice sounding familiar, and I thought I caught a glimpse of deep brown waves, but I couldn't be sure, and I was too lost in the dream to really pay attention or care. My lips were kissed. My body was kissed in the way I was touched, and I could feel silky hair between my fingers as I grasped his head, holding him to me, guiding his mouth to where I wanted—

I woke suddenly, thrust out of the dream and into the real world. An empty bed. No hands or mouth doing decadent and delightfully naughty things. No soft hair gliding between my fingers. I was alone as I stared up at the ceiling, seeing the thin slivers of dawn sneaking through the small gap in the curtains, but my body hadn't recognized that. I felt feverish. Sheets were twisted around my waist. My breasts felt heavy and the tips hard, sensitive against the thin cotton of my shirt. Between my thighs, I ached in a way that felt entirely unfair, and dimly I realized I hadn't been this aroused since Shaun.

Honestly, I didn't think I was ever this turned on by anything we'd done. Not that there had been anything wrong between us, but we were young when we took our childhood friendship and turned it into something more. We fooled around a lot in the first two years, but he . . . Shaun had been a good guy, and he respected Holly and Adrian to the point where I was the one to push the issue. It wasn't until we were eighteen when we had sex, and that was only once. It was good and nice, sweet and awkward in all the ways first times could be when you were with someone who cared so strongly about you. I imagined if we'd been given more time, it would feel like this—like my body was aflame and I'd go crazy if I didn't find release.

I slipped my right hand under the sheets, hesitating as my fingers brushed the band on my shorts. I hadn't done anything since Shaun, not even *this*. I hadn't been enticed to do it, and on the rare occasion when I wanted to, it hadn't felt right. Like I was betraying Shaun somehow, and I realized how dumb that was. But grief twisted things. I knew that.

I bit my lip then let it pop out. Drawing in a shallow breath, I slipped my hand under the band. My stomach fluttered, softly at first, and then deeper. I closed my eyes as I extended my arm.

My breath quickened then caught as the tips of my fingers glided through the wetness and unerringly found the bundle of nerves at the apex of my thighs. A shot of pure electricity lit through my veins as my hips jerked. A soft cry pushed past my lips. I knew what to do. I'd done this before. I'd actually done it with Shaun while we'd existed in the no-sex zone.

But it had been so long.

I ran a finger up my center, and my back arched in response. My toes curled. Without warning, an image of Ren appeared in vivid detail, bright green eyes and a full, sinful mouth. I didn't want to think of him and I attempted to wash his image from my thoughts, but it lingered in the background, and my hips were moving against my hand. The fire inside me was flaming and I was burning hotter and hotter. I tried to keep his image at bay, desperate to not think of him as the ache built and the pressure coiled inside me. My hips rocked, and I pushed my head back against the pillow, losing control of my thoughts. In my fantasy, my hand wasn't my own. My thighs weren't tightening around my hand—but *his*. They weren't my fingers. The tension broke; like a cord pulled too tight, it snapped, the release whipping out through me. I barely swallowed the cry as my body and thoughts shattered into blissful little pieces.

I collapsed back on the bed, my thighs relaxing and my heart rate slowing from its frantic pace. I was staring at the ceiling again, but this time I was wondering why I hadn't done this in three years.

If I woke up every morning like this I'd probably be a better person.

Breaths shallow, I closed my eyes and let the peace drift through my muscles as I told myself I hadn't been thinking of Ren on purpose while I did that. It was purely accidental it was him that appeared in my thoughts. After all, it made sense since he was the last dude I'd seen, not counting Tink. Seeing him in my mind while I . . . while I did that didn't mean anything.

Not a damn thing.

~

I texted Val in the morning, knowing we needed to talk, and I met her at Lafayette Cemetery at noon. The location was her choice. She claimed the peace of the tombs helped her think. She was weird like that, but I loved her enough to make the twenty-minute walk to the oldest of the cities of the dead that existed in New Orleans.

Most people knew not to venture into the cemeteries once night came, but it was usually fine to roam about during the day, especially since they were typically staffed at that time and there were tours in and out.

Plus, she wanted to go to the bookstore around the corner, and I was so down for that. I needed to get another Marked Men novel.

Val was waiting outside, near the archway that led into the cemetery. Today she was wearing a black skirt and a teal green off the shoulder peasant shirt with more ruffles than a wedding gown. Only she could look that good.

She pushed off the wall, coming forward and wrapping her arms around me. "Chéri, you're here!"

Pulling back, I laughed at the French term she only broke out once in a while. "You're calling me darling. What do you want?"

"Nothing." She threaded her arm through mine. "I'm just glad we're finally getting to chat about what the hell is going on." Then in uncharacteristic seriousness she added, "You have me worried, Ivy. Some of the members are talking and . . ."

"And they're not saying great things?" I surmised as we stepped under the iron archway.

She patted my arm. "Well, depends on how you look at it."

I gave her a wry grin. "They're saying I'm crazy, thanks to Trent."

We passed tombs on either side of the pathway. The walkways formed a cross. I wasn't sure if that was on purpose, but I assumed it was. "Trent said you told Harris the night you were shot that it was . . . an ancient that did it," she explained softly as she guided me to the left, and I knew where she was leading us. "And he said you confirmed it Thursday night."

Thursday night seemed forever ago. Straightening my sunglasses with my other hand, I gave myself a moment to change my mind. I hadn't planned on telling Val anything until I talked to Merle, but I needed to talk to someone.

We passed under a large tree with gold and red leaves. The smell of autumn was heavy here. "I did see an ancient, Val."

She didn't respond immediately. "How can you be sure?"

I told her what happened with the ancient. "As you can see, that's not something that would happen with a normal fae." I paused as we passed a group crowding a tomb. "I stabbed him. He pulled the stake out like it was nothing. And I told David, but I . . . I don't think he really believes me. I know he doesn't. He thinks I missed or something."

"God," she said, slipping her arm free from mine.

My stomach dropped and I stopped walking. "I'm not making this up."

Her tight curls bounced as she shook her head. "I know you're not, but . . ."

"But it's hard to believe?" I asked as I stared at her straight back. "I know it is, but he was an ancient, Val. And he's not the only one I've seen. I saw another Friday night in the warehouse district. His name is Marlon St. Cyers, or that's what he's calling himself. He's a freaking huge developer. I'm sure you've heard his name. Fae don't make themselves public like that, but this one— there's no way he cares about someone snapping a picture of him and it resurfacing twenty years from now, proving that he's not doing the whole aging thing."

A moment passed and Val faced me. She was so vibrant amongst all the decaying, gray tombs, but her skin was paler than normal as she stared back at me. "You really did see them."

I nodded, drawing in another shallow breath. "I did."

She walked back to where I stood. "Why do you think they're here?"

"I don't know if they ever left the city or what, but I think . . . I think it has to do with the gates." I glanced as two people strolled passed us and stopped a few tombs down, snapping pictures. I kept my voice low. "I think they might be planning something with the gates."

Her eyes widened, and when she spoke her voice was tense. "Ivy."

"I don't know what, but I'm not . . ." Words left me. Could I tell her about Ren—about the Elite? It wasn't that I didn't trust her, but it seemed wrong to betray his trust.

Val toyed with the bangles along her wrist. "What?"

I'd known Val longer than I'd known Ren, and I trusted her. "What I'm about to tell you cannot go any further, okay?"

"Honey, I'm a vault of secrets." She waved her hands around her midsection. "I could blister your ears with the things I know about some of the members, but I keep them to myself."

I kind of wondered what she knew. Walking past her, I made my way to where we always ended up when we came to the cemetery. The tomb of the first Order member to be killed by a fae in New Orleans was marked by a praying angel that somehow was still a pearly white and almost luminous. The symbol of the Order, the three interlocking spirals, was carved into the center of the tomb. Reaching out, I ran my fingers over it.

"Ren knows about the ancients," I said as Val stopped beside me. I looked at her and forged on. "He's a part of the Elite."

She blinked once and then twice. "What in the fuckity fuck is the Elite?"

A brief smile crossed my lips. I told her what Ren had explained about the Elite and why he was here. She had a suitable expression of puzzlement on her face, and I was sure that was how I looked when Ren told me everything.

Val needed a few moments to soak all that in. She passed in front of the tomb of the fallen member. I stared at the once pristine tombs that had faded to a dull gray, my gaze tracking over them, stopping on one with the entire top exposed down to the worn bricks. The place really was beautiful in an eerie and sad way, but my heart pounded unsteadily in my chest as I waited for her to process everything.

Had I made the right decision?

Unease blossomed deep in my belly as I shifted from one foot to the next. Maybe I shouldn't have told her about Ren and the Elite.

Finally, she stopped and planted her hands on her hips. "You believe him?"

"Yes."

"Okay," she said, exhaling roughly as she scrunched up her nose. "If you believe him, then I believe him. I'm probably more certifiable when it comes to craziness than you could ever hope to be."

Relieved, I felt the tension bleed out of me. The tendril of unease was still there, but that was understandable. I had just told a huge secret.

"So what's the plan?" she asked.

I blinked. "Oh, I don't really have one. David isn't going to say anything if he knows anything. I was thinking about seeing Merle today. If anyone knows about the gates, it would be her . . . depending on her mood."

Her features sharpened. "I'll go with you."

A laugh burst out of me. "The last time you visited Merle and Brighton with me, she called you a harlot."

"Oh yeah, she did." She grinned. "I'm sure she's forgotten."

"Ah, no. Every time I talk to her she asks if I'm still hanging out with the 'slut of Satan' and all that jazz. She hasn't forgotten."

"Slut of Satan? Wow. That's an impressive title."

"It is." I grinned. "Anyway, I think it's best if I do that alone."

She pursed her lips. "Is Renny boy going with you?"

I laughed as I stepped away from the tomb. "No. I told him I might know someone but didn't tell him who."

"Smart girl." She looped her arm through mine again and rested her chin on my shoulder, her curls tickling my cheek. "Thank you for trusting me. I was worried. Well, now I'm really worried, but for different reasons."

"I feel you." As we started to walk back through the cemetery, I asked her, "What do you think the ancients are up to?"

Her forehead wrinkled as her brows knitted. "If they want to open the gates then they would want to bring more ancients through. My maw-maw used to talk about the ancients a lot," she said. That was something I didn't know. "You know, the ones who ran the courts in the Otherworld. She said when they joined the Summer and Winter, there was only one prince, one princess, and the king and queen. That they were the most powerful and they controlled the knights—they controlled all the fae. I don't know if that part is true, but does it matter? What if the ancients here want to *free* them?"

A shiver coursed down my spine in spite of the bright sun. "That would be very bad."

I once asked Tink why the fae didn't stay in their world, why he didn't. He hadn't been all that happy to answer, but he'd explained how the fae had ruled over all the creatures of the Otherworld, enslaving them and nearly killing off entire species. He also said that those actions had severe consequences, but he never elaborated on them. To me, the reason why the fae were here was simple. They'd taken over their realm and now they wanted ours.

With the gateways to the Otherworld closed, they couldn't bring mortals over to their realm to feed on and entertain themselves with.

But no matter what they did, they wouldn't get those gates open.

"Tell me what you find out." Val reached over, slipping my sunglasses off and placing them on her face. I had to say they looked good on her. "I'll help you however I can."

Val and I left Lafayette, heading for the bookstore "Okay. More normal conversations," she said. "You ready for that?"

"Of course," I said, feeling a thousand times better after telling her. Truth kept the soul light.

"So what do you think about this new guy?" she asked as we stepped into the small shopping center across the street from the cemetery.

"Ren?" I looked away quickly because I could feel my cheeks start to heat. I thought about this morning and how his face had popped right into the forefront of my thoughts. "What do you mean? I told you I believe him."

"That's not what I mean. He's hot. Like really freaking hot. And he belongs to a secret organization within a secret organization, so that like tips the scales of hotness. When he was in the meeting Friday night, he smiled and my panties caught on fire." Across from the law offices, Val opened the door to the Garden District Book Shop. "You likie? Because I'd like to get me a piece of that, but only if you're not interested."

I opened my mouth to say no but nothing came out. Nothing. Not a no or a yes. Nothing.

Val spun on me, her eyes wide as she grasped my shoulders. "Oh my God, you're interested in him? You want him to set *your* panties on fire."

"I really don't want my undies to catch on fire." My God, why did everyone want to talk about sex right now? "At all."

She waved her hand dismissively. "You want him. You can have him. You need to break that epic dry spell of yours, and boy that would be one hell of a way to break it." Letting go, she rocked back on her heels and clapped her hands together. "My little girl is going to get laid!" Shimmying her hips, she squealed. "Finally!"

Um.

Looking to the right, I saw a woman behind the counter staring at us. To my left was a man with a small boy, maybe around the age of five or six.

"How do you get laid?" the boy asked the man.

I sighed.

Completely oblivious, Val spun around and headed straight for the romance section. I trailed after her, almost wishing we were still talking about the ancients. "You know," she said, twirling down a tight aisle, her skirt billowed out around her, "I wasn't joking when I offered to end the dry spell for you. I'm equal opportunity."

Laughing, I stopped in the middle of the row and scanned the shelf by authors' last name. "I know."

She danced over to me and draped an arm around my shoulders. "Girls are so much more fun than boys."

"I don't even need to try that out to know that's true. Wait." I bumped her with my hip. "What happened last night with your hot date? That was a guy, right?"

"Oh yeah." Slipping away, she hummed under her breath as she perused the shelves. "He . . . something else." She peeked at me through thick lashes. "I'm surprised I can walk today."

"Thought girls were more fun," I replied dryly, finally finding the last name Crownover.

"Usually." She picked up a book. "But then there are some guys. Like Ren. They are more fun. So when you going to let—"

"Don't even finish that statement." Spying the book I was looking for, I snatched it up and cradled it close to my chest as I turned to Val. "Look, I'm . . . yeah okay, I'm attracted to him. Who wouldn't be? But I've only known him a few days."

"Babe." She skipped over to me. "*Babe.*"

"What?" I shot her a look before starting for the front of the store.

"You do not need to know him, *know him,* to get some. You just need to drop those panties." She paused and her eyes glazed over like she was remembering something pretty steamy. "Actually, you don't need to drop them. He could just tug them aside, and that is really hot."

"Oh my God," I murmured, and then louder, "Can we not talk about this anymore?"

"Whatever. Prude."

I smiled. "Ho."

After we paid for our books, I was sure the employees were happy to see us make our way to the exit. Walking out together, I knew I'd made the right choice by confiding in her. Val needed to know what was out there so she could protect herself. I didn't know what I'd do if I lost her.

We ended up at the coffee shop next door and didn't make it any further than the chairs. She continued on about how I needed to be in a bed or against the wall or on a kitchen counter with Ren by the end of the week until she suddenly jerked straight up in her chair, startling me.

"Are you okay?" I asked, leaning toward her.

"Crap. The time." She jumped to her feet. "I've got to go."

I raised my brows. "Hot date number two?"

"Actually, yes." She grabbed her coffee. "How do I look? Delectable?"

"Hot as usual." I held my hand out. "But can I have my sunglasses back?"

"Oh." She laughed, reaching up and pulling them off her head. She handed them over and swooped down to kiss my cheek. "I'll text you later."

"I have a feeling you're going to be really busy later."

She giggled. "If I'm lucky."

Standing, I picked up my sweet tea and bag from the bookstore. "So do I get to meet hot guy who's going to make you walk funny by tomorrow sometime?"

Val stepped back, her skirt swaying around her legs as she smiled. "You'll get to meet him." Biting down on her lip, she winked. "Be careful, okay?"

I reached out, squeezing her hand. "You too."

Chapter Nine

On the way back to my apartment, I made a pit stop at Brighton and Merle's house, smack dab in the heart of the Garden District, not too far from my apartment. They lived in a true antebellum home, a gorgeous two-story with four large white pillars that supported the sprawling front porch and the balcony above. The shutters were painted a traditional black, but about a month ago, Merle got a wild hair up her rear and hired a contractor to paint the front door a pale blue. I'd thought the idea was odd, especially since the color was such a washed out shade; it was the exact color of fae eyes.

A wrought iron fence surrounded the property, and the gate squeaked like old bones rubbing together as I opened it. The sidewalk used to be cracked, resembling old plaster, but it had finally been repaired about a year ago. I stepped on the porch, wincing as the boards groaned.

Huge ferns swayed in the light breeze, hanging from the ceiling of the porch as I walked toward the wide, blue door. I hesitated for a second then knocked. Merle hated the doorbell, so I resisted the urge to push it. When there was no answer, I knocked again, and finally I had to hit the doorbell. Still, there was no answer.

Stepping back from the door, I looked around the porch. The beautiful wicker furniture was situated a bit haphazardly, and I knew that Merle sometimes moved it around, much to Brighton's dismay. Thinking that they might be in the backyard, I followed the porch around the side and walked down a set of three steps and into a glorious courtyard.

Fruit trees and flowers flourished, scenting the air. I was jealous of Merle's garden. It was absolutely stunning, like something straight off an HGTV show, and I knew both she and her daughter spent a great deal of time keeping it up.

But I didn't find Merle on her knees, yanking weeds or trimming the hummingbird bushes. Brighton wasn't sitting on any number of the thick cushioned lounge chairs or benches with a book in her lap. Flirty jazz music wasn't drifting out from the house. The garden was empty, too.

Geez, the one Sunday afternoon they weren't home was the one I stopped by.

I probably should've called Brighton, but she was terrible when it came to answering phone calls or even knowing where she left her phone. I didn't really have any other choice though. Reaching into my pocket, I pulled out my phone and hit her number.

As expected, there was no answer. At the sound of the beep, I left a message. "Hey, Brighton. It's Ivy. Can you please give me a call when you get this? Thanks."

Disconnecting the call, I turned to walk back up the porch when, out of the corner of my eye, sudden movement caught my attention. I stilled, the bag from the bookstore dangling from my fingers.

Did I see . . . wings?

I swore I'd seen the flutter of wings by one of the bushes with the bright pink blossoms. Not butterfly wings, and they were too big, too transparent to belong to a bird. Pivoting around, I stared at the bush and quietly stepped toward it. I stood still, barely breathing for several seconds—*there*!

Through one of the bushes, I saw the movement again—the flutter of tan, transparent wings about the size of my hand. Was there a brownie in their garden? It was unlikely as hell, but I knew it wasn't impossible. After all, I'd found Tink in a cemetery. There could be more of him hanging around. Maybe even a female. Tink could have a girlfriend.

I wrinkled my nose. What in the hell was I thinking? Even if it was a girl brownie, it wasn't like I was going to capture her and take her home, serving her up to Tink like I was some kind of brownie trafficker.

"Hello?" I called out softly. "I won't hurt you."

A moment passed, and I was just standing in the courtyard, talking to a bush. Kneeling down, I reached out and carefully gripped the branches. I pulled the leafy stems aside and peered into the bush.

Nothing was there.

Letting go of the bush, I sighed as I stood. Either I was seeing things, or whatever had been there, brownie or not, skedaddled on out of there. I puttered around for a couple more minutes, but I didn't catch sight of anything strange. I left their property, closing the gate behind me.

Under the heavy oak trees, it was actually a pleasant walk and I didn't hurry. Too many times I found myself rushing to get nowhere. I didn't have anything planned for the day except to call Jo Ann and maybe grab dinner with her.

About halfway to my apartment, a strange chill snaked down my spine, causing the hairs along the nape of my neck to rise. I stopped at the corner, shivering as the feeling of being watched increased. It was so intense it felt like a person was standing directly behind me. Heart pounding, I looked over my shoulder and found no one there.

The stake inside my boot reassured me as I stood on the street. While most fae preferred the evening and night hours, nothing stopped them from coming out during the day. And the feeling of being watched didn't necessarily mean it was a fae. They weren't the only dangerous things in the city.

Scanning up and down the street, I turned in a slow circle. People were out in their yards, and across the street there was a small group of tourists viewing the homes, but no one was paying attention to me.

The feeling of being watched hadn't faded though, not even when I started walking again, much more alert and at a much faster pace. The sensation remained until I was about a half a block from my apartment. It faded like smoke in the wind, but the wariness lingered.

~

Like Saturday, Ren was waiting for me outside of Mama Lousy, lounging against the wall like he had nothing better to do with his time. I was wary as I approached him and ran a nervous hand over my hair, smoothing the stray curls back into the twist I was trying to keep them in. The humidity was back with a vengeance, and all I really wanted to do was peel my jeans and shirt off and go half naked like everyone else did.

All day a weird knot of nervousness, excitement, and dread bounced around inside me like a rubber ball thrown against a wall. I didn't want to look too closely at the source, but the moment I saw Ren, I thought about what Val had said yesterday and what I'd done that morning.

Heat crawled across my cheeks, and I almost spun around. But where would I go? Hide in an overflowing garbage can? Running from Ren when I'd gladly fight a fae was just stupid. I had no reason to be weird or embarrassed or anything. I needed to chill out. Squaring my shoulders, I tipped my chin as I walked past the entrance of the gift shop.

Ren tipped his head in my direction and smiled. Two dimples appeared as he extended his arm toward me. Between his long fingers was a deep blue, almost violet rose on a single stem.

My gaze flipped from the rose to him then back to the rose. "I . . . I don't understand."

"For you," he said, pushing off the wall and coming to his full height.

I dragged my gaze back to his. "Me?"

His eyes glimmered. "Yes."

"Why?"

"Honey, if you don't want that rose from him, I'll take it," came from a woman, a *random* woman just strolling down the road. She eyed Ren with a saucy grin. "And I'll take him."

The heat in my cheeks increased, and the woman's laugh as she stumbled on down the street was eventually lost in the call of police sirens from somewhere nearby.

"I saw this on my way here, and I thought of you." Lifting the rose, he tapped it on the tip of my nose. The petals smelled fresh. "They almost match your eyes."

My lips parted as I stared at him.

Lowering the rose, he dipped his head as he leaned in. His nose grazed my cheek as he spoke in my ear. "This is the part where you take the rose from me."

A series of tight shivers danced over my skin as my pulse exploded from the slight, innocent touch. I watched him pull back, his green eyes searing. Mouth dry, I took the rose. "Thank you."

He cocked his head to the side. "I'm actually surprised."

"About what?"

"You said thank you. I didn't think you would." He shrugged one broad shoulder. "I figured there was a good chance you'd toss the rose in my face."

Holding the rose close to my chest, I wondered what he thought of me if he honestly expected that. "I must've made a great first impression."

"First couple of impressions," he corrected gamely. "Then again, I don't blame you considering how those instances were initiated."

Incredibly self-conscious, I nodded as I twisted to the side. Shrugging off one strap of my backpack, I unzipped the bag and carefully placed it in the front pocket.

"What do you carry around in that bag?" he asked. "Doesn't look too light."

"Textbooks. Notebooks." I zipped the bag back up. "It's not too heavy."

He shifted closer to me, stepping aside to let someone walk past. "Textbooks? You go—"

"Ivy!" shouted Jerome from inside the gift shop. His roar was so loud I thought it might've shaken the windows. "Get your ass in here!"

Ren stiffened as he turned, his eyes narrowing, but I sighed as I slipped the strap back up my shoulders. "Be right back," I said, turning and opening the door.

The door didn't swing shut. Ren caught it, two steps behind me. I glanced over my shoulder, but he was staring straight ahead at the crotchety old man behind the counter. The playful smile was nowhere to be seen, and his green eyes were cold.

I opened my mouth but Ren beat me. Stepping around me, he stalked up to the counter and planted both hands on the glass case. "Is that how you talk to the lady?"

Oh geez.

Jerome's black brows climbed up his forehead as he met Ren stare for stare. "Who in the hell do you think you are?"

"Someone who thinks you could learn to use a little respect," he fired back.

I wiggled between Ren and a display of voodoo feathers that smelled like patchouli. "Ren, it's okay."

He didn't take that glare off Jerome. "Not okay with me."

Jerome crossed his arms and straightened, expression permanently sullen. I was surprised the deep grooves of his face hadn't truly frozen in a scowl. "No one asked you, boy."

"All right." I held up a hand as Ren looked as if he was about to grab the old man and put him in a chokehold. "Seriously. It's okay. He's not being disrespectful." I glanced at Jerome. "Well, it's not a personal thing. He's a jerk to everyone."

"Not everyone," he replied in a surly tone.

I shot him a bland look. "Your dog doesn't count."

A terse moment passed, and Ren finally looked down at me. Some of the hardness had left his gaze, but he still didn't look thrilled. "Still not cool."

"Ren," I murmured.

"Ivy," he repeated.

Jerome rolled his eyes then lifted his chin. "Hey, you! Yeah, you over by the hot sauce," he shouted. Ren and I turned. A middle-aged white man halted. Two giant bottles of Voodoo Queen Hot Sauce were in his hands. "Those bottles are for buying and not fondling. Either buy 'em or put 'em down."

"Wow," I said, turning back to Jerome. "I'm surprised this place makes any money."

He snorted. "Like I give a shit if it does."

Never really thought that he did.

"Is there a reason why you called her in here?" Ren asked, folding his arms as the customer hurried out of the shop. "Because we actually have stuff to do."

His gaze slid to Ren. "I kind of like you, boy."

"Honored," murmured Ren. "And entirely flattered."

I bit my lip to stop from grinning.

"You owe me." Jerome pointed a gnarled finger at me.

At first, I had no clue what he was getting at, and then I remembered the day. "Oh. Crap." I placed my hands on the counter. "I'm sorry. This has been one hell of a week. I forgot."

"Forgot what?" Ren glanced between us.

"Monday," Jerome grumbled. "Every Monday for about two years, and this is the first time you've forgotten."

"Cake," I said to Ren, letting a little grin peek through.

A brown eyebrow shot up. "Cake?"

"Not just any damn cake!" Jerome slammed his hands on the counter, causing me to jump. "The best damn chocolate cake I've ever had. That girl brings it to me every Monday. I rearrange my points just to have that damn cake."

Ren looked even more confused. "Points?"

"He's on a diet." I grinned then. "I'm sorry. I'll bring it tomorrow. Okay?"

Jerome grumbled something under his breath. "You better not forget. Now get out of here so I can order a pizza."

The thing was, I hadn't been the only one who had forgotten.

Outside the shop, we started toward Jackson Square. We'd made it about half a block before Ren laughed. "What?" I glanced up at him.

"You bake?" he asked, nudging my arm with his. "You bake chocolate cake that's apparently the best in the whole world for a half senile old guy?"

A giggle squeaked out. "Um, yeah. I do. Baking . . . is like a hobby." Okay. That was a total lie. The only cakes I could bake came out of the box. It was Tink who baked the cakes from scratch.

"And why haven't I been offered any cake?"

I wondered what he'd think if he knew the cake was made by a brownie. Sending him a quick glance, I smoothed my hands down my thighs. "You're going to have to get to know me better before you taste my cake."

Ren opened his mouth then closed it a second before he stopped and stepped right in front of me. I skidded to a stop to avoid slamming into him. The guy behind us cursed and shot us a dirty look as he walked around us. Ren ignored him. "Was that an invitation? Because I'm willing to get to know you in any way possible if that means I get to taste your cake."

"Invitation for . . .?" Oh my God. My words replayed. My face turned crimson. "You are such a pervert!" I smacked his chest hard. "That's not what I meant."

"That's a damn shame then," he said solemnly.

I hit him again, on the arm this time, then stormed around him. "You're such a dog."

Tipping his head back, he laughed loudly and deeply, and in spite of my embarrassment, my lips formed a wry grin. I couldn't help it. The laugh . . . it was infectious. He was beside me in a heartbeat. "I really do want to taste the cake—the real cake. Well, I'd also love to taste your cake, too."

"If you stop talking about cake in general, I promise I will get you a slice of cake," I said. "And I won't stab you."

"You'd stab me?" Amusement colored his tone.

I nodded. "Even after giving me a rose."

153

"Okay. Deal. No more cake." He was quiet as we crossed onto Chartres. "Did you do anything on your day off yesterday?"

I almost stumbled as I glanced at him sharply. Brighton hadn't called me back, which was no surprise, and I planned on paying her another visit. But there was no way he'd known that.

A half grin curved his mouth up at one corner. "It's just a simple question. I'll tell you what I did. I slept in until about ten. Then I roamed around, a bit aimlessly to be honest, and found myself buying beignets. Then last night I staked out the hotel we'd seen the ancient fae go into. That's what I did."

Words were reluctant to come to the tip of my tongue. "I didn't do much," I said after a moment. "I met Val and we went to a bookstore. Then I came home and pretended to tidy up. I had dinner with a friend. That's it."

His gaze met mine, and I thought about the sorrow that had been so clear on his face when the man died. "See how easy that was?"

I nodded, but it wasn't easy. Not at all. As we neared Jackson Square, the breeze off the Mississippi was much cooler, stirring the loose curls at the nape of my neck.

"Those textbooks?" he asked, changing the subject. "What are they for?"

Our steps slowed as I considered what I should tell him. Not that going to college was a secret. I ran my fingers along the fence. "I'm going to college—Loyola. Majoring in sociology."

I could feel his eyes on me without looking. "You're actually going to college?" he asked. "You do that and this?"

Nodding, I squinted up at the deep gray steeples breaking the blue skies.

"Do you plan on leaving the Order?"

I laughed. "I think the only way you leave the Order is in a body bag."

"That's not true." Stepping in front of me, he faced me as he walked backward, his hand in front of mine, running along the fence. He was lucky there was a decent space without vendors. "People have left the Order, Ivy."

"I don't want to leave. I just want to . . . I want to do more." My stomach dipped, and I suddenly wished I hadn't said so much.

Ren stopped walking, and our hands collided on the fence.

I started to pull my hand back, but held my ground in front of him. "I know it's strange, but yeah, that's what I'm doing."

His eyes searched mine. "No. It's not weird. It's just different."

Our gazes held for a moment, then I looked away, chewing on my lower lip. When I looked back, he was still looking at me in that way—like he couldn't see through me, but inside me. "What?" I demanded.

"I was just thinking something." His finger had found its way onto mine. I looked at our hands, my breath catching as he drew his finger along my own. "I don't think I've met anyone like you."

"Sounds like a bad thing." I dragged my gaze from our hands.

He smiled. "It's a good thing. I think."

That wasn't entirely a ringing endorsement.

Slipping his hand away from mine, he started walking again, but this time he was going forward, toward the way we came. "Come on. We have work to do."

"Isn't that what we're doing?"

He glanced over his shoulder at me. "What I'm looking for isn't here."

"Oh, is that so?" I caught up to his long-legged pace. "Where are we going?"

"Down here."

My brows rose. "Pirates Alley?"

Ren simply winked at me and kept walking. Having no idea what he was up to, I followed him beyond the entrance of the alley. We weren't heading in there, which was a shame, because the alley was pretty with all its colorful buildings and doors.

He ended up on Madison Street, and I resisted the urge to point out that we could've just gone there instead of heading to the Square, but then again, our job pretty much required us roaming up and down the same streets all night.

Ren walked up to some street kid standing next to a motorcycle. I didn't know what model it was, but it was sleek, black, and looked fast enough to break every single bone if you crashed while on it.

"Thanks, man." Ren handed the kid a wad of cash.

I stared at him as the boy scampered off. "The bike . . . it's yours?"

He nodded.

"What is that?" I stared at the bike like it was a giant two-legged insect.

"Some call it a Ducati." Picking up two helmets, he arched a daring brow at me. "I came prepared tonight. One for me." He raised a helmet. "One for you."

I shot him a dirty look. "And you expect me to get on that?"

"Yes." He handed over a black helmet, and I held it like it was a grenade, away from my body. "Look, like I said, I've got a job to do that doesn't involve tracking down normal fae. I'm here to figure out what the ancients are up to and stop whatever it is that they want. You can come with me or not. I'd prefer that you did." He tilted his head to the side, and the late evening sun glanced off his smooth cheek. "If you're close, then at least I know you're not lying dead somewhere."

My grip on the helmet tightened. "I can take care of myself."

"I didn't say that you couldn't, but even though I've only known you for a short time, I know you're not going to run from a fight. You're going to run to it." The playful half smile appeared as he tossed one long leg over the bike and sat. "And that's incredibly hot, but also incredibly dangerous right now." And you're supposed to be shadowing me, at least until Wednesday. So shadow me on my bike. It'll be fun."

As I stared at him, I wanted to demand that he stop being so damn good looking and charming. It was hard to argue with his logic when he laid it out there with a sexy grin and pretty words.

"Are you coming or not?"

Sighing, I glanced at the helmet then back to him. A slow smile spread across his lips. "Fine."

His eyes deepened to a forest green. "Then get on."

I bristled at his commanding tone, switching the helmet to one arm and flipping him off with my free hand.

Ren laughed, the skin crinkling around his eyes.

"I don't like you," I said.

He grinned as he cocked his head back, eyeing me knowingly. "Don't lie. I know better. You might not want to, but you like me."

Hiding the fact that he'd been unerringly observant, I smirked at him. "You are grossly mistaken."

"Uh-huh." Thick lashes lowered, shielding his eyes, and then his arm shot out. He hooked his fingers through the loop in my jeans and tugged me forward. Balancing the bike with just his legs, he reached up with his other arm and curled his fingers around the nape of my neck.

My breath caught as my eyes widened. I almost dropped the helmet as he guided my head to his. Too shocked to resist, I found myself staring into his eyes, our mouths so close I could feel his warm breath dancing over my lips. He didn't take his eyes off mine as he shifted his head. His lips brushed the curve of my cheek, and my pulse thundered with excitement and dismay. I didn't want him to kiss me. Or did I? His breath tickled the spot just below my ear, and the muscles low in my stomach clenched. I shivered. Okay, maybe I did want him to kiss me.

Ren's lips swept over the line of my cheek and his nose brushed mine. "I bet you have the softest pair of lips out there. And I bet you taste sweet—sweeter than one of those beignets you've got me addicted to." His hand squeezed around the back of my neck. "But you got one hell of a bite—a kick to that sweetness. It'll be rough getting in there, and you're going to fight it every step of the way, but it'll be smooth once I'm there."

My eyes grew to the size of saucers. There were no words. None whatsoever.

"You like me." Letting go, he smiled up at me, that angelic face a picture of innocence. "You just aren't ready to admit it."

All I could think as I gawked at him was, what an observant son of a bitch.

Chapter Ten

The first thing I discovered after ignoring what Ren had just said and done was that there was no graceful way to get on a bike. Not like Ren had done it. I almost kneed him in the back as I climbed up behind him. The second thing I learned came after I put the helmet on and Ren did the same. They were wired with microphones. High tech right there. But the final thing was when I sat rigid behind him, my thighs resting against the outer length of his—I had no idea where to put my hands.

"Ivy," he said, clearly amused. "You're going to have to hold on to me and get closer or you're going to fly off this bike, sweetness."

"Don't call me that." I ignored his answering chuckle as I lightly placed my hands on the sides of his waist—his extremely hard waist. Under my fingers, I could feel the outline of daggers, but I could also tell there wasn't an ounce of fat on his waist.

Ren grabbed my wrists and yanked my arms forward, forcing me to slide on the back until my thighs cradled his ass. My eyes went wide as he folded my arms in front of him, just below his navel. "There," he said. "This is how you ride."

My breasts pressed against his back, and I was grateful for the helmet shielding my burning face. "I'm pretty sure I don't have to be this close."

He chuckled and then the motorcycle hummed to life under us. My heart jumped unsteadily. Out of all the crazy things I did for my job, I'd never been on a motorcycle, and I wasn't quite sure what to expect.

"I'm taking your cherry, aren't I?" he asked.

I rolled my eyes. "Classy."

Another rolling laugh came through the speaker, and then we were off. Ren did not ease me into the experience. He kicked off the training wheels and tossed me face first into it. My arms tightened around him on their own, and at first, I squeezed my eyes shut as he headed for the busiest streets in the Quarter. I didn't want to see all the people I knew we were narrowly missing, but the wind—the rush of air over my fingers and bare arms was too tantalizing. After a minute or so, I pried my eyes open.

Stores and people blurred by in a dizzying stream, and it was frightening and crazy how fast we were going, but it was . . . it was also *amazing*. I turned my head, eyes wide as I soaked it all in. There was something freeing about this. Was that why so many people rode motorcycles? I wanted to know what it felt like to have the wind in my hair. However, I wasn't brave or stupid enough to whip off the helmet. The tension eased out of my thighs and shoulders, and I knew I could lean back without toppling off, but I didn't.

I could feel the power in the corded muscles of Ren's back as they tensed and rolled. Under my folded hands, I felt his taut stomach jump every couple of minutes, as if his body was unconsciously reacting to something.

"Hanging in there?" asked Ren.

I nodded like an idiot at first. "Yeah. I actually . . . I really like this."

"You should be on the back when I get this thing out in the open and really crank up the speed." As he coasted to an idling stop at a light, he reached down and squeezed my joined hands. "It's like flying."

My heart took a tumble. I couldn't find the words to respond as we started moving again, crossing Canal. I knew we had to be heading into the business district, down where we'd seen the ancient that had been masquerading as a developer.

"I've been keeping an eye on our friend," Ren explained as we idled in traffic. "Around seven every night, sometimes at eight, he leaves the hotel and heads to a club called Flux a couple of streets down. Heard of it?"

Sounded like a place Val would hang out. "No. It could be new, but I don't go to a lot of the clubs in town."

"And here I thought you were a regular party animal," he said, tone light and teasing.

"What about you?"

"I did the whole drinking and partying thing before I turned twenty-one." He reached down, patting my bent knee. "Drove my parents crazy. Looking back, I was a fucking brat. They were off risking their lives and dealing with me coming home drunk off my ass. Surprised they didn't murder me in my sleep." He laughed, mostly to himself. "But you know how it was. We went to public school but always had to come home straight afterward."

"To train." I cringed, recalling my high school years. Kids had thought I was weird because I never got involved in any afterschool stuff, didn't go to games, and only hung out with other kids whose parents were in the Order—other kids like me. All and all, it wasn't that bad for me.

"We really didn't have much of a life. So I acted out." His shoulders rose. "At least I got it out of my system. I still like a beer or a drink, but getting shitfaced isn't a priority. What about you?"

"It had its rough moments, but it was okay. I had . . ." I didn't let myself finish. I'd been lucky because I had Shaun, first as a friend and then as more. "I don't drink that much now. Don't really like the taste."

He was quiet, and it was just the idling of the engine. "Your parents still alive?" I asked.

"Yeah. And yes, they're still a part of the Elite." There was a pause. "What about you?"

I bit my lip. "No. Both are dead. My real parents were killed when I was just a baby, and then Holly and Adrian adopted me. They couldn't have kids of their own, so they raised me."

"And they're gone too?"

A familiar burn infiltrated my chest. "They're gone too."

"Damn," he said. "Sorry to hear that you've known such loss."

I really didn't know how to respond to that, but I murmured thank you and wished I hadn't gone that far with the conversation. Sharing things like this bonded you to people, and that made things so much harder when you . . . when you lost them. I didn't know how many times I warned myself not to get close, but I hadn't listened when it came to Val. Not even with grouchy old Jerome or even David.

And now I was doing it with Ren.

Some of the fun was sucked out of the bike ride after that, but that was good. I needed to focus. This wasn't playtime. I wasn't here to get to know Ren and become friends with him, and despite what he believed, it wasn't just because I wasn't willing to admit that I liked him.

I just wasn't willing to go there with anyone.

Ren seemed to sense that I was done with the chatting because he was uncharacteristically quiet. We'd passed the hotel twice before finding a spot down the street to park. There wouldn't be a lot of time for us to wait, but we didn't have to worry about it. From our vantage point, we saw the black sedan pull up in front of the hotel. No more than three minutes later, the ancient came out dressed like he was last week when I saw him. He climbed into the back of the sedan, and then they were off, driving past us.

"Hold on," Ren ordered.

Tightening my grip around his waist, I held on as he made a sharp turn, cutting expertly between an SUV and a convertible. My heart still ended up in my throat. The SUV laid on its horn, but Ren veered to the right, passing the convertible. I peered over his shoulder, spying the sedan four cars ahead. He glided the bike back into traffic, trailing the sedan from a safe distance.

Streetlamps were flipping on as the sun faded into the horizon, the glare lessening as dusk settled around us. The sedan came to a stop in front of a club I'd never seen. Remodeled in one of the older warehouses, Flux was obviously newer, and it looked upscale—the large front windows were tinted out, the sign above was in elegant cursive, and a valet was waiting by the bronze double doors. The building itself was several stories high, and as I looked up, I could see white canopies rolling in the breeze. There was a crowd outside the club, the men dressed nicely and the women in short, slinky dresses.

Ren continued down the street, parking about half a block away as I twisted in my seat, watching the sedan. The ancient—Marlon— got out of the car, and I tensed as I saw another ancient step out from under the black awning.

"It's him," I said into the helmet. "The one who shot me. He's here meeting Marlon."

As Ren killed the engine on the bike, I watched the ancient grip Marlon's hand. A one-armed embrace followed, and it looked like Marlon was speaking to the other ancient. Seeing the two of them together unnerved me. Part of me wanted to hop off the bike and dash across the street, catching them off-guard. But I didn't have the weapons necessary to do any damage. The two ancients strolled inside the club, their heads bent together. Mortals followed after them.

Shifting to the side, Ren hit the kickstand on the bike. I started to take my helmet off, but he caught my hand. "Hold on for a sec." He nodded down the street. The sedan was pulling away from the curb, easing past us. "He's had a mortal driving him. I saw him yesterday.

165

He didn't look as if Marlon was feeding off of him, and it's possible the guy has no idea who he's working for, but let's not take that chance."

Once the sedan turned the corner a block down, Ren let go of my hand and we took our helmets off. He scrunched his fingers through his hair. His waves were going everywhere. "This is the first time I've seen another ancient meet him here. I figured that's what they were doing. This just confirms it."

It was no big surprise that the ancients were hanging out together. All fae stuck close to one another. Rumor had it that they even established communities in some cities, but none of the sects had been able to get an exact location on any of the places.

"There are a lot of people coming in and out of the club." I watched the entrance and then looked at him. "It reminds me of a bar in the Quarter. We thought there might be a fae bartender in there because some of the fae came out of there appearing drunk."

"Must be serving nightshade. Interesting. Let's check it out."

Glad to be off the bike and have some space between us, I tucked the helmet under my arm and started forward.

"Wait," Ren said, moving to my side.

He surprised me by smoothing his hand along the side of my head, tucking back springy curls that had come loose from the knot. "There you go. They were distracting. I wanted to tug on each of them, and really, I can't afford my ADD to be tempted by your curls right now."

A laugh burst out of me. "Your ADD?"

He grinned. "It comes and goes. It's like my ADD has ADD. Actually, I think my ADD has ADHD."

"Oh my." Grinning, I hurried across the busy street beside him. "Sounds problematic."

"Can be." He stopped on the curb, his helmet dangling from his fingers. "See that alley right there? You think it runs behind the club?"

"Probably. Most alleys in the city connect to another roadway eventually. There may be a loading area back there. Want to check it out?"

He nodded. Keeping alert, we headed down the narrow alley. With the sun almost completely set, the lack of any artificial lighting gave the alley a creepy vibe. Potted plants, large and bushy, were placed every couple of feet. There were benches but no one in sight. Weird. It was such a pretty place, rather calming for being in such an industrial part of the city. Our footsteps echoed, and the further we traveled, the sounds of the street faded into the background. Toward the end of the alley, I noticed a door painted the same pale blue as Merle's. Before I could really give that much thought, Ren had reached the end of the buildings and drawn up short.

"Well, hello," he muttered under his breath.

I looked around him and saw two fae standing near a fancy car—a white Benz. These were normal fae by the looks of their silvery skin and pointy ears. They held a human male between them, one that looked like he wouldn't be able to stand if it wasn't for the arm around his chest. Familiar adrenaline surged at the sight of them.

But that wasn't the most shocking part. Standing beside the fae were two uniformed police officers that appeared to be human. One was too short and his stomach too round to be an ancient. The other officer, who looked like he was in his late forties or fifties, laughed at something the brown haired fae said.

The round cop shuffled forward and gripped the jowls of the human male the fae held, turning his head from one side to the next. Words too low to overhear were said, and then the cops left, walking to the third door down from where the Benz sat. They went inside the back entrance of the club.

Holy crap.

Ren and I exchanged looks. Those cops didn't look like they were out of it or unaware of what they were doing. They weren't being fed on, and I had a sinking suspicion they knew exactly what the fae were. This wasn't good.

"Stay back," Ren ordered, and then walked forward before I could respond. The fae watched him curiously. He was halfway to them when he cheerfully said, "Hey."

And then threw his helmet at the fae with brown hair.

The fae caught it, bewilderment flashing across his expression, and then cold, deadly fury as he stepped toward Ren. "The Order," he sneered, "must be getting desperate."

Ren laughed.

The fae threw the helmet back, turning it into a missile, but Ren easily snatched it out of the air and then carefully, almost casually, placed it on the ground. He straightened, reaching to his side and pulling out a dagger.

"Take him out," the other fae said, dragging the human male toward the back of the Benz. "We don't have time for this."

Neither did we.

Instead of staying back as I'd been ordered, I placed my helmet on the retaining wall surrounding a flower box and then slipped the dagger out of my boot, stepping into the open area. The second the other fae realized I'd joined the party, he dropped the human male, letting him slump to the ground, completely out of it.

The brown haired fae threw a punch, and Ren ducked, springing up behind him. Spinning around, he planted his boot in the back of the fae. The creature stumbled forward and then turned. Ren spun out of his grasp, moving fast.

Damn. Boy could move.

My gaze zeroed in on the fae heading in my direction. He was tall with icy blond hair. Sometimes the fae liked to fight hand to hand. Other times, they used their abilities. This one belonged to the latter.

Raising his hand, I felt the charge. Like a jolt of electricity, tiny hairs on my arms stood up. Metal scraped over cement. The bench to my right shuddered and flew into the air.

"Really?" I muttered.

Darting to the side, in front of the Benz, I avoided getting smacked upside the head. The bench crashed into the trunk of a nearby palm, the legs breaking off. The fae raised his hand again, his eyes narrowing. The legs from the bench rose, flipping around. Out of the corner of my eye, I saw a flash of light. Ren had taken the other fae out. Behind him, the legs were flying straight for him.

I had to act fast. Cocking my arm back, I threw the dagger. It spun through the air, hitting the fae in the chest, sinking deep. A startled look crossed the fae's face, and then he too disappeared in a flash of light. The legs dropped to the ground, inches from impaling Ren.

He stared at them for a moment and then turned to me. His head cocked to the side. A sudden burst of bright yellow light lit up the darkened alley.

"In the car!" Ren shouted.

Oh crap. Two headlights blinded me for a moment. The engine roared to life and the Benz lurched forward. My heart lodged in my throat as I launched myself to the side. I hit the ground and rolled, the motion uneven with my backpack. I hoped to God my poor rose was okay. I kind of wanted to keep it.

The Benz came so close I could feel the heat blowing off of it. The brakes squealed and burnt rubber filled the air. Leaping to my feet, I threw my head back as Ren ran up behind the Benz. He jumped, landing on the trunk. The car shook, and the driver's door flew open. The fae stepped out, raising his hand.

A trashcan to my left rattled, lifting off the ground and flying straight for me. I dove for the ground, but the trashcan changed course, slamming into my side. It hit the spot where I'd been shot, and a sharp pain flared. Gritting my teeth, I kicked the can off of me and pushed up.

Ren slid across the roof of the Benz, grabbing the fae. Yanking his head back by the mane of black hair, Ren shoved the stake into the back of the fae, right between his shoulder blades.

Light pulsed and then Ren wasn't holding on to anything other than a stake that looked as if it had been dipped in blue ink.

Rocking back onto my heels, I drew in a deep breath as Ren straightened on top of the Benz. "Well, that was fun."

He wiped the stake on his dark jeans and secured it under his shirt. Then he leveled an intense, angry stare on me. "I thought I told you I had this handled."

"You can take out two fae with a third in a car? All by yourself?" I snorted. "You may be all kinds of special, but come on."

He jumped from the Benz, landing in a nimble crouch he immediately rose from. "I had it. I planned on keeping at least one of them alive to, you know, question it."

"Then maybe you shouldn't have taken out the one in the car then, huh?" I snapped.

"You were supposed to stay back. Last time I checked, you were not to engage until David clears you."

I rolled my eyes. "He's cleared me for Wednesday. That's less than two days from now. I'm fine."

"I don't care if it's tomorrow. If you were told not to risk it, then—"

"Oh, shut up. Geez. I'm okay." I stood up and pain flickered through my side. "Let's—whoa."

Ren was suddenly right in front of me. "I saw that."

"Saw what?"

"You flinched when you stood. You hurt yourself." He grabbed a hold of the hem of my shirt and started pulling it up. "Let me—"

"I'm fine." I grabbed my shirt.

His jaw was set in a firm line as he flicked his gaze to mine. "Let me see, Ivy."

"Jesus!" I all but shouted as I wrestled with the edge of my shirt. "How would you like it if I just went around and started pulling up your shirt?"

He paused, raising both brows. "I'd fucking love it."

"Ugh!" I wanted to stomp my foot.

Chuckling lightly, he almost had my shirt up to where the bullet had hit when his brows pinched in concentration. Without saying a word, he reached out and ran the tips of his fingers along my lower stomach. Gasping, I jerked back, but didn't get very far because he still had a hold of my shirt.

"Your mark," he whispered, and I shivered as his fingers made another pass.

My jeans had slipped low during the fight, exposing just the top of the interlocking circles. The muscles in my belly and much lower tensed, and a heady, pulse-quickening sense of yearning rose. The air around us charged as if a storm was about to move in.

"Stop," I said.

He removed his hand, and I didn't understand the strange sense of disappointment. His gaze was locked with mine, and what felt like an infinite amount of seconds passed while neither of us spoke. I didn't know what he was thinking. I didn't even know what I was thinking, but a sweet heaviness poured into my chest and slipped down, way down.

My phone beeped, breaking up our epic stare down, and then Ren's also dinged. My stomach clenched for a different reason, and a real sense of foreboding rose. He let go of my shirt and I stepped back, pulling my phone out of the back of my jeans. I clicked on the screen, and my breath caught when I saw the text.

Code Red.

"Oh no," I whispered, looking up at Ren. A somber, hard expression had seeped into his features.

Code red could mean only one thing. A member of the Order had been killed.

Chapter Eleven

The ride back to St. Philip was tense. As soon as I got the message, I tried calling Val. When there had been no answer, my stomach twisted into messy knots. As terrible as it sounded, the only thing I could think on the way to headquarters was for it not to be her. I didn't want it to be anyone, but I couldn't bear it if it was Val.

Ren and I didn't talk as we climbed the stairs and waited to be let in. It was Harris who opened the door, and honestly, I'd wanted to punch him in the face since I found out that he ran his mouth, but right then I didn't care.

"They're in the back room," he said, stepping aside.

I almost asked who it was, but I wasn't ready. Nodding at Harris, I crossed the room. There were several doors, and most led to training rooms, but the one all the way to the left led to David's office. We headed for the double doors.

The room was packed with about twenty of the forty-something members that were currently stationed in

New Orleans. My gaze scanned the room, desperately searching for a splash of flamboyant color. When I didn't see her, pressure clamped down on my chest. Panic threatened to take root, and I pulled out my phone, checking it again and finding no response. I tried to prepare myself if it turned out to be her. I'd been down this road before, but I could already feel the bitter bite of pain in the back of my throat. My fingers opened and closed sporadically, and I wanted to be anywhere but where I was in that moment. I knew it was pathetic, but I didn't want to be here if Val didn't walk through that door.

"Not everyone is here yet." Ren placed his hand on my lower back, and my wide gaze swung to his.

His hand stayed there as I stared at the doors, squeezing my hands so tightly I could feel the nails digging into my skin. Faintly, I was aware that other members were doing the same thing, except Jackie Jordan, a tall and sleek woman in her early thirties. She was eyeing Ren with a sense of guardedness I could relate to. When the doors swung open and David strolled in, I almost keeled over from relief. Val was behind him, her gaze searching the room. It took every ounce of control for me to not rush over and squeeze the living daylights out of her. If I did, I knew a lot of the other members would see that as a sign of weakness, even if they were worried it was their friend who wasn't ever going to walk through the doors again. But to them, I was young, and that was strike one. They also thought I was crazy, so strike two.

I didn't need a strike three.

Val saw me standing next to Ren, and her expression relaxed. Stepping around David, she hurried to where I stood. Without saying a word, she found my hand and squeezed, and I returned the gesture.

Aware that Ren was watching us closely, I turned my attention to David. Weariness clung to every step he took as he walked to the middle of the room and placed his hands on his hips. In an uncharacteristic show of emotion, he hung his head.

"We lost Trent tonight," he said, and my mouth dropped open in shock. David lifted his head, his shoulders tensing as he surveyed the room. "He was found just outside of St. Louis Cemetery No 1."

That was the last name I was expecting to hear. Obviously, Trent and I weren't on friendly terms, but he was one hell of a strong guy, and he had a ton of experience. I could not fathom a normal fae getting an upper hand on him.

"How?" Rachel Adams asked. In her late thirties, she was a tall and slender woman who'd been in the city for the last year.

"His neck was broken." David's gaze drifted over the group, stopping and lingering on me for what felt like a second too long before moving on. "But that wasn't all. His arms and legs were also broken, as were his ribs."

"He was tortured," Ren said, his stance tensing, and I immediately thought of the gates. The knowledge of their location would definitely be something the fae would torture for. Val and I exchanged a look.

David nodded. "Appears to be that way."

"He's the fourth to die in what? Five months?" said Dylan. I didn't know his last name, but I was sure it was something French sounding. He was born and raised in New Orleans, and like Val, could track his roots way back. "We suffer losses every year, but this close together?"

Something occurred to me as I watched David. "Were the others like Trent? Were they tortured also?" It had never been said that they were.

As David turned back to me, someone in the back of the group muttered "Crazy" under their breath, and I felt Ren turn, searching out the source, but I ignored it.

"No," David answered.

Standing by the door, Harris rubbed his hand down his face, and instantly, I didn't believe David. I couldn't explain it, but I didn't believe him.

"I'm implementing some changes effective immediately," David continued, pacing. "From now until further notified, you all will be working in groups of two. No one hunts alone."

There were some grumbles from the loners, those who didn't play well with others, but they were quickly silenced by David. He began to team people up. Val was paired with Dylan, and I was left with Ren, which I was sort of expecting. There was a pall over the group as the meeting wrapped up, a heavy somberness that I knew from past experience—too many experiences—would linger for days. It didn't matter how close any of us were to each other. We were family nonetheless, and any loss was a shattering blow, a painful reminder that tomorrow was never promised.

I started to walk out with Val, Ren and Dylan behind us, when David called out my name. "I'll meet you guys outside, okay?"

I headed over to where David stood with another Order member—Miles Daily. Miles was virtually second in command. Though it wasn't entirely official, if something happened to David, Miles would take over until meetings could be held and another leader voted in to cover the sect.

I didn't know Miles very well. He was older than me, possibly in his mid-thirties, and he was quiet, almost aloof. While David looked angry half the time, Miles' expressions were always unreadable. As I approached the men, he looked bored to the untrained eye, but his gaze was sharp. The man missed nothing.

I thought about what we'd seen today behind the club called Flux. I knew I was required to report it to David, but something held me back. It was more than just his dismissal of what I'd experienced last week. Ren hadn't asked me to keep our activities tonight quiet, so it was my choice. I wasn't ready to say anything until I had enough evidence to back me up.

"You wanted to see me?" I asked as they both simply stared at me like they hadn't called me over.

David handed the phone he was holding over to Miles. "Where were you tonight?"

The question was unexpected. "I was out hunting with Ren."

"Where?" Miles asked.

My brows knitted as I shook my head. "We started out by Jackson Square, and then when we didn't see any fae, we headed over to the business district." That wasn't entirely a lie. "We ran into three fae. They had a human male. Ren called an ambulance for him as we—"

"So you weren't in the Quarter tonight, except for the beginning of your shift?" David interrupted.

"No." My gaze darted between them. Hardly anyone was left in the room except for Rachel, who was by the TVs hung on the wall which were showing video feed from the surveillance cameras randomly placed throughout the Quarter, and two more members who spoke privately by the door. I had no idea if they were paying attention to this conversation or not. "Why are you asking me this?"

A damn good question, especially since I hadn't seen them ask anyone else.

"Just checking." Miles glanced up from the phone. I saw that the screen was cracked.

"That's all," David said, dismissing me. When I turned, in a daze from my mind turning their question over and over, he stopped me once more. "Wait. How is your wound?"

I blinked. "Yeah, I barely even notice it." Not exactly true. Since I went toe to toe with a garbage can and lost, it had been throbbing quite steadily.

David held my gaze for a moment and then nodded. A prickling sense of unease washed over me, slow and unshakeable as I walked out of the room and down the stairs. They couldn't be asking me because they thought . . .

No. The idea that they'd think anyone in the Order had anything to do with a death was absolutely insane. I was rattled, which was making me paranoid.

"Everything okay?" Ren asked when I found them standing around Mama Lousy's entrance. Beside him stood Dylan. He was also a tall man, but Ren towered over him.

Smiling faintly, I nodded and then turned to Val. She bounced over to me, throwing her arms around my shoulders. "I just saw your message. I didn't see it."

"It's okay." I hugged her back. "I'm glad . . ." I shook my head as I stepped free. "I'm not glad that Trent is gone, but . . ."

"I know," she said, wrapping her arms around her waist.

Dylan shoved his hands in his pockets. "Trent was a dick, but someone got the upper hand on him? Tortured him? Man, that ain't looking good."

"No doubt." Ren ran a hand through his hair, knocking the wayward curls off his forehead. His eyes met mine before glancing away.

"We better get going before David comes out and finds us all hovered together," Dylan said, pulling his hands free. "Y'all be careful."

"You too." I promised Val I'd call her tomorrow, and we parted, heading in opposite directions.

"You two are close," Ren commented as we made our way toward Royal. The Quarter on a Monday night wasn't too busy. A lot of people were out, but you could walk without too much interference. "You and Val."

"We are. She was the first person I met when I moved down here. And she's really friendly with everyone so it's not hard to become friends with her."

Ren nodded. "I can see that. Seems like a very friendly girl." The way he said the last part made me look at him. He flashed a quick grin that didn't reach his eyes. "I'm pretty sure she's visually molested me a few times since I got here."

I laughed softly. "That's Valerie." I tucked a stray hair back as I blew out a breath. "Trent . . . I don't even know what to think."

"I do."

Deep down, I did too. "You think what has happened to Trent has to do with why you're here—the ancients?"

"Think about it. The identities of those guarding the gates are kept secret for the sole reason that if someone is tortured, they cannot give up the locations. You guys lost four members, and I don't know about you, but I wouldn't be surprised if the other three had similar injuries," Ren said, voicing my earlier misgivings. "For whatever reason, David is keeping that quiet."

"I know." I stared over the people, seeing the Chateau Motel looming ahead at the corner of Phillip and Chartres. "You know, every one of the members killed could've been guards. All of them were highly skilled. With the exception of Cora, they'd been in New Orleans for years."

"But what's the likelihood of the fae or the ancients stumbling across the guardians of the gates?" he asked.

My heart skipped a beat as we both looked at each other. A sour taste filled the back of my throat. Suspicion bloomed. "Unless they knew who to target."

A muscle ticked in his jaw. "There's only one way they'd even have a general idea of who could be guarding the gates."

Meaning someone within the Order would have to be assisting the fae, and God, that was horrific to even consider, but Ren was right if those who'd been killed were guardians. That was a big if, but it wasn't impossible.

"Can we stop for a second?" Ren asked, and then he took my hand, leading me under the balconies of the Chateau. Brown waves toppled onto his forehead as he dipped his chin. "How is your stomach? No bullshit, okay?"

"It's . . . it's a little tender, but it's not a big deal. I'm not bleeding or anything. It's fine." My fingers itched to reach up and brush the curls aside, but that seemed wildly inappropriate. Not that Ren appeared to be the type who cared about that.

"And how are you?" When I didn't answer, Ren reached up, placing the tips of two fingers against my temple. "How are you up here?"

"I'm . . ." It was another question I wasn't sure how to answer. No one really asked any of us that kind of question. We'd been raised in this world, so I guessed people assumed we just dealt with things. "Trent wasn't always easy to get along with. The things he said has half the Order thinking I'm crazy, but I'd never wish him dead."

"I wouldn't think you would," he replied softly.

Swallowing hard, I took a step back and leaned against the wall, suddenly bone weary. "Do you think David knows more than what he's putting out there?"

His shoulders rose with a deep inhale and he lifted his gaze. He didn't speak for a long moment, and the sense of unease deepened. His eyes met mine. "I don't know. Anything is possible, but everything has to be connected. The fae migrating here, the ancients engaging with the Order, members with experience dying and being tortured, and that club where ancients and human cops are hanging out at? Something is going down there. We need to get into it."

I nodded. "We do."

Chapter Twelve

There would be no funeral held for Trent.

As far back as I could remember, the Order did not remember the dead with wakes or funerals. Throughout the years, the bodies of the fallen were buried with little to no fanfare until the Order began cremating the remains some thirty years ago.

I remembered asking Holly once, when I was a small child, why we didn't have funerals. Her response had stayed forever etched into my mind. *"The Order wants to remember the fallen as they were before, all that they have given, and not what remains once the greatest sacrifice for freedom has been made."*

To this day, I still didn't understand how that was a show of respect.

A dismal part of me thought it had more to do with the fact that so many Order members passed in a year's time from all the sects around the world, that if we did have funerals, we'd constantly be attending one.

It was kind of depressing to think about. The world had no idea all that we gave to protect them, and when, as Holly had said, we gave the ultimate sacrifice, not even the Order stopped to remember us. Here one second and gone the next without so much as a few words uttered over our urns.

Brighton called me back on Wednesday while I was in the shower, and it took several hours to reach her on the phone again. Turned out she and her mom were in Texas visiting family. They wouldn't be back for another week, and I made plans to see them upon their return. When I told her about Trent, she seemed surprised and saddened. Not that he and Brighton were close, but like everyone else, she couldn't believe that he'd fallen to the fae.

"Be careful," was the last thing she said to me before we hung up.

Those words haunted me for the remainder of the day and then some, because for some reason, I didn't feel careful. I felt reckless. A week ago, I knew what I was doing and what to expect every day. As crazy as my life was, in some respect, it was static. I got up. Went to class if I had them, and hunted fae if it was my night to work. My job had always been dangerous, but I knew the fae and my own limitations. I didn't keep secrets, especially from David. I didn't have clandestine missions, and I sure as hell didn't suspect any member of the Order of joining up with the fae. There had been no Ren. But everything had changed in a short period of time.

The world as I knew it was different.

On Tuesday, Ren met me outside the café on Canal before our shift. I was slurping away on an iced coffee while skimming notes from class. Like Val had done so many times before, he plopped down, but beside me, not across from me.

"What are you reading?"

Setting my coffee aside, I debated whether or not I should answer him, but decided staying quiet about it seemed dumb. "Notes from my juvenile delinquency class."

"That's right. You're a sexy college student," he said, but I had a feeling he hadn't forgotten that at all. "I do think it's pretty cool that you're doing that."

I picked up my coffee and sucked some down as I eyed him through my sunglasses. "Do you?"

"Yeah. I've never had a real desire to enroll in college. I mean, I know I could if I wanted to, but I never have. So that's just cool to me that you do this." He paused as he watched a group pass us. Then he turned those ultra-bright eyes on me. "Got to take a lot of drive though, to do this plus go out and hunt Monday through Friday."

I shrugged. "I don't have classes Tuesday and Thursday, so it's not that big of a deal, and I want . . ." Blushing for some dumb reason, I clamped my mouth shut.

"You want to be more. I get it." He reached out, found a curl, and tugged it straight. "What do you want to be?"

Staring at him, I wondered if he was able to read minds because it was uncanny how easily he read me. Kind of freaky. "A social worker," I admitted.

"That's good," he said quietly, and let go of my hair.

Unsettled by the entire conversation, I closed my notebook and shoved it in my bag. I started to stand when he spoke. "You don't let people get close to you, do you?"

Again, really freaking uncanny. Sliding my bag over my shoulder, I forced my voice to stay level. "You get close to people and they end up dying on you. Not really too keen on that."

Ren rose. "Not everyone is going to die on you."

"Everyone dies, Ren."

He smirked. "That's not what I meant, and you know that."

I did, but whatever. I walked around the table, and didn't take many steps before Ren caught up to me. I expected him to keep pushing the subject, but he didn't. We ended up making plans to pay a visit to Flux on Saturday, the night both of us were off. We figured it was less risky to put some time between Monday night and when we ventured inside Flux due to the fact they probably realized the Order had killed three fae just outside their doors. Also, since we weren't on the schedule we didn't have to worry about anyone wondering where we were and what we were up to.

Every night that Ren and I worked, we kept an eye on Flux. Twice we saw Marlon there, and he wasn't with the ancient who shot me, but last night, Friday evening, we saw a different ancient arrive at the club with Marlon. Both men were too perfect in appearance, their features pieced together in an extraordinary way that turned their beauty cold and artificial. There was absolutely no doubt in our minds that he was also an ancient. The way he walked into the club was inhuman, just as Marlon did, as if the wind itself moved their limbs. Nothing in this world was as graceful as the fae.

That meant there were at least three ancients in the city. Three fae that even Order members could mistake as mortals. Three fae who held untold power and could not be stopped by an iron stake.

I didn't tell Val about our plans since I had no idea what we'd be facing in there, and I knew if I did tell her she'd demand to be involved. So it was yet another secret I was hiding, but as Saturday evening approached, I knew keeping her out of the loop was the best decision even though she'd be pissed the second she found out.

But I had other, more pressing concerns at the moment anyway.

Standing in front of the full-length mirror hung on the back of the closet door, I studied my reflection with a critical eye. I hated wearing dresses, but I'd seen how the girls had looked going into the club, dressed in a way that ensured men would gladly drop to their knees. They'd looked great—classy and sexy. Two things I wasn't quite sure I knew how to pull off without looking like a little girl playing dress up. A huge part of me wanted to slip on a pair of jeans, but I needed to blend in.

I owned three dresses. One was a brown and white floor-length maxi. The second was in a shorter, peasant style that was definitely not dressy enough. What I was wearing was my final option, the only one that came remotely close, and I hated it.

I'd bought the thing two years ago on a whim while shopping with Val. I don't even know why, but I guess it was some kind of weird fate guiding the purchase. The dress was black, and the material was very thin, one step away from being sheer. Loose at the top, it hung off the shoulders and had short, flirty sleeves, and I had a feeling if I bent over, everyone and their mama would get an eyeful of my breasts squeezed into the most uncomfortable strapless bra known to man. The soft material was cinched at the waist and the skirt was loose. And short. Incredibly short. Only reaching my mid-thighs, I knew that bending over would give the world a show that went further than a glimpse of my breasts.

I felt naked.

Hiding weapons had also proved difficult, and I ended up having to strap a stake to the outside of my thigh which meant I was praying to God no sudden wind blew my skirt up because the scrap of material barely hid what I was concealing. The only other option would've been to wear boots, and I did have a pair of sleek, knee-high boots, but pairing them with this tiny as hell dress would've made me look like a hooker. Actually, I still kind of looked like a hooker.

Hopefully an expensive hooker.

So I went with a pair of black heels I'd owned for a couple of years and worn only once. They were already pinching my toes.

"You look like you're going out trolling for sex. Like the dirty, nasty kind that ends up with a wide array of STDs."

I cast a scowl over my shoulder. Tink was sitting on my dresser, munching on a carrot stick. "Thanks for the input." I turned from the mirror and headed into the bathroom, grabbing a tube of lipstick out of the basket.

"Are you sure this isn't really a date?" Tink called out. "Because it looks like a date."

"It's not a date," I said, and then applied lipstick. Then checked out my mascara and eyeliner to make sure it hadn't smudged, and finally shook my curls out of the clip I was holding them back in. The red ringlets fell over my shoulders, the ends curling just below my breasts. I fluffed my fingers through them and froze, my arms askew, fingers tangled in the curls.

Okay. It kind of felt like I was prepping for a date. It really did because I remembered going through these motions when I knew Shaun was coming over. The all too familiar pang in my chest throbbed, though a bit more faintly this time.

Sighing, I dropped my arms. My blue eyes looked way too big for my face at the moment, my mouth wider and fuller with the red lipstick.

This was not a date.

I left the bathroom, and Tink let out a low whistle. "If you were a foot tall, I'd be all over you."

Giggling at the absurdity of that statement, I gave him a very half-assed curtsy. "So I don't look like I'm going to end up with an STD later?"

"You still kind of do, but one that goes away with treatment. Not the gift that keeps on giving kind of STD," he clarified.

"Gee, thanks."

Tink flew off the dresser and followed me into the kitchen. "Are you sure this is smart?"

No. Heading into the club was wildly dangerous. "I'll be okay."

"If there are ancients there, Ivy . . ." Tink landed on the counter and stared up at me earnestly. "You shouldn't be near them."

Confiding in Tink about our plans to infiltrate the club hadn't been an easy decision, but he hated the fae just as much as I did. Still, being that he was a creature from the Otherworld, there was always that small fear he wasn't what he appeared to be.

"We have to get in there, Tink. It's the best chance we have of finding out what they're up to." I walked around the counter and grabbed the soda I'd been nursing.

Tink cocked his head to the side, eyes narrowed. "I do not like this Ren."

I arched a brow at him. "You've only seen him once."

"There are a lot of people I've never seen that I don't like," he pointed out, storming down the length of the counter. "He's just one of many."

"Tink." I sighed.

"Whatever. I think you should just get some action from him and kick his ass to the curb."

My mouth dropped open. "Okay. That is the most bizarre string of advice I have ever heard. You don't like him, but you think I should have sex with him and then get rid of him? And obviously I can't because he's a member of the Order." That was the one thing I didn't tell Tink—what Ren truly was. "You make no sense."

"I make perfect sense. In my world, you don't even have to like another to have sex with them. It's all about the natural urges to get it on and . . ."

As Tink ranted on about the peculiars of his species' particular mating preferences, I picked up the sugar canister and dumped a small pile of sugar on the counter.

"You just need to let those animalistic—holy brownie balls!" Tink dropped to his knees in front of the pile of sugar. He started moving the tiny granules to another

190

pile, counting softly. "One, two, three, four, five, six . . ." Pausing, he glanced up with a frown. "Where did you learn that?"

I shrugged as I bit down on my lower lip. "Saw it on an episode of Supernatural."

Tink gaped at me.

"What?" I giggled, gesturing at the two piles of sugar on the counter. "I didn't think it would actually work."

"I've been fooled by a Winchester wannabe." He clasped his hands over his chest and swayed before toppling over onto his side. "There is no way to save face. I shall off myself now."

Laughing at the sight of him, I leaned over and poked his leg. He threw up an arm, flipping me off, and then he sat up, starting to count all over again. "I hate you," he muttered. "Look at me. I'm like a crack fiend. I just need to know how many are here. There could be hundreds, or maybe even thousands. I have to know the exact—"

The doorbell rang, and my stomach jolted unsteadily as I glanced at the clock on the stove. It was a little past nine, so it had to be Ren. My gaze shot to the hallway and then to where Tink was meticulously counting sugar. "You need to go to your room."

He looked up, his eyes wide. "But—"

"Forget about the sugar. Ren is here and he can't see you."

Tink scowled. "I'm not afraid of him."

"I didn't say you were afraid of him." Exasperated, I placed my hands on my hips. "You know he can't see you."

The knock came again, and I grabbed Tink by the waist. "Hey!" he shouted, gripping my fingers with his hand. "Careful, Godzilla-sized woman. You're squishing my insides."

"I'm not going to squish your insides, and stop beating my hand with your damn wings. It feels weird." Carrying him around the counter, I headed toward his bedroom as he glared at me. "Stay in there."

His eyes narrowed. "You don't own me."

I rolled my eyes. "Behave, Tink." Opening the door, I tossed him inside. His wings spread and arced as he spun around and gripped the edge of the door. "Tink," I seethed. "Get in there."

"Are you going to have sex with him tonight?" he asked.

"Oh my God, Tink." The knock came for a third time, and I started to pull the door shut.

With surprising strength, he managed to hold the door back and wiggled between it and the frame. I could keep pulling, but then I probably *would* squish him. "I could go with you."

Losing my patience, I counted to ten. I made it to five. "Tink, you know you can't go with me."

He sighed loudly and dramatically. "You're no fun."

I glared at him until he let go of the door then breathed a sigh of relief. "Please behave. Okay?"

A look of pure innocence radiated from his face. "Don't I always?"

This was not going too well, but I was finally able to close the damn door, and I hurried to the front door, yanking it open, ready to apologize for keeping him for so long.

All the words in the world vanished the moment I got an eyeful of Ren.

Holy hotness with an extra side of sexy, when Ren cleaned up, he took his handsomeness into a totally different stratosphere.

The waves and curls of his hair were currently tamed, styled back from his face, showing off the angle of his cheekbones and the fullness of his lips. He was wearing a white dress shirt that showed off the hard lines of his broad shoulders and flashed a glimpse of tawny skin at his neck. I noticed then, somehow never really seeing it before, a leather cord hanging from his neck and disappearing under his shirt. I was sure that was what carried the clover, but as my gaze traveled over him, I quickly forgot about it. The edges of the tattoo poked out of the collar of his shirt, and his sleeves were rolled up to the elbow, exposing powerful forearms. The dark trousers completed the outfit. It was effortless class.

When I dragged my gaze back to his, I realized I hadn't been the only one doing the scrutinizing. He was staring at me in his intense, consuming way, and I stepped back from the door, suddenly feeling very . . . vulnerable. As if I was exposed in front of him.

Heat crept into my cheeks as I plastered my arms to my sides. "Sorry I . . . took so long. I was . . ." I trailed off as he continued to stare at me. "What?"

Ren stepped into the house, catching the door and closing it behind him. His presence filled the living room, and I could barely drag in enough air. "This is wrong," he said, voice thick.

Surprised by the statement, I glanced down at myself. I *knew* I looked like a silly girl playing dress up. "It's the only dress I could wear," I said, feeling the weight of embarrassment settling on my shoulders.

He gave a little shake of his head as his bright green eyes met mine. "Oh, sweetness, you did wrong in all the right ways."

I wasn't following.

"How in the world am I going to pay attention when you look like that?" he chided softly, and my eyes widened. He moved forward, so close that I had to tip my chin up to meet his stare. He reached out, fingering the loose sleeve of my dress. "You are utterly distracting."

"I am?"

A half smile appeared as his fingers skipped off the material and traced the line of my shoulder, sending a tight shiver down my spine. Then his finger wrapped around a curl, the back of his hand brushing the swell of my breast. He tugged it straight like he'd done before. "You are absolutely beautiful, Ivy."

Whatever air was left in my lungs escaped in an unsteady rush. He thought I . . . was beautiful? The heat in my cheeks increased. Not since Shaun had a guy said that to me. Well, there were some random homeless dudes that told me I was beautiful, but I really wasn't counting those moments.

Ren dipped his head, his mouth enticingly close to my ear. "Merida has nothing on you, babe."

My lips curved into a grin at the mention of the Disney chick. "Thanks."

He straightened. "It's the God's honest truth."

A loud thump thundered from the back of the house. I cringed as Ren glanced down the hall, his lips turning down at the corners. "What was that?"

A very dead brownie if he didn't knock it off. "I . . . I have a cat. It probably knocked something over."

194

Ren lifted a brow. "You have a cat?"

"Yeah, a really annoying cat. It's old. Gonna die soon," I said, speaking louder. "I've been thinking about getting it euthanized, you know, to put it out of its misery." The thumping noise came again, and my lips pursed as I inhaled deeply through my nose.

"Well, uh . . . sorry to hear that," Ren said. "What's his name?"

"Tink," I blurted out.

"That's different. Does it stand for anything?"

"Nothing at all. We should be going," I added quickly. "Just let me grab my purse."

Of course, Ren followed me into the kitchen, and I could only pray that Tink stopped doing whatever the hell he was doing in his room. An image of him tossing troll dolls against the wall filled my mind, and I had to bite down on the inside of my cheek to stop the laugh that was building.

"Have a problem with the sugar?" he asked, grinning at the counter.

My gaze fell to the two piles of sugar as I grabbed the black, beaded clutch I'd picked up from a shop in the Quarter and slipped the strap around my wrist. "I'm . . . messy."

He gave a little shake of his head as his lashes lifted. "Doesn't look like that in the rest of the apartment."

I forced a causal shrug. "I'm ready."

Luckily, Ren dropped it and followed me outside. Surprise flitted through me when we stepped out of the courtyard and I saw an older black truck parked along the curb. "Yours?"

"Yep." He stepped around me and opened up the passenger door. "It's been my baby since I was sixteen. It's what got me and the bike to New Orleans."

Biting my lip, I climbed in and smoothed the skirt of my dress. For some reason, a truck fit him. I don't know why I expected him to drive something fancy and fast, but it really did match his personality.

"Question?" he said, tone light. He leaned into the cab of the truck, one arm draped over the door. "You are carrying, right?"

"Yes. Of course."

He grinned as he peered through his thick lashes. "Where in the world are you hiding a weapon, Ivy? I'm dying to know."

I laughed softly and reached for the edge of my skirt. Hesitating for a second, I curled my fingers around the hem and slid it up, giving him a peek of the stake secured to my thigh.

"Damn, girl." He straightened, gripping the door. "That right there is what fantasies are made of."

Blood poured into my cheeks, and I was grateful it was dark out. Muttering a curse under his breath, he closed the door and jogged around the front of the truck. Once inside, he cranked the engine and soft music hummed out of the speakers. As he pulled away from the curb, I realized he was listening to an old Hank Williams' song.

I turned to him slowly.

He smiled crookedly. "Don't knock the music, sweetness. We're off to such a great start tonight. I'd hate to have to kick you out of the truck."

I snorted but didn't say anything as we made the trip into the business district. Since it was Saturday night, the streets were packed and we ended up having to park in a garage two blocks down from Flux.

Ren stopped me as we walked out of the shadowy garage. "Are you ready for this?"

The question humored me. "Are you?"

He grinned. "I'm ready for anything and everything."

What he said came across as meaning a hell of a lot more than what we were about to do, and it brought that reckless feeling to the surface, as if I was standing at the edge of a cliff with one foot dangling off the precipice.

There wasn't much time to really think about that. We were at the club, and I needed to focus on what we were doing. A human male worked the front door, checking IDs, but he appeared to be more interested in the way we looked than how old we were or who we were.

He eyed us like we were cows being auctioned off.

"Have fun," he said, voice sounding like he'd swallowed nails as he handed our IDs back to us.

Tiny hairs rose along my arms as we crossed the deep blue carpet in front of the tinted black double doors. The low, melodic thump of music drifted outside. The door opened before we reached it. Another human male, brawny and rough looking with a shaved head, had opened it.

Ren's hand settled at the small of my back as we stepped inside. I wasn't scared, and I probably should've been, but curiosity was the reigning emotion as I got my first look at the club trolled by ancients.

It looked so incredibly normal, like any upscale club in any large city. Lit with low, flattering lights, there were a lot of dark areas full of shadow-shaped people at the fringe of a large, slightly raised dance floor. On the other side was a long bar with brighter lights showing off the line of high priced liquors. A spiral staircase was near the bar, leading to a second floor. From our vantage point, I could see couches and roped off areas.

But as we walked further in, I began to make out more of the details of those in the shadowy enclaves surrounding the dance floor and the high tables.

I gaped as I stood on the polished floors.

There were mortals in those shadows, their bodies entwined together on the lush couches, a flash of hands moving and glimpses of flesh. But there weren't just mortals. There were fae among them. Their pale blue eyes shined eerily bright in the low light, their skin a beautiful shade of silver. Their hands and bodies moved among the mortals.

Ren lowered his mouth to my ear. "You see what I'm seeing?"

I nodded, unable to speak. My skin felt hot as I stared into the shadows. Some of them . . . they weren't just kissing or touching. Oh no, they were doing much, much more.

"They are everywhere." His hand stayed on my back. "Jesus."

Dragging my stare from the unexpected porn show, my gaze flitted across the dance floor and to the bar beyond. Ren was right. Some were at the bar drinking. Others were on the dance floor. A few lingered on the staircase leading to the second floor.

They were everywhere and there were so many of them. At least thirty.

Instinctively, I knew Ren had stumbled onto something major when he followed Marlon to the club. "I've never seen so many together."

"Me neither," he said grimly. Straightening, his hand slipped off my back and found my hand. He threaded his fingers through mine.

Ren led the way around the dance floor, and I did everything in my power not to look into the shadows. We edged around a group of college-aged girls crowding a table, and a fae stepped out of the shadows, directly in front of us.

My breath caught, and my free hand tingled with the need to grab the stake. Ren's hand tightened around mine as the fae looked us over with pale eyes before moving on to the group of girls.

Ren and I exchanged a long look as we continued to the bar. If we could hear anything, it would be there, but as I glanced at the stairwell, my heart lurched in my chest.

"Shit," I hissed, drawing to a halt.

"What?" Ren turned to me.

Turning to the side, I let my hair fall forward, shielding my face. "It's him. The fae who shot me. He's coming down the staircase."

Ren looked over his shoulder and muttered a curse. Hiding my face wasn't a great shield considering my hair probably gave my ass away. "He hasn't been in here this whole week," he growled. "Dammit."

This was bad. The moment the ancient saw me, our cover would be blown to pieces, and with so many fae being inside the club, I knew we wouldn't make it out. I started to reach for my stake just as Ren started walking toward the shadowy recesses surrounding the floor. My brain balked at the idea considering what was going on in those shadows, but it was either that or throw down in the middle of a fae infested club.

Staring straight ahead, I didn't dare look at the couches we walked past, but I heard the sounds—the soft moans and guttural groans, the panting of many breaths and sharp inhales, the echoes of flesh against flesh mingling with the steady thrum of music.

Oh dear lord in heaven . . .

Couples danced near the couches—uh, on second thought, I wasn't sure what they were doing was dancing. My step faltered as Ren suddenly stopped. He turned to me, and still holding my hand, he hauled me forward against his chest. Throwing my hand to his shoulder, I steadied myself just as he let go of my hand and circled his arm around my waist, sealing our bodies together—front to front.

Immediately aware of the hard breadth of his chest, I stiffened against him. "What the . . .?"

Ren's other hand curled in my hair, scooping it to the side as he lowered his mouth to my ear once more. "He's on the dance floor with another fae."

I swallowed, wondering how well the ancient could see into the shadows. "Crap."

"Yep."

My hands curled around the material of his soft shirt. "What do we do now since this was your genius idea?"

"You agreed."

"Ren," I seethed.

"Blend in." He pressed his cheek against mine, startling me. "We just blend in."

"Blending in means having sex," I retorted. "Or haven't you noticed that's what's happening around us?"

"Oh, I've noticed." The hand in my hair tightened, and I gasped as his lips brushed the skin of my neck. "Dance, Ivy."

Dance? Did it seem like this was the appropriate moment to *dance*? I wanted to push Ren down and kick him in the side, but as I dared to peek at the people near us, I had to admit that dancing was better than just standing here. At a quick glimpse, the couples did look like they were dancing. Maybe some were.

Closing my eyes, I tightened my hands along his shoulders until Ren let out a low growl that was part warning, part something else entirely. The last thing I needed to do was dance with Ren. Or was it? A low hum of excitement trilled through my veins, but I blamed that on adrenaline. I opened my eyes, focusing on the tan stretch of skin exposed through the vee of his shirt.

I started to dance.

My pulse skyrocketed as I swayed my hips, and it was as awkward as a three-legged cat trying to walk a tightrope. Dipping my chin, I hid my flaming face. Between my jerky movements and the indecently loud sighs surrounding us, I wanted to pitch myself in front of a bus.

"He's still talking to the fae." Ren's voice was low and surprisingly soothing in my ear. "He hasn't noticed us. You're doing good, but I know you can do better."

I stilled. "What?"

"Dancing," he replied, and as my gaze shot up to his, he winked. "You own a dress like that, I know you can move that body."

"I *am* moving my body."

He glanced behind me. "You're just moving side to side."

"Screw. You."

He chuckled. "Okay."

"Pervert," I shot back, but without much heat. He was right, though. I was sort of moving side to side, kind of like I was at a high school prom. Actually, they danced better than this. Gathering up my courage, I draped an arm around his neck. "Remember. You asked for this."

He arched an eyebrow.

"Try to keep an eye on the ancient."

Ren's stare turned lazy and wholly arrogant. "Oh, I haven't forgotten why we're here."

Holding his smug gaze, I started to move against him, but not like before. I found the beat of the music, letting it resonate in my veins, through my body, and into my limbs. My fingers found the hair at the nape of his neck. I tugged with just enough force to cause his eyes to open wide.

I smiled innocently up at him but immediately regretted it when he dipped his mouth to my neck. "That was naughty," he mused, his lips brushing the sensitive skin below my ear. "And I liked it."

"Figures," I muttered. Even though I wanted to pull his hair again, I decided that wasn't a wise or beneficial act. "What's he doing now?"

"Still talking. He's at a table now, on the other side."

I resisted the urge to stomp my foot, because the longer I moved against Ren's body, the more I became aware of him. The feel of his hard chest against my much softer one. The way his hand had flattened on my left hip and how the hand in my hair had moved to my back. My heart was beating faster, and it had nothing to do with dancing.

My other hand slipped off his shoulder to his chest, and I felt his deep, sudden inhale. I glanced up quickly, and our gazes collided, held. I was snared. The green hue churned restlessly. His hand on my back slid down the line of my spine and then trailed back up, leaving a wake of shivers behind. With the hand on my hip, he tugged me even closer to him, fitting our hips together. The act left me warm, and that heat spread through me, causing my body to relax and tense at the same time.

The arrogance from earlier was gone from his gaze, replaced by a stark and powerful emotion. Desire. Want. Need. It was all there, and he did nothing to hide it. He didn't shy away from it, but I wasn't ready to see it, to even begin to deal with it. Moving sideways, I turned our bodies so when I gave Ren my back, I wasn't facing the dance floor directly. I could see the ancient, and he was no longer talking to just one fae. Another had joined him.

Swaying to the music, I bit down on my lip when Ren's arm crept around my waist and hauled me back against him.

"Careful," he said, his nose grazing my cheek. "I know damn well he hasn't forgotten that face of yours."

I had no idea if that was just a statement, a compliment, or an insult, but then his hand slid across my stomach, his fingers expanding, and as I danced, I realized this position was a bad idea. Every slight move of my hips sent a jolt of shivery awareness through me. His other hand rested on my hip again, and as he finally started to move behind me, finding the rhythm I'd set, I struggled to remember to breathe.

This . . . this was too much, and yet I didn't pull away. I didn't put distance between us.

Our bodies were virtually one, and the feel of him against my back turned my insides into molten lava that simmered and then flared hotly the moment I felt his mouth, wet and warm against my neck, just below my ear. Ren didn't move those decadent lips. He waited for my reaction, and each second that ticked by I was losing myself to the shadows, to the way we moved against one another, and to the act it simulated.

He pressed a kiss against my fluttering pulse, and another gasp escaped me. My eyes drifted shut as he rained a tiny path of sweet, brief kisses along the length of my throat. This was just pretend. I kept telling myself that as his thumb moved in a slow circle just below my breasts. We were pretending. That was all. But my body didn't recognize that. My breasts ached, and the area between my thighs pulsed. Arousal hummed through my body.

When I opened my eyes, I saw a couple standing across from us. Both were human, and they too were pressed so closely there was no telling where one body ended and the other began. Their mouths were fused together, and his hand was under the skirt of her dress.

God, I wanted Ren to touch me like that. Though that would be entirely wicked and completely wrong, the mere thought of him doing that caused my back to arch and my bottom to press back against him.

Air left my lungs in an unsteady rush. I felt him, and knew at once what I saw in his stare was real. He was not uninvolved in this. He was hard and thick against my lower back as my hips rolled against him.

This was getting out of control.

Ren's hand on my hip moved, inching down my thigh. The tips of his fingers brushed the bare skin of my left leg, and I shuddered. There was no hiding it, no mistaking it. His mouth trailed back up my throat.

"He's still at the table," he whispered, barely audible over the music, the whimpers echoing around us, the sound of my pounding heart.

I opened my mouth, but he caught the lobe of my ear between his teeth, and my words were lost in a moan. He chuckled, and I wanted to hate him for that, but my senses were alive, sending heat through my veins.

His hands were on the move again. The one on my stomach had inched up, his thumb smoothing along the underswell of my breast. Damn that bra, because it proved a formidable barrier, but I could feel the tips of my breasts hardening, and the ache grew stronger. My breath was coming in short pants, and I wasn't sure if we were dancing anymore or just grinding on one another.

My wild gaze flickered to where the ancient was and saw that Ren had not lied. Tiny, delicious knots formed low in my belly when his hand slipped under the hem of my skirt, causing me to jerk against him, losing the rhythm. I gripped his arm, my nails digging into his skin.

Ren waited.

Because I was obviously losing my mind, I didn't pull his hand away, and that was all the permission he needed. His hand swept up my thigh. There was fire in my blood, incensed by the deep sound that rumbled out of Ren from behind me.

His breath danced over the slope of my neck and then my jaw. He pressed a kiss to the corner of my mouth as his chest rose and fell heavily against my back.

"Honored," he whispered.

My heart stuttered blindly. Almost as if I was somewhere else, I watched through a haze as the ancient who could recognize who and what I was stalked across the club toward the exit. He was leaving. We were safe, and it was time to stop this, but his fingers were so close, skimming the crease of my thigh, and I couldn't ever remember feeling like this—like I couldn't breathe. Ren cupped me with his hand, and my entire body reacted to the intimate touch.

The thin scrap of lace was no protection. His hand was hot, and as he pressed his palm against the spot he just seemed to know, against the bundle of nerves, I thought I saw stars.

This was insane.

But I burned for his touch—for him. Thoughts of the fae and the ancients fell away. Being distracted as we were was so incredibly dangerous and ridiculously stupid, but as I held on to his forearm, holding his hand there, I shook with a need I didn't even fully understand.

"Fuck," he cursed. "I want to make you come. Right here. Right now."

The words jarred me into reality, but his fingers had found that spot, brushing over the damp stretch of panties and dragging out a bolt of sharp pleasure. The knot in my belly tightened as he trailed his finger back and forth. Desire clouded all sense of rationale.

"Tell me yes," he ordered huskily. "Tell me yes and I'll do whatever you want. Anything you want. Just let me do this."

Shocked by his words—shocked by the way I rode his hand and by how badly I wanted him, I knew I had to end this because of—because of *reasons*. But I was urging him on, pressing myself against him, wishing deep inside that he'd slip one of those long fingers under my panties. My gaze danced over the club.

"Ivy." He breathed my name like it was a curse.

The word was on the tip of my tongue, forming on my lips as I saw him glide across the floor. Reality rushed me. I jerked forward, breaking free. His hand slipped over my thigh as I whirled around, facing him. I ached—throbbed. My body was screaming what the hell at me, and even my brain was kind of confused. My entire being craved release at his hands.

Ren looked dazed as he stared down at me. He took a step forward, and my heart jumped. Hard desire was etched into his striking features. He no longer looked angelic, but more like a fallen angel hell-bent on claiming me. Two words drew him up short.

"He's here," I gasped out. He stiffened, his gaze never leaving my face. "Marlon is here."

Chapter Thirteen

For a moment, the look that settled into Ren's features said he really didn't give a shit about the ancient, and as my heart raced, I really thought he was going to close the sudden distance between us and we were going to end up like one of those couples on the couches.

But he pulled himself together, and I struggled to ignore the burst of disappointment that lit up my chest. What was that? I didn't need this—whatever this was— with Ren, especially not now.

Dragging in a deep breath, he finally looked away and stared out over the dance floor. A little dazed, I watched the ancient called Marlon take the stairs with long strides. On the second floor, men and women immediately flocked to him, surrounding him near the couches. Two fae joined them, their silvery skin luminous in the brighter lights of the second floor. As Marlon sat on a couch, one of the fae—a tall, elegant blond—sat down beside him, speaking intently.

208

Instinct flared to life. "I need to get up there."

"What?" Disbelief colored his tone.

"He's up there, and that's why we're here, right? To learn something, and he just got here. He doesn't know who I am." The lights over the dance floor changed colors, going from a soft white to a vibrant blue. "I'm going up."

"Ivy." He grabbed my arm, swinging me back against the hard length of his body. "Are you insane?"

I glared up at him. "No. I'm not insane, you dick. I can get up there."

His eyes narrowed. "I have no doubt in my mind that you can get up there. It's really not that fucking hard. You just walk up the steps, but if he even suspects that you are a part of the Order, I won't be able to get to you in time."

"I don't need you to save me, Ren." I yanked my arm free.

A vein thrummed along his temple as he lowered his head toward mine. "It's too dangerous."

I held his stare. "People are starting to pay attention to us." And that wasn't a lie. A couple of the dancers nearby were watching us. "If we keep this up, the fae are going to figure it out on their own. So let me go. I'll head up there, and you'll go to the bar."

Several seconds passed, and then he nodded curtly. "Go."

"I didn't need your permission," I spat back.

Ren smirked. "Honey, I know what you need and you're going to get it."

My body flushed hot with a mixture of annoyance and scalding desire. Raising my arm, I gave him a one-finger salute.

He laughed.

Spinning around, I stalked across the dance floor, easily moving in and out of the gyrating bodies. I couldn't believe what Ren had done—what I had allowed him to do. I had no valid excuse for it. I couldn't even deal with it right now, and I couldn't afford to be so distracted. Shaking off the lingering arousal and confusion, I focused on my job.

A fae stood near the bottom of the spiral staircase, but the female didn't stop me as I started up the steps. I'd half expected her to jump out and demand some kind of code word, but they never expected an Order member to find their way in here, and humans were no threat to them.

But I was.

My heartbeat steadied as I hit the second floor, and I slowed my steps as I neared the group surrounding the ancient. All of them looked out of it, eyes glassed over like they'd smoked a ton of weed. They were clearly under a glamour, and maybe even fed on. I wanted to grab all of them and force them down the stairs, but yeah, that would end badly.

Inching closer to the group, I stopped and grabbed the railing, staring down onto the first level. I sought out Ren, finding him seated at the bar next to a male fae. They were actually talking. I snorted and turned back to the group. Leaning against the railing, I debated my next move.

Marlon sat in the center of the couch, his broad thighs spread wide and his black dress shirt half unbuttoned. The blond fae was on one side, staring at the human female whose cherry red fingernails were sliding mighty close to third base.

"We have a lock on another one," the blond fae was saying.

Marlon smiled at the woman, but the curve of his perfect lips lacked all warmth in a way that concerned me greatly for her well-being. "That's good. How many will that make, Roman?"

"Five, once it's carried out." Roman's pale eyes glittered. He said something else, but I couldn't hear it over the bass of the music. "But we know."

I inched closer, turning sideways as I tried to blend in among those crowding the lounge area. Were they talking about how many members they'd killed? Sounded like it. Trent had made four.

Marlon reached out, curving his hand around the nape of the woman's neck. He said something too low for me to hear as he held her gaze intently. The woman's hand slipped between his thighs. Jesus. I quickly averted my gaze.

"We don't have much more time," I heard Marlon say. "We cannot let him down. Not this time."

Him? My little ears perked way up.

"We know the location," Roman said, his upper lip curling. My chest squeezed. Could they be talking about knowing the location of the gate? "I told you that. The bastard broke, and we will not fail this time."

"And we aren't the only ones who know, either." Marlon's grip on the woman's neck tightened, causing a whimper to escape her lips.

Roman's response was lost in drunken laughter from a nearby couch, but a horrifying notion blossomed in the pit of my stomach. The bastard broke? Trent had been tortured. If what Ren and I suspected was true, that the fae were hunting those who might know the location of the gates, had Trent known and told the fae before they killed him? God, none of this was good, especially if they knew where the gate was.

A human waitress appeared at the top of the stairs, carrying a serving tray full of shot glasses; however, three of the drinks were a strange, vibrant purple color. Was that nightshade? My suspicions were confirmed when she delivered those three drinks, one to the ancient and the other two to the fae. As the waitress doled out the rest to the humans, she glanced up. Her gaze was a clear brown, not muddied or glazed over like the others. She wasn't glamoured, but as she straightened, the blond fae who sat to the left of Marlon snaked an arm around her waist, tugging her back.

Tottering off balance, she dropped her empty tray and landed in his lap. Startled fear flashed across her pretty face as the fae gripped her chin, wrenching her head toward his. She grabbed his arm, her knuckles turning white.

She knew what they were.

Grasping the waitress's face, he moved his mouth over hers. It looked like a kiss—it was a kiss, but a fae's kiss was poisonous. That was how they fed off of mortals, how they hooked them in.

The waitress's hands slipped away from the fae's arm to rest limply at her sides. I stepped forward but stopped myself before I did something stupid. Not intervening was one of the hardest things I ever had to do, and part of me withered, turned black and stale as I stared at her bare arm, saw the veins darken under her pale skin before fading to a faint blue as the waitress was finally let go. She stumbled to her feet, swaying as she reached for her tray. Those brown eyes weren't so clear anymore.

My hands curled into helpless fists, but movement caught my attention. The brunette fae was suddenly prowling around the couch, heading toward me. The look on his angular face was what I imagined a lion looked like when it spotted a gazelle. My heart thumped heavily, but I kept my expression guileless, which meant I probably looked half stupid as he stepped around me, leaning into my back like a total creep.

"Little one," a deep, cultured voice spoke directly in my ear. "You look a bit lost."

Wrapping a curl around my finger, I forced what I hoped was a naïve, harmless smile. "I was looking for the restroom. Do you know where it is?" I added a giggle for extra effect.

The dark haired fae was stunning, the contrast of the silver skin and hair appealing. He stepped closer, his hip brushing mine, and I forced myself not to move, to not even react when he wrapped his cool fingers around my wrist, pulling my hand away from my hair. "This is not the restroom."

No shit, Sherlock. "I see that now."

He tilted his head to the side, the movement snakelike. "What is your name?" When I didn't answer within a reasonable timeframe, which appeared to be a second, he curled his other hand around my jaw, roughly forcing my chin up. Pain shot down my neck. His gaze locked on to mine, those blue eyes unnaturally bright. "What is your name?"

"Anna," I lied, maintaining eye contact.

He dropped my wrist, but his arm circled my waist. He didn't blink, not once, and I knew he was attempting to glamour me. I forced my body to relax, for my arms to hang limply at my sides when what I really wanted to do was gouge out his eyes and force them down his throat. He drew himself up against my body, his shrewd gaze locked on to mine.

"Anna? That's a silly little name." He lowered his head, his breath icy on my cheek. There was a good chance I might hurl in his face. "Perfect for a silly little human."

My heart stuttered to a stop as his cold breath moved closer to my mouth. No incantations or four leaf clovers prevented a fae from feeding. If he got any closer, he would, and I had a feeling that was where he was heading with this. My mind raced. I couldn't let this happen. He could feed, and like the waitress, I would stumble away in a daze that would last for minutes, maybe hours, and if I was lucky, I would come out of it okay. Or he could feed and take *everything*. No way could I allow that to happen, but if I did anything, he'd know I hadn't fallen under the glamour and he'd know what I was.

Shit.

I let my right hand drift to my thigh. There was no way I was going to let this thing feed on me. If I had to fight my way out of—

Suddenly, a loud piercing wail went off, blaring over the music. The fae released me and stepped back, wincing as he glanced up at the ceiling. "What the hell?" he snarled, placing his hands over his ears.

I was jostled to the side as one of the humans staggered to their feet, knocking into me. As if the roof had been peeled open and the sun was exposed, the overhead lights clicked on, casting the club in a harsh light.

The fire alarm continued to roar, and as the fae turned away, I made a break for it. Hurrying toward the stairs, I darted down them, gliding between others who moved much slower due to the glamour, the feedings, or too much to drink.

At the bottom of the stairs, Ren waited. Without saying a word, he gripped my hand, and we joined the crowd stampeding the exits. We were tossed back and forth, and I was sure if we hadn't been holding hands, we would've been torn apart. The scent of sweat and liquor was overpowering as we were packed in.

Shouts rose from behind us, and a shiver coursed down my spine as panic became a real, tangible entity in the club. Someone slammed into my back, pitching me forward. My heels slipped, but I caught myself before I fell. Shooting a look in Ren's direction, I saw his jaw set hard and his gaze fastened ahead. Finally, after what felt like forever, we poured out into the street, into the night air. We didn't wait with those who wandered the sidewalk in front of the club or had stopped, forming small huddles. Sirens blared in the distance. Quickly turning to our left, we made our way to the parking garage.

I waited until we had crossed the street before I spoke. "You pulled the fire alarm, didn't you?"

"How else was I going to get your ass out of there?" he responded without looking at me.

"I totally had it under control."

He snorted. "Didn't look like that from where I was standing. Looked like you were about to become a pop tart."

Irritation prickled from the inside out, mainly because he was right, and because I realized I was still holding his hand. What the hell was up with that? I wiggled my fingers free and resisted the urge to smack the smirk right off his lips. "I think they know where the gate is."

That got his attention. He glanced down at me as we continued to march forward. "What makes you think that?"

I told him what I'd overheard, and he let out a low curse. "If they know where the gate is and we don't, we are fucked."

"Well, don't you sound like a Negative Ned," I muttered, squinting as a cop car raced by. "Let's go ahead and stock up on water and canned beans."

He cast me a sidelong look. "Let's just say that the members they killed were guardians of the gate. That means they are down people, and those the Order promotes won't be as skilled or prepared when—not if— the fae launch their attack. If they open that gate . . ."

We entered the dimly lit garage. "I get it but . . . can't we go to David? I mean, I think we have enough evidence at this point. Together, we can make him understand. He's the sect leader. He has to know where the gate is."

Ren didn't answer for a moment. "What if David is the one working with them?"

I gasped as I stopped near a large cement beam. "Are you serious?"

He turned to me, features shadowed. "We don't know, Ivy. It could be anyone."

"It could be me," I challenged.

"They shot you. For some reason, I don't think they'd shoot the person helping them. At least not yet," he replied dryly. "Plus, you are . . . too strong for that."

Now I was gaping at him for a different reason.

"And don't say how do I know you're too strong. I'm a fucking great judge of character," he continued, and my brows flew up. "It's not you, and I don't trust any other member of the Order, except maybe Jerome."

"Jerome has been deemed trustworthy? Do tell how he earned that honor." I was insulted for the other Order members.

"He's too damn mean to be influenced by the fae," he reasoned, and yeah, I kind of had to give that point to him. "Anyone else I don't trust. And neither should you."

I folded my arms across my chest. "I'm sure they feel the same way about you."

"Do I look like I give a shit if they do? That doesn't change the fact of why I'm here and what I have to do." Turning to the side, he thrust his fingers through his hair. "Tonight wasn't a total bust."

"You're right. It wasn't. Because of me."

Lowering his arm, he looked at me blandly. "Oh, really?"

I smiled widely. "Yep. I'm awesome. Like I put the 'awe' with the 'some.' Admit it. I got the details while you played Chatty Cathy with a fae at the bar."

His eyes narrowed.

"We know that they are picking off Order members and that they most likely know where the gate is. They're working together. That is more than we knew yesterday," I said.

Ren faced me fully. "You know what I'll admit?"

I cocked my hip out. "Waiting."

"I'll admit that you felt fucking sweet as silk against my fingers when I had my hand between those pretty thighs."

Whoa. Totally not expecting that. My eyes widened as warmth invaded me. "I-I don't know what you're talking about."

He laughed. "That's bullshit."

"No it's not!" I unfolded my arms, anger fueling my next words. Anger mostly directed at myself. "What happened inside that club? What do you think it was?"

Ren took a step toward me, lowering his voice. "It was you about five seconds away from having the best orgasm of your life."

Oh my God, he did not just say that. "Y-You," I sputtered. What in the hell did I say to that? "I was acting," I finally spat out. "I was pretending."

He was only a handful of inches from me now, and when he laughed, I wanted to hit him. "Pretending? You were faking inside?"

"Are you a fucking parrot?"

"Oh, Ivy, babe . . ." He chuckled under his breath. "You're a shit liar, you know that?"

My hands curled into fists. "I am not lying."

"Yeah. Okay. Then how do you explain your panties being so wet they were practically drenched?"

My eyes widened. Mortification swept through me, but he wasn't done. His mouth kept on moving. "I bet I could taste you on my fingers right now. But you were pretending? Then that sweetness between your thighs must be one hell of an actress."

I didn't even think.

Stepping forward, I swung at him. No bitch slap either. My closed fist was heading for that jaw. Unfortunately, he was too fast for that. He caught my wrist before my fist connected.

"That's not nice," he said. "No reason to be so violent *and* a liar."

My rage knew no limit. "Oh my God, you arrogant, self-important, mother—"

"You were not acting. You were not pretending." The teasing dropped from his tone as his voice hardened. "You were riding my hand, and Ivy, there isn't a damn thing wrong with that. What's wrong is that you're acting like nothing happened between us. That's total shit. You lit up for me like a damn firework and I barely touched you."

"I—"

My back hit the beam, and before I could take my next breath, Ren's entire hard length was pressed against the front of my body. His head was low, his face in mine. "Do not tell me again you were pretending. You and I both know the truth. I want you. I think I've made that abundantly clear."

"As clear as a damn glass window," I shot back, frustrated for a thousand and one equally important reasons.

His lips twitched. "What is your deal?" One of his hands dropped to my hip. He squeezed gently as he gave a little shake of his head. "Do you still love him?"

I stiffened as if I'd stepped under an icy downpour. "What?"

"Do you still love the guy you lost?" he questioned. "Is that it?"

A huge part of me couldn't believe he dared to even ask me that question, that he would even reference Shaun when we were this close. It seemed so wrong, as if we were spitting on his memory, but the words still tumbled off my tongue. "A . . . part of me will always love him."

"Meaning you aren't still in love with him."

Lowering my gaze, I couldn't respond to that. Losing Shaun had devastated me, and my role in his death had nearly broken me, but I wasn't still holding on to him. Not in that way, and I wouldn't lie and use that as a reason.

"I don't get it then."

"Why do you even want me?" My voice shook. "You barely know me."

He stared at me a moment, incredulity etching into his features. "What I know is that there is no guarantee of tomorrow. There is no promise there will be another day or week for us. When you want something, you go for it. I don't need to know your life story to want you. And don't twist that back on me. I see it already building in those pretty blue eyes. I *want* to know your story. I want to know you. I want—oh, fuck it."

Ren cupped my cheek, his hand gentle as he tilted my head back, and before my heart could take another beat, he kissed me.

It was no slow or seductive kiss.

He claimed my lips as if he were laying claim to my body, to my soul, and every part of me. His mouth was demanding as he tilted his head, his lips moving over mine, his tongue tracing the seam of my lips, willing them to part, and I . . . I opened for him. My lips parted, and he made this sound, this deep animalistic groan that sent flames lapping over my skin. The kiss deepened, and his tongue slid over mine, along the roof of my mouth. He took me with his mouth, tasted me and claimed me.

When he lifted his head, he was breathing deeply as he stared into my eyes. They swirled in a multitude of greens as he dragged his thumb along my lower lip.

"I . . . I've never been kissed like that," I whispered, awed by the way my lips tingled.

"Oh, fuck, Ivy," he groaned, and then his mouth was on mine again.

This time, he explored leisurely, as if he were mapping out the contours of my lips, and I . . . kissed him back.

The hand on my hip tightened as I flicked my tongue along his lip, and he moaned into my kiss. His hand slid down my hip, over my thigh, and then under the hem of my skirt. Those deft fingers glided over my dagger, and a fierce heat built, overshadowing all thought. I didn't understand why. I didn't care. His hand curved over my rear. He lifted me onto the tips of my toes, his hips fitting with mine, and I felt him against my core. Sharp spikes of pleasure shot through me. My arms circled his neck, and that kiss . . . oh God, it went to a whole new level, and what I said moments before was true. No one had ever kissed me with such reckless passion.

His hand worked under my skirt, kneading my flesh, urging me on, and I went. My back arched, my hips pushed against his as I clung to him. He said something against my mouth, between the kisses. I couldn't make it out, but I felt a tremor rock his hard body. I was lost in him, surrendering to the feelings he was creating inside me.

Breaking the kiss, he rested his forehead against mine, but his hand still moved along the curve of my bottom. His voice was thick. "I'm going to try to be the good guy here."

A shaky laugh burst out of me. "I think . . . you are failing at that."

"Nah. If I wasn't trying, I'd have these tiny panties . . ." he trailed his hand up, under the band along my bottom, causing me to gasp, "down by your ankles, and I would be so deep inside you, right here, against a goddamn cement beam."

I shuddered. Part of me was down for that. Lots of parts of me were totally down for that.

"I was raised a little better than that," he added quietly.

The statement surprised me, but he kissed me again, and this time it was different. Our lips brushed once, twice, the act infinitely sweeter and yet as shattering as the deeper, hotter ones. Shivers raced up and down my spine. Ren kissed me gently, tracing the pattern of my lips, and the pressure of his mouth consumed me, awakened me, and it was all I could think about. Deliciously wicked warmth slipped down my neck, spreading across my chest, and then lower.

Laughter suddenly echoed around us, from the entrance of the garage, alerting us that we were no longer alone. With one last lingering kiss, he lifted his mouth from mine and patted the cheek of my bottom and then withdrew his hand. Setting me flat on my feet, he fixed the skirt of my dress. Then he cupped my cheeks with both of his hands.

"Let's not rush forward, but don't let us take three steps back from this. Okay?" His voice was soft, and

God, I wanted to yield to it. "Let's just see where this takes us. That's all we've got. That's all we can promise each other."

Staring into dark, forest green eyes, I found myself nodding. I couldn't believe it.

One side of his mouth creeped up and he kissed the center of my forehead then the tip of my nose. "Let's get out of here."

Like one of the humans from the club, recently fed from, I moved like I was in a daze, walking through water. And as I followed Ren to his truck, I no longer knew what was more dangerous to me—the fae or Ren, because both had the power to drag me under.

Chapter Fourteen

Things were weird for me Sunday morning. Well, weirder than normal. I wasn't even sure what I could categorize as normal when I came home last night from the club and discovered that Tink had set up his own Twitter account and was engaged in a heated argument over which actor made a better Dr. Who. Since I'd never watched an episode and frankly couldn't care less, I didn't even want to touch that conversation with a ten-foot pole.

When I woke up, all I could think about was Ren's touch, his kisses, and I refused to cave to the aching desire. I got up and immediately went for a run, and I ran harder than I ever had before, but the twisty motion in my stomach wouldn't fade. The sensation wasn't unpleasant. A mixture of excitement and confusion, it actually made me feel . . . normal, and that was so stupid. My priorities were goofing off on the wrong playground. I should have been stressing over where the gate was and how we were going to stop the fae when we were only days away from the equinox. I still wanted to go to David, to try and explain what we had discovered, but Ren had been adamant on the drive back to my apartment that it was too risky. It was then that I made up my mind. If I couldn't talk to Merle on Sunday, I was going to David, with or without Ren's approval.

And then my thoughts had pranced right back to Ren.

I knew what the problem was. I hadn't talked to anyone about him, and that was what I needed—to get it out of my head so I could move on and focus on more important things, like stopping a mass slaughter that was bound to happen if one single gate was opened.

But Val bailed on our Sunday coffee and book buying tradition. She had texted that she couldn't make it today, and I was willing to bet it had to do with the guy she was breaking beds with all across the city. I called Jo Ann, and we ended up at the coffee shop near the cemetery.

Dressed in loose sweats and a t-shirt with my hair pulled up in a messy knot, I knew I looked like a hot mess compared to Jo Ann's straight and shiny hair, her skinny jeans and blouse. Looking at her, I didn't get why she was so damn shy when it came to boys. She was really pretty, and she was sweet, smart, and kind.

As she sipped her latte and I chugged sweet tea like it was a college drinking game, we chatted about our classes, and then I finally made myself do it. I didn't know why it was so hard or how red my face was, but I did it.

"I met a guy," I blurted out around my straw.

Jo Ann's brows flew up. "You did? When?"

225

"A couple of weeks ago. He . . . um, he works with me. From Colorado," I told her, feeling bad that there was a lot I had to keep secret.

She smiled as she sat back in the wicker chair, eyes glimmering with happiness. "Is he cute?"

"Cute?" I repeated, wanting to laugh as I toyed with my plastic cup. "I don't think cute is a strong enough word to describe him."

"Oh! Okay, then he's hot?"

I nodded as a small grin pulled at my lips. "Like really hot."

"Okay." She waited as she picked up her latte. "I have this feeling there's more to it. He must be a jerk then?"

"No," I admitted, glancing up at her. "He's actually nice . . . and kind of charming. He's aggressive—not in a bad, creepy way," I quickly added when Jo Ann started to frown. "I mean, he's the kind of guy that when he wants something, he lets it be known. He's not shy about that at all."

"All right." Taking a sip, she studied me. "So, he's hot and he's nice. He's a take charge kind of dude, but not in a creepy way." When I nodded, she asked, "Do you like him?"

My mouth opened, but again, I found it hard to find the right words. They were there, but there was a plug in the back of my throat.

"You like him," she teased.

I snorted. "How do you know?"

"Well, you've never mentioned a guy once to me, so that's a dead giveaway," she explained. Propping her elbow on the table between us, she rested her chin in her palm. "So, you totally like him. Just admit it. Say it. Say it for me, Ivy."

226

I laughed as I shook my head. "Okay. God." Letting my head fall back, I groaned. "I like him. I don't even know why, but I like him."

"You like him because apparently he's hot, nice, and charming."

"And smart," I muttered, rolling my eyes.

Jo Ann giggled. "You sound like that's a bad thing."

"It is." Lifting my head, I exhaled loudly. "I don't really know him."

She stared at me, expression baffled.

"I've only known him for a couple of weeks, and yeah, I have a mad case of insta-lust when it comes to him, but in a way, we're kind of strangers." I shrugged one shoulder. "So it just feels weird."

Her mouth opened, closed, and then opened again. "You know, I'm probably the worst person to get relationship advice from."

"True." I laughed.

Jo Ann's eyes narrowed. "But you do know that people usually are strangers when they meet and then they get to know each other through, I don't know, dating."

"The word 'date' hasn't really come up in conversations."

"Oh." Her nose wrinkled.

"Honestly, I haven't given him a chance to even get to that point, so I don't know if he's interested in . . . dating or just hooking up. I don't even know if I'm interested in dating," I admitted. The idea terrified me because I knew what it led to. A crap ton of heartbreak.

"Then what's the problem? If you both want it, go for it. Who knows? Maybe he wants to date. Maybe you do, and it becomes something serious." Glancing at the front door as it opened, she sighed. "I need to take my own advice."

"You do."

She grinned at me.

Tugging on the straw in my tea, I took a deep breath as my heart turned over heavily. "The last . . . the last guy I dated—the only guy I've been with—he died."

Her eyes widened. "What?"

Since Jo Ann knew about my foster parents' death, I decided it was best to stick with a half-truth. The three of them *had* died together. "He died with my parents in the car accident." I winced, mainly because that was so not how they died. "I loved him like anyone would their first crush, and I lost him."

Understanding flickered across Jo Ann's face, and I felt my cheeks warm. Talking about Shaun was never easy. "I get it," she said quietly. "You're not entirely ready to move on."

I glanced at her and then at the line of people at the counter. I really didn't see them. "It's been over three years, and I . . . I think I'm ready to move on, but does that . . ." Chest aching, I turned my gaze to her. "Is that wrong? Am I somehow betraying him? Because it kind of feels that way, you know? Like why do I get to move on and he's gone?"

"Oh, honey, that is not betraying him. I didn't know him, obviously, but if he cared for you, he wouldn't want you to never go out with another guy or fall in love again." She reached across the table and squeezed my hand. "Moving on is the right thing to do. Deep down, you know that."

"Yeah," I whispered, and that plug had turned into a messy knot, because in that moment, when I tried to picture Shaun's face, the details were all gone. He was blurry and so far away, and that hurt. But she was right. Deep down, I did realize that. "It's just overwhelming sometimes."

"Let me ask you a question," she said, leaning forward. "Do you trust him?"

The question bounced around in my skull. I know she meant it in a different way, since she had no idea what Ren and I did for a living, but her meaning was just as important. Did I trust him with my body? Potentially with my heart and all my secrets? A hard question to answer, not because I didn't know, but because it was what my answer truly symbolized.

Meeting Jo Ann's gaze, tiny knots formed low in my belly. "Yeah, I trust him."

~

A little after twelve o'clock, we said our goodbyes, and as Jo Ann climbed into the back of a cab, I pulled out my cell and called Brighton. When she answered and told me she was home, and that Merle was up for company, I almost hopped down the steps and did a little dance in the middle of the sidewalk.

I managed to control myself though.

Squinting from behind my sunglasses at the screen on my phone, I leaned against the wall surrounding the shopping center. I told Brighton I'd be over in a little bit, but that wasn't the only thing I'd told her.

I'd said that I might not be the only one paying a visit.

My thumb hovered over Ren's number. I trusted him, but this was a big step. Nervous, I glanced up and watched a trolley roll by. Then, without looking, I tapped on his name.

229

Ren answered on the second ring. "Ivy?"

I made a face. "Yeah. That would be me."

His answering chuckle was warm. "Sorry. I'm just surprised that you're calling me. I figured I was going to have to either wait until tomorrow to see you or hunt you down."

Struggling to keep the smile off my face, I paced in front of the brick wall under the oak trees. "Are you busy?"

"Never for you."

There was no holding back the giddy grin at that point, and I was grateful only strangers were walking past me at that moment. "Can you meet me at the shopping center on Prytania Street? There's something I want you to do with me."

A moment passed. "If I told you the images and thoughts flashing through my head right now, you'd probably hang up on me."

"Probably," I said, laughing.

"I can be there in about twenty minutes. Cool with you?"

I nodded and then felt like an idiot because I was on the phone. "Perfect."

The sleek, black motorcycle rumbled up to the curb about fifteen minutes later, and I didn't even want to think about the speed he was driving to make it to the Garden District that fast on a Sunday afternoon.

As I approached the back of the bike, he handed a helmet to me and lifted his. He smiled crookedly, showcasing one of the dimples. "Where are we off to, milady?"

I shook my head at him as I held the helmet. "It's just a couple of blocks down." Giving him the directions, I got on the back of the bike.

"By the way, you look cute today. Like the relaxed Ivy. Never seen her before."

My cheeks flushed and I wanted to kick myself.

"Careful with the backpack," he continued. "There'll be sharp and pointy things in there we can play with later."

That perked my interest in really bizarre ways. I slipped my helmet on and then circled my arms around his waist, careful not to press against his back. It took only minutes to get from the shop and pull up in front of the antebellum home. As he parked the bike and took his helmet off, I removed mine and was about to climb off the bike, but he turned around.

Clasping my cheeks with his large, calloused hands, he swooped in and tilted his head. He kissed me, right there on the side of the street, in front of Brighton and Merle's house. And it was no chaste or quick kiss. I didn't even think Ren knew how to do chaste kisses.

His warm mouth moved over mine, insistent and seductive. With my hands clutching the helmet between us, all I could do was let myself be swept away by the feel of his mouth on mine.

And it did feel damn good.

The bike still hummed under us, and as his tongue glided over mine, I gasped into his mouth. I felt his lips curve into a smile against mine, and I wanted to pitch the helmet into the street and climb all over him.

Ren's mouth brushed mine as he murmured, "Mmm."

"What . . . what was that for?" I asked, blinking.

He laughed as he turned, switching the engine off. "It was a just-because kiss. Get used to it. You're going to get a lot of them."

I stared at his back. "What if I don't want them?"

He looked over his shoulder, arching a brow. "You want them."

I sighed. I did want them.

"So why are we here?" He glanced up at the house, expression curious. "Are we already in the moving in together stage?"

"What?" I scoffed at him as I hopped off the bike. "No."

Grinning, he climbed off and stood next to me, the helmet dangling from his fingers as he eyed the fence. "So what's the deal?"

"A friend of mine lives here. Her name is Brighton and her mom used to work for the Order. She . . . she was caught once and the fae fed off of her, and she really was never the same again." Glancing at the house, I drew in a shallow breath. "Merle knew everything—still knows everything. She was pretty high up there. She might know where the gate is."

Ren stiffened as his green eyes met mine. "Are you serious?"

I nodded. "Just depends on what kind of . . . mood she's in. I tried getting in touch with her before, but they were out of the state."

He tilted his head to the side, and the sun glanced off his cheek. "You've known that this woman could tell us the location since the beginning?"

"Yes." I didn't flinch from his steely gaze. "But when I first went to talk to her and she wasn't here, I didn't exactly trust you."

He dipped his chin. "So you're saying you trust me now?"

"Obviously." I threw up my arms, helmet and all. "Or I wouldn't have brought you here."

"You would've just gathered the info yourself and . . ."

"I probably would've told you we needed to check out the place. I just wouldn't have told you where I got the info."

"Smart girl," he murmured, his shoulders relaxing. "Well, let's do this then."

I frowned. "You're not mad?"

He knocked a wayward curl off his forehead. "I get why you didn't trust me outright, but you do now. That's what matters."

As he started toward the gate, I sprung forward and grasped his arm. "Please remember that Merle sometimes doesn't act right, okay? She may be completely fine or she might not be."

His features softened. "I understand, Ivy."

Relieved, I let go of his arm and we started up the sidewalk. Just as we reached the front porch, the door opened and Brighton stepped out, her golden hair pulled back in a high ponytail.

Brighton was in her late twenties, and as far as I knew, she'd never been married—never got close to that. She used to be active in the Order, but after the incident with her mother, her life revolved around taking care of Merle. It couldn't be easy and had to be lonely.

Wearing jean shorts and a tank top, she came down the steps, her sandals smacking off the wooden boards. Tiny pieces of dirt clung to her shorts. Brighton was gorgeous in that southern way. Like if this was a hundred years ago, she'd blend right in with the belles at the ball; she had that kind of delicate beauty.

Her serious and somber brown gaze moved from me to Ren as she drew up short in front of us. I stepped forward. "Brighton, this is Ren. He's a part of the Order."

She gave him a small, reserved smile that didn't quite reach her eyes. "You're new."

"Yes, ma'am," he drawled, doling out the charm. "I'm from Colorado. Just transferred here at the beginning of the month."

She smoothed her hands along her shorts. "Wow. You're a long way from home."

Ren smiled, the curve of his lips effortless. "That I am. Your home is beautiful. We don't have houses like these back home."

"Thank you." She turned sideways, glancing back at the house before addressing me. "May I ask what you'd like to see my mother about?"

I didn't know how happy Ren was going to be with the amount of info I was about to share, but he was just going to have to deal with it. "There's some crazy stuff going on in the city. As you know, we've lost four members in a very short period of time, and we think . . . we think they were guardians of the gate."

Brighton's eyes widened with alarm. "What?"

"We think the fae are trying to open the gate here," Ren chimed in. "And you know that the gates are weakened on the equinox—"

"They can *only* be opened on the equinox and the solstice," she corrected, folding her arms across her waist. "What does David have to say about this?"

"We haven't told David yet." Here came the tricky part. "Brighton, if the members killed were guardians, and it looks like they might've been, then someone within the Order has to be feeding the names to the fae. We can't—"

"You can't trust many then, if that's the case." She pressed her lips together as she shook her head. "You want to talk to my mom about the location of the gate?"

"If anyone knows, it would be her."

"If she remembers," she said softly, casting a nervous look in Ren's direction. "You know how her head is. Some days . ."

"I know. So does Ren. We're prepared for her not to know, but even if there's a slim chance, we'll take it."

Brighton nodded slowly. "She's having a good day."

"Okay." I looked at Ren and was happy to see not a single look of judgment on his face. Since each of us was raised to value mental and physical strength above everything, so many of the Order members looked down on Merle. "We won't take long."

She hesitated for a moment and then turned. "She's in the garden."

Leaving our helmets on the wicker chair, we followed Brighton around the porch. As we neared the back of the house, the soft thrums of jazz drifted out the back door. We stepped off the porch, following the walkway into the thick of the courtyard.

Merle was kneeling in front of a rosebush, her green gloves covered with dirt as she patted the fresh soil around a newly planted flower. A pitcher of tea sat on a small table, two glasses half full.

Brighton cleared her throat. "Mama—"

"I know we have company, sweetheart. I may have a few bats in the belfry, but I'm not deaf," Merle said, her voice level and sugary sweet. "And y'all weren't exactly quiet making your way into the courtyard."

Ren lifted a brow at me, and I grinned. "Hi, Merle," I announced.

"Hello, dear." Tugging off her gloves, she dropped them on the ground and then stood, turning toward us. Merle was in her mid-fifties, but she could pass for someone a good decade younger. With hair the color of wheat and nearly flawless alabaster skin, I had no idea how she stayed so pale and wrinkle-free when she spent most of her time out in her garden. Only the skin by her eyes and mouth crinkled when she smiled. "It's been a while since I've seen you, and you brought someone other than that hussy with you."

I bit the inside of my cheek as Ren's eyebrow climbed even higher. "She's talking about Val—"

"The hussy," Merle said again, floating over to the chair near the small table. She plopped down with little grace, hooking her knee over one leg.

"Mama." Brighton sighed, moving to stand behind her mother's chair.

"I wish you wouldn't call her that," I said. "Valerie's really nice. Just because she dates a lot doesn't make her a hussy."

Merle tilted her head to the side as she picked up her glass. "Honey, that's not what makes her a hussy."

I wanted to know what did, but the last thing we needed was to get off track, so I decided it was time to change the subject. "Merle, this is Ren—"

"I know who he is," she said, much to my surprise and Ren's. She took a sip of her tea as she eyed him over the rim of the glass. "Renald Owens."

"Renald?" Looking at him, I raised both brows. "Your full name is *Renald*?"

Was that two splotches of pink I saw blossoming across his cheeks? Ha! He was blushing. "Why do you think I go by Ren?" he replied drily. "Ma'am—"

"Call me Merle, sweetheart. And you're going to ask how I know who you are. I know—well, *knew* of your parents. I hope they are still well?"

"Yeah, they are." Ren shook his head, thrown off.

Merle continued to appraise him. "That's a fine looking young man, Ivy."

My eyes widened, and I didn't even dare look at Ren.

She winked at me, and Brighton patted her on the shoulder. "Mama, they're here to ask you about something important."

"Oh, I know they are. Why don't you two take a seat?" She gestured at the chairs across from her. "Cop a squat or so they say."

Ren passed a long, bemused look in my direction as we did as she ordered. Once seated, I tried again. "We're here—"

"Like I said, darling, I know why you're here. It has to do with the Elite." She giggled like a young girl. "Don't look so surprised, handsome fellow. I said I knew your parents. And I know all about the Elite, and if you're here, that means the ancients are up to no good."

Floored, all I could do was stare at her. Holy crap, this whole time Merle really did have this knowledge. Excitement bubbled up, but chasing after it was a great sense of distrust. This was too easy.

"You know about the ancients?" Ren leaned forward, resting his hands on his knees while Brighton shifted uneasily behind her mother.

"I know that not all fae wish for the same." She studied him for a moment while I thought that was an extremely bizarre statement. "Son, I also know why you're really here. I know what it means if you're here."

I tensed, suddenly cold despite the warm breeze tousling the many flowers. Ren sat back, his expression slipping from his face, replaced by a blank look that turned my stomach to ice.

"Ma'am," he began, but she wasn't having it.

"I know what the Elite does. I know that your kind hunts the ancients, but that's not the only duty you have." She shook her glass and the ice clinked loudly. Her smile started to slip as her gaze drifted to me. "What do you want to know, doll?"

Well, hell, now I wanted to know what Ren's other duty was, which was apparently something I didn't know, but Brighton spoke as she knelt beside her mother's chair, drawing her attention. "I think they want to know where the gate is here."

"Of course." Her scrutiny moved to her glass. "I used to be a guardian."

I swallowed my gasp. I'd always known that Merle had been high up in the sect, but I had no idea she was a guardian. Good Lord, if what she said was true, then she really did know the location of the gate, and right now, that piece of knowledge was the most important. I'd deal with Ren later.

"I know about everything," she continued, her gaze fixing on something I couldn't see. "The wards used to seal the gates, the blood required to open them, the crystal that can heal." Her smile was fleeting and quick though I had no idea what the hell she meant about the crystal. "Then I met my match. Or so they say. I really do not recall that day."

"Mama," Brighton whispered, reaching out and clasping her mother's hand. "Do you know where the gate is?"

"My darling girl," she murmured, cupping Brighton's chin as she smiled blithely. "There isn't just one gateway in our city. There are two."

I inhaled sharply. "There are two?"

She nodded as she reached for the pitcher and poured herself another glass of tea. "Yes. Should you be surprised? We're in New Orleans, and well . . . the land here, it's tainted and it's blessed. It is the only place I know where two doorways to the Otherworld exist."

"Are you sure?" Ren asked. "I mean no offense by that question, but I have never heard of two doors being in one city or even within a hundred or so miles of another."

"No offense taken." A wisp of blond hair blew across her face. "One is located in the sanctuary, and the other is in a place where the atmosphere is so unsettled not even the humans or the spirits can rest."

Brighton winced and ducked her chin.

My heart sank. "Merle, I'm not following."

She arched a brow at me. "It's pretty simple, girl. Both are well known, and I don't know how to be much clearer."

I had several ideas how she could be clearer, but as Merle flicked her attention to Ren, I knew her mind had moved on. So many times in the past, she would make a vague statement that made perfect sense to her, and she would not, under any circumstance, explain herself further. It also meant her 'good day' was rapidly coming to a close. Frustrated, I forced myself to sit still in the chair. "Merle—"

"Shush it," she said, and I jerked back, gaping at her while she continued to eyeball Ren. "Back to the more important thing. Have you found it yet?"

Ren's shoulders stiffened, and the tension rolled off of him, settling over the courtyard like a coarse, too heavy blanket. He gave a barely discernible shake of his head.

"You *need* to find it," Merle said, the harmony dropping from her tone. "You know what will happen if they open the gate."

He lifted his chin. "I know."

What in the hell was going on here?

A tremble shook Merle. "If the prince comes through—or the princess—and they find it, everything is undone, Renald. *Everything*."

I looked at Brighton in confusion, but she shook her head. "Mama, what are you talking about?"

Merle stood, her hand clenching the glass in her hand until her knuckles turned white. "Renald, I fear those gates will break this time. It's in the wind. It's in the very song of the birds and in the soil. They will not fail with the gates this time."

Okay, this was getting weird. Typical, but weird, because that was what the ancient had said last night, and when I looked at Ren, he didn't . . . he didn't look too surprised, and the ice in my belly spread to my veins.

Merle stepped toward Ren. "You must find the halfling."

Chapter Fifteen

A halfling? What in the world? All thoughts of everything else vanished. My gaze bounced back and forth between Ren and Merle, and any other time I would've dismissed this as Merle having a bad moment, but Ren . . . yeah, he still didn't look shocked by anything this woman was saying, and I was sure I was rocking one hell of a what-the-fuck expression at the moment.

"Halfling?" Brighton spoke, shaking her head. "Mama, what are you talking about?"

She finally tore her gaze from Ren and stared at her glass again. "It should not exist, but it does. Not for very long. It cannot be. Or at least that's what they say," she mumbled, the hand holding the glass beginning to shake. "There used to be more. Hundreds, if not thousands, but now? Maybe a handful. Maybe not even half a dozen. Because they are a threat to it all. To everything," she spat bitterly.

Ren stood up and shot forward, but it was too late. The glass in Merle's hand shattered. Tea and sharp shards exploded, raining to the ground. Blood mixed in, and I jumped out of my seat, eyes wide.

"Mama!" Brighton gripped her arm, her face paling. "What did you do? You cut yourself!"

Merle frowned as she stared at her bloody hand. Pieces of glass glinted in the sunlight, stuck in her palm. "I'm not sure, darling girl, but it does not feel that pleasant."

"I'm sorry, but I think you two need to go." Brighton wrapped her other arm around her mother's shoulders. "It's been enough for today."

I didn't stop her. Too disturbed by what Merle had done, I watched Brighton usher her toward the back of the house.

"Is there anything we can do to help?" Ren called.

Brighton didn't pause for one second. "Just leave. Please leave."

Squeezing my eyes shut briefly, I bit back a curse as I heard the back door slam shut. "Oh God, that didn't end well."

Ren was quiet as I turned to him. He didn't look at me, his gaze fixed on the broken glass, the spilled tea . . . and the blood. I took a step toward him and spoke low. "Part of me wants to think that what Merle said at the end meant nothing, but I don't think that's the case, is it?"

Casting a sideways glance at me, he gave a curt shake of his head. Dread formed, taking root. "You haven't told me everything."

"No."

Several feelings rushed me at once, and I didn't know what to feel. Disappointment and anger were at the top of the heap. I *trusted* him, but there were also a lot of things I hadn't told him, so it was a pot meet kettle moment, and I struggled to rise above it and boy, that was hard, because I wanted to punch him in the arm. I wasn't the bigger, better kind of person on most days, so I was proud of myself when I held it together. "Is there really such a thing as a halfling? What are you really here for, Ren?"

Tipping his head back, he let out a weary sigh and then nodded to himself. "We should leave."

"I'm not leaving until you tell me what the hell is really going on."

He turned to me. "I will tell you everything, even if it gets me killed."

"Killed?"

"Yeah, it's that big of a deal, Ivy. So I'm not going to do it here. We need to go someplace to talk. You live nearby."

Part of me wanted to dig in my feet, but we did need to leave the courtyard so Brighton didn't have to worry about us setting off her mother even more, but I couldn't take him home. Not when there wasn't any time to warn Tink.

I really needed to get a house phone with voicemail so I could leave him messages. That was getting added to my to-do list.

"We can't go to my place," I said, ignoring the sharp look he gave me.

He studied me a moment. "Then we can go to my place."

243

Nervousness caused my belly to tumble. His place? "I don't know about that."

"Thought you trusted me?" A wry smile appeared on his face.

I lifted my chin. "That was before I apparently discovered that you haven't been a hundred percent honest with me."

"Nothing between us has changed, Ivy. There are— *were*—some things I just couldn't tell you—that you wouldn't just believe." Sighing, he thrust his hand through his hair. "I'm not going to have this conversation in public. It's my place or yours."

My place was out of the question because I had no idea what Tink was doing right now. "Whatever you say, *Renald*." I walked past him briskly, heading toward the porch so we could grab our helmets. "It's your place."

He shot me a mortified look. "I really wish you wouldn't call me that."

I snorted. "People in hell want ice water."

"People in hell are dead and thirst is probably the least of their concerns."

Climbing onto the porch, I shook my head as I glanced at the closed door. Guilt prickled under my skin, making me feel icky. Merle would've never injured herself if we hadn't come here today, but I couldn't go back and change history.

And I had a feeling after this conversation with Ren, I'd never be able to go back to the way things were before.

~

Ren lived in one of the old warehouses that had been recently remodeled into studio and one-bedroom apartments. With its own parking garage, wide industrial elevator, and hallways with exposed steel beams in the ceiling and brick walls, the place had an eccentric, modern feel to it. Definitely on the upscale side, and if the Order didn't pay so well, I doubted Ren could afford the kind of rent this place demanded.

His apartment was on the sixth floor, right outside the elevator, and when he opened the door, I was greeted to a rather sparse place with an open floor plan and the fresh clean scent that reminded me of the detergent Holly used to wash our clothes in.

There was a wide sectional in the living room, a black coffee table with a glass top situated near a large flat-screen TV hung on the gray and white brick wall. Other than a picture on the corner of the coffee table, that was it in terms of anything with a personal touch.

I glanced into the kitchen. All the appliances were stainless steel and new. It was a chef's kitchen, with a double oven and a shiny hood descending from the ceiling over a gas grill top, but there wasn't a table, just two barstools tucked under the kitchen island. On the other side of the living room were two doors. One door I assumed led to a bedroom, and I guessed the other was the bathroom.

It didn't appear as if anyone lived here.

Once inside, Ren shrugged off his backpack and placed it by the couch. Moving to the coffee table, he scooped up an empty bowl. The spoon rattled around as he bent again, grabbing a deep blue coffee cup.

He was cleaning up. That was kind of cute. And normal.

I stepped toward the coffee table, eyeing the picture. It was a family photo, had to be of him and his parents. He was younger, maybe sixteen, and with the wide smile and dimples, he looked adorable standing between a man and woman who he resembled greatly. A snowcapped mountain was in the background, but they were wearing t-shirts. The picture fascinated me—their smiling faces, happy eyes.

Glancing over his shoulder at me, he walked toward the kitchen. "Would you like something to drink?" he offered. "I suggest a refreshment that would be a bit stronger than tea for this."

Tearing my gaze away from the photo, I watched him place the bowl and cup near the sink. He strolled to the fridge, the muscles under the tattoo rippling as he opened the door. "I don't drink."

"Mind if I have a beer?"

I shook my head. "Not at all."

"Make yourself comfortable."

As Ren rustled around in the fridge, I headed toward the door I assumed was the bathroom, but when I opened it, I was staring at the neatly stacked sheets and towels. "You can fold fitted sheets?"

From the kitchen, Ren replied, "Yeah."

I scowled. "Are you even human? No mere mortal can fold a fitted sheet."

"I have mad skills."

That he did.

"May I ask why you're looking in my closet?" he asked, tone light and teasing.

I closed the door, cheeks hot. "I was actually looking for the bathroom."

"Through my bedroom. Not very convenient for guests or my privacy." He swaggered back into the living room, a bottle of beer in one hand and a can of soda in the other. Placing my can on the table, he walked over to the second door and opened it. "Just through here, to your left. The other door is the closet, and no, it's nowhere near as neat as the linen closet. I'll wait for you out here."

Entering Ren's bedroom made me feel weird. I hadn't been in a guy's bedroom since Shaun, and it was like walking through their inner sanctum. Like with the living room and kitchen though, there really were no personal artifacts. Just a huge king-sized bed with a thick, gray comforter left in a pile, a dark wood dresser, a nightstand, and a bookshelf—a fully loaded bookshelf. I wanted to check out what kind of titles he had, but I didn't think it would be cool of me to loiter in his bedroom. I quickly entered a neat master bathroom, did my thing, and then made my way back to the living room.

Ren sat on one side of the sectional, his legs kicked up onto the coffee table. His shoes were off, feet bare. As I picked up my soda, I couldn't help but notice he had sexy feet, and the moment that thought occurred, I decided I needed to get out more if I thought feet were sexy.

I sat against the arm of the sectional, kicking off my sandals and tucking my feet under me. He watched me out of the corner of his beautiful, thickly lashed eyes while he tipped the neck of the bottle to his lips. "I like seeing you in my place," he said. "Just thought I'd share that."

Stupidly flustered, I ignored that comment. "I think we need to start with this whole halfling thing," I decided.

"Good choice. Get the crazy out of the way first." Draping an arm over the back of the sectional, he looked at me. "You're not going to believe any of this, so before I go forward and talk just to take up oxygen, I need you to have an open mind. You get me?"

"We hunt fae, Ren. I have an open mind."

He lifted an eyebrow.

"And I've lived in New Orleans for almost four years. I've seen a lot of weird crap."

"True," he murmured, and flashed me a quick smile. "A halfling is a child of a human and a fae."

Part of me had suspected as much, but I found myself shaking my head despite the fact I just said I had an open mind. "That's not . . . I didn't think a fae and a human could make a baby."

"It's not easy. It's actually kind of rare when you compare it to the billions of people having children, but they can and it *does* happen. As far as we've learned, it can only happen when no compulsion is used, and for all we know, it could have something to do with fae magic. No one knows exactly why one pregnancy happens and another doesn't. Merle was correct when she said there used to be thousands of them but not anymore. There's probably a handful left—a couple dozen at most."

"Why are there so few now?" I asked, deciding to play along with this and hold off on deciding if he was veering into Crazytown until the end of the discussion.

"Our job—the Elite's—is not just to hunt down ancients." His attention drifted from me as tension formed around his mouth. "We are also given the duty of hunting down the halflings."

My lips parted on a soft inhale. "Hunting them down? As in killing them?"

He took another drink of his beer, and when his gaze slid back to mine, haunted shadows lingered in his stare. "There was a magical spell that shaped the doorways to the Otherworld, created by what we assume were the original king and queen of their world. When the doorways were created, they were done so with the ability to be closed and opened. However, there is a loophole in that creation—one act that could open all doorways, all across the world, and we would never be able to close them. Never, Ivy."

"Oh my God . . ." Horrified, that was all I was. The idea of the doorways being opened everywhere and there not being any way to close them was something I couldn't even wrap my head around. All the creatures of the Otherworld, not just the fae and the ancients, could pour out into our world. There'd be no stopping them from coming . . . or from dragging humans back.

"That loophole has to do with a halfling. If the prince or the princess is able to . . . how do I say this? If they are able to procreate with a halfling, the child resulting from such a union—an ancient making a baby with a human half fae—it would undo the original spells creating the doorways." He coughed out a dry laugh as I gaped at him. "You see, a prince or princess should never be in our world. A halfling should not exist. And a baby created between them? Also should not be. It's kind of like dogma—the ideology, the basic fundamentals of our world, the doorways, and the Otherworld, would be challenged, and therefore, the entire paradigm collapses."

"Holy shit."

He chortled. "Yeah. That."

249

My gaze flickered around the room wildly. "It's like the apocalypse baby."

A choking sound came from him, and I blinked rapidly. "It really is. It's so bizarre that it has to be true. God, I . . . I wish I drank."

Ren laughed then, the sound lighter. "Told you that you needed something harder."

Shaking my head, I tried to put all that together in my mind. "So the Elite hunt down the halflings just in case the prince or the princess ever makes it through the gateways. Basically, stopping the problem before it starts?"

"Exactly."

I took a huge gulp of my soda. "And you're here because . . ."

"I'm here because of what I told you before." His eyes found mine again. "All that was true. The Elite fear they will open the gate this time."

My heart skipped a beat. "But that's not all."

"No," he said quietly. "I'm also here because we have evidence there is a halfling in New Orleans."

Swallowing hard, I leaned over and placed my drink on the coffee table before I ended up spilling it on the couch and making a general mess.

"The person probably has no idea what they are. They usually don't." A faraway look pinched his features. "What makes them stand out isn't something that necessarily screams your mama or papa wasn't from this world. Some have never had broken bones because they haven't been in a situation where that's happened, but a halfling is harder to injure. They don't typically get sick as easily. That's about the only thing the fae blood or DNA does for them . . . unless they start feeding on humans, but they don't know how to do that. Another fae would have to show them, and even the fae can't sniff out halflings, not unless they get near their blood, and then they can tell." Pausing, he took another swig of the beer. "As far as we know, the fae have never successfully gotten their hands on a halfling because we've . . . we've gotten to them first."

I shuddered. "How do you even find them?"

A cynical grin twisted his lips. "Because most of them are in the Order."

"What?"

Smoothing his finger along the label of his beer, he nodded. "Remember when I told you that no compulsion could be used for a baby to happen? Order members aren't susceptible to glamour, and every halfling—and I mean every halfling we've found—has been the product of a consensual union."

I recoiled. "You mean that they wanted—agreed to have sex with a fae, knowing what they were?"

"Yep."

"Gross," I muttered.

"So the halfling is usually brought up in the Order somehow. We keep a lot of ears to the ground, but another thing constant among halflings is that all of them have been adopted. So we check out everyone who is."

A cold chill worked its way down my spine. "I was adopted."

"I know." He smiled then, a real one—small but real. "You're not one of them, Ivy."

"How do you know?" I challenged, sickened by the idea—the mere thought that I could be one of them without even knowing. "I was adopted. I've never broken a bone, and as far as I remember, I've never—"

"You haven't broken a bone or gotten sick because you're lucky. And your real mom and dad were happily married before they were killed," he cut in, lowering his gaze while I jerked back from his words. "Their names were Kurt and Constance Brenner, and all those who knew them said there was no marital discord between them. They were in love, Ivy. Neither of them would've gone outside their marriage."

I knew their names, but it had been years since I'd heard anyone speak of them. I'd been too young to know them, to form any bond with them, but they were still my flesh and blood, and it had shaken me to the core.

"Plus, when you were shot, that ancient most likely would've sensed if you were a halfling. You bled. He would've known."

A little bit of relief eased my tensed muscles. I was happy to hear that neither of my parents willingly knocked boots with a fae and produced baby Ivy, future incubator of mass destruction, but still, learning this was . . . fascinatingly horrifying.

"But how would you all know who the halfling is? You just go around . . . taking out people—Order members—that you suspect are halflings?" I toyed with the hem of my sweats. "That can't be all of it."

"It's not." Switching the bottle to the hand furthest from me, he brushed wisps of deep brown waves off his forehead. "The same stakes that can kill an ancient—one fashioned from thorn trees that grow in the Otherworld? If a halfling is cut with one, we'll know they're a halfling."

"How?"

His gaze flicked up to mine. "Their blood will bubble."

I whistled low under my breath. "Well, yeah, that's not normal."

"But I also can't go around cutting people with a stake, now can I?" Something crossed his face, and he looked away. "We know of a couple in the Order who were adopted. One of them is dead. I think her name was Cora."

"Cora Howard." My brows knitted as her freckled face appeared in my thoughts. "She was killed a couple of months ago. Who else?"

"Jackie Jordan. But she's not one. I did manage to accidentally nick her with the edge of my stake during my first meeting. I thought she might punch me. But her blood didn't boil."

A surprised laugh burst out of me, and I remembered the way Jackie had looked at him the night we learned Trent had been killed, like she didn't want to be anywhere near him.

"Really? Wow. Okay. The other two?"

"You sure you want to hear this?"

I arched a brow.

"Miles was adopted.'

"No shit," I whispered. "I'm sorry, but Miles, a halfling? He has the personality of a decade old piece of wallpaper."

A small smile hovered at the edges of his lips. "I don't think his personality disqualifies him."

"Still. I can't imagine it being him. And he's the second in command. How could they allow one to ascend to that kind of position?"

"Simply because they didn't know." Reaching over, he curled one finger around mine, stopping me from tugging on the loose string of the hem. "Sometimes I think it would just make things easier if the entire Order knew that halflings existed, knew what could happen if the prince or princess got a hold of one, but then . . . that kind of knowledge could be destructive."

At first I wanted to argue that point because knowledge was power; it was also a source of safety. But as I watched him drag his finger along my knuckles, it occurred to me why he thought it would be destructive. "You're right," I whispered, stomach roiling. "If everyone knew, it would be a witch hunt. Innocent people would get caught up in it. As soon as someone did anything weird, and all of us are totally capable of some weird shit, they'd be suspected. Guilty until proven innocent."

"Exactly."

"Who else here are you looking into?" To me, Miles was absolutely out of the question. Perhaps my reasoning wasn't the most logical, but I couldn't fathom that, and I didn't know anyone else who was adopted only because that was an uber personal question to just randomly spring on people.

His brows furrowed as he tapped each of my knuckles. "The Elite is still pulling research on the rest who might . . . fit the description."

"In other words, you don't want to tell me who else it could be."

He lifted his gaze to mine. "It's nothing personal. I'm just not going to put thoughts in your head that might not need to be there."

"I don't know anyone else who's been adopted," I persisted.

Several seconds passed. "I don't like the idea of keeping you in the dark, but like I said, I'm not going to put shit in your head that might not need to be there."

Annoyed, I started to pull my hand away from him, but I held myself still as his finger followed a bone up my hand, to my wrist. Behind the irritation was apprehension. Obviously there was something he wasn't telling me, but there was a reason other than him not wanting to put shit in my head. Could it be that I was close to whomever he— and the Elite—suspected? Immediately, my thoughts went to Val, but I dismissed them. She hadn't been adopted, and both her parents were alive and still active within the Order.

"When you find the person . . . you're going to kill them, aren't you?" I asked.

Several seconds passed then he leaned back, his fingers trailing off my hand. Taking a drink of his beer, he nodded. "That's part of my job, Ivy."

A shudder danced across my shoulders. Although I killed fae every night I hunted, to me killing a human—half fae or not—wasn't the same thing. "I've never killed a human."

His gaze flicked to mine but he didn't respond, because deep down, I knew that he had. A lot of Order members had. Not because they wanted to. Sometimes it was a human who'd been fed on too long, like the woman in the Quarter the other day. Other times it was someone who knew about the fae and worked alongside them. Or it was an innocent person who got caught in the crossfire. I knew that sometimes it couldn't be helped.

"David says that makes me weak," I added quietly.

The emerald hue brightened as he said earnestly, "That does not make you weak, Ivy. Not at all. And be glad that you've never had that kind of blood on your hands, and I hope you never do. It may be our duty—my duty—but it's not something I look forward to. It's not . . ." He looked away, a muscle thrumming along his jaw. "It's not something I'm entirely okay with. Not even when they're halflings."

All too easily I recalled the solemn expression that had been carved into his features when the man died in the Quarter. I didn't know what to say to him because I didn't know what it was like to kill someone whose only crime was their mixed heritage, and I wasn't even sure if I was okay with that. How could I be? If what Ren said was true, most of them, if not all of them, had no idea what they were. On the other hand, I understood the risk they posed. Conflicted, I tried to sort out what I thought. The only thing I did know was that what Ren said was true—he wasn't okay with it. Instinct told me that.

I studied the hard set of his jaw, the straight and proud nose, the flat line of his lips that were usually curved in a teasing smile. "Can't you leave the Elite?"

He coughed out a dry laugh. "You could leave the Order, but you can't leave the Elite. They'd never trust us with the knowledge we hold. I was born into this." His gaze found mine once more, and the shadows I'd seen in his eyes before had only increased. "And I'll die in this."

My chest tightened with those words. I didn't like to hear him say that—didn't want to hear him say anything like that. I inhaled, but the air got stuck in my throat, lodged up against the bitter ball of panic.

I closed my eyes.

God, I was so dumb. I'd allowed Ren to get under my skin, just like I had let Val in, and I knew better. Was I some kind of sadist? Hell. Why couldn't I be the fun kind of sadist, enjoying bondage or some freaky stuff like that?

"You are handling this well—better than I thought."

When I pried my eyes open, he wasn't looking at me. He was staring at the bottle of beer he held, at the label he'd almost peeled off. "Maybe I'll freak out later. I don't know. This was a lot of info to swallow."

"It is," he agreed pensively, and I hated that tone—and I *hated* that I cared enough to feel that way. "We still have to figure out the gates," he added, finishing off his beer. Leaning forward, he dropped his feet on the floor and placed the bottle on the coffee table. "Do you think she was actually telling us where the gates were, in her own way?"

"I think so." Running my hand down my face, I sighed wearily. "Something about the last thing she said, about no spirits or people being able to rest there? It sounds familiar. I can talk to Jerome. He's lived here his whole life. He might know of a few places we could check out."

"Sounds good. Bring him cake." He flashed a quick grin. "Butter him up. But save me a slice."

A reluctant smile appeared. "I still don't know if you can have any of my cake."

"Babe, I'm gonna get a piece of it, all right?"

I laughed, shaking my head. "So cocky."

The grin stayed on his lips for a few more seconds before slowly fading, and then it was gone, like it had never been there. Curled up against the arm of the couch, I let everything he told me sink in. My thoughts whirled from one direction to the next. I couldn't help but obsess over how much David was aware of. Did he know that Miles was adopted, a potential halfling? Did he know anything about the halflings in general, and if he did, was he prepared? He had to be.

Ren tipped his head back against the couch. "I let my best friend die."

Startled, I blinked. "What?"

Exhaling harshly, he stared at the blank TV screen across from where we sat. "My best friend—his name was Noah Cobb. We grew up together, always around each other. Hell, we were like brothers. Getting into trouble, staying out of it. If you saw one of us, you saw the other shortly afterward."

A sick feeling descended upon me. "What happened to him?"

Ren's jaw flexed as he stared straight ahead. "He was a fluke. Raised in the Order, both his parents were alive, and they were happy, you know? Never would've even suspected anything. His father hadn't stepped out on his mother. It wasn't like that. From what we gathered later, Noah came into the picture around the same time his father met his wife. It was a one night stand, and they'd hidden what he was very well. After . . . after what happened, we learned that the fae his father slept with brought Noah to him. The fae know what a halfling can do, but they can't raise a child that has mortal blood. They don't have the compassion or the humanity it takes to not neglect a child, for it to even survive a week.

258

Jennifer L. Armentrout

Anyway, the woman his father married accepted Noah as one of her own. They had no idea what being a halfling meant."

An ache lit up my chest as I listened to him. Human compassion—his father's love and his wife's acceptance had saved the boy, but I knew where this was heading, and although I wanted to hope for a different outcome, I knew it wouldn't change how this story ended.

"Noah was . . . God, he was a good guy and would've made one hell of an Order member. Loyal to the fucking core, and I . . ." A harsh laugh thundered out of him. "He even knew what I was being trained to do. Shit. I wasn't supposed to tell him, but man, there were no secrets between us, and I was so damn proud back then. I thought I was special." His lips curled into a mockery of a smile. "The way we found out was a fucking accident. My fault really. I brought the thorn stake out."

Shoulders tensed, he rubbed his hand along his chest, over his heart. "My parents lived just outside the city on several acres of land. They had the targets set up and we'd practice knife throwing. That kind of shit. He was over at my house, and we were in our backyard screwing around. My dad was there. So was another member of the Elite—Kyle Clare." His tone was tight, edged in bitterness. "My dad had no idea I had the thorn stake out there, and I let Noah pick it up. Nicked himself. Just a tiny cut, but that's all that was needed. I saw it. So did my father and Kyle."

My chest constricted, ached from what he was telling me. Out of all the loss I'd experienced, I had no idea what I'd do if I learned that my best friend, someone like Val, was what I was being trained to hunt—to kill.

259

"He knew," Ren said, his voice hoarse. "Noah knew when he saw his blood bubble, because I'd told him. He looked at me, as if he was sorry. I'll never forget that look." He cut himself off, clearing his throat, and I squeezed my eyes shut against the sudden burn of tears. "I was shocked. I didn't do a damn thing as I stared at him. My dad saw it, so did Kyle. They . . . pretended not to notice, but I knew they did. Noah left, and I just . . . I just stood there in that damn backyard."

"Oh God," I whispered.

"Kyle? He left then too, and a part of me deep down knew why he was leaving. This whole time a halfling had been right under our noses. It takes years sometimes to get info on potential targets." Drawing in a shuddering breath, he shook his head. "When I snapped out of it, I tried to go after them. I was going to go after them. I didn't know what I was going to do, but I couldn't just stand there. My father stopped me, and . . . Noah never made it home. I never saw him again."

"Oh, Ren, I'm so sorry." My voice was thick. "I don't know what to say other than I'm sorry."

He nodded, but guilt chewed out his next words. "To this day, I think about all the things I could've done differently. Like if I hadn't told him about the Elite, then I would've never had that stake out there with him. He never would've cut himself, and well, shit would be a lot different."

"Wait. What happened to him wasn't your fault."

"I knew better."

"How old were you when this happened? Sixteen? We didn't know jack shit at sixteen, Ren. What happened wasn't your fault."

"I didn't stop them from killing Noah."

"But you tried," I reasoned.

His heavy, tortured gaze swung in my direction. "Did I try hard enough? I'm not sure. And was I even supposed to try? I grew up knowing halflings had to be dealt with. There's no gray area there."

"No matter what, it wasn't something you did or didn't do. His death wasn't your fault." I reached over, wrapping my fingers around his forearm. "God knows, I understand what that kind of guilt feels like."

A flicker of understanding crossed his features. "You do?"

Realizing what I'd admitted, I quickly forged on. The last thing Ren needed to hear was how I actually was the cause of three people dying. "You don't need to carry that kind of guilt around, Ren. What happened was terrible, and there are a lot of things that could've been done differently, but I doubt it would've changed the outcome." I paused, wondering when was the last time I sounded so mature. "It's not your fault, Ren."

He searched my face carefully, and then he placed his hand over mine. "I don't ever want to be in that situation again."

My heart squeezed, forcing out a promise I knew I couldn't back up and had no control over. "You won't."

Ren was quiet for a moment, his stare locked onto mine with an intensity that caused my breath to quicken, and then he moved. Closing the distance between us, he kissed me.

The brush of his lips was the last thing I was expecting, but the sweet, almost shy way he did so snagged me. I opened to him, and his other hand settled at the nape of my neck. I kissed him back, still feeling a little out of my element when it came to doing this, but after a few moments, I wasn't thinking about whether or not I was doing it correctly. I wasn't capable of a lot of thought when all I could taste was him.

My heart rate sped up as he tugged me toward him. Sliding his hands to my upper arms, he lifted me onto his lap, my knees settling on either side of his hips. Never once did he break contact with my mouth, and well, that took talent.

I shouldn't be allowing this, but I was trembling and I wanted so much more. Every time he touched me, and with every brush of his lips, I was dragged under a little deeper, but I couldn't make myself stop. I was starved for this contact, the red-hot sting of pleasure and the breathless bliss that awaited.

I was starved for *him*.

Chapter Sixteen

Ren needed it—needed me. I could feel it in the way his hand trembled as he slid it over my hips to squeeze my bottom, and in the fierceness with which he kissed me. His hand gripped the back of my neck again, holding me in place, but I wasn't going anywhere. Behind the heat in his stare was such sadness it tugged at my heart, and I wanted to erase it, to take it away. I wanted to bring back that teasing, smiling Ren who excited and infuriated me.

I skimmed my hands down his chest, wrapping my fingers under the hem of his worn shirt. I tugged up and Ren pulled back. A moment passed and he asked, "What do you want, Ivy?"

My breaths were coming out fast and shallow. "Ren . . ."

He didn't respond. His eyes were a heated shade of green as he cupped my cheeks, smoothing his thumbs along my jaw as he tilted his head, kissing me once more. Our kisses were deep, slow, and it left me shaking and wanting so much more.

Pulling on his shirt again, I exposed a glimpse of his lower stomach. "I want to take your shirt off."

A semblance of a grin appeared. "Who am I to argue with that?"

As Ren lifted his arms, I took off his shirt, letting it fall beside us on the couch as I rocked back, getting my first really good look at Ren. He was . . . utterly breathtaking. His pecs were hard and his stomach a series of tight ridges that begged for me to touch and explore them. There was a faint trail of dark hair that started under his navel and disappeared below the band of his pants, but it was the sprawling artwork that encompassed his entire right arm and shoulder, the right pec and down the side of his body that blew my mind.

I knew what the tattoo was now, and I wanted to cry and lick every square inch of it. The vines were inked into his skin, forming endless knots, and those vines twisted together over his chest, where blood red poppies formed. There were dozens of them, up and down the side of his body, and mixed among the flowers were letters—a phrase that brought tears to my eyes.

Lest We Forget.

The flowers were a symbol of remembrance, of never forgetting a loved one. I knew those flowers were for his friend, and there was something incredibly honorable about the homage he paid with his body.

Dipping my head, I kissed the one above his heart. My gaze flipped to his when he sucked in a sharp breath. "That tattoo . . . it's beautiful. Does it go down your back?"

He nodded, and I glanced down, running my fingers over the vines, and then I saw that the tattoo bled into three interlocking circles next to his hip, over the lickable indent. "We're marked in the same place."

"I know."

Of course he'd seen it, and I guessed that was why he touched it then. A shudder worked its way through his large body as I trailed my fingers over the vines.

"May I?" Ren caught the edge of my shirt, and with a deep breath, I nodded. He pulled my shirt off, easing my arms out of it. I had no idea where the shirt ended up. His lips parted. "You're beautiful, Ivy."

The way he said it made me feel beautiful—the way he spoke made me feel like a goddess even though my bra was white with yellow daisies on it. Really. I did own sexier stuff. But his hands traveled from my hips, over my stomach, to my breasts. The feeling he left in their wake was a bit frightening and exhilarating. He cradled my breast, his thumb smoothing over the top, teasing the hardening tip through my bra. A moan rushed out of me, and his eyes burned a deep forest green.

"I like the way you look at me," he said, his lips brushing mine. "But do you know what else I like more?"

"What?"

His fingers moved in a slow, torturous circle over my tip. "The sound you make when I please you."

My cheeks burned as I tried to catch my breath. His mouth left mine, trailing a path down my neck, nipping at my skin. He trailed the lacy edges of my bra, then his agile fingers made their way inside the cup, and my back arched, pressing my breast against his flesh. The skin on skin contact thrilled me and heated my blood. When he caught my nipple between his fingers, the sexiest sound I'd ever heard rumbled out of his chest.

I reached for the button on his jeans, popping it through its hole, then I tugged his zipper down. I glanced up when he caught my wrist.

His eyes were on fire. "Are you sure?" he asked.

"I . . . I just want to touch you."

Those thick lashes fluttered, then he guided my hand inside his loosened jeans. My fingers brushed the hot, hard thickness, and I gasped. "You're not wearing . . ."

The grin he gave me was mischievous as his hand moved to my other breast. "I was still in bed when you called. Left in a hurry."

"I'd say," I murmured, turned on in a ridiculous way with the knowledge that he'd been bare under his jeans the whole time.

I stilled as he slipped both hands under each cup. He tugged the bra down, baring my breasts, and he shuddered again, the act making me hot.

"Fuck," he murmured. "I am not worthy of this."

Before I could respond to such an untrue statement, he lowered his head to my breast and took one aching tip into his mouth. I cried out, my senses twisting with each hot, wet pull. My hips rotated, and using my other hand, I pulled on his jeans. He lifted his up, helping me ease them down, baring himself.

Lost in the sensations he was stirring inside me, I rested my cheek against his as he moved one hand down my stomach, inside my loose sweatpants as I wrapped my palm around the base of his hardness. He jerked, his entire body responding to my touch. A teasing bite caused me to cry out, and then I shuddered when his fingers brushed the center of my panties.

His breath was warm in my ear. "I'm going to make you come."

A tight shiver racked me, and I closed my eyes. I stroked him slowly, unsure of what to do because it had been so incredibly long since I'd last done something like this. He groaned against my neck, skimming a finger over my center. A knot tightened low in my belly.

"Am I doing this right?" I whispered.

"Fuck, Ivy. You're doing it perfect." He drew back, scorching a path of kisses along my cheek. He captured my mouth, taking me deeply. "Anything you do is going to be right. *Anything.*"

Encouraged by that, I leaned back and looked down—and then stared, gawked at him like a total idiot, but I couldn't help it, because he wanted me and I wanted him. There was a power in that I had forgotten all about, and probably never fully understood anyway, at least not until now.

"I have a secret to admit," he said, curving his hand over mine while he continued to tease me with his other.

"You do?" I asked, breathless.

He eased my hand up his length. "I did this last night when I got home. I was so fucking turned on by you. I had to."

Oh God.

Turning my head, I found his mouth and kissed him, overwhelmed by what he'd admitted. My grip on him tightened, and he rocked against my palm. Both of us were breathing fast as he gripped the back of my neck while he slipped his fingers under my panties. My heart stuttered as he eased a finger through the wetness gathering between my thighs and then inside me.

"You're so tight," he said against my mouth. "You're not—"

I shook my head, but he'd stopped moving. Taking it on myself, I pushed down on his hand, forcing his finger in further and his palm against the bundle of nerves. "Oh God," I gasped. That was all I was capable of saying as he worked his finger in and out, in and out.

Every nerve ending felt like it was on fire. My body tingled as pleasure shot through me. We kissed deeply as I rode his hand and stroked him, our rhythms matching until the tension built to an unbearable point. I pushed against his hand frantically, and he groaned into my mouth. Wetness gathered at his tip, and I knew he was close—I was close—no, I was *there*. I kicked my head back, crying out as the knot quickly unraveled, spiraling pleasure throughout me. Tremors rocked my body, and then his hips thrust up, his thickness spasming against my hand.

I don't know how much time passed before either of us seemed capable of moving, of withdrawing our hands from one another's bodies, but we didn't part. He gathered me in his arms and held me tight against him as my heartbeat slowed. His breathing was deep, ragged, as he pressed a kiss against my temple.

"Stay for a little while and I'll take you home?" he asked.

The smart thing for me to do was to say no and skedaddle on out of here as fast as my feet would carry me because I'd accomplished what I set out to do. He wasn't sad anymore. Bonus points for both of us getting off, but I was warm in his embrace. My muscles didn't want to do the running away thing, and I felt cherished, not alone, and that was an amazing feeling I wasn't ready to give up yet.

Even knowing my head was now fully under water, I snuggled closer. "I'll stay."

~

It was late when Ren drove me back to my apartment, switching out his bike for the truck because it had started to rain, and it took me quite some time to make my way out of the cab of his truck.

Totally not my fault though.

I tried to slip out, but before my fingers even brushed the handle of the door, Ren snaked an arm around my waist and hauled me across the seat. Fat drops of rain pelted the window and coursed down in tiny rivers as he captured my wrists.

"Ren?"

With a half smile, he guided my hands to his chest, and I could feel his heart pounding under my palm. "You've got to learn something, Ivy."

I raised my brows, desperately trying to play it cool even though my pulse had picked up. "Learn what? You're grabby and touchy-feely? I already know that."

"Smartass." He chuckled, lowering his head to mine. "You don't leave without a kiss."

My breath caught. "Oh."

"Yeah, oh."

In that lovely truck with the windows fogged over, he held my hands to his chest as he kissed me like he was dying of thirst and I was his own personal bucket of water. He made that sound—that masculine, deep growl that rumbled out from him and caused a rush of heat to flood my senses. Our kisses burned between us, turning into touching. His hands drifted under my top and his fingers followed the length of my spine. Mine found their way under his shirt, mapping out the dips and planes of his stomach. I had no control of my fingers, especially when they became super interested in getting under the band of his jeans.

"We need to stop," he said, voice thick as he lifted his mouth from mine. In the soft yellow glow of the dome light, I could see his lips were as swollen as mine felt. "Or I have a feeling we're going to get arrested for lewd behavior."

Cheeks heated and body burning, it was hard for me to pull away, but I did and I said goodbye. We had plans to meet up after my classes to talk to Jerome. "Tomorrow?"

He swallowed hard and nodded.

I climbed out of the truck and hopped into the cold rain. My mind raced as I darted across the sidewalk and through the gate. What was I doing with him? Getting off, obviously, but it was more than that. Oh God, it was so much more than that, and instead of being completely nauseated over it, there was excitement and a burgeoning hope that I could have a taste of normal amongst all the crazy.

Did I dare to even have it? Today was the closest to normal I'd known in ages. We hung out on the couch, ordered takeout, and watched a marathon of some reality show on a cable channel. We didn't talk about our jobs—the ancients or the doorways—even though we were only three days away from the equinox and that should've been our priority. We just . . . hung out like anyone our age would, and I wouldn't change—

Heavy footsteps behind me were my only warning as I neared the stairs. I turned, ready to kung fu someone into next week, but it was Ren. I lowered my hands. "What the—?"

Ren was on me before I could finish whatever it was I was about to say. His hands landed on my hips, and he picked me up as he pushed me back against the stone. My body's reaction seemed immediate. Legs wrapped around his waist and arms around his neck, a strangled gasp parted my lips seconds before he was kissing me again. I could feel him against the center of my legs, and in spite of the cold rain, it heated my skin.

Ren's hips pressed against mine in all the ways that were fun and naughty and totally led to lewd and lavish acts, but I wasn't thinking about possible jail time or fines as his hands cupped my face.

Lightning split the sky and thunder crashed, but all I could hear was my pounding heart. All I could feel was Ren pressed against me as our lips melded together. I was so ready to lose myself in him. Our bodies rocked and our hands became slippery. I don't know how long we kissed, but our clothes were soaked and my body was trembling by the time we came up for air. His lips skated over my cheeks, and his hands drifted to my throat, tipping my head back.

Hair plastered from the rain and rivulets running down his face, he looked like a god of the sea. "Thank you for today. You have no idea how much you being there meant to me." He kissed the tip of my nose, pulling back and gently setting me on my feet. "Tomorrow."

Then he was gone, disappearing into the rain like some kind of phantom lover.

"Jesus," I whispered. Lightning cut the sky open, quickly chased by a thunderous boom.

I ended up stumbling into my apartment half out of it and totally drenched. Tink was in the living room, and he took one long, strange look at me and said nothing, fluttering into his room. And that was fine by me. My head was in a thousand places, and I didn't have the mental fortitude required to engage with Tink.

I slept like the dead Sunday night. Actually, I slept like someone who just experienced an orgasm that wasn't self-induced for the first time in years, which was totally accurate. Either way, I woke up quite refreshed, but as I did my morning run and got ready for school, something nagged at me, a shadow of a thought that lingered just at the fringes of consciousness. I couldn't quite grasp it each time I reached for it.

Before I headed to class on Monday I managed to sway Tink into baking a cake by promising to provide him with a buffet of beignets when I got home from my shift. I hoped the baked goods would warm Jerome up enough so he would be of some help. It was a long shot assuming that he knew anything, but there weren't many other options left.

Tink flitted from the small pantry to the cabinets, grabbing flour and brown sugar. "You're lucky I always demand we keep a stash of baking powder and baker's chocolate."

"That I am." I backed out of the kitchen, my thoughts tiptoeing over the recent events. I remembered something I'd forgotten while I'd been at Merle's yesterday. The first time I tried to visit her, something had been in her garden. It could've been a sparrow for all I knew, but what if it were another brownie? How long had it been here? Better yet, how in the world had Tink gotten here without us knowing something had come through the gate? It's not like I never thought about this question before, but now knowing everything that I did, the flaws in Tink's story seemed more visible.

I think he lied to me. It was difficult to believe that, but there was a lot I just discovered recently that one would think a creature from the Otherworld should know.

Not paying attention to me, Tink lugged a mixing bowl out of the cabinet as I watched him. I hesitated at the entryway to the kitchen, wincing as the metal bowl clanged off the counter when he dropped it. For some reason, I thought about how he got here—the location of the cemetery. "Tink?"

He didn't look over at me as he pulled a spatula from the drawer and buzzed around the kitchen. "You're interrupting my me time. And you know baking is my me time."

Leaning against the doorframe, I didn't rise to the bait like I typically would. My thoughts were too conflicted. Did Tink not know about the halflings? Because if he did, why hadn't he told me? And what about the gates? I glanced at the clock, seeing that I needed to leave soon so I would make it to class on time. "When I found you in the cemetery, do you remember how far away from the gate you were?"

Tink turned around, clutching the spatula close to him. "No. I told you before, I don't even remember coming through the gate. I woke up in the cemetery, my poor wing snapped, my leg broken, beaten like an orphan kid in regency England. I was a pitiful wee creature."

"Um, okay. Anyway." I straightened the strap on my bag and shifted my weight. "Did you know there were two gates in the city?"

The spatula slipped an inch between his hands as his pale eyes widened to the size of nickels. "What?"

"Remember Merle?" When he nodded, I continued. "She said there were two gates in the city—one in an old sanctuary, and the other in a place where no spirits or humans could rest."

A frown marred his face as he placed the spatula on the counter instead of dropping it. Hovering in the air, his translucent wings moved silently. "No. There have never been two gates."

"Could there just be two gates and you never knew? I know the fae only know the gate they come through, so maybe there are more cities with more than one gate."

He shook his head. "No. That can't . . . well, nothing is impossible. I mean, look at you. You spent all of Sunday with a guy, and I never thought that would happen."

I started to scowl.

"But two gates? That would be . . ." His gaze drifted to the window, his brows furrowed. "That would be very bad."

"Yeah," I said, pushing off the doorframe. I started to leave but stopped. Tink was still focused on the window, expression surprisingly serious. "Do you know about halflings?"

His head swung toward me sharply, and he didn't have to say a word. I knew that he was fully aware of halflings. It was written all over his face, in the way his jaw had dropped, and the slight flare of understanding in his big eyes.

My stomach sunk like it was full of sharp stones. Our eyes met, and I found it hard to breathe around the knot in my throat. "Why . . . why haven't you told me about them before?"

Tink stared back at me wordlessly.

"Having that kind of information would've been helpful to know because I'm assuming you're aware of what could happen if the prince or the princess gets a hold of a halfling." My voice was strangely thick. I tried to tell myself I didn't care if Tink hadn't been forthcoming with information, but I was angry. Angry because I willingly brought him into my house and I never really questioned him. I blindly accepted what little information he'd told me, and I don't even know why I had done so. Looking back, there was no simple justification as to why I never pushed Tink.

God, the answer to why was so glaring and right in my face. Ever since I'd lost my adoptive parents and Shaun, I'd closed myself off to everyone in a distressed attempt to never feel that kind of hurt again. Val had wiggled her way in, and so had Jo Ann, but that hadn't been enough. Deep down, I knew that. I'd still been so desperate to be close, to forge a bond to anything, and I still was. Look at Ren.

And as Tink continued to stare back at me helplessly, I knew—dammit, I *knew* he wasn't being upfront with me.

He lowered his gaze and heaved a great sigh. Floating down to the edge of the counter, he sat, his wings drooping on either side of his bent back. "You would not understand, Ivy."

Closing my eyes, I took a second before I reopened them and responded. "Why don't you try me, Tink? For once?"

His face flinched. "I haven't lied to you. Not really." As I cocked my head to the side, he pressed his hands together under his chin. "I just haven't been entirely communicative."

"Do not try to act cute right now," I warned him, letting my backpack slip off my arm and land against the door.

"I'm not. I swear." He lowered his hands to his lap, his shoulders slumping. "I had one job. And I failed."

"You're not an Internet meme."

He shook his head. "My job was to destroy the gate in New Orleans."

I stiffened. "What?"

Tink lifted his chin. "Your guardians basically only guard those gates—their positions are virtually useless except for the fact that they hold knowledge of the location, and that makes them only valuable to the fae. One does not simply walk to a gateway and open it."

All I could do was stare at him.

"If the blood of an ancient is shed on the doorway from inside the Otherworld, it destroys the door. If the blood of an ancient is shed on the outside, it opens the door," he explained. "We knew what the fae would do if the ancients ever crossed over to this world en masse. They would destroy it like they've been destroying the Otherworld. You see, our world . . . it's dying, because of what they're doing. They need to get out, but we . . ." He balled up a fist, pressing it to his chest. "My kind have done everything in our power to stop them, and two and a half years ago we believed we had succeeded in destroying the gates from the inside. It's a suicide mission to do so, but one we gladly take."

"Wait. Are you saying all the gates have been rendered useless?"

Tink lifted his wings and stood. "We found all of them in the Otherworld, and we destroyed them by luring ancients to the gates and killing them. Or being killed. A lot of us have died that way, and we would have to send another." He frowned as his arms hung limply at his sides. "I should've died that day. I wasn't lying when I told you I don't even remember coming through the gate. I don't even know how it happened. Must have been a freak occurrence, and I was sucked through when the door was destroyed. And I would've died if you hadn't saved me." Those big pale eyes met mine. "I didn't tell you because I saw no point. The door was destroyed, and Ivy, it was the last door in the Otherworld. Or at least that's what we believed. We had no idea there were two here. It should've been the only one in that church—the one across from the cemetery."

"Our Lady of Guadalupe?" I cursed. Dammit. The location of one of the gates had been right in front of my face. It made perfect sense, especially based on what Merle had said. That church had been a sanctuary at one time, and it was the oldest surviving church in the city. And Tink had been found in the cemetery right across the street. "Why didn't you just tell me you came through the gate there?"

"What was the point? I destroyed it, Ivy. Nothing is getting through that gate. Maybe the fae and the ancients on this side don't realize that, but they aren't opening it."

I folded my arms, struggling to stay calm. "Why didn't you tell me that all the gates had been destroyed? We have lost Order members because they are guarding something that doesn't even work."

"But if you're right, that there are two gates in the city, then it is a good thing that it has guardians," Tink argued, his cheeks flushing. "And I swear to you, I had no idea there was a second. That is why I've never been too concerned about what the ancients were up to, and I saw no point in bringing up the whole . . ." He looked away, lips forming a flat line. "The whole halfling stuff, but I'm telling you, believe me or not, if they have discovered a second gate, it's come from someone within the Order. It's the only way, because we didn't even know it was there."

I shook my head, floored.

"What good would it have done if I told you about us destroying the gates? Do you think the Order would've believed you? Would you have told them that you learned it from me, and would they have trusted you?"

"And I'm supposed to trust you now?" I asked.

He drew back like I'd smacked him.

For a long moment, I did nothing but stand there, and then I turned, walking down the hall. I sat down on the couch and put my head in my hands, rubbing my fingers along my temples. I tried to make sense of everything.

If what Tink was saying was true, then that would also explain why so many fae had migrated to New Orleans. One gate left open? They'd throw all their force into opening it, and it also added to our fears that someone within the Order was working with the fae.

"I'm sorry."

Laughing hoarsely under my breath, I slid my hands over my eyes. A stab of terror lit up my stomach as I realized that if what Tink was saying was true, every single fae nearby was going to go after one gate. Those guarding it would not survive. Balling my fists, I lowered them and looked at Tink. He hovered just over the edge of the coffee table looking contrite.

"Do you know where the other gate is?" I demanded. "I mean it, Tink. If you know, you need to tell me right now."

Crestfallen, he shook his head. "If I knew I would tell you. I swear! But you need to find out, Ivy, because if there is a gate still in operation, they will open it, and the knights will come through. They will bring the princess. They will bring the prince, and you . . . you do not want that to happen."

Chapter Seventeen

I didn't end up making it to class Monday morning, and when Jo Ann texted to check in on me, I lied and told her I'd overslept. There was a lot of lying going on these days, and I was just as guilty as everyone else, I supposed. I spent the bulk of the morning trying to figure out how I was going to broach this subject with David. I had to, but I couldn't tell him how I found out.

I couldn't even tell Ren the truth.

For some dumbass reason, I was still protecting Tink. If I told anyone in the Order about him, they'd raid my house like they were the police, and they'd kill him.

Who knew what I was going to do with Tink? Part of me wanted to pitch him headfirst through a window. The other half understood why he hadn't been forthcoming. By the time I left to meet up with Ren at headquarters, Tink had been sulking around in his room for a while.

The only thing I could do was lie about how I found out the info, and that knowledge sat bitterly in my stomach. I climbed the stairs to the second floor and was buzzed in by Harris.

"You're early today," he said, closing the door behind me.

"Meeting Ren." Without my backpack, I felt naked.

"Hmm. You and the new boy seem to be getting along fine." He ambled back to his office. "Good for you."

"Thanks," I mumbled, unsure of what to make of that comment. "I think."

A giggle from my left drew my attention, and I turned to see Val walking out of one of the meeting rooms, her phone plastered to her ear. "Everything's fine, babe." Smiling with a slightly dazed look about her, she veered toward me. Of all the guys Val had dated in the past, I couldn't remember her looking this way or even talking to a guy on the phone. She'd been more of a text me and leave me alone kind of girl, and I had to wonder if Val had finally found the one—if she was in love. "I have to go now. Yeah, I'll call you and let you know. Bye."

Hoisting myself up on the edge of an empty conference table pushed against the wall, I grinned at her. "Sounds like an interesting phone call."

She shrugged as she slipped her phone into the pocket of her orange jeans. I didn't even know they made jeans in that color. "Sorry about yesterday."

"It's okay. You were with that . . ." What did I call him? Her boyfriend? Guy? Friend with benefits? Heck, what did I call Ren and me? "You were with the guy you're seeing?"

Leaning against the table next to me, she stretched out her long legs as she tipped her head back. Tight curls tumbled over her shoulders, and she sighed.

"Actually, I was asleep. He worked me so hard Saturday night. I can still feel him in—"

"I get the picture," I interrupted with a laugh as I swung my feet. I glanced at her, lowering my voice. "I need to talk to you later."

She straightened, the easy smile fading from her heart-shaped lips. "About what you were telling me before? The gates and stuff?"

I nodded, but before I could go any further, the buzzer went off and Harris made his way to the entry once more. Ren strolled through the door, and my breath caught. He looked like he'd just stepped out of the shower, hair damp and curling along his temples, face freshly shaven. A light, three-quarter sleeve thermal in charcoal gray clung to his broad shoulders and defined pecs. The black tactical pants fitted to his strong thighs.

God, he looked too good to be real, to be stalking toward where I sat, his stunning, emerald eyes fixed on me like I was the only person in the room.

"Wow," Val murmured under her breath.

I sat up straight, eyes widening as he advanced on me. I opened my mouth to say something—I don't know, a hello would've worked—but all the words died a quick and painless death. Ren clasped my cheeks in his hands and tilted my head back as he got right up on me, his legs spreading mine. His mouth was so close that we shared the same air.

"Uh," Val said, and she sounded so far away.

Ren kissed me, and there was nothing tentative about it, as if he didn't care that Val was sitting right next to us. He boldly parted my lips, and his tongue danced over mine as my grip on the edge of the table tightened. If I wasn't leaning against the wall, I probably would've fallen right over.

My lips tingled when he cut the hot kiss off, and I forced my eyes open. All I could see was green fringed behind black.

"Um. Wow. I think I just got pregnant watching that," Val said, breathless.

Ren chuckled. "I've been waiting all day for you to text or call me," he said, lowering his mouth to my ear. "I know you didn't forget about me."

Wincing, I drew back with my cheeks flushed bright red. I hadn't contacted him this morning, and it wasn't like I hadn't thought about doing it before everything went down with Tink, but I wasn't sure if he would've been cool with that. Like were we at that stage? I had no idea how many stages there were or at what level texting each other for no reason other than to say hi was acceptable and not an act of neediness. Now I kind of felt like a douche.

He pressed his lips just below my ear. "It's okay. You're out of practice, so I'll tell you how it is with me."

"Do tell," Val coaxed.

I shot her a dark look, but she ignored it as Ren placed his hands on either side of my legs. "I want to hear from you—whenever. Day. Night. Morning. After you get out of the shower, and especially any time you're naked." He winked, and I rolled my eyes. "And I have no problem with anyone knowing what you and I've got going on."

"Really? Never would've guessed that," I responded dryly.

I dared to take a peek at Val, and she was watching me expectantly. "So when did this happen?" she asked, moving her finger in a giant circle.

"Oh, it's been happening." Ren patted my leg as he straightened, folding his arms. The look on his face dared me to disagree.

So I did. Naturally. "Actually, we hung out yesterday."

"Wow," Val said. "I should bail on you more often."

Ren nodded. "I can agree with that."

I immediately thought of what happened the night we went to the club. I narrowed my eyes at him, and one side of his mouth curled up in a teasing grin.

"You two." Val shook her head, tsking under her breath. "You've been up to no good, knocking booty boots."

Warmth swept across my cheeks and down my neck. "Look, guys. There's some serious stuff going on—"

"Like what you two have been doing?" Val added, grinning when I groaned.

"No. Not that."

"Actually, I think what we got going on is pretty serious," Ren chimed in, and I wanted to bang my head on the wall.

Val pushed off the table, clapping her hands together as she twirled to face us. "I'm proud of you, Ivy." Then, completely shameless, she gave Ren a long, appraising look that was one step away from a visual molestation. "Really proud of you."

Thank God David decided to enter the room because I really had no idea where this conversation would go, and I didn't want to be there whenever it got to its pervy destination. I hopped off the table and stepped around Ren. "David, you got a minute?"

He stopped, shoulders tensing as he turned to us. "Do I want to have a minute?"

"Yes. Yes, you do."

Ren's hand landed on the small of my back. "What are you doing?" he asked in a low voice.

Glancing at him, I took a deep breath. "We need to talk to him."

"Ivy—"

David frowned, which wasn't entirely unusual. "Talk to me about what?"

"I found some stuff out this morning," I told Ren, willing him to understand. "We have to talk to him. Trust me."

A muscle ticked along his jaw as his gaze held mine. I could tell he wasn't at all happy about this, and when he looked away, flipping his eyes to the ceiling, I wondered if he was praying for patience. I wanted to tell him that I wasn't going to force him to talk about the Elite, but there was no way for me to bring that up without broadcasting it to the entire world.

"What in the hell is going on?" David demanded. "I don't have all day."

I took a deep breath. "Trust me."

His gaze shot back to mine, and another moment passed while I held my breath. Finally, Ren nodded. "Well, let's do this then."

Relieved that I wasn't going to have a major fight on my hands with him yet, I started toward David. "I think we should go into one of the rooms."

Val followed us, much to David's chagrin. "I didn't invite you to be a part of whatever the fuck is about to come out of their mouths."

She shrugged. "I'm inviting myself." She flopped down into one of the metal folding chairs as David closed the door behind us.

Ren eyed her with a measure of distrust. "Whatever is said in this room goes no further."

An elegant eyebrow rose as she met his gaze. "You're hot and obvious. A winning combination."

David looked half done with the conversation already. "Make this quick. I have to meet with a couple of potential new members that are being transferred here."

I glanced at Ren, but he'd taken up a silent stance in the corner of the room, arms folded over his chest, as still as a sentry. "There are ancients in the city, David."

"Oh, for fuck's sake—"

"Listen to me." I cut him off abruptly and in a way that would probably end with my butt getting written up. "There are. I've seen at least three of them, and they are planning to open the gate on Wednesday."

David's face darkened as he took a step toward me, and that's when I saw Ren move. Lightning fast, he leaped out of the corner and gripped David on the shoulder. I sensed no real threat from the sect leader, but Ren wasn't having it.

"She's not bullshitting you, man. I've seen them myself," Ren said. "They are here. They've been in a club downtown—Flux. And that place is most definitely catering to the fae. Not only that, but we've seen them talking to the police there."

Shrugging off the younger man's hand, David scanned the whole room with an annoyed gaze before landing on Ren. "First off, that's not a huge surprise. We've had situations before where the fae fed off humans who were police. And mostly importantly, I'm surprised you've actually seen a fae since you've been here, because boy, I'm pretty sure the only thing you've been concentrating on since you got here is how to get in that girl's pants."

"Oh my word," mumbled Val.

My jaw dropped, but it was the eerily calm smile that graced Ren's lips that concerned me greatly. "Now that's an unjust observation, David. I can multitask."

That statement wasn't helping things. "David, you need to listen to us. Those police officers didn't look like humans who were being fed on."

"They could've been compelled."

"Does that matter?" I shot back. "The ancients are planning to open the gate, and we know there are two in the city. But the one in Our Lady of Guadalupe Church isn't a functioning gate anymore. They can't get through that one."

Everyone stopped and stared at me.

"What?" Ren said softly.

David's response was a bit harsher. "How the hell do you know the location of that gate?"

"There is another gate in the city, right?" I persisted.

He looked down his nose at me. "There are two, but what I want to know is how the fuck you learned where one of them is and why you think it isn't functioning."

"Does that matter?" I snapped. "I also know about the halflings and what will happen if the prince or the princess comes through the gate and gets their hands on one of them."

"Halfling," repeated David. "What the hell are you talking about?"

I glanced at Ren, and the hardness in his expression said he was a second away from putting David through a wall. "You don't know about the halflings? I'm talking about a half human, half fae."

He stared at me like I sprouted an arm out of the side of my head and was waving at him. "Have you lost your fucking mind?"

"And do you know how to speak to a lady?" Ren fired back.

"A half fae?" David said, throwing up his hands. "Need I really say more?"

Ren cursed under his breath. "This is pointless, Ivy. I told you there was no reason to bring this up to him."

"A half fae does sound kind of crazy," Val said from her chair. "I mean, I'm not taking sides, but seriously?"

Frustrated, I curled my hands into fists. "If you don't listen to me and put every single member you have on the other gate in this city, they are going to get through, and whether you believe in halflings or not, we're going to have one huge fucking mess on our hands."

"I'm with the Elite," Ren announced the moment David opened his mouth to respond, and those four words silenced everyone; even Val quieted. All I could do was stare at him. I couldn't believe he'd just thrown that out there. Granted, Val already knew, but he didn't know that. Once he had David's attention he continued. "Do you know what that is?"

A tense moment passed, and then David said, "Yes. I know what the Elite is."

Well, la-di-da.

"Then if you know what I am, you know damn well that there are ancients still walking this realm. You might think since the Elite have been hunting them they are not a concern. Maybe you just don't want to send your sect into a panic by openly admitting that there are fae they cannot kill with iron. And maybe you don't know about halflings. I honestly don't give a flying fuck why you don't want your group to know, but I am telling you that I was sent here because you have a huge population of fae and ancients that have been heading in this direction."

Ren stepped up, and since he was a good head taller than David, he towered over the sect leader. "But if she's saying that there are two gates and that one of them is not working, you need to tell me where the other gate is, pull your fucking resources, and get that other gate guarded. Now."

The only thing that could be heard was the clicking of the clock on the wall, and then David said, "Everyone but you out of the room."

He meant Ren. I held my ground. "I'm not leaving."

"You're leaving." David glanced back at Val. "So are you. This is between Ren and me."

"That's bullshit! This—"

"This is an order, Ivy!" David thundered. A vein along his temple throbbed. "Or have you forgotten that I'm your boss?"

I sucked in a sharp breath. What could I do? Stand here and get myself suspended or kicked out of the Order? What good would that do? However, standing here and punching David in the face would make me feel oh so good. Calling on every bit of restraint I had, I walked out of the room behind Val, not even looking in Ren's direction, but I did slam the door behind me.

"What a bastard," I fumed, striding past an Order member who was coming down from the third floor. Walking to the window that overlooked the street below, I gripped the windowsill and focused on breathing instead of running back there and smacking someone.

Val stood beside me. She reached up, pushing a wayward curl off her forehead. "What do you think they're talking about in there?"

"I don't know." I glanced over my shoulder, keeping an eye on the members roaming around. "You know what the really bad thing is? We're sure that someone in the Order has been working with the fae. It's the only thing that makes sense."

Her eyes widened. "How does that make sense?"

"It's a long story." I turned around, leaning against the wall, and pushed my hands through my hair. "You know the members that have been killed? We think all of them were guardians," I explained, speaking barely above a whisper. "And remember how they said Trent was tortured?" I licked my lips and dropped my hands. "There's this club in the warehouse district. We've seen the ancients there. I was *this* close to them. They said they knew the location of the gate, and that they would not fail this time. I also heard them say they had a lead on another person. I think they were talking about an Order member."

"Holy crap," Val said. She stepped to the side, her hands on her hips, several seconds passing. "You know all of that sounds like random ramblings, right?"

"I know. It's just . . . a lot going on. This is a big deal. They open that gate, we are so screwed." I looked at her.

Val cast her gaze to the floor, her brows furrowed. Neither of us spoke for a couple of minutes. "Hey, I've got . . . I have to go." She backed away. "I'll call you later."

She left me. Not that I blamed her at this point because that was a lot to dump on someone, and she didn't even know the half of it. There was a lot of potential what the fuckery for her to sort through.

I paced in front of the window, wanting to know what David was saying to Ren—what Ren was saying to David. Why would he kick me out of the room? And would Ren tell me what was said inside? If not, I was going to punt kick him into next week.

Because my annoyance wasn't already at an all-time high, Miles appeared, having walked down from the third floor. As soon as I saw him, I turned away and pretended to be engrossed in staring out the window.

Of course, that didn't work.

"Have you seen David?" he asked.

I glanced at the closed door. "He's in there with Ren."

"Huh." Miles frowned. "Why?"

Like I was going to answer that question. As I studied Miles from the veil of my lashes, I tried to picture him as a halfling, and I almost laughed out loud.

His frown increased. "What are you doing out here?"

"Waiting on Ren," I answered. "We were paired up together."

"That you were." Miles eyed me closely. "You know, we found Trent's phone near his body. It was damaged, but not destroyed."

I thought about the phone I'd seen him holding last week. "Okay."

His light brown eyes were guarded. "There were pictures of you on his phone—you and Ren. You guys were by Jackson Square, looking mighty close."

At first, I didn't think I heard him right, then I pretty much just gave up on the day right then. "Well, that's kind of creepy."

"True," agreed Miles. "That was the night he was killed. You know why he was taking those pictures? He didn't trust you."

Tiny hairs rose on the back of my neck. "He thought I was crazy, so I'm not surprised."

Miles smiled slightly. It was forced, barely changing his expression whatsoever. "He was worried that you'd become . . . influenced by the fae."

I balled my hands into fists. "Why the hell would he think that? I'd have to be without a clover for that..." I trailed off, my stomach dropping.

"He looked into your past, Ivy. He raised some interesting questions about what happened the night the fae attacked your home," Miles continued. "Pointed out things that just didn't add up."

My stomach kept falling, and I didn't know what to say as I stared at Miles. Horror was like ice slushing through my veins. No. There was no way Trent had found anything out.

The door opened, and I'd never been more grateful to see Ren stalking out, not looking nearly as angry as he had when I left the room.

David stood in the doorway. "Miles. I need to see you. Now."

I turned to Ren, about to stop him, but he gave a quick shake of his head. "Let's head out," he said.

Beyond impatient, I followed him out of headquarters and onto the sidewalk. "What's going on, Ren?"

He reached down between us, wrapping his hand around mine as we started down Phillip, toward Royal. My step stumbled, and he squeezed my hand gently. I looked up at him and he lifted a brow. "Holding hands is something that people do when they like one another."

"I didn't know we were at the stage where we hold hands," I replied, trying to get my bearings as Ren led me around a group of tourists. The panic was still clawing its way through me, dragging me down as my past threatened to meet my present.

It took everything in me but I managed to shove all of that back, locking it up, and forced myself to forget what Miles had alluded to. I had to do that. It was the only way I could focus on the now.

"I'm pretty sure that everything we did yesterday is a good indication that we like one another, Ivy."

I pursed my lips. "I don't think liking one another is necessary for all of that."

"It is for me." He passed me a quick, meaningful look. "You feel me on that, right?"

Oddly flustered by that statement, I quickly looked away. "Why are we even talking about this right now?"

"Because you seemed so shocked by the act of holding hands, it distracted me, and I needed to make sure you and I are on the same page."

"Ren . . ."

Squeezing my hand again, we turned onto Royal. "David wants to take down Flux Saturday. He's talking to Miles, and they're going to round up a group of members they trust. But we're going to have to get past

Wednesday night first. He will have the gates guarded, but not just one. Both of them. He doesn't believe that one isn't working, and he's not willing to risk leaving one completely unguarded during the equinox."

I almost got down on my knees and kissed the street out of thanks, but then that would be entirely gross considering the kind of stuff that went down on these streets. "So he believes us?"

"I'm not entirely sure what he believes, but he does know about the Elite. He doesn't know anything about what we do, but since he knows the only way I could know about the Elite is because I'm a part of it, he's willing to listen to me."

"Well, that's just nice," I said snidely.

"Hey, at least he's freaking listening to us. Like us, he knows there's someone in the Order that is working with the fae. That's why he wanted you and Val out of the room. I don't think he suspects you, but . . ."

Cold air hit the back of my neck. "I think . . . I think he does."

"Wouldn't make a damn bit of sense if he did. You were shot by one of them. He can't ignore that."

I wasn't sure. Why else would he make me leave the room? A sick feeling of betrayal twisted up my insides.

"He does know about the ancients, but since they've never been active, he and Miles have kept them quiet. They apparently feared that the fae would be going for the gate, and David was already pulling in extras to cover them, but I don't think they realized until tonight the seriousness of what is happening. I don't even know why he is giving you so much shit about it."

Probably because I have a vagina, and that was just flat out bullshit. This whole *thing* was bullshit.

"Either way, he wants us at the gates." Tugging me to the side and out of the path of foot traffic, his gaze found mine. "Where did you hear about the other gate not working?"

My stomach roiled even further. This is where I had to lie. I hated it, but I couldn't tell him the truth, and I loathed that I was about to bring my friends into this. "I talked to Merle this morning. She said that the gate in the church no longer worked—that all the gates had been destroyed except the second one." As I spoke, I could feel anti-karma points stacking up. "I figured that if she's been right about everything else, she'd be right about this too."

"All the gates have been destroyed?"

I nodded. "Yeah. I guess that's not something the Elite knows then?"

"No. Never heard that in my life." He dropped my hand, thrusting his fingers through his now dry hair. "How does she know this?"

"I don't know," I said quietly. "But if it's true, then . . . what if the fae know that?"

He shook his head. "I hate to say this, but I don't know, Ivy. That doesn't make sense. Not at all."

How could I convince him without telling him about Tink? There was no way around it. "Did he tell you where the second gate is?"

Ren nodded. "We're standing right in front of it."

I jerked, looking around. "What?" My gaze fell to the gray, three-story building. Understanding sunk in. "You've got to be kidding me."

"Wasn't this one of the houses that TV show used on their horror show?" Ren asked.

295

I stared up at the famous haunted house on Royal Street, reputedly the *most* haunted house in New Orleans. A place that harbored a terrible, brutal history. What Merle had said came back to me. The second gate was located in a place where no humans or spirits could rest.

In other words, a haunted house, but ninety percent of New Orleans was rumored to be haunted. "Is this the...?"

Ren shook his head then placed two fingers under my chin, turning my gaze to the brick building beside the grandiose home. "That's where the gate is."

Chapter Eighteen

Monday night was dead. Not a single fae was roaming the streets of the Quarter or hanging out in the club in the warehouse district. Instead of that being a thing of relief, it brought forth a great sense of foreboding. Monday nights weren't hopping by any means, but not a single fae? Something was very wrong with that.

As our shift drew to a close, we ended up back in the Quarter, on Phillip Street, where Ren had stowed his bike. My head was in a thousand different places—the location of the second gate, the possible traitor, what would happen on Wednesday—when Ren asked, "Come home with me."

Standing on the corner of the street, under the faint flickering glow of the streetlamp, I frowned. "What?"

Ren smiled faintly. "Come home with me tonight, Ivy."

I shifted my feet, taking a step back. The request thrilled me . . . and frightened the holy hell out of me.

With everything that happened today, I hadn't had much time to think about what Ren and I were doing, even with the panty-dropping hot kiss he unloaded on me at headquarters or the way he held my hand as we walked to the old brick home on Royal Street.

My heart kicked around in my chest as I stared at his shadowed face. "I'm not sure if that's a good idea."

"It's a great idea. Possibly the best idea I ever had."

Off in the distance, someone howled with laughter. "I don't think—"

"Stop thinking." Ren took my wrist, gently unfolding my arms. "You do that too much."

"I don't think you can possibly think too much," I reasoned as my gaze dipped to where he held my wrist between us. Truth was, I didn't want to go home yet. Since I had no idea what to do with Tink, my apartment above the lovely courtyard was a very lonely place to be.

Ren sighed as he smoothed his thumb along the inside of my wrist. "I'm not going to take you to my place and ravish you, Ivy."

My mind was full of images of him stripping my clothes off, holding me down and doing whatever he wanted to me, and parts of my body got really excited about that prospect.

"Unless you want me to, then I'm all for it," he continued, his tone light. "I'll do whatever you want, just . . . come home with me."

I lifted my gaze to his, and his stare was unflinching, open and honest. The laughter was drawing closer. "If you don't want that from me, why do you want me to come home with you?"

A look of confusion flashed across his face and then he gave me a half grin. "First off, Ivy, I do want *that*

298

from you. Always. Hell, it's what I've been thinking about since the first time you took a swing at me."

"That's . . . kind of demented."

He ignored that. "But it's not the only thing I want from you. I like hanging out with you. I like spending time with you."

Weirdly, that never really occurred to me, which made me feel kind of stupid, like why wouldn't that have ever crossed my mind? Sometimes I felt like I had the experience of a fifteen year old. To be honest, I liked hanging out with him. These last couple of weeks working with him had made my shifts more enjoyable. Not that I didn't like doing my job, but he made things . . . *different.*

Looking up at him, I almost said no—almost. "Okay."

The slow grin spread into a full smile that showed off those dimples, and the urge to stretch up and kiss each of them was hard to ignore. The ride home was as uneventful as the evening, but it was strange walking into his apartment at night, as if we were going there to engage in some naughty behavior.

I was nervous as he flipped on the overhead light then headed into the kitchen, grabbing us something to drink. With a beer in one hand and a soda in the other, he swaggered over to the couch, placing both on the coffee table.

As he toed off his boots and socks, he eyed me through his thick lashes. "You know, you can sit on the couch."

I sat on the couch, folding my hands together in my lap.

He shook his head at me. "There's something I actually want to show you—give you. Be right back."

Give me? What could he possibly want to give me? A kiss? I doubted he had to go into his bedroom to get that. And did I want a kiss? I had no problem with those kisses yesterday. God, I didn't know what I wanted.

Or I wasn't ready to acknowledge it.

Either way, Ren returned and sat on the couch beside me, a slender ashy colored wooden stake in his hand. "It's a thorn stake. It'll kill ancients." He placed it in my hand, wrapping my fingers over the smooth, thicker end. His eyes met mine. "I wanted you to have this. I meant to give it to you yesterday, but we kind of got distracted."

Oh, we'd gotten way distracted. "I can't say a guy has ever given me a weapon of stabby awesome before."

That mouth curved up on one side. "Obviously you've never met a guy like me before."

That was so true, in a lot of ways. The stake felt light, but it was sturdy. He slowly slid his fingers off mine, leaving behind a wake of shivers. "Are you sure you want to give this to me?"

"It's my extra. I'm not using it, and I want you to have it on you, especially going forward." He leaned over, grabbing his beer, then settled back against the couch beside me. His thigh rested against mine; the nearness was comfortable to him, and I imagined if I stopped thinking about it, it would be to me too. "You have to hit them in the chest. As if they were vampires."

I turned the stake over, respecting the craftsmanship it took to whittle this baby into such a sharp, destructive end. "Thank you."

He nodded and tipped the bottle to his lips.

"I mean it." Gingerly placing the stake on the coffee table, I grabbed my soda and sat back. Around midnight we received a mass text from David advising us of an emergency meeting Tuesday afternoon. We knew it was about the gate. "How do you think the other Order members will respond to what David's going to talk about?'"

"I don't know." He grabbed the remote off the cushion next to him and flipped on the TV. "Let's not talk about any of that, okay? I know that's probably not the smartest decision, but babe, there isn't anything we can do at this point that's going to change things."

I hesitated as I studied his profile. "But what about the other halfling? If that gate opens, it becomes even more imperative that we find out who that is."

"We?" He grinned as he took a drink. "I like that. We. Sounds good."

My cheeks heated as I glanced at the TV. He'd turned it on to some movie channel.

"We know there's at least one more member that fits the bill, but I haven't been given the details just yet. They won't say the name until they have something on them," he said, and for some reason, unease blossomed in my stomach.

I didn't have any reason to think he wasn't telling me everything. He'd been pretty upfront. "I'm sorry for not warning you ahead of time about talking to David and putting you in the position of having to tell him about the Elite."

"It's okay."

I shook my head and avoided his gaze. "Actually, it's not. Val . . . she already knew because I told her the weekend after you told me. I had to talk to someone so I could wrap my head around it. I know that doesn't justify doing it, but I wanted to be upfront."

When I dared a quick look at him, he didn't look too pissed. His expression was virtually blank. "Did you tell her why I was here?"

"To hunt the halfling? No. You heard her. She didn't know about the halflings until now."

A moment passed and then he nodded. "Have you've told anyone else?"

I shook my head.

He seemed to mull that over. "Well, honestly, it doesn't really matter now. Even if you didn't tell her, she would've heard about it when she was in that room."

No real measure of relief was felt even though he handled it a lot better than I probably would have. "I should've called you this morning and gave you a heads up or something."

"Hey," he said, curving his free hand around my chin, turning my gaze to his. "A heads up would've been nice, and I would've preferred for that conversation to go down when there wasn't anyone else in the room, but it's over and done with. David knew about the Elite, so it wasn't like I was dropping some big bomb or breaking the rules."

"You already broke the rules with me."

"I did." He dragged his thumb along my lower lip, and if I were a braver girl, I would've caught that wicked finger with my mouth. "For tonight, let's just . . . be normal."

I pulled back, eyes wide. "What?"

"Normal. Like those people we saw at the diner the night you almost slit my throat with your stake," he explained, and I remembered the girls and guys we'd seen in there. "Let's just not talk about any of that shit. Okay?"

I bit down on my lip and nodded as I returned my attention to the screen. A knot formed at the back of my throat, and I downed half my soda to get rid of it. He had no idea how wanting the same thing I did, even in the littlest way, affected me.

As he ended up settling on a Vince Vaughn movie, I relaxed, one muscle at a time, sinking into the couch beside him, his shoulder pressed against mine. We laughed at the same jokes, shook our heads at the same scenes, and it didn't take long for me to realize just how badly I needed this—both of us did.

After the movie was over, we ended up chatting through the credits, and another older eighties flick came on. It was late, well past three in the morning when Ren flicked his tired gaze to mine and sat forward, dropping his bare feet to the polished, cement floor.

"Ready for bed?"

My eyes opened wide.

"It's really late. I don't feel like going back out there, and I'm not cool with you doing it alone. I'm not suggesting anything. Just stay with me."

"Just stay with you?" I repeated. "In your bed?"

"It's a big bed. Like three people could sleep comfortably in there, even if you add a large dog at the foot of the bed." Smiling slightly, he patted my leg while I stared at him. "Come on."

Ren stood, picking up our empty drinks and taking them into the kitchen. Then he headed into the bedroom, holding the door for me.

One would think I didn't face cold-blooded killers all the time by how weak my knees felt when I stood. What was I doing? I decided I didn't know as I walked across his cool floor, my shoes and socks tucked against his couch.

Letting the door drift shut behind us, he crossed in front of me. Next to the bed, he flipped the lamp on. "I have a shirt if you want to change into it. Should work for you." He went to a dresser, pulling open the second drawer, and took out a dark shirt. He walked it over to where I hovered just inside the bedroom.

Amusement danced over his face as he placed the shirt in one hand and took the other, guiding me toward the bathroom. "You can get changed in there. Or out here. I would totally prefer it to be out here."

Snapping out of my frozen stupor, I pulled my hand free. "I'll get changed in there."

"Sad face," he murmured, and then louder, "I'll be waiting."

I shivered as I closed the door behind me and turned the light on. For a moment, I froze in the bathroom, my heart racing with . . . excitement. I hadn't slept with a guy since Shaun, with or without sex. I honestly had no idea what I was doing, but I stripped down to my bra and panties, and then quickly rinsed my face with a splash of cool water.

The last thing I wanted to do was sleep in a bra. Heck, I hated wearing a bra ninety percent of the time. I didn't have small breasts and they weren't huge, but they did like to jiggle when they had a taste of freedom. As I debated whether I should leave the bra on or not, I caught a glimpse of my ultra-bright blue eyes and flushed cheeks in the mirror. I closed my eyes, my fingers trembling as I reached behind me and unhooked the bra. The straps slipped down my arms, and I quickly grabbed the borrowed shirt, slipping it on over my head.

It reached just below my thighs, and I'd definitely not be doing any jumping jacks anytime soon.

Before I left the bathroom, I snagged the bobby pins holding my hair up in a twist, and sighed the moment my hair was loose. Curls fell in every direction, and my scalp tingled with happiness. Gathering up my clothes, I opened the bathroom door and came to a complete stop.

Holy fae on fire, Ren was shirtless, standing with his back to me, and I got to see the rest of the tattoo.

He'd changed into loose cotton sleep pants that hung indecently low on his hips, and that was all. His muscled back was on display, and those vines from the front of his chest and arm crept over his shoulder, tangled down the right side of his back. In vivid detail, peering out from the vines was a black panther, its eyes the color of amber, and its mouth open, tongue a crimson red, sharp teeth a brilliant white

All I wanted to do was run over and touch it.

"I was starting to get worried about you in there." Putting the pillow in place, he turned around. "Thought I might . . ." He trailed off, lips parting.

Both of us were staring at each other, and I didn't know what he saw in my expression, but he was gazing back at me like he'd never seen me before. There was such concentrated intensity in his stare that it felt like a physical caress. The tips of my breasts hardened, straining against the shirt.

"God. Damn," he said, voice husky. "Wearing my shirt might not have been one of my brightest ideas."

"I'm . . . sorry?"

He ran his hand through his hair, the muscles in his arm and stomach doing amazing things as he clasped the back of his neck. "You were in a serious relationship before, right? The guy you lost?"

Not knowing how that had anything to do with his shirt, I nodded.

"You were really young," he said quietly. Ren moved toward me, much like I imagined the panther on his back would've if it was stalking prey. Stopping in front of me, he plucked up a curl that brushed my cheek. He tugged it straight as his gaze swept over my face. "It's a good thing—a powerful thing to see a female you like wearing your clothes. I'd forgotten that until now."

Heat traveled down my neck. "Oh."

"Yeah." Letting go of my hair, the curl bounced back into place. "I'm guessing you've never worn a guy's clothes before?"

I shook my head as my gaze dipped to his throat. The leather string of the necklace was entirely too tempting against his golden skin. "Shaun and I . . . we didn't get a chance to get to that point, I guess."

His head tilted to the side as he curved his hand around my cheek. "So that's his name. You've never said it before."

"I haven't?"

With a shake of his head, he trailed his thumb along my cheek. "You really haven't been with anyone since him?"

"No." Why would I lie about that?

He smiled faintly then lowered his head, dropping a kiss against my forehead, eliciting a shaky breath from me. "Make yourself comfortable. I'll be right out."

He left me standing there as he disappeared into the bathroom, and I tried to make sense of what just happened. All I knew was that the punch-in-the-chest sadness that came whenever I thought of Shaun wasn't there. And I didn't know what to make of that.

Or anything.

Taking a deep breath, I put my clothes on his dresser and all but dashed into the bed, and good Lord, the mattress was comfy! I scooted to the middle and froze, having no idea what side he slept on or if he had a side. I totally had a side—always the furthest away from closet doors because I was a dork. Straightening the shirt out so my undies weren't saying hi to the world, I tugged the blanket up to my hips and lay flat on my back.

I so needed an adult to explain to me what the hell I was supposed to do from this point on.

There wasn't much time to stress over it because Ren returned from the bathroom. His ever-present half grin spread as he saw me. I clutched the blanket, my breath caught in my throat. My heart pounded so fast that I wondered if I was going to have a heart attack, and God, wouldn't that be embarrassing. I swallowed nervously and willed my heart to slow.

Turning off the lamp, shadows fell around Ren, but when he faced me, I could tell that he'd frozen. I couldn't make out his expression as he bent, taking a hold of the covers on his side.

"Ivy?"

"Hmm?"

He slowly edged the covers back from his side and climbed in, and although I couldn't make out his eyes, I knew he was watching me. "I'm happy that you're here."

My fingers eased off the blanket.

As he stretched out beside me, my eyes adjusted to the lack of light, and I could see that he was smiling. "Are you?"

"Yeah," I whispered.

"Good. That's all I wanted to hear."

Wow, the warmth that flooded my chest could've turned me into a puddle of goo in that bed. I waited for him to make a move on me, but seconds ticked by. He seriously was behaving himself. I dared a quick peek at him, and found I could not look away.

Ren lifted his arm closest to me, and a heartbeat passed. I hesitated for a moment, and then, my heart pounding even more, I slid over until my leg brushed his. He curved his arm around my waist and drew me up against his side, guiding me down until I was nestled against his warm, bare chest. Another moment passed and then I lowered my cheek, and the simple pleasure of lying like this nearly broke me right open.

Neither of us spoke after that, and I thought I'd never fall asleep as I felt every deep, slow breath of his. In the darkness and the quiet, I closed my eyes against the tears that rushed me. I never thought I'd feel this or that I would ever lay in another boy's arms and be thinking only of him.

~

I wasn't sure what dragged me awake, but I woke up with a ball of molten lava simmering low in my stomach and the blankets pulled aside. Lips brushed the curve of my cheek, my chin, and then down my throat as the hand at my breast mercilessly teased the hardened tip.

Slowly, my eyes opened as my hand fluttered to the back of Ren's head, my fingers slipping through the soft strands. "What . . . what are you doing?" My voice was raspy, strange to my own ears.

"Waking you up." Ren kissed me, nibbling on my lower lip, and, still half asleep, I gasped. He took advantage, deepening the kiss, replacing the cobwebs of sleep with those of hazy desire.

His hand was under my shirt, his fingers against my bare breast, kneading my flesh, and then his hand slid down below my belly, between my thighs. "You were all tangled up with me when I woke up," he said in the space between our mouths. Rubbing his fingers against my center, he drew a low moan out of me. "Your arms around my waist. Your leg in-between mine."

"Yeah?" I said, barely knowing what in the world he was talking about. Sleep fogged my brain. All I could concentrate on was how he was dragging his fingers. My hips moved of their own accord, rolling up to meet the slow glide.

He inched down my body as he pushed the shirt I wore up. Cool air washed over my heated skin. "I like it," he continued, pressing a kiss between my breasts. "You're a cuddler."

"Nuh-uh," I murmured, and then my back bowed off the bed when his mouth latched on to my breast, sucking hard and deep. Curling my fingers through his hair, I cried out.

"Oh yeah. You're like a little monkey when you sleep." His kisses went lower, and I opened my eyes, watching him in a daze as he kissed just above my navel then circled it with his tongue before plunging in.

My toes curled as an unexpected blast of pleasure rolled through me. "Oh my . . ."

Ren chuckled against my stomach. "You know what that did to me?"

Swallowing hard, I had to catch my breath. "No."

He was below my belly button, trailing a new path of kisses, and my fingers slipped from his hair. He gripped the sides of my panties as his gaze flicked up to mine, his green eyes deepening to a forest green and full of wicked fire. "It made me so fucking hot for you. I couldn't help myself. I had to kiss you—touch you." His voice sharpened. "Lift up."

With my brain somewhere in la-la land, my body was on autopilot. My hips lifted, and Ren cursed swiftly as he tugged my panties off. "God, you're fucking beautiful." He placed his hand between my thighs. "Everywhere."

Ren lowered his head, dropping his mouth to the tattoo on the inside of my hip. He traced the lines with his tongue, and I felt every stroke all the way to my core. Then he kissed the insides of each of my thighs, moving closer and closer. Self-conscious and unnerved by the intensity of the feelings growing inside me, I tried to close my legs, to scoot back, but his hands clamped down on my hips. He lifted them, and my pulse skyrocketed.

His eyes met mine for a second and he said, "You have no idea how long I've wanted to taste you."

Then he kissed me in a way I've never been kissed before. My chest heaved as he parted me, and he drew every moan, every whimper, and every cry with each lap of his tongue. I didn't know if I could take it. The tension built to a point that was almost painful.

I reached for him, to either push him away or pull him closer, I wasn't sure, but I didn't get the chance. He let go of my hips, catching my wrists and holding them against my belly with just one hand. I could barely breathe as he grinned and slipped one finger inside me.

Body jerking, my fingers curled helplessly. "Ren."

"You like that, don't you?" His breath brushed the damp curls between my legs. "More?"

I nodded.

"Say it, Ivy."

God, seriously? His hand stilled. He was totally being serious. "More," I gasped out.

That smile was pure sin as he worked another finger in. "How about that?"

The pressure increased, but then he hooked his fingers slightly, and a strangled sound came out of me as I angled my hips.

"Ah, that's the spot, right?" He sounded proud, smug as he worked with an ease that was actually impressive. "I want to hear you scream my name when you come. Remember that."

I didn't think I'd ever screamed a name, but then his mouth clamped down on the bundle of nerves. Mind blown, I was a writhing heap on the mattress, my hips shamelessly thrusting up to meet what he was doing. My head thrashed as he pressed against a spot deep inside me and sucked on the tiny piece of flesh that seemed to become the epicenter of everything.

The tension inside me snapped, and I did scream his name as release powered through me, starting from my core and radiating out to the tips of my toes and my fingers. I was shaken and panting, his name echoing over and over in my head even as he slowly eased his fingers out of me.

He got up and I could see the bulge in his pajama pants. Caught up in the pleasure he gave me, I met him halfway, gripping his hips as I found his mouth and kissed him. Tasting myself on him, I think I might've been a little drunk on pleasure, a little out of control with the idea of giving him what he'd just given me.

He groaned into my mouth, and my heart pounded as I balled the material of his sleep pants in my hands and dragged them down his lean hips, stopping just below his belly. "Ivy, what—?"

Freeing him, I wrapped one hand around the thick, hard base. His hips jerked and he rasped out, "Fuck, Ivy." He stared down at me, his eyes hooded, his taut stomach rippling with tremors. "You want to do this? You sure?"

Instead of answering, I showed him. Dragging my hand up his length, I reveled in the way his back arched.

"Damn, girl. I didn't do that for this."

Finding my voice, I tightened my grip on him. "I want to do this."

He groaned as I stroked him with my hand. "Move back," he ordered in a gruff voice. "Against the headboard."

I scooted until my back was against the wooden frame, and he moved, placing his knees on either side of my hips. His body caged me in. One hand landed on the headboard behind me and the other curved around the nape of my neck.

I'd done this a handful of times before with Shaun, but that had been so long ago, and it seemed like nothing compared to this. Ren was a man, and Shaun . . . well, he never got the chance to become one.

Pushing those troubling thoughts aside, I kissed him like he kissed me, and at the first taste of him, Ren's hips moved and the hand on my neck tightened. He made a deep guttural sound that told me that even though I was sure there were a whole lot of chicks that could do this better than me, he was right there with me.

I drew him in as deep as I could, and though his body shook, he was careful as he rocked his hips in short, quick motions, holding back even as I found my rhythm. "God, Ivy, you sweet, sweet thing," he groaned. "I can't take . . ."

Ren tried to pull away, but I was latched on to him, and he shouted my name as he came, his large body shuddering as his release rolled through him. I stayed with him until his body arched and he slipped out of my hand and mouth. He kneeled in, capturing my head and tilting it back, kissing me deeply despite what we'd just shared, and he didn't stop as he shifted off of me, dragging me down beside him.

Ren gathered me close, tucking me to his side as he rolled onto his back, his arm furthest from me thrown over his face. All I could see was his warm, sated smile.

His curls were mussed from sleep, adorably disheveled from what we'd just done as he turned his head to me. "Can I keep you?"

My heart skipped, and the first thought that flounced into my head was that I wanted to be kept by him.

I stiffened and my skin chilled like icy water had been doused over my head. The pleasure that I'd been given—that I'd given—cleared, and as I lay burrowed close to Ren, the most horrible thought crossed my mind.

How could I go back to what life was like before Ren when I lost him? Not if, but when, because I would lose him eventually. That was how things worked for me. I loved and I lost, and I cut off that train wreck of a thought before it could become something more, something entirely too powerful.

"Hey," he murmured softly.

My heart was pounding in my chest again, but for different reasons. Nausea turned my stomach. Back before I lost my family and Shaun, I hadn't thought my days with them were numbered. It hadn't crossed my mind, but things were different now, because our days were not infinite, they were most likely numbered down to one day.

Wednesday was a haunting shadow that never truly faded away, and I knew it was the same for him. After all, why else had he asked me to stay the night? There was a chance that we were going to see a lot of death—we might not even come back from it. Ren might not survive.

Panic seized my insides, sinking its bitter claws into my skin. I couldn't do it—couldn't face the soul-crushing grief again, and if things with Ren carried on—hell, even now, losing him would have a shattering impact.

I sat up, tugging my shirt down so my lower half was covered. Oh God, I really had screwed up—fucked this up. I wasn't supposed to let him get close. We couldn't be normal. Order members didn't *have* normal. Out of everyone, I knew that, and here I was, in bed with a guy who could very likely die by the time the moon rose tomorrow.

"Hey," he said again, following me. "What's wrong?"

"I . . ." In the back of my head, there was a part of me telling me to stop, to take a deep breath, but acid filled my mouth. I needed to get out of here. This was a mistake. "I have to go."

"What?"

Tossing my legs off the bed, I stood and headed for the dresser. I stopped halfway, but didn't see my panties, and decided I really didn't need them.

"Whoa. Wait a sec, Ivy. What's going on?" Ren was off the bed, hitching up his bottoms. "Talk to me."

I grabbed my jeans off the dresser, tugging them on without looking at him. "I just need to go home. That's it."

"Okay. That's so not it. You were fine, fucking sweetness in my hands a couple of seconds ago, and now you won't even look at me." Ren came toward me, and I backed up, bumping into the dresser. A look of confusion poured into his face. "What the hell?"

Turning away, I pulled his shirt off and slipped my bra and shirt on faster than I ever put clothes on in my entire life.

"Did we move too fast?" he questioned, putting his hand on my shoulder.

I reacted, born out of a keen sense of desperation. I spun around, swiping my arm, knocking his aside. "Don't touch me."

He took a step back, hands at his sides. Concern filled his emerald gaze. "Okay. Can we just talk for a second?"

"There's nothing to talk about." I started for the bedroom door.

"Did I hurt you? Dammit, Ivy, answer me. Did I hurt you somehow?"

Pushing my hair out of my face, I shook my head. "No," I croaked, turning to the bedroom door. "You didn't hurt me. Not yet." I pulled on the handle, found it locked, then cursed under my breath. Unlocking the door, I threw it open.

"Not yet?" Ren followed me into the living room, staying back a distance as I sat, grabbing my socks and shoes. "Baby, I would never hurt you. Why would you—?"

The words burst out of me, coming from a dark place I tried to stay away from but could feel myself slipping into. "You wouldn't mean to. You'll promise me that everything will be okay, and then it won't be because you can't control it."

His brows knitted as he moved to the other side of the coffee table. "Ivy, I'm not following you."

"It doesn't matter." I slipped my shoes on and stood, swiping the stake off the table and shoving it in my back pocket. I pulled my shirt down to cover it.

"Let me get dressed. I'll take you home, okay?" he reasoned gently. "Just give me a couple of—"

"No! No. I don't need you to take me home. I don't need you to do anything, all right? You're a great guy, but this—whatever this is—isn't going any further. This was a mistake."

Ren straightened as he eyed me. "Dammit, Ivy, what the fuck is going on? This was a mistake? This morning was anything and everything but a fucking mistake."

I wrapped my fingers around the handle, heart racing, and I stopped for just a second, my throat burning. "Maybe for you it wasn't," I said and then walked out.

As I crossed the hall and hit the button for the elevator, part of me expected, maybe even hoped, that he'd come after me, which was so sick and twisted. But the elevator came, and as I stepped inside, the door across the hall didn't open.

Ren didn't come after me.

The elevator doors slid shut and I backed up, hitting the wall of the elevator. I smacked my hands over my face, smothering a raw sob. I pushed it down, I pushed it all down until there was nothing.

Until I felt nothing.

Chapter Nineteen

Tuesday was a fucking mess and a half that went from shitty to shittastic in a matter of minutes. I tried to get a hold of Val, but she wasn't answering her phone, and I thought about calling and dumping all of this on Jo Ann, but she had a pretty packed schedule on Tuesdays.

Tink was still holed up in his room, and the only reason I knew he was in there was because he had The Cure and Morrissey on repeat, and I was about to lose my ever loving mind if I had to spend another second in my apartment.

After showering and changing into fresh clothes, I still couldn't get rid of the scent of Ren or the taste of him. What we had done this morning, what I'd done . . .

My body heated even as my chest ached. I'd never felt like that before, never so out of control and turned on, but those feelings stirred up this morning had run deeper than lust. And maybe I could've handled it if it was just about getting off, as crude as that sounded, but it was more than that.

More. Hadn't I wanted more out of life? If so, this was like taking a class on stupid and excelling at it.

I sat at the edge of the bed and placed my head in my hands. Okay, I couldn't go back and change anything that had happened between us. I just had to deal with it, and I had to be stronger. I had a job to do and I needed to focus.

I'd done what I needed to do, right?

There was no answer, only the droning of The Cure. I got up and strapped the iron stake into one boot and the thorn stake into the other. Picking up my phone, I tapped the screen. There were no texts or missed calls from Ren—not that I expected any to be there. Not after telling him that the morning was a mistake. I slid my phone into my back pocket and hooked my keys to the loop on my jeans, starting toward the front door, but I stopped. Turning around, I faced the hall that led into the kitchen and Tink's bedroom. I started toward his room, but I still had no idea what to say or do with him. I wasn't even sure if I was angry anymore or just disappointed.

I left my apartment without saying anything to him.

With a couple of hours to waste before the meeting David had called, I took a cab to Canal then slowly made my way toward Royal. Skies were overcast, the clouds fat with rain that would soon fall, and the streets weren't nearly as congested as they normally were. I ended up in front of the nondescript brick building.

Based on what Merle had said about the spirits, did that mean the ghosts of the mansion beside it had traveled into this house? Or maybe it was the gate that affected the area; after all, the gate would've been here before any of the houses were built.

I lingered under the painted green iron balcony of the house next door. I wasn't sure about ghosts. I'd never seen one, but that didn't mean they didn't exist. I mean, fae were real and so were halflings, so why not ghosts?

There were iron bars on the windows and the door, and to the untrained eye, that might look like the custom of the houses in the Quarter, but those bars were made out of iron for a reason. I hadn't even noticed the little old house before. God, how many times had I hobbled up and down Royal Street, walking right past this gate? The same with the church?

I would fail as a detective.

Who was in the house right now? Would they answer the door? Probably not. There was no space between the buildings, and the only way to get to the back of the house was through the home itself.

I lingered around Royal until it was time to head to headquarters, my stomach in knots knowing I was going to have to face Ren. As I passed the front of the gift shop, I saw that Jerome was behind the counter, flipping through a magazine. I hurried by in case he caught sight of me. I really owed him a cake.

Upstairs, the second floor was packed with Order members, most in groups of two or three. I lingered on the fringes, away from the door as I kept an eye out for Ren. Avoiding him would be pointless since we had to work together tonight, but I was in total delay mode.

David and Miles were at the front of the large open space, both conferring with each other quietly, and I slinked over to a window, leaning against the ledge until

I caught sight of Val walking out from one of the rooms, her chin down and her curly hair falling forward, but that didn't hide the dark purplish bruise circling her right eye.

"Oh my God." I pushed off the window. "What happened?"

Val reached up, touching the skin under her eye. "I was going for a new look. What do you think?"

I gaped at her as I grabbed her arm, pulling her aside. I dropped it the moment she winced, and I realized there might be more bruises, ones I couldn't see. "Seriously. What the hell happened, Val?"

She sighed as she folded her arms across her fuchsia colored shirt. "I ran into a fae last night that didn't want to go down easy."

"When you were with Dylan?"

"No. It was after my shift. It's not a biggie, though." She smiled, but it sort of looked painful. "I'd say you should see the bitch, but there's nothing left of her to see."

"God. Do you need anything?"

"Nope," she said, then her gaze drifted over my shoulder. Her features were pinched. "Odd."

"What?"

One dark brow rose. "Yesterday you and Ren were locking lips, and today he's standing over there, against the wall, looking like he wants to put his fist through said wall."

My stomach dropped, and I almost looked over my shoulder. Val's gaze moved back to mine, and I sighed. "It's a long story. I called you earlier."

"Yeah. Sorry." She patted my arm. "We can talk later?"

I nodded. David clapped his hands together, drawing everyone's attention. I was surprised to see his wife was here, standing at the front of the group. Compared to his grumpy ass, she looked serene.

"We have a potential emergency situation," he began, and then he launched into a rather blunt breakdown of what could happen tomorrow night. Basically a Fae Apocalypse for Dummies sort of explanation, leaving out any discussion about halflings, which was understandable. At this point, that wasn't relevant.

Needless to say, the proverbial poo hit the fan. The Order members knew all about the ancients, and apparently some had even believed that the almost fabled form of fae had been hanging around, but none of them seemed prepared for the idea that there were several in the city that could be gunning for the gate Wednesday. Neither David nor Miles mentioned the clubs, and keeping that on the down low made sense. If someone among us was working with the fae, we didn't want them to discover that we were on to them.

"The equinox happens at 9:29pm, give or a take a few minutes," David said, arms folded across his chest. "We have to be prepared for anything. Nothing may happen. Or we may be facing the ultimate fight. We cannot allow an ancient to get near the gate. Their blood will open it. No matter what, we need to keep them back."

Both gates were discussed, and I wasn't surprised when names were rattled off, half assigned to the church and half going to the house on Royal Street. Val and Ren were assigned to the house, along with me and twenty other members. One look from David warned me to keep my mouth shut about the belief that the gate at the church was destroyed. Even knowing that he wasn't ready to accept that or take a risk and leave it unguarded, I still bristled.

Nothing seemed to shock the group more than the locations being openly discussed, but at this point there was no risk because there was no doubt that the fae already knew the locations. The only small hope any of us could hold on to was that they'd go for the gate at the church, not knowing it was be destroyed. Still, even if that happened, there'd be a significant loss of life tomorrow night no matter what.

My stomach dropped as what I was thinking seemed to settle across the group. Everyone knew what was at stake.

David cleared his throat. "With all that being said, there will be no patrols tonight."

In front of us, Dylan scrubbed a hand over his jaw and cursed under his breath while I openly gawked at the sect leader. Damn. Surprised, I glanced at Val, but she was staring off into nothing. David and Miles were giving us all the night off. Holy crap, I couldn't remember when that happened. We even patrolled on Christmas.

"If you have families, I suggest you go home and spend time with them," David continued. "If you don't have anyone special, I suggest you use tonight to find someone. Some of you will not be coming home Wednesday night."

Well, wasn't that just motivational?

The meeting was over pretty much after that, members filing out, some somber while others were gearing up for the fight. I turned to Val as I tucked a stray curl back behind my ear. "Got plans for tonight? I can't promise you'll get laid though," I joked.

"I . . . I think I'm going to go see my parents," Val said quietly, and I squelched a burst of disappointment. She had every right to want to spend time with her family. "Maybe we can get together later."

I nodded even though I knew not to count on that. Smiling, I hugged her carefully. Part of me expected her to make some sort of joke about getting the night off in spite of the seriousness, because that was Val, but she didn't. When she slipped through the crowd, heading for the door, I wasn't the only one watching her. David's keen gaze followed her out. Dylan was behind her, and he watched until they both disappeared. Then he looked at me.

I wiggled my fingers at him.

David's frown turned severe.

It was time for me to make an exit. I glanced around but didn't see Ren. I guessed he'd already left. Disappointment bounced around inside me again, and I had no ownership to that. Maybe he was going out to find someone to spend the night with, and boy oh boy, I so did not like the thought of that. Jealously wasn't a green-eyed monster but a fire breathing dragon when my mind produced an image of Ren this morning, his muscled thighs blocking me in, his hips level with my mouth. Thinking about another girl made me want to cut someone.

I needed help.

Maybe if I survived Wednesday, I could check out some therapy. Or at least acupuncture or something.

The clouds had darkened when I stepped out of the building, and I turned to my right, immediately coming face to face with Ren.

I stumbled back a step. Heat rushed my face and then quickly dropped when my eyes locked with his. Standing in front of Ren was about seven different kinds of awkward.

"I was waiting for you," he said. "Though I'm sure that's obvious."

At a complete loss for words, all I could do was stare up at him. The green-eyed fire-breathing dragon was demanding that I ask if he planned on listening to David's advice, but luckily, common sense told the dragon to shut the hell up.

"We need to talk." Ren's eyes never left my face.

I found my voice. "No. We don't. We don't have to do anything." I forced myself to turn away then, because I feared if I did stay, if I did talk to him, I wouldn't be able to distance myself. I wouldn't walk away and I'd . . .

I'd keep falling underwater when it came to him.

"You're a coward."

I froze as those three words washed over me, then I whipped around, facing him as the first drop of rain smacked off the sidewalk. "Excuse me?"

Ren lifted his chin. "You heard me right. I hate saying it, but it's true."

Anger rose in me like thick smoke. Though I shouldn't be surprised that he was finally going to confront me after this morning. He had a right to say whatever he felt was necessary, but that didn't mean I had to stand there and listen to it. "Whatever, dude. Think what you want to think. I'm going home."

"For someone who is so strong and so brave, I never would've thought you'd be such a coward when it really counts," he continued. "I get that you've been hurt before. Guess what? All of us have lost someone close to us, but—"

"You have no idea what you're talking about," I snapped, raising my hand and pointing at him. "You know nothing about what I've lost."

"Then tell me, Ivy. Make me understand."

My mouth opened, but there were no words, just silence and a deep cutting shame when I thought about the night I lost everything. How could I tell him? How could I tell anyone? Pivoting around, I started walking.

"That's right," Ren called out. "Just walk away."

And that's what I did.

~

The distant rumble of thunder matched my mood as I roamed aimlessly through my apartment Tuesday night. The sun had long since disappeared, and I'd seen on the TV that severe storms would be moving through the area the next two days. Perfect.

I stared out the French doors leading to the balcony, watching the rain pound the wooden boards as I counted the seconds between the flash of light and answering thunder. Twenty seconds. When I was younger, Adrian taught me to count the seconds between the strike of lightning and the boom of the thunder to tell how many miles away the storm was. Probably wasn't the most correct method of judging where a storm was located, but to this day it was an old habit.

But one thing Adrian hadn't taught me was what to do with those seconds.

I never knew what to do with those seconds.

Oddly, as I rested my forehead against the cool glass, I wasn't afraid for myself. The fear churning through me, despite the fact there was a good chance I wouldn't survive tomorrow night, had nothing to do with my own fate. We lived with death and we knew it waited for each and every one of us. We were taught not to fear the inevitable, but again, what we were never taught was how to live on when those around us left. The fear I tasted in the back of my throat was for all those who might not survive tomorrow night.

For Val, and even David and Miles, and Ren.

I feared for *them*, but not myself. And I feared what would happen if we weren't successful tomorrow night. Knots tightened in my stomach at the mere thought of the gate opening. Mankind had no idea how frail their position of power was, and once the knights came through, their position would be even more precarious. If they managed to find the halfling and knock boots, producing a baby, then those doors would never close. Nothing would stop the fae from taking humans back to their world again or from coming into ours in far greater masses.

Over the hum of the TV, I heard Tink's bedroom door close, and I turned around. He'd been in the kitchen, making himself a hot pocket or something. Living with him right now was what I imagined a couple faced when going through a divorce. Awkward as hell.

My gaze fell to where my phone sat on the wooden chest. Under the fear was a sour taste of regret. If I were to meet my end tomorrow night, would I do so without remorse? No. Regret filled me, and God, I didn't want to go out that way. I'd made major mistakes in my life and people paid the price in blood, and that was something I could truly never undo, but everything with Ren felt like

I was just stacking on the regret, and the weight was suffocating me.

I slowly walked over to the chest, my bare feet padding across the wood floors. My heart jumped as I reached for the phone, coming up short. If I called him, what would I say? What would I do? Admit that I was a coward, because in a way I was. So afraid of allowing anyone to get that close that I had shut him out. He was right. I'd been slamming the door in people's faces the entire time, and Jo Ann and Val were the only ones to squeak through.

Next to my phone was one of my textbooks. Statistics. Man, I hated that class. As I stared at the book, a sort of epiphany slammed into me with the force of an ice cream truck being chased by overheated kids in the dead of summer.

I wanted more from life than my duty to the Order. After all, that was why I was taking a class I hated to earn a degree that I hoped I'd be able to use while I worked for the Order.

I wanted more.

But I wasn't allowing myself to have more—not really. Not the intangible things that counted most, like friendship with no walls, and real human contact. Lust. Love.

A clap of thunder boomed, causing me to jump. I didn't need to count anything to know that the storm was closer. Sitting down on the edge of the couch, I picked up the remote and flipped the TV off. I looked at the phone again, my lips pressed together.

Could I let go of the fear of losing Ren so I could at least experience him?

I wasn't sure or if it was an option at this point. I'd walked away from him twice already. Tucking my hair back behind my ears, I leaned against the cushions and sighed. I sucked. I sucked huge—

A knock on the door jarred me.

I sat up as my heart lodged itself in my throat. I waited there for a moment, and then the knock came again. Jumping to my feet, I hurried over to the door and stretched up, peering through the peephole.

"Oh my God," I whispered.

Although it was dark, I could make out Ren's profile. He was standing sideways, his head tipped back, and I thought maybe his eyes were closed. Ren was here—he was actually here, and I couldn't believe it.

And I was just standing there, my palms pressed flat against the door, my mouth hanging open, looking like a complete goober.

I glanced down the hall to make sure the door to Tink's room was closed. As I opened the door, I hoped Tink stayed in there.

Ren turned, lowering his chin and dropping his hands from his hips. He was drenched from the rain, the shirt clinging to his body, his hair a wet mess. Our eyes collided and held. Lightning cut through the sky behind him, casting his features in an eerie glow before it fizzled out.

He placed his hands on the doorframe and leaned in as his chest rose with a broad inhale. "If you tell me to leave, I'll turn and walk away. I swear that, Ivy, but I had to try one more time. I'm not going to possibly go to my grave without trying. Please. Don't let me go."

Shaken by how closely his words matched my own thoughts, I didn't move for what felt like forever, and then I did. As if I were in a dream, I stepped aside, allowing him in.

Acute shock splashed across his striking features. He must've thought I'd slam the door in his face. After all, that was what I did, and I was good at it. It was probably the one thing I was best at doing.

I was rather tired of excelling at it.

Ren walked in, and I closed the door behind him with trembling hands. I didn't look at him, but he was standing close enough that I shivered, almost able to feel him. So many thoughts raced through me.

Neither of us spoke for several moments, and then I exhaled a shaky breath. What I said, it came from the darkest part of me. Words I'd never spoken to anyone before, and never thought that I would.

"I'm the reason why Shaun was killed," I said, barely above a whisper. "I got him killed and I got my adoptive parents killed. Their deaths were my fault."

He inhaled sharply. "Ivy, I don't think—"

"You don't understand." My voice was flat and I closed my eyes. "It really was my fault. I did something so stupid, so fucking stupid."

There was a moment, and then he said, "I would like to try to understand then."

I almost laughed, but then I figured if I did, it would sound slightly crazed. If I told Ren how incredibly reckless I'd been, he probably would walk right back out this door. I wouldn't blame him. One could never go past the acceptable level of stupidity, and I'd blown right on by that unspoken line.

Sometimes stupidity killed.

Like the people who thought one more drink didn't mean they couldn't drive. Or the ones who thought sending one quick text while driving wouldn't end with them smacking into someone head on. All bad, stupid decisions.

Mine was pretty epic, all things considered.

"I was two weeks shy of turning eighteen, and I'd already taken the mark of the Order. I know that's not common, but Holly had talked to the sect. Shaun was getting his done and I . . . I wanted mine. They agreed. I don't know what about taking the mark made us feel like we could actually begin hunting. I mean, we'd been training since forever, but none of that mattered. We were young and dumb, I guess."

Opening my eyes, I edged past Ren and walked to the French doors. "Three nights before my birthday, I was supposed to meet Shaun at this restaurant in the city, and I'd dressed up for it. You know, being cute, and instead of wearing the clover necklace, I put on this silver chain thing because it matched the dress." I laughed then, and it sounded harsh. "I left the house without a clover. Seriously. Darwinism at its finest. I guess I thought I wouldn't run across any fae, and maybe I wouldn't have if Shaun and I hadn't been hunting before we were supposed to. We didn't know that once we hunted—"

"You can easily become the hunted," he finished quietly for me.

I nodded as I traced a raindrop down the glass with my finger. Most fae stayed away from the Order, wouldn't dare track one home. I assumed the ancients would probably be different, but Shaun and I had looked as young as we were. One glance at us, and the fae knew we were untrained. "We just didn't think about the fact that if we were engaging fae, we could be seen by other fae, you know? How incredibly stupid was that? Anyway, I left the house and I was almost to the train station. I was going to catch a way into the city through the metro, and I saw a fae. She must've recognized me, because all I remember is her making a beeline for me at the station, right in public, and before I could do anything—which was nothing, because I didn't even have a stake with me . . . I'm sure you can guess what happened next."

Ren didn't answer for a moment. "The fae compelled you?"

"Yeah," I whispered, leaning back against the door. I finally looked at him, and his expression cut through me like a blade. Sorrow dampened his eyes to a mossy green, his lips pinched with bleakness. "You know, I guess it's why I can relate to Merle. She made a dumb choice, went out unprotected. I don't know what happened to her. No one really talks about the details, and I think in a way I was lucky. Not those around me, but I was."

"Ivy," he said softly.

"I don't really remember much after her telling me to take her to my house, and all I do remember was that I was back home, in my living room. I remember seeing Adrian lying on the floor . . ."

Pushing away from the wall, I walked to the back of the couch. A ball formed in my throat. "He was dead, stabbed with his own stake, and for a second I thought I'd done it, but there was no blood on me. His blood was on the fae, and Holly was in the kitchen. So much was being broken." I frowned as the noises of the night resurfaced. Wood splintering. China shattering. The screaming. "I tried to help. The fae—she practically put me through a wall, and Holly . . . she dropped her guard. She came for me, and the fae sneaked up behind her. Snapped her neck."

I didn't realize I was crying until I felt the dampness on my cheeks. I swiped at the tears angrily as I backed away. "Then Shaun showed up, looking for me, and the things she did to him. She didn't outright kill him. No. She toyed with him. Didn't even feed on him or Holly or Adrian. But after she was done with Shaun, she did feed on me."

With measured steps, Ren walked around the couch, approaching. "Honey . . ."

I kept backing away. "Have you ever been fed on?"

He shook his head.

"It hurts at first. Like your insides are being pulled out, and then it stops, and it really doesn't hurt anymore. She probably would've drained me if one of Adrian's friends hadn't shown up—another Order member. They never figured out how the fae got in the house or why it was there. Like we all know, it was unheard of for them to come after Order members, and I never told them the truth. I was so ashamed, and I knew if I did, they would've kicked me out. So instead of them rightfully scorning me, they all felt sorry for me." Humiliation stung my skin. "I think . . . I think Shaun and I killed her partner. She kept mentioning his name. Nairn. I don't know. I guess that part doesn't matter." I paused, sliding my hands over my cheeks as I stared at the floor. "I don't even know why I'm telling you any of this. It's not a justification for how I behaved toward you this morning or earlier. It's not an excuse and I don't expect you—"

"I get it. I know you're not making excuses, but I get it." Ren continued toward me. "God, Ivy . . ."

"I don't want your pity or for you to tell me it wasn't my fault. That's not why I told you." My back hit the wall behind me and the pain of that throbbed inside me. "So don't lie to me."

"Okay. I won't lie to you." When I started to sidestep him, he caught my hands and held them between us. "You made a shit choice when you were seventeen years old. God knows I made some shit choices when I was that age."

"It's not the same."

"It's not? My best friend was killed and I did next to nothing to stop it. No," he interrupted when I started to disagree. "You can't tell me my situation is different, and I have no reason to feel guilt over what happened to my friend if you can't forgive yourself. Maybe neither of us can truly forgive ourselves. Sometimes we do things or we enable things to happen that we can never go back and change. Maybe our shit choices aren't truly forgivable, and the only thing we can do is learn from them and not make them again."

Breathing became hard as the knot in my throat expanded. "I . . . I've lost everyone I loved." My voice broke, and his stark expression wavered. "I've lost everyone."

"Do you really ever lose anyone, Ivy? They may be gone, but they still exist." My lips trembled as I struggled to keep myself under control. He brought my hands to his chest, above his heart. "They still live here. They always will."

I could feel the hold on my control snapping, one fragile strain at a time. I started to pull away, but he let go of my hands and clasped my upper arms. "Ren . . ."

"I'm still here." He dipped his head, his eyes meeting mine. "You haven't lost me."

"But what if—"

"Sweetness, you can't hold your life back on a bunch of what ifs. Who the hell knows what could happen? Either one of us could walk out of this house and get struck by lightning, or both of us could live until we're ninety. Tomorrow we could die or we could come back here. We don't know." Sliding his hands up to my cheeks, he lowered his forehead to mine. "But we're both here right now and that's all that matters. The right now."

"The right now?" My heart raced.

"Yeah. Right now. We're both here. That's all that matters, and I can't promise that I'm not going anywhere, but I'm going to try damn hard not to. That is one thing I'm going to tell you to trust."

A hailstorm of emotion rose up in me, like the thickest barricade finally cracking open. My face crumpled, and I couldn't stop it, didn't even try. Tears streamed down my face, and Ren made this raw sound that came from deep within him as he gathered me against his chest, tucking my head under his as he held me tight, whispering words I didn't understand but were soothing nonetheless.

I didn't know what did it—Ren saying he wasn't going anywhere or the fact that he couldn't promise that he wouldn't. He hadn't even tried, but he was here, and maybe that was what set me off.

Burrowing my face against his damp chest, I let it out. Like a plug being pulled on an overflowing tub, it was slow and choking at first, as if it would never end, then it was gone fast with a trickle of tears and a stuttered breath.

Time had passed and when I finally lifted my head, he smiled at me, one dimple appearing. He swept his thumbs over my cheeks, erasing what was left of the tears. "You're even pretty when you cry," he said.

A laugh escaped me, throaty and flimsy. "Now you're definitely lying. That was ugly crying."

"Nothing about you is ugly."

There was a lot of ugliness in me and I think he knew that, deep down, because he carried the same, but I appreciated the kindness he doled out like candy on Halloween. On the spur of the moment, I stretched up and kissed him. It was a chaste kiss, a benediction and a thank you, nothing more than a brush of my lips against his, but there was a spark between us that lit up every cell in my body, and I knew he was just as affected. A slight tremor coursed through the hands that held my cheeks. I lowered myself onto the soles of my feet and stared into his eyes as a different kind of storm sieged me.

The heat flushing through my body told me that I wanted him. Badly. My mood whiplashed me, but there was nothing I needed more than him. Surprisingly, it had nothing to do with what David had said earlier about us finding someone to spend the evening with in case we didn't survive the following night. Yeah, what I was feeling . . . it had been there before David's less than motivational speech, under my skin, building around my heart. Wetting my lips, I trailed my hands down to his hard chest, and he must've read what I wanted in my eyes.

"Ivy," he all but groaned.

I repeated his words from earlier. "Don't let me go."

His eyes flared as he stared at me intently. "Never."

Chapter Twenty

Ren didn't let me go. Oh no, he did the exact opposite. Gripping my hips, he lifted me clean off the floor, and instinct drove me to wrap my legs around his lean hips. One of his strong, grounding hands cupped the back of my neck, guiding my lips to his. There was an artless, questioning quality to the kiss at first, gentle and sweet before it changed, becoming needy and demanding. I felt the sweep of his tongue all through my body.

His hands roamed to my bottom, rocking me against his hips, pressing his arousal against mine. I moaned into his mouth, and in the back of my head, I really hoped Tink didn't wander out to investigate what was going on in here. But then Ren started walking, all the while laying claim to my mouth and so much more than that.

"Bed. Now," he growled.

I clutched his shoulders. "Agreed."

Ren's mouth moved over mine once more as he carried me to my bedroom. I reached out blindly behind me, finding the doorknob and wrenching it open. Once inside, I tore my mouth free. "Let me shut the door."

He raised an eyebrow, but closed the door with his booted foot instead of turning me so I could. Then he walked over to my bed and dropped me. I landed with a bounce and a giggle.

He kicked off his shoes and socks and was on me before I could take my next breath. My shirt came off in a heartbeat, and then my bra. His hands were everywhere, roaming up my stomach, caressing the hard and aching peaks of my breasts, and then back down, to the button and zipper on my jeans.

Ren had superpowers when it came to stripping my clothes off. Somehow, within mere seconds, he had my jeans off and his hand was under the band of my panties. I moaned and raised my hips as he slipped a finger inside me. I was already so hot and so ready that when he started to pump his finger in and out, I almost toppled right over the edge, but I wanted more. I wanted to feel him inside me.

Reaching between us, I rubbed his hard length through his jeans, and his answering groan turned me on even more. I caught the buckle of his belt and tugged it free. I tackled the zipper, but it took longer than it should have. Ren was thoroughly distracting with his hand between my thighs and the trail of kisses he blazed down my chest to my breasts.

"God," I cried out as he caught my nipple between his teeth playfully.

He chuckled as his liquid gaze met mine, searing me. "You like that?"

"Yeah. Yeah, I do."

He nipped at my other breast. "Never thought you'd be the praying type."

"Never thought you'd be a tease." I pulled on his jeans. "I want you."

"You have me," was his immediate response.

My breath caught as my chest swelled. "Prove it."

Ren let out a ragged breath then lowered his mouth to mine, kissing me with a hunger I had little experience with, the kind of kiss that erased all those that came before and ensured that nothing in the future could ever live up to it.

Wow. He was definitely proving it.

Finally, I got his jeans down his hips. He helped me out then, withdrawing his hand from my wetness. As he stood over me, he took off his pants and the tight, black boxer briefs. Completely naked, he was awe-inspiring. There wasn't a drop of fat on his bones, but his skin was far from flawless. Like mine, there were tiny scars all over his body, nicks from training sessions gone awry and battle wounds that never faded.

"You're beautiful," I said, meaning it. His smile turned crooked and his cheeks flushed. "You're blushing, *Renald*."

"Oh, you call me that again, and I will turn you over my knee and spank you," he warned, and when I bit down on my lip, he narrowed his eyes. "I think you'd like that," he said.

I might, but I wasn't thinking of that when he circled his hand around the base of his length. Mouth dry and the area between my thighs pulsing, I watched him stroke himself from base to tip. I clenched my thighs together, squirming on the bed. I'd never watched a guy do this before, and there was something entirely arousing about it. My skin flushed, and I dragged in shallow breath after shallow breath.

"Take your panties off," he ordered.

Normally taking orders from a guy was the least attractive thing ever, but coming from him, in this moment, if I could wrinkle my nose and make my underwear disappear, I would. Leaning back, I lifted my hips and slipped the thin material down my waist and then my thighs, the scrap of lace landing on the floor.

His gaze slid over me in a slow perusal that set my skin aflame. "Let me see."

Primal instinct told me what he wanted, and the flush deepened as I obeyed once more, spreading my legs. His gaze dipped and his hand swept over his length again.

"Now *that* is beautiful."

The air was so laden with sexual tension that I thought I might combust, and I'd be very frustrated if that happened before he got down on this bed with me, but I didn't have to wait long.

He placed one knee on the bed, on the outside of my thigh, still gripping himself as he cupped me between the thighs. "Please tell me you have a condom," he said as he slipped a finger inside me.

I gasped, back arching. "No. I don't have any. Haven't needed them."

"Fuck." He slowly added another finger.

"You don't have any with you?"

"I didn't come over here, expecting this to happen. That would make me a douche." He flashed me a grin. "We don't—"

"I'm on the pill," I said quickly. "Have been since I was seventeen. I take it every day."

His green eyes pinned me with a molten stare. "I'm clean."

I believed him, and truthfully, after what I'd done this morning, it was a little late to be worried about that, but I really did believe him. I trusted him. "Please?"

"God." He closed his eyes briefly. "Ivy, you don't have to beg me. I'm already there."

My stomach hollowed as he let go of himself and placed that naughty hand beside my head and lowered himself between my legs. Staring up at him, he was a study of proud perfection. He returned to me, sucking and nipping, exploring every inch of my body as if he sought to memorize it with his mouth.

And I was totally down for that.

I arched against him, aching and throbbing as he mastered absolute control over my body. Powerful desire consumed me, and as he brought his mouth back to mine, I felt him glide through the wetness.

Ren lifted himself up, staring down at me in a wild, intoxicating way that mirrored everything I felt inside. Shifting his weight onto one arm, he moved his hips forward.

I gasped, digging my nails into his arm.

"You okay?" he asked, his eyes searching mine.

I nodded. "I'm okay. It's just that I haven't . . ."

"I know." He kissed me softly. "I know, Ivy."

I held on to him as he inched his way inside, taking his time even though his body shook, being so incredibly gentle. Tears pricked my eyes, and I blinked them back. This was like my first time . . . basically because it was only my second time, but this—this was beautiful because it was my first time with Ren.

The exquisite feeling of him stretching me and doing so in such a careful way consumed me, and then he was in, all the way, and the pressure made my body come alive.

Ren was still inside me, his eyes glowing like emerald jewels as he slid his thumb along my lower lip. I moved, tilting my hips up, and we both groaned.

"That's it," he rasped. "God, you're so tight, so fucking perfect."

Hearing that was wildly erotic, and maybe later I'd be embarrassed, but right now all I wanted was to feel more—feel everything. He let me set the pace at first, letting me move under him as I kissed his cheeks, his throat, and followed the leather strand of his necklace, kissing the encased clover before I moved on to each of those poppies.

"You're driving me crazy," he growled against my temple. "I have to take this deeper, harder."

And Ren did.

His restraint broke and he began to thrust deeper, harder, just as he promised. I'd never felt so full, so out of control as his hips pistoned. Each plunge drove up the intensity until it became a feverish pace, and the only sounds in the room were our breathing and the music of our flesh meeting. Wrapping my legs around him, I took him to the hilt and nearly broke the hold. My head spun with bliss, and this—oh God, this was more than just two people coming together and getting off. No question about it. He moved faster, grinding his hips against mine as he wrapped one hand around my chin, bringing my mouth to his a second before the tension was unleashed.

Ren's lips smothered the cry he elicited from deep inside me. The release was an incredible moment, as shattering as it was healing. Spasms rocked my body as I shuddered around him, thrown so high from the tight waves of pleasure rolling over me.

He cradled my hips as he lifted up onto his knees, powering into me, heightening the rioting sensations. For a moment, all I could do was watch the muscles of his stomach ripple and flex, his chest tense as he took me, then I kicked my head back. I bit down on my lip until I tasted blood. It was too much, like being pitched into heaven, and there was no escape. He thrust once more then twice, and then snaked an arm around me, sealing our bodies together as he came, his large body shuddering around me, in me.

My arms fell to my sides, limp and useless.

For long moments, he didn't move. His head was buried in the crook of my neck, and I could feel his heart pounding against my arm. A fine sheen of sweat covered both of us, and I didn't care. Lifting his head, he nipped at my shoulder, chuckling when I whimpered.

"You okay?" He kissed my chin, then my cheek.

"Perfect."

He kissed my temple and then the space just below my eyebrow. "That was amazing. Honestly. Like honest to god, honestly."

A slow, sated grin pulled at my lips. "It was. You . . . you really are wicked."

His gaze slid to mine. "You have no idea." Carefully easing himself out, he frowned when I winced. "Are you sure you're okay?"

"Yes." I forced my arm to move and patted his cheek. "Come on, I'm like a born again virgin. It's quite possible my hymen grew back, but I'm fine."

Ren tipped his head back and laughed. "I don't know about that, but I do know I might've tasted heaven there for a moment."

I laughed again.

"Look at you. Your cheeks are flushed all pretty like." Rolling onto his side, he gathered me close to him. "You're fucking adorable."

"Shut up."

"You're as adorable as a—"

"If you say a Disney character, I will kick you out of this bed."

Throwing a leg over mine, he buried his head under my chin, kissing my neck. "I'm not going anywhere. You're going to have to pry me from between those even more pretty thighs."

"Oh my God."

"True story."

We lay there in each other's arms for what felt like forever, talking about nothing important. There were no thoughts of the past or the future, and for the first time in a very long time, I was right there in the moment, and I didn't want to be anyplace else.

~

Ren woke me Wednesday morning much like he had the morning before, his mouth hot and insistent on my breast, his fingers dancing between my legs. I came fully awake in a sensual haze, threading my fingers through his hair. He knew exactly how to touch me, to bring me to the edge of control, as if he'd been doing it for years.

I guided his mouth to mine. "Goodness, you're a morning person, aren't you?"

Using his knee, he pushed my legs apart, and I felt him easing into me. "Only when I have a gorgeous girl tangled up with me when I wake up."

My back arched as he thrust all the way in. "Any girl?"

"Nah, not any girl." He put his forearms by my head and shifted his weight onto them as he rocked his hips slowly. "Just you."

"That's sweet of you to say." I slid my hands down his strong biceps, curling my fingers around them.

His lips brushed mine. "It's the truth and I'm going to prove it."

And he did with every stroke of his hips and every kiss, his large body covering mine as he rocked into me. There were no words in the early morning hours, and the world didn't exist outside of that bed. My moans and those deep, sexy sounds of his filled the space between us. My heart was thundering, a flutter spreading its wings in my chest and stomach. When I came, I pressed my mouth to his chest, muffling my scream as an explosive and consuming release took me.

Lightning zipped through my veins as Ren pulled out of me. Gathering me in his arms, he sat up and hauled me into his lap. My knees dragged along the comforter as he lifted his hips, impaling me once more. This position was something new, and it seemed to extend my release, setting off quakes deep inside of me as he moved my hips over his. His embrace was tight, and when he came, he sealed us together, hands pressed against my back and my cheek on his shoulder.

Neither of us moved for a while. We were spent and breathless, and I didn't want the next minute or hour to come. I wanted to stay here, like this with him, as long as I could.

But then my stomach grumbled.

Ren chuckled as I ducked my head. "Someone's hungry." Cupping my cheek, he tipped my head up. "You know what?" He kissed the tip of my nose.

I grinned, feeling absolutely boneless. "What?"

"You owned me with just one kiss," he said, and my chest clenched with the most exquisite pressure. "I just wanted you to know that."

Emotion clogged my throat, and when I spoke, my voice was hoarse. "Okay."

A crooked smile appeared and he kissed me softly. "Stay here. All right?"

I nodded, and when Ren withdrew from me and left the bed, I settled against the pillow, closing my eyes as I stretched my arms and legs. A big, goofy smile pulled at my lips. Parts of my body were sore in the most delicious way, and I couldn't remember ever feeling this relaxed. Like I'd spent the week getting a deep tissue massage and now—

A sudden shout from the kitchen, followed by the sound of something crashing to the floor jerked me into a sitting position. Heart pounding, I threw my legs off the bed and grabbed Ren's shirt. Tugging it on over my head, it fell to just above my knees as I grabbed the stake off my dresser and hurried out into the hallway. I came to a dead stop in the entry of the kitchen.

Holy granola bars.

Somehow, in my post-coital blissed out mind, I'd forgotten all about my very special roommate.

Ren had Tink pinned to the counter, a kitchen knife at the brownie's throat, and his large hand wrapped around Tink's midsection. A large bowl was on the floor, brown flakes scattered across the tile like a cereal murder scene.

Oh crap.

Tink's wide gaze found mine as he twisted his head to the side. "I wasn't doing anything!"

"You were in her kitchen," Ren snapped, eyes glittering dangerously. "Eating her Frosted Flakes. What in the actual fuck?"

"Uh . . ."

"I always eat her cereal!" Tink flailed his little arms. "And you're naked. You're completely naked!"

Oh my, Ren *was* completely naked. My gaze dropped to his butt, and good Lord and *Mamma Mia*, so help me, he had a nice behind. Shapely, firm globes—

Fear for Tink's life snapped me out of it. "What are you doing, Ren?"

He sent me a dubious look. "I was going to make you breakfast, but I found this little freak in your kitchen."

Tink curled his lip. "You were going to make her breakfast while naked? Your junk out and everything?"

Ren's grip on Tink's midsection tightened, and the brownie squeaked like a toy. The whole breakfast thing was kind of sweet and Ren cooking naked was really hot, but I needed to regulate.

"Okay." I placed the stake on the bistro table then reached up, tucking my hair back. "I can explain, Ren, but I need you to let him go."

"You heard the woman," Tink said. "Let me go."

Ren's gaze flew from the brownie to me. "You want me to let this thing go?"

"He's my thing—I mean, he's not a 'thing.' He's a brownie, and he's okay. He's not going to hurt anything. I swear." Walking over to where Ren stood, I ignored the way Tink glared at us. "Please."

"He's a brownie, Ivy. What in the hell is he doing here?" He turned his gaze back to Tink, and the brownie paled since the edge of the knife was still near his throat. "And what do you mean he's yours? I come into the kitchen and he's sitting in a bowl of Frosted Flakes like a walking, talking rat."

"I am not a rat, sir! I am a brownie and damn proud of it, you overgrown—"

"Tink," I warned, then wrapped my hand around Ren's wrist. His emerald gaze flicked to mine. My heart was slamming against my ribs. As upset with Tink as I was, if something happened to him . . .

"His name is *Tink*?"

I nodded. "Well, that's what I call him."

"Am I high? I've got to be high." He glanced back down at Tink and scowled. "Is he wearing doll pants?"

"What's it to you?" Tink challenged.

Ren's brows flew up.

God, this was so not how I wanted Ren or anyone to find out about Tink. Drawing in a deep breath, I tried again. "I'm sorry. I should've warned you—"

"You should've warned me," Tink muttered crossly. "I'm the one who had to see his dong swinging around—"

"Tink!" I snapped, sending him a glare that let him know I was seconds away from letting Ren do his worst. "Okay. I can explain everything, but I need you to let him go, and you should . . . um, put some pants on."

"I second that," the brownie said under his breath.

349

Oh my God, Tink had a death wish. "Please, Ren. Tink isn't bad. Brownies aren't bad. I can explain everything. Please, just let me explain."

For a moment, I wasn't sure if Ren was going to listen, but then he flipped the knife in his hand, slamming the sharp end into the cutting board next to Tink. The knife trembled from the impact as Tink flew off the counter, zooming up to the ceiling lamp. The fixture swung as he peered over the edge.

Tink raised his hand and his middle finger.

I sighed.

Ren turned a disbelieving stare on me then stalked out of the kitchen. I'd be lying if I said I didn't get distracted by that ass.

"You got some last night," Tink called from his perch. "You hussy."

I turned my glare on him. "What were you doing? You had to know he was here."

"Oh. I know! I heard him," he yelled back, and my cheeks heated. "I didn't think he'd stay the night. One night stands don't stay the night!"

"Not a one night stand, asshole!" Ren shouted from the hallway.

My heart got all happy about that, but then Tink lowered his voice. "Him? Really? You decide to dust the cobwebs off and you do it with *him*?"

"Nothing is wrong with him, you little jackass."

Tink gaped at me. "I'm the jackass? He manhandled me! While he was naked!"

Shaking my head, I started out of the kitchen. "Get down from there. I need to go talk to him."

The brownie muttered something under his breath, but I ignored him as I went to my bedroom just in time to see that wonderful behind disappearing into jeans. Ren faced me as he tugged the zipper up. "I really don't know what to say," he said.

"I . . . I don't know either, to be honest." I walked over to my dresser and opened the drawer, grabbing a pair of shorts. "No one knows about him. Not even Val."

A shadow passed over his face. "He's a creature of the Otherworld, Ivy."

"I know." I pulled the cotton shorts on then grabbed a cami with a built-in bra. I turned to the side, tugging the shirt off, and quickly slipped the tank top on. I faced him and saw that he still hadn't buttoned his jeans. The cut of the muscles near his hips was extraordinarily distracting. "I haven't told anyone about him, and maybe one day I would've told you, but . . . he's a brownie and I know people like us would judge him on just that fact and nothing else."

Ren thrust his hand through his hair, causing the waves and curls to stick up. "How else are we supposed to judge them?"

I picked up my cardigan from the chair and slipped it on. All I could hope was that Ren would tell no one about Tink. Hoping for anything else seemed foolish. "I don't know? Maybe understand that not all creatures from the Otherworld are like the fae?"

He stared at me like I just flashed him a third boob.

"Maybe I should start at the beginning?" When he didn't respond, I sat on the edge of the chair. "I found him a couple of years ago, in St. Louis Cemetery No. 1. He was hurt badly. His wing and leg were broken, and I don't know why I didn't finish him off like I knew I was supposed to, but I'd never seen a brownie before. Didn't even think any of them were in our world. I couldn't kill him. I know it's a weakness, but—"

"It's not a weakness, Ivy."

Hope that he'd understand everything sparked in my chest. "Anyway, I just couldn't do it, and I couldn't leave him there, so I took him home and healed him. He's been with me ever since, and he's never done anything to put me in danger or hurt me. Well, he does try to bite me every so often." I frowned and shook my head. "I think that's just a weird brownie thing."

"Do you have any idea how powerful brownies can be?" he asked as he glanced at the open door. He took a step toward me. "Do you have an inkling of what is living in your home?"

Tink was powerful when it came to ferreting out my passwords and ordering shit off of Amazon, but other than that, I think he got hit with the short stick when it came to having useful powers. "He's really good at cleaning the house," I said lamely.

Ren stared at me. "So you basically have a pet brownie?"

Thank God Tink wasn't here to hear that. "I wouldn't necessarily call him a pet." He was more expensive than a pet.

"Then what do you call him?"

I shrugged one shoulder. "I just call him . . . Tink." Pulling the ends of my cardigan together, I looked up at Ren. "He's my friend."

"And I protect her," Tink said from the hallway. He was peering around the edge of the door.

"I wouldn't go that far," I said dryly.

Ren looked down at the brownie. "Protect her from what?"

352

Tink was rebelliously silent as he marched into the room, creeping over to where I sat. He ended up clutching the leg of my chair, his body half hidden behind my leg.

"Brownies hate the fae, Ren." I fiddled with the buttons on my cardigan. "They aren't the enemy."

"Is that so?" murmured Ren, watching the brownie.

Tink cocked his chin up defiantly . . . from behind my leg. "They killed my entire family. There is nothing more I hate than the fae."

"The brownies have destroyed almost all the gates from inside the Otherworld. They've been doing more than what the Order has accomplished when it comes to the gates, and none of us ever knew," I explained quietly. "That's how I know about the gates being destroyed. Merle didn't tell me."

Ren's brows lifted. "It was him?"

Tink glared at me. "Oh, so it's okay for you to lie?"

"Shut up, Tink," I snapped.

Ren sat down on the edge of the bed, resting his elbows on his knees as he studied the brownie. I was relieved to see that he no longer looked like he wanted to murder the little guy, but wariness was etched into his features.

"I couldn't tell you how I knew. If I did, then well, I would have to tell everyone about Tink, and as much as I want to punt kick him across the room sometimes . . ."

"Uh," muttered Tink. "Love you too."

Ignoring him, I took a deep breath. "I will protect him with my life."

Ren's head jerked up and his crystalline gaze found mine. His lips parted, and I held my ground. "Please," I said. "Don't tell anyone about him."

A tense heartbeat passed, and then he said, "Well, at least it's not like you have a pet snake, because that shit would be weird. And I guess there are people who have more annoying roommates. I'll be honest, though. I don't trust the little shit, but I respect your decision."

"Well, I don't trust you either, so what-the-fuck-ever," Tink replied with a saucy grin as he stepped out from behind my leg.

Grabbing a scarf off the chair, I threw it at him.

He caught it, clutching it to his chest as he flew into the air. "You gave Tink a scarf. Tink is free!" He flew out into the hallway like a little cracked-out fairy, screeching, "Tink is freeeeee!"

Ren looked at me. "What in the actual fuck?"

I sighed. "He's obsessed with Harry Potter. I'm sorry."

Tink darted back into the room, holding the scarf to his bare chest. "There is no reason to apologize when it comes to Harry Potter."

"You do remember what happened to Dobby, right?" I said.

"Shit." Tink's eyes widened and then he dropped the scarf. "Fuck that shit. I'm hungry. Someone—no name mentioned—ruined my breakfast. So I'll be in the kitchen." He stopped and looked pointedly at Ren. "I got my eyes on you, buddy."

Ren lifted a brow.

Once I heard bowls clanging around in the kitchen, I focused on Ren. "Are you really okay with this? Because I need to know if you're not."

He stood. "Honestly? I think I'm a little dumbfounded by it right now." He walked toward me, snatching the fallen scarf off the floor then kneeling in front of the chair I sat in. "You have a brownie living with you. *I've* never even seen a brownie before."

"I didn't tell him about what you are," I whispered. "The Elite? Any of that? I don't think he knows."

He smiled crookedly, glancing at the door. "I thank you for that. God, I have so many questions I actually want to ask the little punk. Sorry, I—"

"No. He's a punk. He's proud of it." I smiled a little. "He'll probably answer your questions. He likes to talk, especially about himself."

Ren laughed under his breath as he placed the scarf on the arm of the chair. "A fucking brownie. Jesus. Not expecting that."

I didn't know what to say, so I said nothing.

His brows furrowed, and he looked like he was about to say something then shook his head. "You know," he said after a few moments. "I wanted to make today— well, what we have left of today—special for you. I thought I could make you breakfast and then maybe we could go somewhere. I don't know where, but anywhere." As he talked, my eyes widened and my heart squeezed like it had been put through a juicer. "Tonight is going to be hard, and I want you to have this day to just be happy." A flush crept over his cheeks. "Kind of sounds stupid now that I say it—"

"No. Not stupid." Scooting forward, I placed my hands on the sides of his face, the slight stubble tickling my palms. "It sounds brilliant." He turned, pressing a kiss against the palm of my hand and then the other. "You still up for it?"

"Most definitely."

"And if you make breakfast and save a little bit for Tink, he'd be really forthcoming with any information," I advised him.

Ren tilted his head against my palm, rubbing back and forth. Part of me was still worried over how Ren truly felt about Tink, but I did trust him to not say anything, and I could only hope that if Ren . . . if he stuck around, he would grow to accept Tink, maybe even like him. The latter was a long shot, but he was handling this better than I expected, and for that I was grateful.

"Let's do this then."

I let him pull me out of the chair, and still holding on to my hand, he guided me toward the hall. As I followed him, an unexpected cold chill snaked down my spine. Looking back into the bedroom at the rumpled bed and clothing strewn across the floor, all I could hope was that today wouldn't be my last happy day, that I'd have many more.

That I would have a tomorrow and so would Ren.

Chapter Twenty One

Surprisingly, Ren made breakfast and the three of us managed to eat the fluffy omelets without him trying to kill Tink once, and I was kind of amazed by that. Tink had answered Ren's questions about the gates and what the brownies had been doing in the Otherworld, but Ren didn't push beyond that. I could tell that he wanted to, but for some reason, he held back.

After we showered—separately, because it would've been weird at that moment knowing that Tink was fully aware of what Ren and I had done last night . . . and this morning—Ren and I spent the better part of the day along the Mississippi, doing the tourist thing. I skipped classes again, knowing that I'd pay hell when it came to catching up, but I was doing the whole here and now thing. I wasn't going to stress about it.

Although it wasn't the first time I'd ever been on a date, it was sweet and fun and so different to me that it did feel like I'd never done this before. Through idle chatter, Ren discovered that Tink was a baker and the reason for my late night trips in search of beignets.

"You really do care about him," he said, sounding stunned.

It struck me then how much I did, and I should've realized that when I hadn't turned him into a shish kabob when I found out he hadn't been upfront with me. Or when I'd laid out a thinly veiled threat that I would protect Tink.

The day passed by too fast, and when it came time for us to get ready for the night, we parted ways just as the storm clouds were starting to roll in again. Moments after I hailed a cab, he hauled me up against his chest and kissed me deeply, soundly, on the curb of Canal Street, and that kiss was like waking up in the sun. I was hot and bothered the whole ride back to my apartment.

Getting dressed for the night felt strange. As I buttoned up a worn pair of tactical pants, it felt surreal putting them on. The same when I strapped the thorn dagger to the inside of my forearm and tugged the sleeve of my lightweight shirt down, covering it. When it came to everything with Ren, I was most definitely still floating underwater, but I wasn't alone. Ren was with me. I never thought I'd have a day like today. That I'd get to experience that kind of bliss enabled by companionship that only came from being with someone that you cherished and cherished you in return. And being with Ren? Yeah, I did feel precious, and after Shaun I honestly hadn't believed I'd feel that way again.

Or that I deserved to experience that kind of wealth.

But today was like taking the first deep breath of spring. All the simple things we shared today were priceless. I . . . I lived, really lived, for the first time in almost four years.

Staring at my reflection, I didn't let my mind wander too far into the future. I was taking this literally one minute at a time. I tugged my curls up, twisting the long lengths into a bun I secured with bobby pins.

Thunder rumbled off in the distance, and I inhaled deeply, letting my breath out slowly. I was ready for tonight.

"Don't go."

I started at the sound of Tink's voice. He was hovering in the open bathroom door. "What?"

"Don't go tonight," he repeated.

A frown pulled at my lips. "I have to go. It's my—"

"I know it's your job, but just . . . don't go. You don't need to be there," he insisted. "You don't have to be *there*."

Unease curled in my chest like a snake. Tink had never asked me to not head out and hunt—never once. Tonight was different though. We wouldn't be hunting fae. I knew they'd be coming right at us.

I shook my head. "I have to, Tink. It's my job. You know that."

He looked as if he was going to say something else, but he snapped his jaw shut and his wings drooped as I stepped around him. He followed me to the front door, saying nothing while I picked up my keys and cellphone.

Tink landed on the chair normally stacked with Amazon boxes and clutched the back of it. "Ivy?"

"Yeah?"

His pale blue eyes were wide and solemn. "Please be careful, because there . . . there are worse things than death if that gate opens."

~

Tink's parting words haunted me as I made my way to Royal Street. Not exactly the thing I wanted to be thinking about as I dodged tourists caught in the rain and nearly lost an eyeball a couple of times when the sharp pointy ends of the umbrellas got up close and personal.

As the brick house on Royal Street came into view through the drizzle, I saw Dylan standing outside, under the balcony. I thought about the way David had watched him leave the meeting Tuesday afternoon. Did they think Dylan was the traitor? I didn't know him that well, but he'd always seemed like an okay guy to me. Then again, what did I know? Even though the members were like a family to me, they were more like distant cousins I saw on holidays. I wasn't close to a lot of them.

Dylan nodded at me as I passed him. The door was unlocked, and as soon as I stepped inside the foyer, it was like being transported back in time.

A time where it was in fashion to have homes that smelled like mothballs and furniture that looked like something you'd find in a *Pride and Prejudice* movie.

An ancient chaise lounge and couch were situated in the middle of the room, in front of a fireplace I really hoped wasn't in use based on the condition of the crumbling chimney.

There was an archway leading into what I assumed was a kitchen. I could hear members in there talking. I turned to the steep, narrow stairway. David stood at the top, arms folded over his chest as he spoke to Ren.

My heartstrings felt like they were strings on a puppet. They danced and shook the moment I saw him. *He's mine*. Those were the words that crossed my mind, and the tips of my ears started to burn. But it was true.

As I slowly climbed the stairs, I knew beyond a doubt that he was mine.

Ren turned as I neared the top, his mouth tilting up to reveal the right dimple. I didn't know how to act in front of David, so I stopped a good foot away from Ren.

David gave me his typical angry face stare as we eyeballed each other, and then he said, "You make sure you walk back down those stairs, Ivy."

Surprised, I stuttered out, "Y-You too."

I watched the sect leader stroll into a room catty-corner to the stairwell. "I think he likes me. Deep down, I think he really does."

"He does." Ren touched the curve of my back lightly. "Because who doesn't?"

"A lot of people."

"I don't believe that," he replied. "You're just too damn likeable."

I smiled at him when all I really wanted to do was stand on my tiptoes and lay one on him. Funny how a month ago, laying one on Ren equaled punching him in the face and not kissing him. I grinned. My how times had changed.

He stepped closer. "What are you grinning about?"

"Nothing." My grin spread into a smile.

His gaze drifted over my face. "God, you're beautiful when you're not smiling, but when you are? Fucking breathtaking."

I flushed at the compliment and was aware that the Order members roaming around on the second floor were giving us the side eye, but I wanted to say something to Ren just in case . . . in case we didn't get the chance later. Looking up, I met the brilliant hue of his green eyes. "Thank you for today. It was . . . wonderful."

"You don't need to thank me," he said in a hushed voice.

"No, I do. It was probably my favorite day in, well, forever." The heat had moved from the tips of my ears to my face. "I just wanted you to know that." He smiled, showing off both dimples, and I decided it was way past time to change the topic of conversation before I was lost to that smile and ended up acting like a goober. "So, the gateway? Where is it?"

Ren glanced at the doorway across the room. "It's in the master bedroom. Want to check it out?"

Nodding, I followed him across the hall and into a large room that was empty. I imagined that at one time, back in its heyday, it probably contained a four-poster bed and beautiful, handcrafted furniture, but now its bare floors were dusty, its fireplace cold.

I started to ask where the gateway was when Miles turned sideways, responding to something Rachel Adams said, and that's when I saw it with my own eyes.

I assumed it was the door to a closet or maybe another room, I wasn't sure, but there was no mistaking that it was not a normal doorway.

The shimmering blue light shining through the cracks all around the door might've given it away. Or it could be the numerous locks on the outside, because seriously, who had deadbolts on doors inside a house. And if none of that was glaringly obvious, it could be the fact that the door was shaking and rattling, as if something on the other side was trying to get through.

That was because something *was* trying to get through.

Holy crap. That was a legit doorway to the Otherworld. Part of me couldn't believe I was actually seeing one. As terrible as what the gateway represented, I was still awed being in the presence of one.

I stepped forward. "Is it . . . is it always like that?"

Miles answered. "Normally, it's quiet, but as it gets closer to either the equinox or the solstice, it starts to act up."

"And it was always here?" I glanced at him. "This doorway, even before the house was built?"

"I imagine so," he explained. "Before the house, I have no idea how it appeared, but it would've been on these grounds somehow. Once the house was built, our records indicate that the doorway appeared in this room. People never lived long in this house."

Obviously.

Before the Order discovered the door and closed it, the fae had used it to move back and forth between the realms. Coming through the door with humans living in the house had to have been mighty convenient for the fae.

I saw Val walk into the room, her red shirt standing out so brightly amongst the darker tones everyone else was wearing. She headed in my direction, but like me, she was staring at the door.

"That is crazy," she said, stopping between Ren and me. "It's like an episode of *Ghost Adventures* or something. I mean, can you imagine moving into this lovely two-story home and it comes with a door that glows blue and shakes just four times a year?"

I snorted, but Ren appeared largely unamused as he glanced down at Val, but she seemed unaware of the coolness radiating from him. I frowned, having no idea what the deal was with that, but this wasn't the time to question it.

Downstairs, Order members were forming a first line of defense, so to speak. Their job was to block the stairs, and our job was to keep the door protected. I assumed the same thing was happening at the church, as needless as that was.

Something struck me then, and I turned to Miles. "How active is the door at the church? Is it like this one?"

He scowled at my question but nodded. That didn't make sense to me. If the brownies had destroyed that door, why would it be like this one? Or did destroying the door even affect the light show going on right now? I'd have to ask Tink later.

"We can't let an ancient near the door." Miles was talking, but my gaze was fastened on the door. The light was deepening into a sapphire blue. "If one happens to get close, do not cut it. Remember, their blood opens the gates. Push them back."

There were many nods, and as the clock ticked away, the idle chatter ceased, and with the exception of the rattling door, the room became so quiet you could hear a fly sneeze. It was the same downstairs until David announced that it was five till the equinox.

Every muscle in my body tensed as I tried to prepare myself for anything. I reached down, unhooking the iron stake from my boot and clenching it tight. I wasn't going to break out the thorn stake until I needed it. Not even a tiny part of me believed that they wouldn't come in full force, but when we were a minute away, I looked at Ren.

He was looking at me, and I buried my concern and fear, buried it so deep that I felt nothing inside me.

Doing so was the only way I could do my job tonight and not end up in a corner rocking.

Ren winked at me.

My lips twitched into a small smile.

"It's time," David announced.

I held my breath as I faced the closed bedroom door. Seconds tiptoed into minutes, and when nothing happened, those in the room began to shift. The door was still rattling like an army wanted out, and I exchanged a quick glance with Ren, the tension in my back starting to ease.

A shout rose from downstairs, sudden and violent, followed by more. My hand tightened on the stake.

"They're here," whispered Val.

Rachel started for the door, but David called out, "Stay."

She sent him a wide-eyed stare as the shouts turned into screams. "But they're . . ."

I winced. She didn't finish the sentence, but there was no need. My breathing hitched as the sounds from downstairs turned wet and sickening. How could we stand here like this? Ren shifted a step forward.

"Hold," Miles urged from behind us.

His shoulders bunched, and I knew he was having just as much trouble as I was standing here, but then the noises from downstairs stopped. There was nothing—it was tomb quiet below.

Thump!

A loud bang against the hallway door caused me to jump despite all my training. Then another thump and another, shaking the door. A crack formed in the center.

"Uh, guys . . ." I stiffened.

David stepped forward. "This is about—"

The door splintered, shooting large chunks of wood through the air as several bodies thudded against the wood floors. My mouth dropped open. Blood was pooled on the floor, chests ripped open, exposing pink and jellylike tissue. They were Order members—all of them.

A guttural, heart-stopping roar deafened us. Shivers of dread dug deep into my muscles as shapes poured into the room like a wave of death no one could escape from.

Fae—a truckload of fae—flew through the now shattered opening.

There were so many—silvery and coolly beautiful, their eyes pale blue and their gazes sharp. There was at least a dozen and a half, maybe more—probably more. But behind them, I saw him—the ancient who'd shot me—and another I did not recognize.

For a moment I froze as Ren and the other Order members rushed forward, disappearing into the mob. Iron stakes glinted and stabbed, some clattering to the floor. Screams and shouts mingled with the sound of tearing cloth and snapping bones. *Dear God*, the fae were breaking necks like they were nothing more than matchsticks.

I caught sight of Ren as he engaged a fae, slamming his booted foot into its chest in a stunning display of brutality and grace. He whirled, moving like a dancer, shoving the stake where his foot had been seconds before.

I'd never seen anything like this.

Instinct finally kicked in. Fighting was in my blood, in my heritage. Hundreds of years' worth of generations rose inside me, stampeding the icy fear that had settled in the pit of my stomach.

I whipped around. The fae stalking Rachel didn't see me coming, and I shoved the stake deep into its back. A flash of light blinded me for a second then I spun back. A female fae dove at me like some kind of pro wrestler, but I danced out of her grasp. Spinning around, I kicked her back, knocking her down onto one knee. I drove the stake down, and the skin and muscles gave way. Shimmery blue blood sprayed, covering my hand as I leaped back.

I was grabbed from behind and tossed to the side, hitting the floor and nearly sliding into the mess they had made of the Order members from downstairs. A fae charged me.

"Ivy!" Ren shouted.

Scrambling across the floor, my hand brushed something wet and soft, and I swallowed down the nausea as I shot to my feet. I feinted to the right, but the fae was fast, swinging at me. I blocked his punch then whipped the stake down. He dipped quickly, springing up beside me.

"You're about to die," he said.

"So cliché," I retorted, then dipped down. I swept his legs right out from underneath him. The fae went down, and before he could retaliate, I went all Van Helsing on his ass.

I jumped up and started toward Ren. Two fae had him in their sights. I checked the door. The ancient who shot me was stealthily prowling toward it. I changed direction and was cut off by a fae I recognized from the club.

Roman.

He smiled at me. "Hello there."

As I rushed him, I caught sight of Val. She stalked forward with a purpose, darting around Miles, and at first, I thought she was going to help Ren, but she ran past him, the stake clutched tightly in her right hand. Dipping under Roman's arm, I grabbed him from the back and fell, bringing him down with me.

I rolled, bringing my knees up and planting them in Roman's back, flipping him off of me. Jumping to my feet, I slammed the iron stake in his chest as he rose. "Guess what? You failed."

Roman staggered back, but instead of a look of horror on his face, he smiled before exploding in a burst of sharp light. I turned, about to go to Ren's side, when I saw that Val had reached the ancient who'd shot me.

He was squared off with Dylan who was blocking the rattling door. Val would help him, so I started toward Ren, but out of the corner of my eyes, I saw Val grab the ancient's shoulder from behind. Oddly, he did nothing. He stood there as Val yanked his head back, exposing his throat.

I skidded to a stop, my boots sliding through a wetness I didn't want to think too hard about. Time seemed to slow to a crawl as Val swung the stake around in a wide arc. Dylan lurched forward, trying to stop her.

"Val!" I shouted, my heart stopping. The blood of an ancient opened the door. She had to know that. The ancient was too close. "No!"

She didn't seem to hear me. Slicing the stake along the ancient's throat, blood sprayed. Droplets hit Dylan's face as Val let go of the ancient. Stunned, Dylan didn't move fast enough when the ancient swung his arm out, knocking the Order member aside.

Horror propelled me forward, but I couldn't move fast enough. There wasn't enough time in the world to stop what was about to happen. I heard a scream ringing in my ears and only dimly realized it was coming from me. The ancient lurched forward as he swept his hand across his bloodied neck then slammed his palm on the shaking door.

Bright blue light flared behind the door, shining out through the cracks. The ancient that shot me fell to his knees in front of the door, arms spread wide. A heartbeat passed, and then there was a clap of thunder, a sonic boom blasting from behind the door, throwing me off my feet. I hit the floor and air punched out of my lungs. Dazed, I sat up slowly and saw that everyone had been knocked down, and the ancient was gone, as if he'd never been there, but his bloody handprint burned on the door, an unholy blue.

My wild gaze found Ren on the other side of the room. He too was sitting up. Our eyes locked, and whatever relief we saw in each other's gazes faded away. A soft breeze swept over my skin, tossing the loose curls across my face. I turned slowly to the door, inhaling the sudden honeysuckle scent.

The blue light was gone. The door no longer rattled, but every hair on my body rose as an icy chill snaked down my spine. Carefully, I rose to my knees and stood up. I saw Val do the same thing, but she . . . she was backing away from the door and she was . . . *smiling*. I didn't understand, couldn't fathom it, even as she looked over her shoulder, her gaze finding me. The smile only faltered a little.

Oh no. No, no, no.

369

I couldn't be seeing this. It had to mean something else because there was no way—absolutely no way. They had to have gotten to her somehow, but I saw that she wore her bracelet, the one that held the clover in it. I'd never seen her without it.

A lock turned and clicked, the sound echoing through the room like a gunshot. Pulse pounding rapidly, I swallowed hard as another lock unclicked. The doorknob rattled once, twice, then turned slowly.

My heart stopped as I tightened my grip on the stake.

An unnatural hush settled over the room as Order members and fae alike rose to their feet, and then the door swung open.

Chapter Twenty Two

Darkness like I'd never seen before hovered inside the empty doorway. A shadow so deep and thick, it pulsed as it moved out from the entry, the thick edge of it latching on to the wall above the door. It moved, fluid like oil as it climbed the wall and seeped forward. The tin material popped under the weight as it slid over the ceiling. Tendrils of black smoke extended out, whipping into the air. The scent of honeysuckle grew.

"Oh, that's so not good," I murmured, taking a step back.

Wisps of black smoke funneled down from the ceiling, several columns forming at once. I lost count at ten. The shadows spun dizzyingly, revealing a bright blue light from the center. The light pulsed once and the shadows dissipated, as if a great wind had scattered the smoke.

In the place of the shadows stood tall men wearing some kind of dark pants, maybe leather. Their feet and chests were bare. On their right arms was a band with some kind of writing I didn't recognize. All of them had short hair, nearly black, buzzed close to the skull. Their eyes were like frozen lakes as they surveyed their surroundings.

The fae in the room suddenly dropped to their knees, bowing their heads, oblivious to the Order members still standing.

And that was a really bad sign.

I drew in a sharp breath then it caught as another shadow moved from the doorway. A man walked through, not a cloud of evil mist, but a man well over six and a half feet. He wore the same kind of black breeches, but a white linen shirt clung to his broad shoulders. As if he'd grown bored of buttoning it, half of his bronze chest was exposed. His raven colored hair was longer, brushing his shoulders, and his features were astoundingly angular. All the raw beauty the fae seemed to have pieced his face together. He was so beautiful he was almost hard to look at, and it was unnatural, too unreal.

And there wasn't an ounce of compassion or humanity in his features.

I didn't need anyone to tell me who or what he was. The way he held his head high, the slight curl of distaste to his full lips, how he cast his gaze around the room with a look of arrogant dismissal.

The prince.

The prince had arrived.

And the men before him were the knights. They were free, and before the full horror of that could be recognized, one of the knights stepped toward the closest Order member and thrust his hand out, shoving it clean through the man's chest.

Chaos ensued.

Order members charged the knights as the fae remained in their obedient, kneeling positions. Instinct guided me. I reached for my left arm, unhooking the thorn stake strapped there. Grunts of pain and the wheezing sound of last breaths being taken surrounded me as I stepped forward, preparing to engage the nearest knight.

Then I saw Val.

She was walking at a rapid pace behind the prince, who with a simple raise of his hand, sent anyone standing in front of him flying to the sides. The show of power was shocking. Within seconds, he was at the entry to the hallway and then he was gone from my sight, Val right behind him.

I hesitated, my frantic gaze finding Ren ducking under the outstretched arm of one of the knights and popping up behind him. He slammed his booted foot into the knight's back, bringing the powerful creature to its knees. A second passed and then Ren saw me, and I knew what I had to do.

I spun around and raced for the hallway, darting around those who had fallen—some injured, some never getting back up again. I thought I heard someone shout my name, but I threw open the door and crossed the short hallway, peering over the railing. Down below, I saw the bright red of Val's shirt slipping through the front door.

"Val!" Taking the steps two at a time, I rushed through the foyer and caught the front door before it swung shut. I burst outside, startling a group of teenagers standing on the curb.

Looking left and right, I caught sight of Val heading toward the French Quarter. My brain had clicked off.

Duty demanded that I go after the prince. I'd been the closest to the door, and I knew others would soon be in pursuit—if they could get out of that house, but it was more than just duty.

I had to get to Val. Maybe it was shock, or maybe it was denial that she had purposely enabled the ancient to open the door—that she had willingly left with the prince. Deep down, I knew that she was a traitor, that she had *already* betrayed us, but some little part of me thought I could fix this, if I could just get to her. Because she had to have been compelled. Maybe she'd been caught without protection like Merle—like I had been.

Picking up speed as they turned onto St. Phillip Street, I feared I knew where Val was leading the prince. All I could hope was that I was wrong. Legs aching, I pushed, dodging streetwalkers and panhandlers. My lungs seized when I passed the Irish pub and saw Val's red shirt a second before it disappeared.

No. No.

I pushed harder than I ever had before, nearly out of breath when I reached the side entrance of Mama Lousy. Heart sinking, I yanked open the door and peered up the staircase.

The normally closed, secured door was open.

Dread settled like a cannonball in the pit of my stomach as I climbed the stairs. As I neared the top, the metallic scent was so strong that I could taste it in the back of my throat. Clearing the stairs, I stepped into the room and swallowed a hoarse cry.

Harris lay on his back, his eyes glassy and unfocused. The front of his shirt was torn and covered in red. A puddle of blood seeped out from under him, spreading across the beige carpet.

Anger and horror warred inside me as I stalked forward, toward the back of the room and the stairwell that led to the third floor, clenching the stake until my knuckles hurt. "Valerie!" I shouted.

A door to my right slammed shut, and I whirled. Val stood there, holding something the size and shape of a bowling ball in her arms. It was covered with a black cloth. I had no idea what she was carrying, and in that moment, I didn't even care.

"Why?" I asked, my voice cracking halfway through the one single word.

Tight curls bounced as she shook her head and edged toward the door. "I wish it hadn't been you that came after me."

Before I could respond, cold air danced along the nape of my neck. I spun around, my breath catching as I saw the prince standing before me. Two words pretty much summed up how I felt about that.

Oh shit.

I heard the door close behind me, and even though I knew Val had made her escape and she had left me with this—this thing, I didn't take my eyes off of him.

The prince cocked his head to the side, studying me intently like I was an odd bug under a microscope. "Your hair," he said. His voice was odd, an accent that reminded me of someone from England, but different, more lyrical. "It is the color of fire."

Uh.

"It's rather . . . abrasive," he added, almost as an afterthought.

I blinked, kind of stunned because there was a good chance that the prince of the Otherworld just insulted my hair color. Frankly, I couldn't believe I was even standing in front of the prince. "I'm not here to talk about my red hair."

He stared at me with icy eyes. "You're here to fight me then?"

"I'm here to end you."

A soft, musical laugh radiated from him. "You humor me, and I am feeling . . . kind." He spoke the last word like he was unfamiliar with it. "I shall let you live."

When he stepped to the side, I blocked him. His gaze flicked to the stake I held, and his lips curled into a slow, utterly creepy smile that did nothing to add warmth to his face. "A thorn birch stake from the Otherworld, I assume?"

"You betcha."

"You think just because you hold one of them that you can use it successfully against me? That is silly." He dipped his chin and long strands of black hair fell against his chest. "And fatal."

My heart was thundering in spite of my words. "You talk a lot."

He drew back, surprise flashing across his features. "I do not wish to harm a female," he said in his weird accent. His cold gaze drifted over me. "I find that there are more pleasurable things to engage in with the fairer sex."

"Ew," I spat. "Gross."

He lifted a dark brow. "My kindness is rapidly diminishing."

There was a significant part of me that wanted to turn and run. This was the prince, and despite the situation I just put myself in, I wasn't stupid. Trained as I was, squaring off with the prince was tantamount to suicide, but my duty—what I'd been raised to do—was that I *never* ran from the fae. I had committed an act in the past that had gone beyond dereliction of duty, and I would not do that again.

I held my ground.

The prince sighed heavily then snapped forward, gripping my wrist. The contact made me gasp. His skin was cold. "I give you one last chance." He increased the pressure on my wrist, but I held on to the stake. "You will not like how this ends, my lovely little bird."

"I'm not your anything, buddy."

"Too bad." Then he pushed me with just a flick of the hand, but it was enough force to send me skidding across the carpet.

Apparently, his creepy Casanova speech wasn't all pageantry. I caught myself before I fell. He hadn't hurt me, and it seemed like he was giving me one last chance, but too much was at stake for me to turn and run. "What did you do to Valerie?"

"Who? The little girl who was just here?" He tipped his head back. "I did nothing. I think she is . . . perhaps intelligent? She knows we cannot be stopped."

"No." I shook my head as fury built inside me. "She would never willingly help your kind. She must've been compelled to do so."

"If that makes you feel better."

Holding on to the disbelieving anger, I launched forward and spun to my left. I swung with the stake, but the space where he'd stood was empty. I stumbled back. "What the . . .?"

"Too slow."

I spun around and found him standing there, a small smile on his face. I dropped, sweeping my leg out, but hit nothing but air again.

"You cannot fight me, little bird."

Now I was starting to get irked. Jumping to my feet, I spun, about to deliver one hell of an awesome roundhouse kick, but the prince popped out of existence and then his arms were around me. He lifted me off my feet like I was nothing but a small child troubling him.

"I no longer have any more patience," he said into my ear, sending an icy chill down my spine. "Or kindness left in me."

Oh damn.

Throwing my head back, I hit his chin, snapping his head to the side. The prince dropped me and my knees cracked off the floor. I lifted my head to find him standing directly in front of me.

Double damn on a Sunday.

There was no time to react. His hand was suddenly around my throat, and he lifted me clear off the floor. I swiped out with the stake, grazing his chest. Blood hissed out from the shallow wound, bubbling like lava.

Speaking in a language I didn't understand, he caught my wrist holding the stake and twisted until my hand opened despite my frantic attempt to hold on to it. The stake slipped from my grasp, falling harmlessly from my fingers, and then both hands were around my neck.

I'd taken my last breath before I realized it. Panicked, I kicked at him and clawed at his grip, but his fingers dug in deep. "Fly, little birdie."

I was suddenly soaring backward through the air. I hit one of the empty folding tables, toppling it over. I landed on the floor on my side, dragging in deep breaths around the pain lancing up and down my ribs.

Jesus, I could barely breathe through it. I pushed onto my forearms, my body trembling with the effort to stand. My chest felt too constricted as I lifted my head. One second he was across the room and the next he was right in front of me. Reaching around blindly, I grabbed a metal chair and swung, crying out as the pain in my side knocked the wind out of me.

"Please," the prince said, catching and ripping the chair out of my hands.

Blazing pain rushed across my jaw and the side of my face as I was served an epic backhand with a metal chair. I stumbled to the side, dropping to my knees. Blood pooled in my mouth, spilling out between my lips—my torn lip. Something—his foot?—slammed into my stomach, flipping me onto my back. Before I could taste the raw fear building in the back of my throat, the panic that surely came seconds before you knew you were in trouble, there was a flash of bright light behind my eyes as another wave of pain burst along my cheek.

I was going to die.

In that moment, the clarity of the situation rang out. Before, I believed I hadn't been afraid of dying but of living while everyone else perished around me, but I was wrong. A terror I never knew before rose like insidious smoke, choking me. I didn't want to die. Not now. Not when I'd just started to really live again. Not when I was falling for Ren, falling in—love? Oh God. The too little, too late realization cut deeper than the physical pain, lighting up my chest. Tears rushed my eyes, but I could barely see out of them as it was. They didn't seem to be working right.

Pain . . . pain was everywhere. With every breath I took it overloaded my senses. Something important inside me had come unhinged, split wide open. A searing hurt roared through me as I felt the prince kneel over me, his knees on either side of my body. I tried to lift my arms, but every nerve ending was firing in rebellion. A darkness clung to the edges of my consciousness, outlining the world around me in a smoggy haze. My tongue felt too heavy as the prince's blurry face came into view.

"You should've left when you had the chance, little bird." Disgust cloaked his tone, and then he leaned down, his face in mine. "I gave you the . . ." He trailed off, inhaling deeply, audibly.

I sensed that the prince had frozen above me, and then I felt his hand on my cheek. He raised it to his mouth, his fingers tipped in red. The encroaching darkness was spreading, but I thought . . . I thought he had tasted my blood, and that just put the fuckity in the fuck.

He jerked back, and I had the distinct impression that his skin had paled and then he was in my face again. "No," he said.

Then he made a sound that reminded me of a curse before whispering a word I didn't understand—a word that was English, but couldn't have been what I thought he'd said.

Reaching between us, he gripped the collar of my shirt with both hands and tore it open like it was made of tissue paper. My heart, weak and spent, stuttered as a different kind of panic set it. He placed his hand on the center of my chest, and his hand didn't roam, but his . . . his palm warmed and the heat scalded my skin, burning deep into the tissue and muscles. The strangest fire rushed through me.

A door somewhere burst open, wood splintering against the wall. There were shouts—some recognizable but sounding so very far away. The prince rose with a rush of chilled air. He seemed to collapse into himself, and where a man once stood, there was only a raven.

The creature spread its majestic wings, like two feathered arms. The raven rose to the ceiling, disappearing out of my sight, and that . . . that one word cycled over and over in my scattered thoughts as someone hit the ground next to me. The voices increased, and I thought that maybe it was Ren beside me, that maybe he was the one touching me so carefully, but all I could hear was that one word the prince had whispered.

Halfling.

Chapter Twenty Three

Time . . . time moved strangely for me. I had no real concept of it. All I became aware of at some point was that I'd been moved from the rough carpet and placed on something much softer. A bed maybe? Then I'd eventually heard a low beeping that was persistent, ticking away in the background—a heart monitor. Once I managed to open my eyes—my one eye actually— through my blurred vision I was able to make out the off-white drop ceiling and low lights. There was a distinct antiseptic scent permeating the air. Dumbly, I realized I must've been in a hospital, and if I was here instead of headquarters, then things were serious, but I was too tired to chase that thought.

I had no idea how much time passed like that, when I would become aware of my surroundings for a few moments here and there. Once I thought I *felt* Ren near me. Another time I thought I heard Val's laughter, but that thought didn't make sense to my addled mind. There were reasons why I hadn't heard Val's laughter. And then there were other moments when I woke up and the only thing I could think about was what the prince had said to me.

Halfling.

This time, though, as I crawled through the darkness, I was about to pry one of my eyes open, and when I blinked, bringing the ceiling back into focus, I didn't fade away immediately.

I drew in a deep breath and winced as dull pain radiated up and down my sides. I tried to swallow, but my throat felt raw like I swallowed a mouthful of nails. The more moments that danced on by, the more pain I became aware of. My face *hurt*. Hurt like I'd run face first into a brick wall then motor-boated it. My jaw ached, so did my left eyeball—like my entire eyeball. A steady throbbing emanated from my right wrist. A fire burned bright in my ribs.

Waking up sucked. God.

I wiggled my fingers, relieved to find that they worked. Next, I would attempt my toes, but before I could do the system check, there was movement in the room.

The bed dipped slightly, and then I saw the most beautiful green eyes, two emerald jewels plucked out of a mine and placed behind thick lashes, shining out from a striking set of features that I'd come to . . . love. My heart started racing, and the beeping matched the pace. I loved him. I did. Somehow it had happened in the mix of all of this.

"Hey," he said softly, staring at me like a man who never thought he'd be holding this conversation. "There you are sleepy-butt. You gonna stay with me this time?"

I focused on him with my one eye as emotion built in my throat. What put me here, in this bed, lingered in the back of my mind, not forgotten, but just . . . *there.* "Hey," I managed to croak.

A relieved smile appeared on his face, softening the dark shadows under his eyes. His hair looked like he'd run his hand through it many times. He stared at me a moment then reached for the stand next to the bed. "You thirsty?"

I started to nod but realized that wasn't a smart idea. "Yeah."

Ren poured water from a pitcher into a plastic cup. "Okay. Just a little." He slipped one hand carefully under my head and lifted, bringing the cup to my lips. The cool water stung my mouth and throat, but it was like swallowing heaven. He pulled back before I could chug it like a college drinking game. I glared at him with one eye.

"Slowly." He laughed, his eyes lightening. "I don't want you to get sick on top . . ." His jaw flexed as he thrust those fingers through his hair again. "On top of everything else."

Everything else—my aching face, battered ribs, but I was alive and that shocked me, because I'd felt something serious break inside me. Something really bad. My brows pinched.

"God, Ivy . . ." Clearing his throat, he leaned down and kissed me gently on the tip of my nose. "I haven't spent one moment not freaking the fuck out. I thought . . . when I saw you in that room . . ."

The raw pain in his voice hurt to hear. "I'm okay, I think."

"You think?" He laughed outright at that, his laugh deep and throaty. When he lifted his head, I thought there was a sheen to his eyes. "You're in the hospital near your house—Kindred Hospital. We couldn't keep you at headquarters."

After another slow drink of water, I managed to get my tongue working. "How . . . what's happened?"

"Ivy." He carefully brushed back a wayward curl as a look of deep pain sliced through his features. "Do you not remember?"

"I . . . remember." I settled back against the pillows, strangely exhausted despite the fact I had a feeling I'd been playing Sleeping Beauty for a while. "What day is it?"

He didn't look like he wanted to answer at first. "Saturday night."

"What?" I started to sit up, panic exploding like buckshot, but he gently pressed down on my shoulders.

"It's okay. You need to stay in this bed. Just for a little longer. You were hurt pretty badly, Ivy." His hands lingered.

"But . . ." I glanced around the room, seeing that we were alone. "But the knights—the prince, they got out."

He shook his head. "Strangely, it wasn't the giant apocalypse that we thought it would be. The Order—what's left of the Order—has been on patrol every night since then. We haven't seen a single knight *or* that motherfucker. David and a few are heading to Flux tonight, but I have a feeling they aren't going to find anything there."

My thoughts were sluggish, trying to follow what he was saying. "That doesn't make sense."

"No, not really, but wherever they are, whatever they're doing, they are in hiding." He smiled at me, but the act didn't reach his green eyes. "We were able to get the gate closed again."

I let that sink in, but what stayed at the forefront of my thoughts was what he'd said. *What's left of the Order.* "How many did we lose?"

Ren cast his gaze to the side, the muscle along his jaw working. "Sixteen."

Oh my God, I couldn't even . . . I squeezed my good eye shut. The rising sorrow nearly made me wish I was still swimming in that darkness. "Have you all found her . . . Val?" It hurt even saying her name.

"No. No one has seen her either, not even her family."

God, what had she done? My thoughts roamed back to seeing her at headquarters. "She was carrying something, Ren. She went there for a reason. She had something covered in black."

Ren nodded slowly. "I know. Remember Merle mentioning some kind of crystal? David had one stored in a room on the third floor, among other weird shit. I don't know what the importance of the crystal is." He looked away, his shoulders rising with a deep breath. "David hasn't said what the hell it is, and I have no idea."

I thought about the room that David never allowed anyone in, but how had Val known it was there? To be honest, I'd forgotten about the crystal the moment I learned about halflings.

"I figured Merle might know, but I haven't . . . well, to be honest, I haven't really cared about that right now. I've only cared about you," he said, and my gaze drifted over him. His brows furrowed as he wrapped his hand around my left one and squeezed gently. "I know you don't want to hear this, but I want to kill her for doing that."

Yeah, I didn't want to hear that.

"You could've died and I—" He cut himself off, and when I reopened my eye, he was staring at the space near me, at the monitor. "I wouldn't know what to do."

My breath hitched. "I'm . . . I'm here." It sounded lame, but it was all I could say.

His gaze flicked to mine. "You are, but you should have never had to face the prince—any of that. What were you thinking?" He swallowed. "Going after him was like putting a loaded gun to your head."

"It was my duty."

He shook his head slowly. "It was suicidal. You're incredibly brave, Ivy. You're strong and courageous, but that was insane, and I wish you never had to face that."

I wished that too. My thoughts floated back to headquarters, and I wondered if I'd ever be able to walk in there again and not think about fighting the prince or what he said.

Halfling.

A shudder rolled through me. Did the prince think I was a halfling? There was no way—no way. An ancient had been near me when I bled before, but . . . but the prince had been right on me when he sensed it.

He'd tasted my blood.

"Hey, let's not talk about any of this." Ren brushed his lips across my temple. "Okay?"

But I had to ask. "Do you think she was compelled? Val?"

"I don't know, Ivy. It's possible, but . . ."

I suddenly wanted to cry. The likelihood of her being compelled was slim. Compulsions didn't last forever unless they were feeding on her, and if that was the case, she was probably already too far gone.

She was already gone.

Without asking, I knew orders to bring Val in had been placed by the Order, and it would be a dead or alive sort of thing. Mostly dead. Because other Order members would be gunning for her ass. Her betrayal hurt just as badly as the prince opening a can of whoop ass on me.

Ren swept his thumb over my hand, and I forced a smile even though it wasn't the most pleasant of all feelings. "How bad do I look?" I asked.

"You never looked better."

"You're such a liar. I can *feel* how much of a hot mess I am right now."

He raised my hand to his lips and kissed the center of my palm. "You're here. I don't care how you look. Not when I thought I'd lost you."

My heart expanded in my chest, and I almost—almost—said those three little words. Our gazes collided and held. "Did you think you'd get rid of me that easily?"

Ren smiled, showing off his dimples. "Honey, that's the last thing I ever want."

~

Sunday evening I was discharged from the hospital and was immediately whisked away to my apartment where I discovered that while I'd been out like a burnt out light bulb, Ren had actually checked in with Tink.

That alone almost sent me back to the hospital.

According to the hyped up brownie, Ren had stopped by daily, giving him updates and had not once been 'naked' or tried to kill him. When I looked at Ren, he'd actually looked embarrassed as if he'd been caught fraternizing with the enemy.

While my injuries could've been worse—should've been worse—I was exhausted and ended up spending most of Sunday through Tuesday in bed with both Ren and Tink catering to my every need, which was interesting to see those two sort of working together.

I had no idea how I was going to make up all the time I missed in class. Talking to my advisor was on my immediate to-do list once I didn't look like I shoved my face through a meat grinder.

Tuesday evening I'd migrated out to the living room. Ren sat at the end of the couch, and I was tucked between his legs, resting against his chest. I'd finally upgraded from soup to real food, which meant I'd devoured half a box of pralines while Tink forced us through a marathon of Harry Potter movies.

"Do you need to repeat every single line from the movie?" Ren asked at one point.

Tink huffed. "It increases the enjoyment of the film."

"Maybe for you, but not for the rest of the world," Ren muttered, and I smiled.

I ended up falling asleep there with Tink sitting on the other arm of the couch, and Ren with his arms looped carefully around me. Every night since I got out of the hospital Ren had stayed with me, and he'd been there when I woke up in the middle of the night, a scream echoing in my ears. And he'd been there to ease the terrors that plagued me in my sleep. I had no idea what I was dreaming about. Each time I woke, there were no images.

On Wednesday, Ren headed back to work, and tomorrow, if I was feeling up to it, I would head into the Quarter to see David. With us losing so many members,

I needed to get back out there. Not that anyone was pressuring me, but I needed to.

I needed to find Val.

That was going to be priority number one, and while I knew David and the Order members were looking for her, no one knew her better than I did. No one. I didn't plan on telling Ren, since I knew he'd flip, but I had to try and find her.

Shuffling into the bathroom, I cringed as I got a good look at myself. My left eye was now opened to a thin slit. The entire left side of my face looked like someone had smacked me with grape and strawberry jam. My lower lip was swollen and torn in the middle. I looked like road kill with greasy, limp curls. Hot.

I heard the front door open then Tink shouted, "Aren't you supposed to be at work?"

"You're not my keeper," was Ren's response.

Curious why he was here as it was only seven in the evening, I ambled out to the bedroom just as he filled the doorway. Concern immediately blossomed in the pit of my stomach. "Is everything okay?"

He grinned as he strode toward me, one arm behind his back. Over his shoulder, I saw Tink hovering in the air. "I just wanted to stop by real quick. Make sure you're okay."

"You could've texted me . . . wait." I sniffed the air. "What is that I smell?"

He stopped in front of me, moving his hand out from behind him. He was holding a bag from Café Du Monde.

Tink squealed like a fifteen-year-old girl at a One Direction concert. Zooming into the room, he snatched the bag from Ren's hand and flew out. Ren turned, frowning. "Save one for her, you little ass!" He turned back to me, narrowing his eyes. "I really don't like that thing."

"I'm sure the feeling is mutual, but thank you for the beignets."

"It was really just an excuse to see you." Reaching out, he started to unbutton my cardigan. "I hate the idea of leaving you alone right now."

I watched him as he lined up the buttons with the correct holes since I'd haphazardly clasped it together. "I'm not alone."

"That little freak doesn't count."

"Hey. He's my freak."

Ren shook his head then cupped my unmarred cheek. "Are you sure you're okay? I can talk to—"

"I'm okay. I swear. I plan on taking a shower, then crashing on the couch, and hopefully, if Tink doesn't devour all of them, eat sugary goodness until I pass out."

"Okay." Dipping his head, he gently kissed the corner of my lips. "I'll be home as soon as I can."

Home? Here? Here was home to him? Oh my God, my heart swelled to the point I thought I'd float up to the ceiling. I don't even know what I said to him when he left, but I was still standing in the middle of my bedroom like a doofus.

Oh God, I was head over heels, drowning underwater, in love with Ren—with *Renald Owens*. I was in love with a dude whose real name was Renald. This wasn't the first moment I realized that, but each time I thought it, it shocked me straight to my core.

Shaking my head, I turned to head back into the bathroom when my gaze danced over the dresser. I stopped, my heart feeling like someone had taken a tack to a balloon.

Ren had retrieved the thorn stake I'd dropped during my fight with the prince. Right now, it was on my dresser, lined up with my iron stakes.

Halfling.

I shut my eyes. It didn't make sense. The prince was just being . . . creepily weird. But that didn't explain what he'd done before Ren and the others showed up. He'd . . . put his hand on my chest and I felt this warmth inside me. I think he'd healed me. I know he did. That was the only reason why I was standing right now and not in an urn. But there was no way. I took a step toward the dresser, then another.

There was one way to find out. I knew what would happen if I cut myself with the stake. Either I would bleed normally and end up feeling stupid—ridiculously stupid but happy. Or it would . . .

I reached out, picking up the stake. I shook my head again and started to put it back on the dresser, but I cursed under my breath and opened my left hand, palm up.

"What are you doing?"

I gasped, turning around to see Tink in the doorway. Powdery sugar covered the front of his doll shirt. I started to say nothing, but the words tumbled out of my mouth. I hadn't told him anything of what had happened beyond what Ren told him. "When I fought the prince, he said something to me—I think he *did* something to me. You see, I was . . . I was really hurt. Worse than this." I gestured at my face with my free hand. I think he healed me. Is that possible or am I crazy?"

Tink said nothing and the sense of dread grew. I drew in a shuddering breath.

"He was going to kill me. I know he was. Even though he gave me a chance to leave, he was going to kill to me. But he healed me, and he . . . the prince . . . said halfling. When I was bleeding, he said *halfling*."

Tink's expression fell, and my heart followed. "Ivy."

I couldn't catch my breath. My skin suddenly felt cold.

He flew into the room and several moments passed. "We—the brownies—have always been able to sense the Otherworld in other creatures, no matter how minimal. In a way, it made us valuable to the others," he explained quietly, his pale gaze sharp and fixed on me. "Fae, ancient or not, aren't bloodhounds. They have to be right on someone to scent the half in them."

And the ancient who'd shot me, the one who opened the gate with Val's help, hadn't been standing right by me. He'd been several feet away. Was that something that the Elite hadn't realized?

"But you . . ." I couldn't even finish the thought. In the back of my mind, I knew Tink had been keeping even more information from me, but at that moment, I didn't care. That wasn't what was important right now. Maybe later I'd punt kick him through a window, but at this second, horror consumed me. "It wasn't a coincidence that I found you, was it?"

Tink cast his gaze to the floor, and the stake trembled in my right hand.

"Don't do it, Ivy."

And because he asked that, I did it. I had to. I had to know, and I swiped the sharp edge of the stake right across my palm. I didn't even feel the pain, but my skin split with a hiss, and my blood immediately bubbled and popped.

"Oh my God," I whispered.

Dropping the thorn stake, it clattered off the wood floor as I stepped back from it. I lifted my head, staring at Tink. His wings drooped to the side as he lowered himself to the foot of the bed. My heart was thundering, pounding so fast I thought I'd be sick.

"No," I whispered.

Tink looked up soberly. "I told you not to do it."

A raw sob rose from the depths of my soul. "*No.*"

There was no response from Tink, and as my gaze crawled back to my palm, to where my blood still bubbled like it was being boiled, I staggered under one horrifying realization after another.

I was the halfling.

I was the halfling the man I'd fallen in love with had been sent here to kill.

Jennifer L. Armentrout

The *Wicked* Saga continues with the sequel
TORN
Coming July 2016

*A*cknowledgements

First and foremost, I want to thank Stacey Morgan for listening to me ramble on about a dream I had and how I wanted to write a book loosely based on it. Because she said I should do it, I did it. And another big thank you to my agent Kevan Lyon, who being her usual awesome self, listened when I said I wanted to self-publish this book and got right behind me. People, she totally rocks. Thirdly, another thank you goes out to Sarah Hansen from Okay Creations, and her beautiful cover design, and to Kelsey Kukal-Keeton for being excited about doing an underwater photo shoot and pulling off an amazing job. Thank you to the awesome models—Justin Edwards and Heather Noel MacDonald for also being willing to jump into the water and still manage to be incredibly sexy doing so. That's some real talent right there.

Thank you to Kara Malinczak for her awesome editorial powers and cleaning up this book so it's not a hot mess.

KP Simmons—thank you for doing your PR thing like a chicken wing.

Without Laura Kaye, Tiffany King, Wendy Higgins, Sophie Jordan, Jen Fisher, and Lesa Rodrigues, I'd probably go crazy. Or stop procrastinating so much and get more work done. Cora Carmack—you rock. Sarah Maas—I still have a total girl crush on you. Jay Crownover—let's make book babies one day. Thank you to Jamie McGuire for giving me the courage to do something. She knows what it is. Thank you.

Last but not least, a thank you to all the reviewers, bloggers, and readers of my books. You guys are why I do this. I love all of you. Seriously. THANK YOU.

Jennifer L. Armentrout is the # 1 New York Times and International best selling author who lives in Martinsburg, West Virginia. Not all the rumors you've heard about her state are true. When she's not busy writing, she likes to garden, work out, watch really bad zombie movies, pretend to write, and hang out with her husband and her hyper Jack Russell named Loki.

She writes young adult contemporary, science fiction, and paranormal romance for Spencer Hill Press, Entangled Teen, Disney Hyperion, and Harlequin Teen. Don't Look Back was nominated as Best in Young Adult Fiction by the Young Adult Library Association. Her book Obsidian has been optioned for a major motion picture and her Covenant Series has been optioned for TV.

Under the name J. Lynn, Jennifer has written New Adult and Adult contemporary and paranormal romance, including the # 1 New York Times best seller Wait for You. She writes for HarperCollins and Entangled Brazen.

CPSIA information can be obtained
at www.ICGtesting.com
Printed in the USA
LVHW021608170921
698105LV00007B/672

9 780988 982956